I0761482

CANTICLE

CANTICLE

Janet Rich Edwards

Spiegel and Grau

S&G

Spiegel & Grau, New York
www.spiegelandgrau.com

Interior design by Meighan Cavanaugh

Library of Congress Cataloging-in-Publication Data Available Upon Request

ISBN 978-1-966302-05-6 (hardcover)
ISBN 978-1-966302-06-3 (ebook)

Printed in the United States

First Edition
10 9 8 7 6 5 4

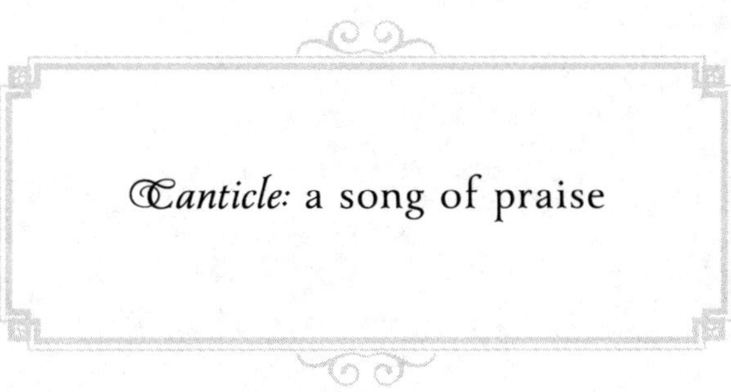
Canticle: a song of praise

Brugge, County of Flanders

1299

The young woman appears in the square, wearing neither veil nor wimple, her short brown hair plaited behind her neck. She's covered by a cloak of fine maroon wool; specks of white ash have drifted to land on her shoulders like snowflakes. The acrid smell of bonfire is already in the air. Witnesses will later swear the girl was lit like a taper, and some will claim she had a halo. They'll say the brass steeple cocks spun as she entered the square and the clouds broke apart, fleeing south, fleeing north, at once all directions, impossible. Church bells snapped their stays and a wild clanging rose from every corner of the great city. No one is quite sure what happened.

As the crowd parts before her, Aleys sees the path of gray cobblestones receding to the stake. Parchment is piled high at its base. Smaller fires have already been lit, dotting the plaza. They're burning her words, too.

A chant of "Sint! Sint!" rises from the crowd. Even now, even though the Church has named her heretic, the people still call her saint. It's true and not true. They are all saints. They are none of them saints. They think her a miracle worker. They think she speaks with God. But really, everyone does. It's just so hard to hear.

She takes a step, another step, her heart hammering.

Adieu, she thinks, I go to God. This time, truly, I go to God.

Liber Primus

1

ALEYS

Damme, 1295

Aleys has fallen behind the group of children running along the canal. She stops abruptly. Maybe she's dropped something, or perhaps she's studying her feet, which would be strange enough. She's thirteen years old and powerfully odd. The others glance back, but they're used to Aleys freezing in mid-sentence, in mid-chore, in mid-anything, and they move on as a pack toward the bridge, where they'll chuck pebbles onto barges headed south to Brugge or back to the North Sea and jeer at the raised fists of English skippers.

Aleys looks around to be sure she's alone. She crouches to examine a caterpillar crossing the towpath. Aleys knows she's getting too old to care about something so small. It's nothing special, just a green cabbage worm, not even the length of her thumb, the kind she knows will turn into a plain white moth with tiny spots as black as monk's ink. Aleys watches it creep across the path. It's a miracle that the stampede of children didn't crush it. She rises and walks over to a bush and breaks off a twig and returns to the creature, coaxing it onto the stem and bearing it carefully to the side of the path. She bends to deposit it in the undergrowth and watches it disappear beneath a leaf. Funny, how God makes creatures blend in where they belong. How strange they are when out of place. Aleys looks up after the children. They've forgotten her. She lifts the leaf, but the caterpillar is gone, too. She worries she might not have put it back in the right spot; she hopes it finds its friends. She hopes it gets to fly.

Aleys considers, for a moment, whether to chase after the others. By now, they'll have reached the intersection of the canals, where they'll wait for the old lockmaster to turn his back so they can teeter across the gates as the water fills. They might now be running up the towpath of the Zwin toward the sea or they might have veered onto the Lieve Canal that goes all the way to Ghent. She doesn't really want to follow. "Aleys!" they'll say, turning, laughing, toward each other. "Did you get lost?" She won't want to tell them about the caterpillar. Not even her brothers or sister, who laughs at everything. So Aleys straightens and turns back. A bee trails her, and another joins. Bees love her like she's a tulip. They don't sting her. She doesn't know why.

Mama will be at home. Papa's gone to the cloth hall in Brugge to get the guild's stamp on their spring wool. The Lakenhalle has a new belfry as grand as that of any cathedral, and louder, too. Mornings and evenings, it clangs out the hours that wool production must start and stop, as if there's a race on. Papa says that even God stops work when the Lakenhalle tolls. Mama slaps him when he says this, but she smiles all the same.

Aleys scuffs her shoes along the path. It's a pretty spring day, one of those that carries the smell of the sea and the rasp of gulls from the coast. She passes homes with yards facing the canal. The spinsters have moved their stools outside and are hand-spinning thread from clouds of fleece atop long poles nestled against their shoulders. The women tip their faces to the sun and call out greetings. Aleys knows them all from collecting the skeins that Mama sorts on their kitchen table. Papa takes the best yarn, creamy and smooth, for the weavers in Brugge. The rest is used for felting or sold to carpet makers. Aleys and Griete play cat's cradle with the cheap stuff, full of knots and noils, beside the hearth. Or they used to, anyway.

Aleys finds Mama in the vegetable garden, sprinkling carrot seed along the furrows with one hand, supporting her swollen belly with the other. Farrago, their dog, is beside her. He follows her mother everywhere.

"Mama, you shouldn't be doing that."

Mama dusts the last of the seed from her hands and leans back, bracing her palms in the small of her back. "I couldn't resist. It feels like the first day of summer." *Any day now*, Mama's been saying for a week. They pulled the cradle from storage and placed it on the hearth. When no one's looking, Aleys sits on the stool and practices rocking it with her foot. It might be all right, Mama having a baby. Aleys can't remember an infant in the cradle. Griete's nearly eleven. It's been empty a long time.

Mama straightens and brushes her braid over her shoulder with the back of her hand. Aleys got Mama's blue eyes, but not her fair hair. Her own is a glossy brown, almost black, like Papa's.

Mama looks beyond Aleys for the others. "You've returned alone?"

Again, Aleys hears her think, though she knows it contains no judgment. Mama says she was the same as a girl. Sober, stubborn, wondering. Different. Mama's the only person in the world who understands.

"What marvels did you find?" Mama asks.

"Just a cabbage worm."

"You saved it?" Mama slaps her palm to her forehead. "You know it will eat this garden empty."

"Not this one."

"No? Well, better than wool moths, I suppose." Mama gazes off over the fields that run behind their yard. She has that faraway look, brings both hands to her belly. Then she sighs. "Be a good girl, Aleys, will you, and bring in the washing?"

"Mama, I thought maybe we could . . ."

"On such an afternoon?"

"Please? They'll be back soon. And any day now . . ."

"What a strange child," says Mama. "God's glory on earth all round us, and my daughter wants the prayer book." She is shaking her head, but she's smiling. Mama loves the book as much as Aleys does. "Never mind the laundry. I'll get the psalter." Mama trundles into the house, Farrago at her heels.

For as long as Aleys can remember, she and Mama have read the psalter together. Well, not exactly read. Mama isn't lettered, and it's in Latin, anyway, which not even their priest understands. Mama inherited the little book from her aunt, abbess of a convent near Sint-Truiden. Aleys wishes she could read it. But Mama knows all the prayers and the lives of the saints, no matter what the Latin says. She spins them into stories for her children. Henryk and Claus will sit still only for the goriest of her tales. Saints rarely end peacefully, and Mama sends them to their deaths with relish, leaning in to the stonings and hackings, flayings and clubbings. Aleys frowns at her sometimes. It seems impious. Mama sighs. "Aleys, I have to give your brothers some kind of Christian education. Those rascals aren't about to become monks."

And Griete? She's all about the drama. Aleys's younger sister likes to act out the stories, flinging her golden hair all over the place. Griete's favorite is Saint Ursula, who led eleven thousand of her best friends on pilgrimage. When the Huns attacked, Ursula and her maidens chose to die by the sword rather than submit their virtue to the soldiers. Aleys wonders what it would be like to have so many friends. What it would be like to have just one good friend you could take on pilgrimage.

Her siblings seem to think that martyrs exist solely for their entertainment. Just yesterday Griete hopped up when Mama closed the psalter and went back into the kitchen. "My turn," she announced. "I'm the saint today."

"No," said Aleys. Sometimes Griete was imperious. "It should be Claus." He was the only one who could remember his lines.

"He's *always* the saint," whined Griete. "Can't we do Ursula? I'll be the virgin. The boys can be Huns."

"You're not that good a virgin," said Claus with a lopsided grin. He was right. Griete was an unconvincing Ursula. She just flirted with the Huns, glancing back over her shoulder and giggling as they gave chase.

"Virgins are boring," declared Henryk, who made a decent soldier but not much else.

"How about Saint Laurence?" Claus nodded with his own enthusiasm. "You can grill me to death over a pit of flame." He threw himself to the ground. "Watch." He rolled on the floor as if on a spit. "I'm well-done!" he shouted. "Turn me over!"

Privately, Aleys thinks they should take the saints more seriously. It would be marvelous to be a martyr. So sure, so full of passion. Everyone loves them, despite how strange they are. Maybe because of how strange they are. She tries to convince Griete to join her. "Straight to heaven," she says. "No purgatory. It'll be easy." The problem is, how to get yourself martyred? You might become a pilgrim and hope to be beheaded or burned for your love of God in the Holy Land. Or better yet, you could be shot through by a pagan arrow en route to Constantinople; that seemed a tidy, even cut-rate, entrance to heaven. Given the alternatives. But then Papa told her that he had no plans to take them farther than Brugge, let alone Byzantium. "You and your mother," he said, chucking her under the chin, "are all the saints we need."

Aleys is convinced she'll live her life and die in triviality. There must be other ways to get God's attention. Aleys tests her faith like she's wiggling a loose tooth. She tries fasting, but after a day or two, though she pinches her thighs and is sure she's wasting away, nobody notices. It's a great disappointment.

Aleys needs a hair shirt. She collects the shed fur of Farrago and painstakingly glues it to a belt that she fastens beneath her girdle and under her nightdress. It works beautifully, it itches horribly. Aleys breaks out in bright pink welts and can hardly keep her hands from clawing at her torso.

"What is that?" Griete shrieks in revulsion when Aleys lifts her shift to show her.

"My penance," supplies Aleys.

Griete wrinkles her nose. "What for? You've never done anything wrong in your life."

The hair belt develops fleas, so Griete bans it from their bed, and that's the end of that.

Aleys has tried everything she can think of to prove herself to God. She can't help but feel her talents are wasted. The saints get all the adventures. All the friends.

"You're a strange child," says Papa, "but you'll save us in the end."

It started with the pictures in the psalter. When she was small, Aleys would sit on Mama's lap and grip her braid as ballast to lean over the book and fall into its miniature world. Illuminations, Mama called them, paintings that bring light to the prayers and psalms lettered on the page. Even now, when Aleys leans her cheek on Mama's shoulder, she loses herself in colors so vivid they seem to vibrate. There are ladies who might suddenly speak or bend to feed a green apple to a ruby deer. Turn the page, and there are sinners with bug eyes peeping from cauldrons or pleading from dark pits guarded by scaled beasts. Aleys has to look at the demons through her fingers. Angels land on the pages, too, trailing banners with tidings in Latin that Mama can't read. Somehow Mama knows what the angels think.

Mama's psalter holds the real world, too, not just trees and birds, but things Aleys has never seen, mountains and waterfalls and strange fruits from faraway lands. She wonders how they'd taste if you touched your tongue to the page. Aleys wants to dive into the paintings, to swim in the crimson and blue, the willow, the traces of gold. The psalter holds prayers for every hour of the day, precisely lettered across the page. Mama knows that Aleys loves the psalter more than anyone, even if neither of them knows exactly what the words mean. *Someday this will be yours, but you must be very, very good.* When they finish looking, Mama will slip the psalter back into its silk pouch and place it out of reach. Aleys's eyes will follow, her imagination caught within the pages of a small book on a high shelf. Sometimes, as she's dropping off to sleep, the illustrations waver before her. Birds fly through forests of inked letters and she wakes wondering what the bristly shapes could possibly mean.

Today, though, Aleys wants a particular story.

"Perpetua?" Mama looks at the book in her hand. "You're sure?" She puts her other hand back on her stomach. *Any day now*. "It won't be too much?"

It's not actually the tale of Saint Perpetua that Aleys craves, it's what Mama always says at the end. Aleys could recite the story herself, though never as well as Mama. It brings tears to her eyes when her mother describes Perpetua unlatching her newborn from her breast and handing him to her brother. Perpetua holds her head high as she strides into the arena where wild beasts wait to tear her apart for the emperor's birthday. All because she refused to renounce the one true God for the emperor's menu of Roman gods. Aleys wonders what it would be like to be so brave, has imagined herself as Perpetua. But not today. Today it's Mama about to enter the arena. Aleys isn't exactly sure what happens when you have a baby, but she knows it's dangerous. Last year they lost a neighbor, one of her favorites, to childbirth, a woman whose three sons would dash laughing to see Aleys when she came to pick up the yarn. She remembers the armful of blood-soaked rags the midwife carried from their door.

Reading her mind, Mama pulls Aleys into a tight embrace. Aleys can feel the baby kick through Mama's dress, right into her own belly, and she feels a surge of anger. They don't need a baby. They're fine as they are, the six of them. She wishes the baby away. It's a wild beast, it doesn't belong.

Mama whispers into her hair. "Remember, you still have your wishes ahead of you." Every girl receives three charmed events, almost like wishes, in the three years before she weds. They might be subtle, so you have to be alert. Aleys is in no rush to marry, but she likes the thought of spontaneous gifts.

"Maybe one of them will be the baby," says Mama.

"No." Aleys doesn't want to waste one of her wishes on an infant. She wants to spend them on herself. "Mama, what if the baby . . ." Her glance strays toward the neighbor's yard, then back to her mother.

Mama draws back and holds both her shoulders and looks Aleys right in the eye. "Listen. I delivered the four of you. I'm strong." Then Mama pulls Aleys close again and whispers in her ear the words she always says—her very own words, just for her daughter—at the end of Perpetua. "Never could I leave you, child. Not even for God." But it doesn't comfort Aleys the way she wanted, and she goes to bed uneasy.

That night a steady rain creates a dense hush around the house, punctuated by the occasional slap of the shutter against the window frame. Aleys sleeps fitfully, in and out of dreams, finding no rest. In the small hours, a shriek pierces the quiet. Aleys starts awake, gripping the sheet, her heart racing. Maybe it was an owl. The cry comes again, from inside. Downstairs. Aleys sits up, hugging herself. The shutter gives a loud snap, and Aleys looks over at Griete. She's sound asleep. Her sister sleeps through everything. She could wake Griete, ask what the cry was, hold hands and huddle beneath the bedclothes. But Griete would only stoke her fear, and Aleys feels her heart can't beat any faster. She slips out of bed and down the stairs. The floor in the hall outside her parents' chamber is cold beneath her feet. Farrago waits in vigil. He's shivering. His eyes are worried. His tail gives one short wag when he sees Aleys, then stops.

Aleys puts her ear to the door. For a moment, she thinks a wild animal has gotten into the room, but then she understands that the growling is human, the laboring breath is Mama's. It's here. The baby is coming. The sounds are terrible, inhuman moans and grunts, as if Mama is wrestling with a dark angel from the psalter. An image invades her mind of the leathery, winged beast from the book, the king of the abyss, sprung to life in Mama's chamber with his terrible clawed hands and thrashing tail. The baby is breaking her mother, and demons are waiting to seize her.

Another cry, more panting. Aleys feels a chill course her limbs, like she's freezing from the inside out. She braces her hands against the doorframe. Within the chamber are horrors, things she shouldn't see, things she's afraid to see. She should be fearless, like Perpetua. She should go to Mama's aid. But she can't. She just can't. The demons. Aleys stands locked in terror outside the door, her feet frozen to the ground. "Mama," she whispers.

Aleys begins to pray. *Please, Lord, hear me.* She slides to her knees and presses her forehead into the door. All she wants is her mother. She doesn't care what happens to the baby. *Take it, just spare Mama.* She concentrates everything into this one desire, until her need is a hot coal in her belly. *Send the angels.* She prays to the saints, she prays to Mary. She leans into the door, all her small weight, as if she could push the monsters back to hell. Light breaks around the frame. Is it a sign? *Bring more light, Lord, more angels.*

She prays harder, scarcely breathing, the words in her mind frantic, each one crashing into the next.

Her wishes. If ever there were a time for them, it's now. *Dear Lord, I wish Mama to live*. It's not just her first wish, it's her every wish. *I'll give them up*, she prays, *all my wishes. Just not my mother*.

Then it grows quiet, so still that Aleys can hear the tumult of her blood in her ears. A flicker of hope kindles within her. She takes a breath, holds it, listens. Then a whimper, long and plaintive, so unlike her mother, so strange, snakes under the door. It's the worst sound she's ever heard. She clenches her fists against the noise. There are other murmurs, voices Aleys doesn't know, a few urgent words in Papa's familiar voice. And then a terrible silence. There should be a baby crying. There should be sounds of joy, of relief. The quiet is all wrong. Aleys clenches her fists as the knowledge seeds itself. No. No, no. The silence seems to swell, until it is vast and bottomless, until it opens into the dark abyss of the prayer book, and Aleys pictures Mama falling, falling away from her, into the pages of the psalter, forever. *Mama*. Aleys can't draw breath, doesn't want to draw breath. *Take me with you*. She shuts her eyes and wills herself to leap into the darkness. Farrago releases a howl. Someone opens the door. Aleys falls forward onto her hands and knees. Inside, on the floor by the bed, is a heap of bloody linen. The dog is keening. Her wishes were worthless. Mama is dead.

2

ALEYS

A fog descends on their house, curling through the rooms, filling every space with its blank white face. Aleys can barely see through the dank mist. No one speaks. Hours go by and no one speaks. There's nothing to say.

Aleys is surprised, when she goes outside, at the sun. A group of children run the towpath, children who still have mothers. News has spread. They slow as they pass the grieving house, out of respect or maybe fear that the sorrow is contagious. I didn't pray hard enough, thinks Aleys. *Be careful or you'll end up like me. Go home to your mothers.* The children don't dare to look at her, and their relieved whoops and shouts trail behind them as they head up the canal.

That afternoon, Papa burns the cradle in the yard. The laundry is still on the line, flapping senselessly. Papa weeps as the wood cracks, but Aleys is glad to see it go.

"We have to eat," Griete says, and tries to make a meal, though she's just ten years old. No one eats it, and Aleys takes their plates out back and scrapes them for the pigs. She notices that the friars have not come to the gate, as though they've heard that no one eats here, that to hold out their bowls for food would be pointless and cruel.

But there are things that must be done. Claus remembers to feed the chickens. After a few days, Henryk hitches the horses to the wagon. Papa must go to the Lakenhalle, he must go to the dye yard, he must go to the fullers. A draper's work never stops; wool won't produce itself. He sends

Griete on the rounds to collect the skeins from the spinsters, without Aleys, as if Papa knows she's the worst affected, can't look upon other mothers. And so Aleys is left alone at the kitchen table, her hands deep in skeins of wool, dun-colored figure eights that loop endlessly. She weeps as she sorts them, pauses often to put her head on the table. There is something solid, something comforting in the feel of yarn between her fingers, the animal smell of it, that allows her to breathe. Farrago follows her now.

She doesn't understand why God took Mama. Aleys wanders the empty house, stops in her parents' bedchamber. Mama was so good. Kind and generous and devout. Aleys eyes the prie-dieu where Mama prayed twice a day, knees on the kneeler, elbows on the sloping shelf, psalter open before her. Aleys grips the frame and shakes it, as if she could force answers to rattle out. It makes no sense. Mama was perfect. Why would he take her when she was so needed on earth?

God should explain himself.

The psalter sits above the prie-dieu on a high shelf, secure in its scarlet pouch, untouchable. Aleys yearns to open it, to search the pages for her mother. "Papa?" she starts to ask. But she can't. Their grief is a fragile tower. One more stick, one more reminder, and he might collapse. She could lose him, too. So the pouch remains, gathering dust, closed and knotted, as Mama left it.

Summer turns to fall. Aleys sees a white cabbage moth with inky spots and smiles for the first time in weeks. Fall turns to winter. The friars return to the back gate, murmuring blessings as they hold out their bowls. They lean over the fence while Aleys spoons out porridge for them. If no Franciscans happen down the road, she tosses the offering into the slop trough and the pigs feast like preachers.

"It's always friars. Why don't priests come begging?" Griete asks Papa one day, as he loads the cart with finished lengths. "Or monks?"

Papa looks over his shoulder. "They're not hungry." Griete screws up her face. Papa sighs. "Mama taught you all about the saints in heaven but not about the Church on earth?" He puts his hands on his thighs and crouches to speak to her. "Here's my lesson. There are three kinds of churchmen. First, the priests in the churches, they're the bottom rung of the ladder that stretches all the way to the pope's throne. The higher you climb—your bishops, archbishops, and all that—the richer you get. Too rich, if you ask me. Now, monks"—Papa pauses to rub his beard—"are different. They live in the monasteries, and most of them are well-off. They own fields and livestock and learn Latin and copy manuscripts."

"Like Mama's psalter," says Aleys.

"And they make the best ale," adds Henryk.

"That, too," says Papa. "Come on, boys, let's finish this." He turns back to the work.

"You forgot the friars," Griete insists.

"Ah, well, the friars, they're something new." Papa leans against the cart. "Those men mean what they say. The Franciscans and Dominicans have taken vows of poverty. Won't even touch money. They preach on the street corners, though nobody pays them. The friars live on the providence of God and depend on our alms. That's why they come begging at our gates."

Aleys likes the friars. If she were a boy, that's what she'd be. "What about women?" she asks.

"Don't be stupid," says Griete. "Women have to be nuns."

"Be they nun, monk, priest, or friar, they all answer to the pope in Rome," says Papa, hoisting the last pallet onto the cart. "And we to the guild in Brugge." He wipes his brow with the back of his hand. "Claus, hitch the horse, and let's get going."

A cold wet winter cedes to spring, and Papa says he needs help with the wool—it's become all too obvious how much the family business relied on Mama. Receipts have faltered. At least he thinks they have. Papa can't take on all her work negotiating with spinsters and local shopkeepers and keep up the books, too.

"You'll have to learn to read," he announces, "and write. All of you."

Aleys snaps to attention. Read? It's like getting a wish she never even hoped for. She didn't think it possible. Girls don't read unless they're schooled in a nunnery. She squints at Papa. "Truly?"

"I've hired the tutor." He smiles at her eagerness. "You'll start tomorrow."

Aleys remembers the three wishes and frowns. They were nothing but a story for children. She abandoned childish things the night Mama died. But learning to read? It's like something from a fairy tale.

The tutor comes twice a week and teaches them to read and write ledgers. Aleys learns quickly, faster than her brothers. But it's dull, even disappointing, all the repetitive words: fleece, bale, skein, bolt, dye. What she longs to read isn't written in Dutch. It's not line after line of transactions and weights and expenses and income. She wants to read the psalter. Mama's voice, even Mama's face, has begun to dim. If Aleys could open the book, she's sure that memories of Mama would fly out like birds. If she could learn Latin and read the words, maybe she could bring Mama back.

Aleys begs Papa to bring in a Latin teacher, but there's no money for that. Her brothers declare church language a waste of their time. They'll read and write in Dutch to draw up a contract or a bill of sale. "*Miserere mei*," says Henryk, swirling the beer in his mug and showing off one of the few phrases he knows. He downs the drink and slams the mug on the table like a grown man. "Forgive me. What more do I need than that?" Mama was right, their religious education is truly lacking.

Aleys strains to recall the saint stories for her siblings, but she can remember only Perpetua and Ursula, and the boys quickly lose interest. Without an audience, Griete does, too. Aleys tries to pray for them all. She prays in the root cellar, with pebbles beneath her knees. It feels like penance, like a cleansing to wash away the stain of the night she failed Mama. She knows she's not supposed to hold that thought. Papa has said that God took Mama for his own reasons. What those could be, why he would want to fill her with an unfillable hunger, Aleys has no idea.

Eventually, her siblings leave her alone with her saints. Griete discovers the looking glass, Claus deserts martyrs for marbles, and Henryk, growing firm of jaw, decides that virgins are, in fact, interesting. It's as if they've all moved on from Mama and Aleys is stuck behind in the mud, straining for a glimpse, searching.

A year passes before God delivers her second wish.

It's late afternoon, and Papa has been watching Aleys chop onions into a stew. Onions that she planted and tended in their side garden, as she has every year. Griete is out back skipping rope with her friends. Papa's in a thoughtful mood. "We should have had a maid," he says. "You work so hard." Papa is the fourth son of the third son of a once-noble family. They even have a crest, a lion rampant. Henryk likes to think of it as a kind of glory, but Papa says that family honor doesn't pay anyone's wages. Nor will it win him a spot in the Lakenhalle, which would make it easier to sell their wool, and at a premium. Lately, there's new competition from Florence, where they've devised clever mills that render the wool just as dense and soft as handwashing it in old urine. Money's been getting tight. They may have to sell Claus's horse that he loves so much. Papa works hard, and it's clear, in this moment, that he knows Aleys does, too.

"Come," he says, rising.

Papa leads Aleys to his chamber and reaches to the top shelf. Aleys catches her breath. What's he doing? Papa retrieves the scarlet pouch and gently turns it in his hands, blowing off the dust. Where his breath brushes the silk, it glints ruby in the afternoon light.

Aleys wipes her hands on her skirt. "That's Mama's." Her fingers itch to grab the book.

"Just so." Papa's smile is rueful. "The first time I saw her psalter was at our wedding. I was almost jealous, she loved it so much."

Aleys thinks of Mama, not much older than she is now, clutching her book at the altar. What painting illuminated her mind in that moment? Was she picturing an angel alighting before her or the pits of hell? Did she know death was waiting, not so many years off? Of course not, Aleys tells herself. No one expects that.

"Mama meant to give this to you on your wedding day."

Aleys retracts her fingers as if Papa's offered her live coals. What's he saying? They've never discussed this. Surely, he doesn't expect her to marry. He knows she belongs at home, with him, with them, with Farrago and the wool and the garden and the chickens. Aleys looks down. She's standing where the midwife dropped the soiled linens. She backs away.

"Papa, no." The words come out fast. "Who'd run our home? And the business—you can't manage without me." She can sort the strong yarn from the weak, can weigh a skein with her eyes and select a dye for a monk or a marquise. He needs her. Doesn't he? Her throat clenches. "I don't want a husband." Papa is smiling like there's a joke only he knows. She feels panic rise. She's only fourteen years old. "This is my home."

He nods and assesses the book in his hand. When he looks up, his eyes are bright. "You know, when your mother prayed, there was something so sure about her." Papa regards the prie-dieu beside their bed, as if Mama were right there, and Aleys realizes that, for him, she still is. "So intimate." He shrugs. "Most people pray because the priests tell them to, like they're checking off a list. Your brothers, for one. Or they're afraid of the hell the priests whip up." Papa shakes his head. He doesn't much care for priests, agrees with those who complain the Church has grown corrupt. "And then there are those," he says, "like Griete, who get down on their knees to deliver God their list of demands. But your mother was different." He looks out the window at the fading light on the field. "When she prayed, she raised her head as if she were listening. Like she was trying to catch a melody just beyond reach."

Aleys imagines Mama in prayer, the house asleep, the candles flickering. "She prayed from love."

"More like curiosity, I think. She wanted to know God." He smiles. "She used to take my hand and reach it out like she was pressing against an invisible cloth. She'd say, 'It's here, husband. Right here. God's will. If we could just see the weave.' Sometimes I thought she missed her vocation. She would have made a happy nun."

"Mama, a nun?" Enclosed within the walls of an abbey? Aleys doesn't agree. Mama loved the world, loved her neighbors, loved Papa. She loved the waves of the North Sea. She wouldn't have wanted to be a nun.

"Your mother had a talent for prayer," says Papa. He shifts the pouch from one hand to the other. "Aleys . . . you have no idea how like her you are. So I have to ask. Do you want to join the convent?"

Aleys shakes her chin rapidly, almost a shiver. She has no more desire to live behind walls than Mama did. "I'd never see you again."

"And you don't want to marry?"

"No! I told you. I don't want to go anywhere. I'm happy here."

"But you'd never have children."

She shudders. "Papa, I don't . . ."

"I know," he says, putting out his hand. He won't make her say it. "No one's going to force you."

"You promise?"

"I promise." He nods. "Then, if you have no intention of leaving, this should be yours." He puts the pouch into her hands and holds them for a moment. "From Mama."

Aleys can hardly breathe. She gently loosens the drawstring and eases out the prayer book. It's exactly as she remembers. The psalter fills her hand the way it once filled Mama's. She traces her fingers over the vine that runs around the edge of the supple green leather. "I can open it?"

"Of course. It's yours."

Aleys opens the book at random, to a painting of an enormous oak. Her breath catches. She remembers this, how the tree spreads across the page, how every branch holds a different bird. The leaves are light green and dark green, and the birds' wings are tipped with gold. Mama's voice comes to her. *The blackbird. And the cardinal. You see the sparrow?* Below the tree, auburn foxes poke their noses from dens in the earth. Aleys can't read the words of the psalm, but she knows every single bird on every single branch.

"Oh, Papa." She holds the book to her heart. She can say no more.

One hunger begets another. At night, while the others sleep, Aleys sets a taper on the kitchen table. She washes her hands thoroughly in the bucket and rubs them on her dress until they chafe, and only then does she loosen the drawstring on the pouch and extract the psalter. She pauses with her hands on the cover, and she swears she can feel the imprint of Mama's fingers. Then she opens the book like she's raising the lid of a treasure chest. Each illuminated psalm is vibrant as a sunrise. She pictures the monk who copied the verse and decorated the margins, but instead of ink, she imagines him dipping his quill in the colors of bluebirds and holly berries and bright spring moss.

Look, Mama had said. *How the wind stirs the trees.*

The vivid images wake something in Aleys, as if her own senses are tipped with monk's gold. The sun in the psalter lights the fields outside her window. She pours water from the ewer and stands still, hearing cascades from the hills. A hawk's cry becomes the call of an angel. The world of the psalter and the world around her begin to merge, and she wonders how much she's failed to see, right in front of her. The marvels Mama spoke of, the beauty of God's world. It comes back to her. Aleys tips her tongue to the grapes and tastes wine. It's hard to know what's real and what's not. If she could read the verse, Aleys feels, she could understand. She aches to understand. She wants more. She reaches her hand out to touch God's fabric and thinks she feels him pushing back.

As the fire settles in the hearth and the pewter ticks with the night chill, Aleys works to decipher the Latin. She starts with the *Ave Maria*, the song of Matins, the first hour, which even a milkmaid can recite. Everyone knows at least a few Latin words from the prayers they chant by rote in church. It's just that there are so many words. Aleys starts by translating the handful she recognizes. *Ave* means *hail*, *mater* is *mother*, *benedicta* is *blessed*. She teases apart the Lord's Prayer, too, figures out that *terra* means earth, deduces bread from *panem*. But she can get only so far without a tutor. She'll never read the psalms or the saints unless she learns Latin.

And then, out of nowhere, from the least likely of places, Aleys receives her third wish. It's January and frigid, ice slicking the roadways. Henryk is sick and Papa needs help delivering fabric to the dyers. Aleys thinks Henryk is perfectly fine. He's just afraid the fumes from the dye yard will stink up his cloak. Recently, Henryk has become a bit of a dandy. His loss. She's glad of the chance to ride out with Papa. He piles the bench of their cart with sheepskin and Aleys draws over their knees a heavy blanket made from coarse cast-off yarn. She wraps her hands twice in the wool, but the chill finds its way through the weave. She doesn't mind. The sky above is so pure blue it looks like it could crack with the cold.

They smell the yard before they see the enormous cauldrons that emit great plumes of steam like the devil's vats in her psalter. The yard smells like hell, too, but at least it's warm, with fires stoked high. Papa gets down to negotiate with a large man and his sons, a matched set of hulking twins, one whose hands are blue with woad dye, the other's scarlet with madder. Aleys unloads the bolts of wool onto a wooden pallet. They're talking about the drapers' guild and whether the head of it, a man named Mertens, will ever grant Papa a license to sell in the Lakenhalle. "Our best fabric dyed in your royal blue? How could he refuse?" asks Papa. They'll be bargaining over the price of that blue for a while. Aleys wanders off among the steaming vats.

Men in leather aprons wield long wooden paddles, stirring lengths of wool through the dye. Boys scurry like squirrels, adding wood to the fires. Aleys lifts her skirt above puddles streaked with purple and red. Colored vapor lifts from the vats and drifts off like carnival smoke. Aleys turns the corner of a shed and nearly trips over a boy.

"Oh. Hallo." The boy is seated on a low crate, hunched over a hornbook. She peers at the tablet. A sheet of finely shaved translucent horn traps and protects a piece of parchment. Aleys starts to ask why he's studying outside, then stops. "You're reading Latin." The surprise in her voice comes out before she can disguise it. A dyer reading Latin?

"What of it?" The boy is skinny, but he'd be taller than her if he stood up. He shows no sign of doing so. He places his forearm over the hornbook to shield it from her eyes, but his arm is too thin to hide what he's reading. He looks like a younger version of the dyer's twins, with large gray eyes and long fingers. But his are clean. She wonders why he's not stirring a vat. Maybe he has more brothers than there are colors.

"You're reading that?" she asks.

"Obviously." He doesn't move his arm.

"You must go to the monks' school." The monks teach boys whose families can't afford tutors. Girls aren't welcome. She leans over him. "Can I see?"

The boy tilts his head at her, not quite smirking. "You wouldn't like it. There aren't any pictures."

"I can read."

"Latin?"

"Yes." It's a bold claim. Sure, she's worked out some words from prayers she knows by heart: give, day, bread, kingdom, power, glory. She can map out the sounds of the other words, too, but she has no idea what they mean. It's just gibberish to her, even if she can pronounce them. Might as well be Portuguese or English. She doesn't understand those languages, either.

"Prove it." He shoves the tablet at her.

Aleys shakes her sleeves from her wrists and takes the paddle and presses her hand down on the horn sheet so she can see through it. She recognizes *give* from the Lord's Prayer. It's enough of an anchor to decipher the first sentence. "Give, and it will be given to you." She hands the hornbook back to him. "See?"

The boy squints skeptically at the tablet. It dawns on her that he can't read it. So she makes up the rest. "Take, and it will be taken from you." Sounds about right. "Teach, and you will be taught."

He looks at it dubiously. "It says that? Exactly?"

"That's the general idea."

He turns to a leather bag at his side and pulls out another sheet of parchment. "I know this one." He doesn't bother to slip it under the horn sheet. He doesn't even look at it. The Latin flows off his tongue: "*Numquid potest caecus caecum ducere nonne ambo in foveam cadent.*" He's clearly memorized the passage. Showing off, he repeats it in Dutch for her benefit. "Can the blind lead the blind? Shall they both not fall into the pit?" She bristles at his condescension. So the boy is fluent in Latin and can commit passages to memory. It doesn't mean he can read.

"Show me where it says *pit*," she demands.

The boy points, but his finger wavers between words. He's guessing.

Aleys squints at the sentence. By process of elimination, she should be able to get it. She knows *fall into temptation*; *fall into the pit* can't be that different. She picks one of the words from the end of the sentence where she knows *pit* ought to be. "*Fo-ve-am.*"

"Pit," he says.

"Pit," she agrees. She points at the word.

"How can you tell?"

"I figure it out."

"That's a trick." He's looking at her like she's just blown flame from her mouth. "Girls don't read Latin."

"Nuns do. If I had a tutor, I'd speak Latin like you." It dawns on her that he has the opposite problem she does. She reads the words but can't understand them. He speaks Latin but can't read it. She gestures at the page in his hand. "So how do you know what that says?"

"I memorize it."

"Don't the monks teach you to read?"

"They will, once we're fluent. And after we master copying. That's what they mostly care about, getting the manuscripts done for their patrons."

"But you want to read what you're copying."

"Of course I do. I'm not just some monkey with a quill." Suddenly, he's up on his feet, thrusting the page at her. "Show me how you do it."

She steps back. "Why should I?"

"If you do, I can read the text that the monks set us to copy." He looks at her from the corner of his eye. "Plus the scripture they don't want us to read. I can get that."

Well, good for him. "But why should *I* teach *you*?"

"Because I understand Latin and you don't."

A path opens before Aleys. He's proposed a *quid pro quo*. If she shows him how to sound out the Latin words, he'll be able to read whatever he wants. And if he teaches her what the Latin words mean, she'll be able to understand everything in Mama's psalter.

"What's your name?" she asks.

He doffs his hat like he's a courtier, not a dyer's son. "Finn," he replies. "They call me Finn."

Aleys becomes Finn's reading tutor, and he becomes her Latin tutor. Finn has a donkey he can bribe with stale turnips to make the trip to Damme, so they meet in the root cellar after her family is abed. Shoulder to shoulder, they learn like wildfire. He sneaks out the manuscripts he's supposed to be copying for the monks. By spring, Finn can sound out words and Aleys can tell him what they mean. By summer, they trample down a nest for themselves in a nearby field, the wheat turning from green to gold, stars emerging above. He curves his lanky body over the parchment, his sandy hair falling over his gray eyes. She brings a leather cord and plaits it for him. "There," she says. "Now you can read."

She finds she's happy. She has a friend. She thinks Finn would go on pilgrimage with her if she asked. He's as curious about God as she is.

"When you grow up in a dyer's yard," he says, "you don't need to be told what hell is. But there's supposed to be a kingdom of heaven on earth, too." Finn's been getting worked up since he can read for himself. "So where is it? The priests are hiding something. Why won't they let people read for themselves?"

"We have our prayer books."

"But there's so much more, Aleys, than is in your mother's psalter."

For now, Aleys is happy to decipher the prayers for the hours in the psalter. The words, to her surprise, are as beautiful as the illuminations. The prayers seem to pare her senses, leaving her raw and open. And closer to Mama. How she'd have loved to have been able to read. Aleys tries to pray as Mama would have. She tries to listen for both of them.

In chapel, when all necks are bowed and the priest raises the host to the cross, Aleys lifts her head. She sees, just over the field of downcast heads, in shafts of sunlight, and everywhere, really, dust motes winking, heedless of prayers. No one sees them, unless there's a shift in the light. They're everywhere, buffeted by the breeze, in the sap of the pines, in the crunch of leaves underfoot, in the way the bread tears in the hand, the way the bread knows to tear in the hand just so. The treaded path, the burst of grape on the tongue, the sudden flood, it is all thus, and there is a hand behind it, a design, a pattern so diverse and particular that it seems no pattern, but it is, she knows it is. The air, the stone, the pearl, the cry of jay, the smell of moss, all of it, all of it, sings with joyful, dancing bits of God. It is there, just beyond reach. She knows it. Something is waiting for her.

Finn understands. Finn feels something coming, too.

Her brothers are playing chess in the kitchen and Griete is fumbling with the pots, having promised to do the cooking, for once. "Just today," asks Aleys. "Please."

"So you can pray?" Griete is incredulous. "More?" They share a little altar in the corner of their bedchamber. After he gave her the psalter, Papa let Aleys move the prie-dieu upstairs. Griete has scant use of it. She veers wide of the shrine, performs a knee bob from a safe distance, crosses herself as if in protection from all virgins, and runs to the sunshine.

"Please, just do it." Aleys doesn't say that last night she dreamed of Mama. It was so real, Mama looking up from the kitchen table, her hands deep in yarn. "What is it?" Aleys had asked. Mama had said nothing, but Aleys could read her eyes. *Come meet me*, they said, *in your prayers*.

Domine labia mea aperies. Thou O Lord wilt open my lips.

Rain spatters the windowsill, making little pools. Aleys positions herself on the prie-dieu. She places the psalter before her and opens it to the illustration of the Virgin receiving astonishing news from the angel. She's pregnant. Mary looks strangely happy about it, almost like she saw it coming. Aleys chose this page because Gabriel seems like the best messenger between heaven and earth.

On the page, God shines down from a disc of gold and Gabriel has just alighted before Mary, his wings rigid and high. *Come to me*, *Gabriel*, Aleys prays. *Let me see you. Just once*. Mary has been praying at her prie-dieu, just as Aleys is. Though it's sunny in the psalter and cloudy on earth, Aleys knows that God's favorite angel wouldn't be deterred by rain. She recites the first line of Mary's prayer over and over again: *Ave Maria, gratia plena. Dominus tecum*. Hail Mary, full of grace. The Lord is with thee. In the repetition, the words begin to blur and lose their meaning. Her head swims a little. She can no longer feel her feet. She repeats the verse until it seems the words might thin the veil between this world and the next. She wants to reach out and test it, but she keeps her hands clasped tight. Send the angel, she prays. Bring Mama to me.

And then it happens. The roof lifts away. Aleys grips the stand and looks up to an open sky, where the sun hangs swollen and beating like an enormous heart. Clouds flee in all directions as if frightened, until there's nothing but gold above her. She has entered the psalter. All falls silent and an unbearable sweetness fills her limbs. She doesn't exactly see the angel, but she feels him behind her shoulder. She wants to turn and look but fears he will disappear. Or that he might tell her she's pregnant.

Time stops on a pinpoint of glory. She feels herself breathe, but all else is still. One breath, two, three. Then the angel speaks. She can't say what language it's in, or whether Gabriel speaks aloud. She will remember only one word: *Seek*.

It's a message from Mama.

When the door bangs open and it is Griete, Aleys whispers, "Behold!" But when her eyes return to the ceiling, she sees only rafters.

"Supper is ready," says her sister. "We're all waiting for you."

Aleys goes down in a daze, can barely lift her spoon. The pewter gleams like silver, for hours, until it fades. But her heart holds the glow.

Until it doesn't. For she can't seem to bring the angel back. She prays at the same time, with the same words, in the sun and in the rain. It never happens again, and there is a corner of her that wonders whether maybe, just maybe, she dreamed it.

3
FRIAR LUKAS

Brugge

One league up the canal, in a quiet church in the mercantile capital of the Low Countries, Friar Lukas is at prayer. He's a small man of great faith. *Bring me Martha*, he prays. *Bring me Mary. Send me Ruth, or Miriam, or Esther. A woman of virtue, a woman of learning, who can lead with humility, who seeks material poverty to reap spiritual riches. Bring me a woman with the faith of a saint.*

He has never met a woman like this. Nor a man, he thinks. To be fair.

Friar Lukas, the leader of the Franciscan preachers of Brugge, has sent his band of men into the lanes to fill their begging bowls from the back gates of households. He's stayed behind to pray. *Help me serve you, Lord.* I've spoken to shopkeepers and seamstresses, examined the daughters of merchants, queried midwives and nuns. I have looked high and low to find a woman able and willing to establish a new order in Flanders. A woman who can lead the humble life of Saint Clare, in its pure austerity, to inspire the women of Brugge to the utmost edge of devotion. We need a dedicated, fearless Franciscan woman to lift up this city of greed.

"You want what?" the women say.

Poverty, chastity, obedience. To renounce the material world for a life of prayer. To seek God above all else. To spread his word.

Even the nuns think he's extreme.

Lukas sits back on his heels and sighs. All he wants is to bring God's kingdom to this particular corner of earth, the wealthiest city in northern

Europe. It's been twenty years since he renounced his life as a banker's son and took vows with the Franciscans. Twenty years of preaching on street corners, five as the head of the band of brown-robed friars. He loves his men with their empty bellies and full hearts. He just needs more of them. It's his mission to expand the order. But the people of Brugge are hard with greed like they hunger for hell. They've had no new recruits since Lukas took charge. People love the brown friars, but they don't want to join them. At least, not under him.

But then it struck him. There's another half of the population. When Saint Francis founded their order in Assisi, not so very far away and not so very long ago, he had only a handful of followers—until the arrival of Saint Clare. Upon hearing Francis preach, young Clare gave her possessions to the poor and fled her noble family to join him. Hers was a true faith, and the people responded. Under Francis's guidance, Clare established a large order of Franciscan women. She healed the sick, she fed many from little. Saint Clare's prayer was so powerful she saved Assisi from an attack of infidels scaling the city walls. Dazzled by her, the invaders fell from their ladders and fled. The pope attended her funeral. That's the kind of woman Friar Lukas needs.

Saint Francis had Clare. Abraham had Sarah. Adam had Eve. Well, that didn't work out so well. But that's the point. He needs a rare woman, a woman of virtue and faith, to bring Brugge to God.

4

ALEYS

Damme

As the days grow long, Aleys finds she understands the priests better than they understand themselves. She cringes as their village pastor stumbles through the readings. The Latin syllables wash over the rest of the congregation like a cleansing burble of river water over a bed of stones, but not Aleys. She wants to correct the priest—he stresses all the wrong words—but she can't explain how she knows, so she bites her tongue. Finn is her secret.

But then their priest takes ill, and a substitute, one of the Franciscans, is sent from Brugge. Everyone is impressed by the wandering friars who strive to live like Christ's apostles. Everyone watches to see if they can succeed with so little; there are those who take bets whether they'll survive another year. The friars own nothing but the robes on their backs and the bowls in their hands. They're the begging preachers that Papa admires. No monastery lands. No vineyards. They collect no rents and no taxes, not like the bishop's priests, who grow fat on fees for baptisms and burials, whose trade in indulgences is so brisk that rich patrons purchase forgiveness before they even commit their sins. Claus and Henryk bought discounted pardons from a priest in the next town, stocking up for a life of depravity. "*Miserere mei*," Henryk intones piously, rehearsing.

No, the friars are different. They're like the common people. That's why she loves them. Why everyone loves them.

So the parishioners of Damme welcome this visiting friar, who they say leads his order in Brugge. He's a middle-aged man, rather meek seeming for the head of an order, the fringe of his tonsure starting to gray. He gathers himself as he surveys the congregation. He takes a deep breath and opens the day's scripture and begins to read the Latin verse. Aleys looks up. The man reads like he knows the language. Really knows the language. He probably assumes no one else does. Nevertheless, he starts to redden. A flush creeps over his Adam's apple. He intones, "*Ecce tu pulchra es amica mea*" and buries his head in the book to hide the rest of the line. Aleys stares at him. What did he just say? *Behold, you are beautiful, O my love. Your eyes are those of a dove.* He looks up, and their eyes meet. The friar runs his hand over his bald pate, which glows bright with perspiration, but he doesn't stop. He's actually reading it; he's not making it up. It's like a play about a pair of lovers: *Behold, you are handsome, O my beloved, and graceful. Our bed is flourishing.* In the church! Who is this beloved? The friar is sweating, the congregants are nodding off, and Aleys can't wait to get her hands on the text. She runs from the church to find Finn.

"Oh!" says Finn. The tips of the wheat behind him catch the last of the sunlight. "The *Canticum Canticorum*."

"The Song of Songs?"

"Mmm." He scratches his nose. "I'm not sure we should . . ."

"It's a proper psalm, isn't it?"

"No, it is. It is. It's part of the Old Book. The Canticle is the most beautiful, the most poetic psalm." He looks a bit misty eyed. He's seen it already, she thinks. He can get a copy. She wants a copy. She needs one. Aleys knows, somehow, that it has answers to questions she doesn't even know yet to ask.

"We should read it." She leans in. "For the vocabulary."

When he returns the next day, Finn places the parchment in her hands. The words are astonishing, seductive. *Sicut vitta coccinea, labia tua. Your lips are a scarlet ribbon. And your cheeks are like pomegranate, except for what is hidden*

within. There is a pomegranate in the pages of her psalter, the fruit broken open and garnet seeds spilling down the page, but she'd never thought of it like this. The words make her yearn, make her grow warm, make her push herself against her pillow, which is full of devils. *Fulcite me floribus, stipate me malis. Prop me up with flowers. Close me in with apples. For I languish through love*. She imagines herself on a bed of roses, or shut within a bower of apples, the scent like wine. She yearns to languish with love. Of God, of course.

About her, the colors brighten. The sparrows sing like nightingales; the nightingales sing like choirs. Leaves shiver on the trees as they've never shivered before. Something is happening. Aleys feels she has woken up. She hopes the angel will return. Just so long as he doesn't announce she's pregnant.

Finn feels it, too. He lies beside her in their snug hollow in the field, the soil warming their backs, their hands pressed into the earth. "Do you sense it?" he asks. "The world moving beneath us?" She turns her head and watches an ant climb a stalk, reach the seedhead, put out its feelers. "I do," she says. She senses other things, too. Finn's shoulders broadening, the hair on his forearms turning the color of brass coins. She can smell him now, in their nest, a scent of earth and leather. She thinks he's unaware of it. She wonders if she, too, has a scent.

Summer deepens to fall. Aleys turns sixteen. She wants to cry when their nest is mown down, but they move to the orchard. Finn places rough-sawn planks between the branches of an apple tree to form a hidden bench among the leaves. Our couch, he calls it, and she knows what he means. Right there, in the Canticle: *Our couch is green; the beams of our house are cedars, and its rafters are firs*.

Some passages of the Canticle elude her. She asks Finn what they can mean: *I rose up in order to open to my beloved. My hands dripped with myrrh, and my fingers were full of the finest myrrh*. Finn withdraws quickly, reddening. "Maybe you should ask your priest." Aleys can hardly look at him, is embarrassed by his blush. "I have to go," he says abruptly, jumping from their platform and landing awkwardly, squashing fruit beneath his knee. He takes a few paces, wipes apple pulp from his pants, then turns. "See you tomorrow?" Aleys stays in their tree a while, stroking the backs of her fingers over her cheeks to cool them.

The next day, Aleys arrives in the orchard as shadows from the trunks glide into each other like dark paths. Like invitations. Aleys jumps from one to the next until she gets to their tree. More apples have fallen, and bees buzz around the bruised fruit, the smell sweet as brandy. She pauses, looks around to double check no one's passing on the road, and pulls herself into the tree. Aleys leans back against the trunk and lets her legs dangle, knocking at the apples with her toes. Finn appears suddenly, swinging his leg up to the platform.

"Where were you?" He's not usually late.

"Oh just"—he hesitates—"just at the monastery." He scratches behind his ear. "Aleys, I've been thinking—"

"Me too," she says, "about the verse, what it means." She doesn't elaborate. It feels dangerous, like they're teetering on a knife blade between sacred and sinful. One false step and they'll plummet—or, possibly, fly. But she can't say that. She can't say that she's begun to reconsider her position on marriage. That her fear of bearing children might have an exception, if they were Finn's. He doesn't know that he was her third and final wish. So instead she asks, "Did you bring more?"

Finn pauses, then pulls the parchment from his bag, tender with the page like it's a newborn. The sun casts freckles of light on his face. He's careful not to touch her hand as he passes it to her, as if he, too, feels the live sliver of space between them. Aleys looks down to read and a lock of hair falls from her braid. She shoves it back in and hopes he doesn't notice how awkward she is. She reads aloud: "As the apple tree among the trees of the wood, so is my beloved among the sons." She looks up at the ripe fruit hanging around them. "An apple tree? Truly?" She gives a little giggle, but Finn doesn't respond. He's lost in thought, half listening. She remembers the time they couldn't stop laughing, when she showed Finn that the raindrops suspended from the tips of grasses each held a tiny world. How he'd touched his tongue to a drop and swallowed it. "I am the devourer of worlds," he said, and they rolled around their nest, licking up globes. That was a while ago. They're older now.

Aleys bends her head to the page. This time, she skims the Latin first. She almost can't say the words. They turn her liquid inside. When she speaks, her voice is hoarse. "His fruit is sweet to my taste." She stops. She can't look up or she'll lose her balance. Does he feel it, too?

The leaves stir. She thinks, God has written this for us, God has made this orchard, has set us in this tree, has placed these words of his passion on our lips. Surely, he means us to fly.

Finn reaches up to twist an apple from the branch and holds it out to her. "Sweet like this?" he asks.

Aleys meets his eyes and shakes her head. "No. Like this." She leans in, parting her lips, thinking of pomegranate. She's about to taste the ruby fruit.

"Aleys, I can't." He can. The pulse in his throat, his heartbeat, says he can. He's there, right there.

She lets her lips graze his. "Can't bear the sweetness?"

But Finn stiffens and grabs her wrists, pushing her back. "No." His voice comes from far away. "Stop." Her eyes fly open. It's like he's slapped her. "Aleys, I can't." He looks at his hands, drops her wrists. "I was going to tell you. I . . ."

"What? Tell me what?" She feels herself flood with shame.

He takes a deep breath. "I'm joining the monastery."

She's stunned. "To become a monk? You can't. I thought . . . we would be together forever."

"Aleys. I'm called."

"By whom? By God?" She's incredulous.

"The monks say I have a gift."

"A gift I taught you."

He ignores that. "Aleys, there's an opening in the scriptorium in Ter Doest. They'll teach me, lead me further."

"And what about me? Who will lead me further?"

"I don't know. You're a girl. Join a nunnery."

"I don't want to. Besides, I promised to care for Papa. I thought you and I would . . ." She had thought Finn could move in, that she could keep Papa and her best friend. Her only friend.

"Well." He looks at his hands. "You'll marry."

She brandishes the page before him. "And do what? Read scripture between nursing babes, and spinning, and turning the joint? Finn, I'll be in another man's bed!"

He flushes. "I can't—I can't think about that. I have to go where I'm called."

"Well, so do I." Aleys jumps from the platform and lands hard on both feet. She picks up her skirt and dodges apples as she runs toward the woods so he can't see her tears.

But where? Where can a girl go?

And why hasn't God called her?

The sting of Finn burns like swallowed lye, like her blood has turned molten and everyone can see the fire in her cheeks. Even though Griete's the only one who knew about him, Aleys is sure her shame is stamped on her. She avoids her reflection the way Griete avoids the shrine. There's something deficient about her, something unwomanly that would drive a boy to become a monk. Although that's not fair, and she knows it. Finn loves God as she does. It's just that she loved Finn, too. What a fool. She thought she could have them all: Papa, Finn, and God. It was like the trinity, Father, Son, and Holy Ghost. Only false.

Aleys takes the leavings to the gate, shielding her head with her apron against the rain. A pair of Franciscans appears, their brown robes flapping about their skinny ankles. They have each other, she thinks, always two by two with their begging bowls and shorn heads. No one ever heard of a friar abandoning another, not ever. She wonders if they can see in her face that she's been betrayed. But they murmur the same benediction they always do, like nothing's changed. *Amore Domini Dei.* For the love of God.

She wonders what it would be like to be a friar, to have your mission spelled out for you. To commit to the *vita apostolica*, the life of an apostle. There are Franciscan sisters in other lands, a friar once told her, though not in Flanders. Here, a woman's only choice for fellowship is to vanish behind convent walls. And the nuns aren't that serious, anyway. Everyone knows the abbey is for surplus daughters. God didn't call them; their wealthy fathers sent them. At least Papa wants her to stay.

Aleys studies the eyes of the friars as she ladles soup into their bowls. They mostly look hungry, but what a holy hunger it must be. So unlike Henryk and Claus, who wolf down their food and grab for more. She thinks of Finn eating in the monastery refectory and banishes the image of him. Unlike him, too.

The friars, the monks, the nuns all have companions. Only she has to go it alone. She watches the friars recede down the lane. The rain has stopped. Farrago nudges her and she bends to pat him and then drops into a crouch, hugging him close. She buries her face in his graying fur. The dog leans into her as she whispers how much it hurts to be human. Farrago understands. If only he could speak.

Above, the piercing cry of a hawk. Girl and dog lift their heads. The sound makes Aleys think of angels, armed and angry. She scans the skies.

"Mama," she says to the empty air, "what now? I'm sixteen and out of wishes." If Mama were here, she'd take Aleys in her arms and stroke her hair. But she's not. The only way Aleys can find Mama is in her dreams, like when she prayed and the roof dissolved. That messenger, standing behind her, bearing one word from Mama: *Seek.*

Mama would tell her to seek. No, she thinks, I can't. I'm in too much pain. She buries her head back into Farrago. The dog raises his muzzle to sniff the air. Aleys takes a deep breath. She looks up again.

The hawk threads circles above them. When its scream comes again, terrible and near, Aleys feels the raw broken thing inside her rise to meet the hunting angel.

They are telling her. She's meant for God, not man. That the three wishes lead to a sacred union, not an earthly one. She takes a deep breath.

God is her beloved now.

Show me how to find you, she prays. *I will seek. Show me the way.*

But God sends trials, not road maps. Aleys is rinsing out the small beer jugs when Griete rushes from the side yard holding a leaf that looks like lace. "Our garden!" Aleys throws down the towel and races outside. Decimated leaves litter the ground. The broccoli, the lettuce, even the tomatoes are gone. Bent stalks lean from the soil like wounded soldiers. Cabbage moths. All the crops that they were about to harvest, all of it, eaten overnight. She imagines their root cellar in February, empty. Her heart falls.

Oh Mama, this never would have happened if you were here. Then she thinks, Where there are cabbage moths, there are clothes moths.

Griete has the same thought. They sprint toward the storage shed. Aleys gets there first, rattles the door. Of course it's locked. Griete runs back to the kitchen, grabs the key, fumbles with the padlock, throws open the door. A small cloud of moths puffs out. Griete looks back, ashen, shaking her head.

"How bad?" asks Aleys.

"Bad."

They push into the storage room, sweeping through billowing moths and grabbing stacks of dyed wool and running to the yard and dumping them into the sunshine, piles of red and blue and black. The edges of the fabric crumble in their fingers. They run back and forth until the shed is empty of everything but fluttering gray insects. Aleys bends to pick up a length of indigo wool and lifts it to the sky. Spots of light glare through like evil stars. She drops her arms and looks around. Maybe half their wool is salvageable. Maybe.

"I thought he took it to Brugge last week." Aleys scans the yard. Ravaged plants, ravaged wool. Oh, why hadn't she checked her plants for worms? She'd been so caught up in her fantasies and her broken heart.

"He went to the Lakenhalle, but the guild had lowered prices." Griete wipes her forehead with her sleeve. "Papa thought it better to wait. He thought Mertens might finally grant him a stall." She presses the heels of her palms into her face. "It was such good wool."

Aleys could curse Mertens. They've been waiting on him as long as she can remember. The last time they went to the city to get their wool stamped, she'd sat in the back of a draper's shop, leafing through her psalter, daydreaming of Finn. She barely looked up when a middle-aged man emerged from behind a curtain. He had a pink face, with skin that shone as if polished. The man spoke of weft and warp, but his eyes kept roaming to Aleys. Aleys frowned and turned a page. She saw Griete tilt toward the merchant, tip her blonde head and dimple at him. *Regard my sister, not me.* But Griete's languid blink went unnoticed. Even if she was a flirt, Griete was still nearly flat as a board.

When they left, Griete turned to Papa. "Who was that? He was so comely."

Was he? Aleys didn't find him so.

Papa laughed. "Comely? That was Pieter Mertens, the head of the guild."

"Oh." Griete was no fool. "Who runs the Lakenhalle. He sells wool to princes." Aleys could tell that Griete was thinking she'd like to meet a prince.

They all knew it was Mertens they needed, Mertens who could grant them the license that would allow them to grow. And now, looking at the remains of the wool, she knows they need that license to survive. They'll have to scrub and brush what's left and sell it fast. Aleys looks from the ruined garden to the ruined wool. They've already sold Claus's horse. What's next?

Winter approaches. Her brothers hire themselves out as barge workers, Aleys and Griete take in washing, their knuckles growing raw with lye. Papa sells the salvageable wool, the best they've ever produced, smooth and fine with a graceful drape in royal blue, at a fraction of its value. He's back and forth from Brugge all the time now, trying to negotiate credit with the guild. Aleys promises the spinsters they'll be paid in the spring, once her family sells the next season's wool—if only they can have this yarn now?

Winter settles in. Aleys pulls the last shriveled turnips from the cellar. The friars skip their home. Word is out that hunger is at their back gate.

Aleys finds Griete at the prie-dieu. She tiptoes away. She hopes God hears her sister's list of demands, because they need his help now.

It's just after dawn that Aleys hears hooves in the courtyard. She raises herself to her elbows. A door opens and closes. Papa is speaking in urgent tones with someone in the kitchen. Aleys descends quietly, avoiding the step that squeaks. She peers around the corner just as the messenger leaves. Papa has his sleeves rolled up and his elbows on the table, his head in his hands. He looks at her, then quickly away. He can't seem to speak.

"Papa, what is it?"

"An offer from Mertens."

"And?" Aleys places her hand on his. "The license?"

He nods. "We will join the Lakenhalle."

"At last!" She claps. They're saved. More than saved, they are made. If they can just make it through the winter, they'll sell next year's wool at a premium. With the guild's approval, credit will flow, and they'll be back in production.

Claus appears, rubbing sleep from his eyes. "We got the stall?" Papa nods and Claus lets out a whoop. The others crowd into the kitchen. Henryk is slapping his forehead and Griete is jumping up and down. Old Farrago has heaved himself to his feet and is weaving between their legs, tail flapping.

"Can I buy back my horse?" asks Claus.

Henryk claps him on the back. "You'll buy two, brother." He looks up at the old family shield above the fireplace. "Get that down. I'll polish it." The crest won't be a joke anymore. "We're about to become a major house."

"Aleys." Griete grabs her sleeve. "A dowry! I could have anyone!" She turns to Papa, who's still sitting at the table, looking at the letter in his hand. "Do you think . . ." She breaks off. "Papa," she asks, "what's wrong?"

"Aleys." He looks up, eyes stricken. "He wants to wed Aleys."

Everything stops.

"Mertens does?" asks Henryk.

"He can't do that," says Claus. "She doesn't want to marry."

They stare at her. Griete puts her hand to her mouth.

Henryk speaks. "But she has to." He turns to Papa. "Right? She has to. Or we won't get the license?"

Papa closes his eyes and nods.

"Why her?" asks Griete.

Papa finally regards Aleys. "He wants a wife who knows the draper's business. Who can teach his children to read."

"But I . . ." starts Griete.

Papa puts his hand up. "Griete, this is about your sister."

This can't be real. None of it can be real.

Papa is looking at her, saying something. Something about Mertens being a good man, a wealthy man. She can't hear it. She's looking around the kitchen, at the hearth that needs sweeping, at the familiar blackened pots, at the spot where Farrago sleeps. This can't be happening. She's meant for God, not for men. Marriage will kill her. Papa's voice is far away, still speaking. We need this, he says. I'm sorry, he says.

"I gave him my answer." He places his hands flat on the table. "You'll marry Mertens."

Everything comes into focus, as if a stagehand has yanked away a screen. There was a marketplace behind their kitchen, and she never saw it. Where there had been the hearth, the low stool by the fire, Farrago at their feet, Aleys sees stalls and inventory, account ledgers and scales. She looks back at a father who is suddenly a stranger. Aleys feels, in this moment, transformed from a girl to a bolt of cloth. A daughter whose value has been weighed in the balance. A daughter who's been sold.

5

ALEYS

Pieter Mertens comes from Brugge, dressed in his finest, and spends an hour with her in the garden. It's a warm day with the promise of spring, but Aleys still hugs her maroon cloak tight. Griete watches from the kitchen window. Aleys toes the greening moss by the well while Mertens speaks of mercantile interests, of horses, of tapestries and pearls. He stands too close. He assumes too much.

As soon as he leaves, Aleys runs to her bedchamber and bursts into tears. They can't make her do this. They can't.

Griete enters and leans against the door. "He's not that bad, Aleys. He's healthy, he's tall. He obviously wants a wife."

"But I don't want a husband." Aleys starts pacing back and forth in front of their altar. There must be a way out.

"You could become a nun," says Griete. She sounds hopeful.

Why does everyone want Aleys to become a nun?

"You know, you're not the only daughter in this family." Griete plays with the tassel on her belt. "I'm only two years younger than you. I'm nearly of age."

Aleys ignores this. How can she marry a man like Mertens? She imagines his shiny pink body on a fur-draped bed. She shudders. Perhaps she could be like Saint Cecilia, who converted her husband to chastity on their wedding night. But Cecilia wasn't faced with Pieter Mertens. His heavy breath, his damp fingertips when he ran his hand from her cheek to her neck before she could pull away. Nuptial conversion is not a solid plan. Aleys will have to drink poison the night before. That's how she'll do it. They'll find her at dawn, dark hair strewn across the pillow, pale and pure. Like Saint Ursula. Her suitor isn't exactly a Hun, but still. She'd rather die on the sword than submit to Pieter Mertens.

She prays for guidance. She wants to ask Mama, but she's afraid of the answer. Mama would put the family first. *Never could I leave you, not even for God.* What if Mama expects her to sacrifice herself by marrying Mertens? It's hardly the martyrdom Aleys had hoped for. But Mama also told her to seek. Aleys is so confused. One moment she burns with shame that she would even think to abandon her family. The next, she's furious at Papa's betrayal. She can't look at him, has to leave the room when he enters.

She is sure of one thing. Marrying would break a promise she made to God. Aleys has to leave. But where can she go? She could pound on the doors of a convent, beg to be admitted, even though it's about the last place she wants to be, even though she doubts they'd take her without a dowry. Besides, how would God find her among all those women?

Then she has another idea. A better one. That visiting friar from last summer, the one who blushed as he read the Canticle, is the head of the Franciscans in Brugge. It would be marvelous to be a Franciscan, though she doesn't really know what their women do. Of course, she won't baptize souls or shrive sinners. She's not naïve. In the brown robe, though, she could travel, she could debate, she might even preach. The *vita apostolica*. The open road, the sky, the marketplace, the stink of fish canals, not the walls of a cloister. Or the bed of a merchant.

She confronts the next set of friars she sees. Friar Lukas, she learns, preaches at noon on the corner of the Markt, as reliable as the Lakenhalle bell. So, when the family hitches their newly purchased horses to set up their new stall in Brugge, Aleys grabs her cloak and sneaks into the plaza as the church bells begin to toll.

It's snowing lightly. She spies Friar Lukas preaching to a knot of widows. He's smaller than she remembered. She can't hear his voice over the commotion of the market and the clamor of bells. When he reaches for the sky and his brown sleeves slip to his elbows, she can feel his yearning for God. Aleys has no idea who this man is. But if she's to leave home for the unknown, better this mystery than the certainty of damp breath and sweaty paws.

Friar Lukas sees the girl at the edge of his sermon, feet square on the cobblestones. The marketplace is veiled with delicate snowflakes, the gray of the stones merging with the gray of the sky. He's been preaching on this corner for years, yelling over the constant rumble of carts on the cobbles. He has to compete with hawkers and jugglers and street players, but where better to preach truth to commerce? Lukas once brought a tambourine to get attention, but the people wanted him to do a jig. Christ suffered mockery, he told himself, but no one asked him to dance.

The morning started like any other. "Vrouwen ende mannen!" He waved his arms. "This very house"—he gestured behind him—"is a nest of devils!" As he spoke, merchants in velvet and fur entered and exited the cloth hall, eyeing him as though he might barge in and flip over tables. They'd hired a steward to fend off the beggars, but Lukas knows the man is too afraid of hell to shoo away a friar. The paupers figured this out, too. They use Lukas as a screen to get close to money. He forgives them; he just hopes they absorb God's word as they pick men's pockets. Maybe there is a lenient corner in purgatory for half-enlightened thieves.

"Pity these men you see coming and going. They are like foxes who chase pheasants, though the honeycomb lies broken open at their feet. They pursue gold and neglect the treasures of heaven at their fingertips." He extended his fingers as if heaven could be glimpsed in his palms.

A few people gathered, the regulars. Aside from the pickpurses there were the widows, rapt at his words no matter what. He could read the city charter aloud, and the elderly would gaze upon him with their insatiable appetite for the young—or, in his case, the not yet old. A few others stopped to listen. They stood in a half ring, shifting their weight. Some drifted away almost immediately, looking for better amusement. Well, it's truth he was offering, not entertainment. A pair of workmen paused and put down their heavy sacks. Lukas raised his voice in his most fervent tone, cupped his hands and lifted them: "God grant us the gift of poverty!" He opened his arms in a gesture to shower the congregants with God's love.

The larger of the workmen slapped his thigh. "You can keep your gift, Friar!" he shouted. "I have all the poverty I need!" The smaller one tossed his hands toward Lukas. "Here, take mine, too!" The crowd laughed. Lukas's arms sank to his sides. He had no retort. His throat tightened about his silence, a thick plug in his chest. *Lord, give me words to answer the mockery*. None came. One of the widows shook her fist. He hated when they came to his defense. It made him feel like a child. The workers bowed like players, flourished their caps, hoisted their sacks, and waved as they retreated toward the harbor. The noon bells began to toll.

"The end is upon us!" Lukas shouted. He'd lost his crowd. The paupers peeled off toward the money changers, hands outstretched like dowsers for water. He needed to say something, anything. "The date is known only to the Lord, when the pure shall rise and the wicked shall tumble." It was only the widows left. His voice petered out as he cried, "How long, O Lord, until thy judgment?"

That's when he saw her. She came from nowhere, alighted in the middle of the plaza, bright snowflakes like stars on her maroon cloak. Something wild in her eyes that he recognized, a hunger as clear as water. He thought of Ezekiel. He thought of the gate through which the Lord entered creation. And he wondered for the first time if Mary had been odd in this way, if she had seen right through the world around her. If the angel Gabriel had glimpsed the burning bushes in her strange prophet's eyes and thought, Yes, this is she.

The girl approaches now. "When will it end?"

He frowns.

"The world. You said the world would end."

He smiles. "Soon," he says, looking up to the belfry. "Any moment."

"Yes, I have seen it," she replies. "The apocalypse of every stroke."

He looks deep into her eyes and sees that she, too, is made of prayer. That she belongs to God.

"Father," she says, straightening, "you don't know me." Though I do, he thinks, I do recognize you. "I'm an apostle, willing and devout." She lifts her chin. "My heart is Franciscan. I want . . ."

He squints at her. "What are you asking, child?"

"I want to join your order."

It comes to him. "I saw you. When I preached in Damme."

"Your eyes are those of a dove?" Her small smile tilts into a question.

"Yes! You did understand. I looked for you, after the service. You know Latin? How?"

"I taught myself to read. My psalter. I read it every day."

"That's remarkable." He puts his hand on his heart. "And you seek a life of prayer?"

"Yes."

He nods to himself. "We should talk. If you are in earnest—"

"Please," she interrupts, "there's not much time. Can you come tomorrow?"

6

Aleys

Aleys listens and waits and listens some more. A cool breath sighs down the chimney, stirring the ashes in the grate. Henryk and Claus are finally gone to bed, the dregs of wine silting in their cups. Her brothers were all too happy to start celebrating on the wedding's eve. Papa was unusually quiet and retired early. None of them know that a few days ago, Aleys slipped a scrap of paper to the friars at the gate. "Get it to Friar Lukas," she whispered. "Quickly." Now or never.

The moon traverses the window impossibly slowly, as if it will never reach the peak of the sky. Her fingertips tingle with anticipation, and she bites her palms as if to taste the coming glory. She's about to enter the psalter. She can feel the kingdom around the corner, the armies of angels waiting just beyond sight. From the corners of her eyes the six-winged seraphim flee like wisps of cloud before the storm. *Wait for me!* She knows there is more to this life. She's about to give everything for a sip of the secret honey. Everything.

Beside her, Griete snorts and turns away, pulling the bedclothes with her, creating a chill hollow in the small of Aleys's back. She watches the rise and fall of Griete's round shoulder, forces herself to bear the raw ache of it. *I'll miss you*, she thinks. *I wish I could save you, little sister.* Griete's hair is loose against the bolster. Aleys reaches out to stroke it, to feel it slip between her fingers. She'd like to plait the fair silk strands and loop them into a crown, the way Griete prefers, one last time. Aleys lets her hand fall to the pillow. She's about to ruin them. Griete won't understand. Griete will never forgive.

Stop, Aleys tells herself. You're committed. You're almost there. She shakes herself and checks the window. Now, she thinks. It is spring, the moon is risen, and my new life awaits.

She parts the bed curtains and swings her legs out, one at a time. Griete doesn't stir. Aleys shrugs off her chemise, slips into her linens. She glances at the finery laid out for the wedding, the embroidered sleeves with their intricate metal buttons, long enough to sweep the chapel floor. The buttons wink in the moonlight like mean little spirits. She pinches one and twists it. If only she were wearing it to chapel with Finn. She releases the button. In this world, men—lovers, friends, fathers—abandon women.

Forget men. She has a new beloved now.

Aleys turns from the wedding finery to her wool dress. Her most plain dress, still not plain enough. It should be brown, the color of beasts, not dyed blue to flatter her eyes. Aleys belts the girdle around her waist and reaches for her psalter. She hesitates. The book, vivid with lapis and leaf, is anything but plain. But she can't leave it behind. Aleys slips the psalter into its scarlet pouch and presses the silk to her cheek, feels the smooth slip against her skin, then kisses it and loops the pouch strings around her girdle with practiced fingers. She ties on her stockings and slides to the hall, shoes in hand, down the steps to the back door, the door never opened, unless to let out a casket. She will be dead to them, she knows, once they discover what she's done.

At the back door, Farrago comes to say goodbye. *You alone wait up this hour with me*, she thinks. She scratches him behind the ears. "Adieu, Farrago," she whispers. "I will miss you, dear friend, but I go to God." She swings her cloak over her shoulders, lifts the latch silently, and is free.

She needs no light; she knows the beaten path. At the bridge, she stops. Her hand travels her dark braid, thick and sleek as a living thing, one last time. Then she picks up her pace and her joy bubbles forth, and Aleys runs, she flies toward her beloved. A pair of birds bursts startled from roadside grasses, and she stops to watch their silhouettes wing away. Angels, she thinks, this time I follow.

The church rears before her, large and close. Her feet falter, even as her heart propels. Her step stutters. Why should her feet object? She knows this church, where she was baptized, where the butcher's wife sings off-key, where there is a drafty spot toward the altar. It is a stout and homely village church. Tonight, though, the familiar gray stone feels somber and strange, like a widow at a wedding.

A blemished moon watches through new leaves. Aleys shivers as if the moon's gaze might freeze her to the spot. There is God, there is the devil, and there is the witness moon. It looks skeptical, somehow, like it mocks her commitment. If only the church itself didn't look so cold. She shakes herself. God has called me here. My beloved is within. That thought lightens her heart, and she sprints across the yard and pushes into the church.

The oak doors bang against the walls. At her feet, rose and brown tiles stretch in a diamond path to the apse. A lone taper burns vigil on the altar cloth. Vaulted wooden ribs press from above, a known weight. Her rapid breathing fills the space. She's never seen it empty. The merchants, the baker, the blacksmith, their wives in their woolens. They are all abed, safe. It's rather exciting, being alone in the church. It makes her want to dance.

She closes the doors softly, and the flame reaches toward her. A faint honeyed fragrance, beeswax, floats down the aisle. It's her bridegroom beckoning. Aleys presses her back against the door. She wants a sign. She wants to see him. *Show yourself, my Lord. I am offering my life to you. Show yourself to me.*

And, quietly, before her, she beholds a small miracle, the tiniest of miracles. The flame atop the taper deepens from shivering primrose to something lustrous and deep, a burnished copper. A radiant halo graces the snowy altar cloth, the oak prayer rail, the high cross. The candle burns so vivid it seems alive, both flame and more than flame. It leaps out in sudden relief, borders distinct in the air, colors more brilliant than gems. It is singular. The flame seems not of this world, more real than reality, so real that it throws everything else in doubt. Aleys looks down at her hands, solid and true, and back to the altar. The halo of light is still there. She's not imagining it. He is here.

Her breath comes quick and shallow. She wants only this grace. She feels the kernel of fire deep in her chest, the hiddenmost desire, rush to meet its marriage in the flame, and the joy within her expands and breaks her surface. She will inhale no doubts, exhale no questions. It is all she needs, this sign. She runs to the altar as to an embrace of light.

7
Friar Lukas

Friar Lukas starts at the sound of the church doors banging open. He can't see the girl from his vantage in the side chapel, but he can hear her. Her ragged breath fills the space, fast and urgent, as if she's run like a fox along the canal. He is slightly shocked but corrects himself. After all, he brought her to Christ's chamber door. So the bride is keen, he thinks. I should not begrudge my Lord an eager spouse. Her shallow breaths, coming so urgent, have an almost marital intimacy, as if she and Christ were already joined. A warm shame ascends his throat. He hears her close the doors quietly like she's sealing a bedchamber. He wants to see her face.

Lukas rises from his knees and steadies himself against the wall. He creeps along the passage to its intersection with the nave. He keeps to the shadow, he knows not why. When he peers around the corner, he sees he would have been invisible to her, even in broad daylight. The girl is aglow, her eyes glittering and greedy, her braid glossy, her cheeks burning. Her gaze is fixed on the flame of the taper he lit for her, as if it were a living thing. As if, he thinks, she is witnessing angels.

He glances to the crucifix above and back to the girl, who is under the candle's spell. An annoyance flicks through him; it seems a small heresy to ignore Christ for a candle, but nor can he tear his eyes from her light. The flame burns and she burns with it, and the sweet smell of beeswax seems to come from her and the candle. The air thrums with desire. *What do you see?* He wants to ask. *What do you feel?* His longing is an ache at the base of his spine. His hands dangle cold at the end of his wrists. If he could reach her, touch the back of her hand, her heat would travel his arm and scorch his heart. Her passion would engulf him, would burn away his failures. His sins, his doubts, would become light as cinders. He wants—he holds his breath at the thought—to be consumed in the bonfire. He doesn't move. He watches her from the shadow, his cheeks hot with shame. He can't say which is worse to witness, Aleys's ardor for Christ or Christ's ardor for Aleys.

She sprints toward the altar. Lukas reaches for the robes and the knife and steps to meet her.

8

Aleys

In the morning, as Aleys prays before the cross, there is a commotion. She hears hooves outside. The doors to the church burst against the walls. She rises from knees bruised with prayer. Friar Lukas stands wide-eyed as her father and brothers spur their horses up the aisle. The animals jostle each other before the altar; there's no room for such a snorting cavalcade. Henryk is in front, brandishing the old shield with the lion rampant, as if he's a knight on crusade. Claus pouts, dragged reluctantly from bed. Papa is behind them. She can't look at him.

"She is ours!" Henryk shouts. "Aleys is to be married. Today."

Henryk, she thinks, *you're no knight. Put down the shield.*

Friar Lukas is about to speak, but Aleys raises her hand. The moment is hers. She grasps the altar cloth with one hand. With the other, she sweeps off her new woolen veil. She holds both cloths, brown and white, and drops her head. Aleys imagines their shock at seeing her, crucified, the virgin bearing witness. The men fall silent. Henryk lowers his shield and blinks stupidly, as if she's a stranger. Papa frowns as if he doesn't recognize her. Claus shudders with revulsion. For Aleys is shorn. She looks, as mournfully as she can, at Friar Lukas. A little late to his role in the pageant, Lukas lifts the thick snake of Aleys's gleaming braid like the consecrated host and says, "This night, the maid Aleys has vowed poverty, chastity, and obedience. See here her humility." He waves the braid in the air. It's a bit much.

"Vows, daughter?" Aleys sees the sadness well in Papa's eyes. He tips his head back, addressing heaven. "Let her be God's child, then," he says. "She's no longer mine."

Oh, Papa. If only you'd let me stay. I'd have been yours forever. You gave me no choice. You betrayed me.

Her chest swells with righteousness and cracks in pain. Aleys has never felt so heartbroken. Or powerful.

Later, Aleys sits on a wooden bench in the garden outside the church. Bees buzz about her, not quite a cloud. She ignores them. Her eyes are on Friar Lukas, who's been pacing for what seems like hours. Aleys rubs her temples. It's not even noon, and doubt is already beginning to soil the edge of her triumph. She's not sure what she expected the morning after, but more than this. Maybe a celebration with the brown friars. She feels a twinge of remorse, thinking of her brothers headed home with Papa, outsmarted and defeated. Correction: former brothers. She has an entire order of brothers now, every one of them pledged to God.

Where are they? Shouldn't there be another ceremony? Or even more prayer? She's been sitting forever on a bench in hot wool on a spring day that feels as warm as apples in August. The halo on the altar last night, the flame . . . well, at noon, you can't see the halo. She's not sure it was real. Like the day she prayed the roof from its rafters. The glow fades so fast.

Plus, she's hungry. She forgot about hunger when she vowed poverty.

One of the bees lands on the back of her hand, a tiny winged tiger. With a free finger Aleys strokes his furry back. He tries to crawl up her sleeve, and she shoos him off.

She watches Friar Lukas bend to pluck a dandelion. For a moment, Aleys thinks he might eat it. Lukas has a starved aspect to him, like an underfed wolf. His hair is graying, but his tonsure is freshly shaved. She's noticed how it blushes pink when he's not looking at her and crimson when he does. Friar Lukas should move into the shade.

Aleys runs her fingers beneath her veil, over the damp, bristly hair at the nape of her neck. She imagines the neighbors' surprise when she appears at their back gate, draped in brown, bowl in hand. She thought they'd ply for alms this morning. But Friar Lukas seems sunk in meditation, beating a path between gravestone and lilac, occasionally raising gray eyes to consult white clouds, as if they bear a message. She wishes the clouds would say something about breaking fast. Her stomach growls. She presses her forearm into her new robe to make it stop.

Last night, when Friar Lukas grasped her braid with one hand and sawed through it with the other, she bowed her head to make it taut. The hairs prickled as they snapped under the knife, each one a release: gone husband, gone mewling children, gone chains of lace and pearls. Gone cooking, gone cleaning, gone . . . Her old life fell away as the braid hit the church floor. Aleys lifted her head and savored its cool, light absence, nothing catching, nothing tugging. She felt herself knighted, an honorary male. One with her new brothers.

Papa will have to tell Mertens that his wife has run off with the wandering preachers. She hopes Mertens will let them keep the place in the Lakenhalle, but she knows better. She forces her thoughts elsewhere. She can't think about them now.

Aleys knows she'll be the talk of the town. Friar Lukas will expect her to set an example. He said as much last night. "You'll be like Saint Clare." The women of Assisi flocked to Clare like doves when she joined Francis. Princesses left their palazzi to bathe the feet of lepers. Though, thinks Aleys, Clare didn't live in Flanders. The Brugge city wives would sooner sell the lepers' shoes than wash their feet. It's not like she's become the Clare of the North overnight. Just what does he expect of her?

She cracks her psalter. It falls open to the illustration of Gabriel and Mary. Aleys reads the angel's words in the curling banner that unfurls above him: *Do not be afraid, Mary, for you have found favor with God*. She sighs. She will have to trust them both, God and Friar Lukas.

9

Friar Lukas

Sister Aleys is studying her psalter, her lips moving as she reads. Her hand slips beneath her veil. He's seen this before. The sap of youth rising. The dew on her cheek. The young are all the same. The novice friars can't keep their hands off their shaved skulls, as if they've discovered a new body part. They're blind to their own presence, the way their loud steps announce their arrival, how their cloud of lemon zest assaults everyone around them.

He turns at the end of the path, resumes his pacing.

Friar Lukas feels relieved to be clean of the desires of youth. His body's needs were loud once, but his appetites have dried. When hunger arises in him now, it hovers for a moment, then passes like a wasp from a spent vine. Through discipline, he has become undistracted, a temple dedicated to spirit. He rubs his fingers together and the dry flesh does not grab. He pities the young. Green as weeds, they walk too fast with their begging bowls, duck into alleys to shove a crust of bread into their mouths. Eventually, they master the body. Eventually, they become free of it. She will, too. He knows she's hungry; this is part of the discipline. He's asked Brother Hervé to bring food to the church, but not before the sun is high.

Lukas thinks back on his own induction. It feels like yesterday. The brown friars had no church, so the boys took their vows in a glade. Lukas was the last in line, his knees pressed into damp soil. He heard the others' voices catch, one after another, on the last vow. The first vow, poverty, was nothing to those who'd never tasted it, a glamorous badge of defiance in a mercantile town. Chastity seemed, in the moment, a minor inconvenience and lust a twitch that could be ignored. It was the third vow, obedience, that made a boy's blood freeze in his veins. Lukas looked to his right, at the sons of commerce in their velvet tunics, saw their throat apples bob. Obedience was a futures contract, an unspecified price for goods unseen. It was hard to imagine obedience, let alone pledge it. It was bottomless. The first boy tossed his flaxen head, then accepted the yoke. The second screwed his eyes shut as if jumping from a cliff. Only Lukas accepted obedience gladly, felt his knees root into the dirt. It was a test, he knew, a chance to prove himself. Obedience was the discipline. Obedience was the way. It still is.

Lukas watches the girl stand and stretch, arching her back and looking toward the sun.

It will be harder for Sister Aleys than for his brothers. Women are easily tempted, prone to deception by demons. It's hardly their fault. They're daughters of Eve. He passes his hand over his bald pate. Goats are cropping grass at the edge of the garden, the females among the males. Sister Aleys is an altogether different creature than his brown friars, but he trusts the Lord will show him the way. He cinches his rope belt. He will guide her.

As if she's read his thoughts, she starts to follow him through the garden. This all happened so fast. He's not sure what to do with her. He wonders how Saint Francis handled Clare, who, of course, wasn't a saint when she showed up with more passion than common sense. What did they do that first day? Where did Clare sleep that night? Maybe Francis had a sister or a cousin she could stay with. But he has none. Perhaps he can ask the local convent to house Aleys until he figures it out.

He turns abruptly, and there she is, holding out a sprig of lavender. A piney smell rises from her fingers and pricks the back of his throat. He reaches to accept it, then restrains himself, placing his hands on his belt.

"Give your flower to Christ, not to me."

"Will we not eat?" she asks.

They are standing there, the two of them, when Brother Hervé enters the garden holding an alms bowl. He stops short. Lukas steps back, suddenly aware of what this looks like. He's mentioned this induction to no one, not even to Hervé, his least impressionable friar, a large man whose silent presence deepens the thoughts of all around him. But even Hervé can't hide his alarm. "Lukas?" He raises heavy eyebrows. "What have you—"

Lukas cuts him off. "Brother Hervé, let us step aside." They move to the end of the garden. Aleys follows them with her eyes.

"You've recruited a woman?"

"I wanted to inform the brotherhood, but I had to move quickly." He sees Hervé swallow a protest. "Listen. The order is pressuring us to expand. And she just appeared, like a"—Lukas's eyes rise to the sky—"like a gift from God. She can read and write. In Latin! She doesn't butcher her *pater nosters*. She'll attract followers. She'll be an ornament to the order."

"We need ornaments?"

Lukas sighs and glances over his shoulder. His actions made sense in the night. In daylight, he's already questioning whether this induction was premature. And here's the girl coming toward them in one of their own robes. "Well, it's done, anyway. She's ours now."

Lukas turns and announces a bit too brightly, "Sister Aleys, Brother Hervé has brought you food."

Hervé makes the sign of the cross over the bowl, passes it to her, then stands well back.

Aleys tips the bowl back and drinks avidly. Lukas thinks he should have brought a wimple to cover her throat, but he's a friar—where is he supposed to find a wimple? When she's done, she runs her tongue inside the bowl. Hervé looks away.

"Lukas, she can't join us in the friary." Hervé says this in a low voice, the voice that gentles horses. "She'll create a disturbance."

"I know that."

"So where will she go?"

"I thought the Benedictines."

At this, Aleys looks up, licks her lips, and protests. "The nunnery?"

"You can't expect to live with the men," says Hervé.

"But I'm not Benedictine." She grabs a fold of her brown robe and raises it to show them. "I'm Franciscan." You can't do this to me, her eyes declare, you can't shear off my hair and then pawn me off on nuns from another order. "They're not properly poor, the Benedictines. I'm meant to be with you. With my brothers."

She looks from him to Hervé, who's regarding her like an oddity of nature, a two-headed calf or a fish with ears.

Lukas states what should be obvious: "Aleys, what better place to pray than enclosed with sisters in Christ?"

"No. I won't go to the nuns. They're not serious."

Obedience is going to be more of a challenge than he thought.

"The beguines would take her," murmurs Hervé.

"What?" cries Aleys. "You can't do that." Her blue eyes dart between their faces like a startled moth. "They're even worse."

"Sister, have you already forgotten the vows you made last night?"

She bristles. "Which one? Obedience or chastity? Everyone knows the beguines are wanton."

"The beguines are pious women!" Friar Lukas is their pastor. He's sick of people slandering good women who seek a Godly life, though they lack either the dowry or the desire to become nuns. They live without men, but the town gossips about the begijnhof like it's a brothel.

Aleys is staring at them open-mouthed.

"They run a school and a hospital," offers Hervé, as if virtue and lust were incompatible.

"But their charity's just a cloak for their sins. They hold strange rites in the begijnhof. Lewd rites. It's common knowledge."

Lukas and Hervé exchange exasperated glances.

"They're jades," she insists. "People say they lead honest men astray."

"People say many false things. Have you ever set foot in a begijnhof? You won't find a single man. Aside from priests."

"I hear they choose their own." She waits for that to land. "Priests."

Hervé laughs and puts a hand on Lukas's shoulder. "Usually one of us."

"The bishop doesn't like them," she asserts.

"No, he doesn't," agrees Hervé. "The women prefer our friars to his church clergy. The beguines, you could say, are rather independent."

That much is true, thinks Lukas—they are ungoverned. The beguines of Brugge have never accepted a monastic rule, unlike the nunneries regulated by the Church. The beguines write their own rules. They're not cloistered. But that doesn't make them loose. On the contrary. Lukas knows many beguines more devout than nuns, and they work much harder, since they have to make their own living. He has great respect for the beguines.

"Sister," he says. "You do understand you're on probation."

"I am?"

"Of course. You're a novitiate."

He sees the surprise in her eyes. Did she think she'd proven herself just by running from home? Hadn't they discussed this? He thinks back and realizes he'd spoken at length about the beauty of the *vita apostolica*. Not so much about its duties. "You must demonstrate that you're suitable to join the order."

"Oh."

"You will emulate Saint Clare. You'll draw other women to the Franciscan way."

"But . . . how?"

"Well, Saint Clare asked her sister, then her mother, to join her. Others followed."

"My mother is dead."

He winces. He softens his voice. "Then you'll win women over with your faith. Starting in the begijnhof."

"She'll have to work," says Hervé, "if she joins the beguines."

Aleys shakes her head.

"You refuse to work?" asks Lukas.

"No. It's not that." A bee has landed on her brown sleeve. She looks at it with something like sadness. "I mean, the beguines are not"—she searches for the right word—"that holy."

"They're humble," he says. *Unlike you*, he thinks.

But her eyes plead with him, and he glimpses again her wild desire. The beguines don't soar, her eyes seem to say. They can't teach me to fly.

Lukas understands. He does. But first she must crawl.

He claps his hands. "The swiftest path to God is obedience. You will live among the beguines. I give you two months, until Midsummer, to recruit the first sisters to our order. Consider this your first test."

Liber Secundus

10
Aleys

The begijnhof turns its brick back to Brugge, facing inward, each house tight against the next. Here and there, windows push open above a canal that swells into a pond before the entrance. An arched footbridge cinches the middle of the pond like a belt. Half a dozen vigilant swans patrol a miniature island. Others stand guard on the bank. Each twists its thick neck to fix Aleys with inked eyes, feathered soldiers defending a moat.

It's not what she expected. Aleys thought the beguines would live in lopsided, debauched houses, loose beamed and flapping open to the town. Hardly. The cobbled entrance to the begijnhof seems like a drawbridge to a tidy fortress. It's entirely enclosed. The busy square outside is crammed with the shops of butchers and bakers, a tailor and a chandler, mostly fronted by brick, but some in beam and plaster, and one in ramshackle wood that leans over the canal. Inside the begijnhof, across the bridge and through doors the height of two men, Aleys senses something different.

She follows Friar Lukas over the bridge. He never told her that she'd be a novitiate, like the new girl at a nunnery. What if she fails? She can't go home. Her stomach clenches. Not even a convent would take a failed Franciscan who ran away. She adjusts her robe, rubs her arms to calm herself. She will hold her head high as she enters this arena. The beguines aren't wild beasts, she tells herself, just wild women.

They pass through the entrance and the sound of carts and commerce falls away. Aleys stops short at the scene before her. Within the contained court, all is white and green and breeze. A ring of whitewashed homes, maybe twenty or thirty, each capped with red-tile bonnets, hugs a large grassy yard lined with tall trees strung end to end with linens. A faint smell of brine gusts over the rooftops.

They've stepped into another world. Papa once brought home a decorated egg; you peered through a small round window in the shell, and beheld inside a miniature scene of the nativity, perfect and complete. Aleys had wanted to enter that world, to dig her fingers into the sheep's wool, to gaze into Mary's eyes, to lift the infant from the cradle and sniff its milky skin. Papa let her keep the egg on her altar for a week before he returned it to the sailor he'd met on the wharf. She mourned its loss. Aleys would have crept inside that egg and never come out.

The wind shifts, a change in tempo, and the sheets on the lines begin to rise and fall in waves, a billowing ocean of snow, and Aleys imagines she could swim from one end of the courtyard to the other, where a gray stone church rises like a headland. The breeze shifts again and the sheets snap like the wings of gulls rising from the sea. She can't tear her gaze from them.

"Sister." Friar Lukas is speaking. "Aleys?" It seems the sheets have a message for her. What is it? What is God saying? Lukas should stop interrupting.

All falls silent. The spell is broken. The linens settle back to their lines. Cloth alleys appear between trees. Between them, brown-stockinged legs kick a ball. Giggles rise from the bleaching.

"Ach! Don't you muddy my sheets with that ball!" Across the courtyard, an exasperated young woman stands from her stool and waves bristled paddles at the children, fine strands of wool trailing down her wrists. She and two others are carding outside one of the houses, a black cat stretched on the sill behind them. The rhythmic *scritch scratch* halts as all three look at Aleys and Lukas. The giggling stops. A ball rolls from the linen alley as if presenting for punishment.

One of the carders pushes aside a blonde braid with the back of her wrist as she looks up at Aleys. The third woman elbows the first: "Look, see? That must be her." Aleys is suddenly conscious of her monkish robe, her smudge of brown amidst the green and breeze. They are staring at her, three young women in simple dress and aprons, judging Aleys in the strange robe with the thrice-knotted belt. I'm wearing linens underneath, just like you, she thinks. You don't need to stare. Aleys lifts her chin. She will be as brave as Perpetua entering the arena.

Then the church bell rings, the three turn in unison toward a house, a door opens, a tall woman exits, the cat hops down, and Aleys feels gears whirring, like she's stepped inside a well-tempered clock. She half expects the woman in the doorway to chirp the hour. Instead, the woman pauses to kick the ball back to the children. Small hands show under the sheets, grasp the ball, throw it down the linen alley. The children are off again. Laughter resumes from the laundry. All is set right, the hour resumes. Straightening, the woman notices them.

"Friar Lukas. I thought we might see you this morning."

The woman's bearing is elegant and brisk, her eyes clear and intelligent. In a simple white veil and wimple over a plain gray dress, she could pass in town for a widow. A happy widow. Her face bears the creases of contentment.

Friar Lukas places his hands inside his sleeves, gives a small bow. He has obvious regard for this woman. "Magistra." He turns to Aleys. "I introduce to you the magistra of the Wijngaerde, Grand Mistress Sophia Vermeulen."

The magistra inclines her head. "Introductions are unnecessary, Lukas. Your young sister is the woman of the hour." Her eyes rest on Aleys's face. "Everyone is talking about you." She seems more amused than shocked. Raising an eyebrow, she inclines her head toward the women who've set down their carding paddles and are drawn into a knot, simply gaping. "It's not every day someone runs from her betrothed to join a band of friars."

"I didn't run from him." Even as Aleys blurts the words, she wonders if they're true. "I was running to God." Lukas shifts, embarrassed, like she's said something indecent.

Sophia regards her with a steady gaze. The moment stretches, the older woman studying the younger one. Finally, the magistra nods. "Yes, child, I think you were."

Sophia shifts her focus to Lukas. "You would have her stay with us? Your brown—what do we call her? Nun?"

"I'm not a nun."

"Friar, then?" Sophia purses her lips to hide a smile.

Lukas interrupts. "Sister will do."

"Certainly. We are all sisters here." Then, as if she detects Aleys's reluctance, "This is your wish? To live with us?"

Of course not, Aleys thinks, but Lukas's stare binds her like a commandment. She nods.

Sophia's cheeks hollow slightly. "Of course, you've heard tales about the begijnhof."

Aleys feels a blush rise to her cheek. Here, in this crisp courtyard, the rumors seem implausible. She's heard strange things about these women. People say beguines are not just immoral in the regular ways, vice and lust and wickedness. They're immoral in ways no normal person would even want. They pray at the bedsides of the dying, for nothing. It's too virtuous, such charity. A priest will mumble last rites and leave with your coins in his pocket. The beguines will stay at your deathbed and pray in low voices, ushering you from your last breath in this world to your first breath in the next. People call them the midwives of death. Claus used to stumble about the yard, pretending to be a beguine, arms outstretched like the reaper. Henryk claimed their prayers were as potent as those of virgins, but he still wouldn't want to touch one. Only Papa thought it unfair that the healthy were quick with their insults but quicker still to call the beguines to their deathbeds. *Oh, Papa. You never imagined me here.*

Sophia sees her blush. "Yes, I can see you've heard about us. People will sow rumor like spring seed. They need better stories." She presses two fingers to the edge of her eyebrow. "The truth of the begijnhof is too plain for a good tale. We commit to three things: simplicity, charity, and chastity. They're not formal vows, nor lifelong ones, but we pledge them to each other. And we support ourselves, so of course we value industry." She looks at the carding women. "More industry than gossip," she says loudly, and waves the back of her hand at them. The three resume carding, though not without frequent glances their way. "You'll join us in work, as well as worship?" She raises her eyebrows at Lukas.

"Sister Aleys will do what you require," he answers.

Aleys bites her tongue. She can't fail her vow of obedience on her first day. But she left home to pray, not card wool. He's presenting her like a draft horse. He might as well have a switch in his hand. The magistra looks pained. As she starts to say something, they are interrupted.

"Friar Lukas!" Behind them, a large woman in gray strides through the arch, a leather purse slapping against her thigh. The chink of coins accentuates her step. As she bears down on them, heat lifts from her in waves.

"Lukas, how could you do this to us?"

She stops just short of Sophia. The two women are of similar age, but where character has written grace on Sophia's face, it has chiseled indignation into this one.

"Magistra, this morning I had a meeting with Pieter Mertens. Or should have had"—her jaw tightens—"to set the summer wool price. Then the van Bruyk daughter, from Damme, this one"—her hand chops at Aleys—"jilts him." She glares at Lukas. "To become one of yours. That's what they're saying." She appeals to Sophia. "Pieter's in a foul mood. He's a laughingstock from here to the sea. And Lukas would deposit her in the begijnhof?"

Lukas opens his mouth, but she rounds on him. "Did you stop to think how this would affect us? Did you even think to clear it with the bishop?" She spits out the word. "What will your brother say?"

Aleys isn't sure she's heard right. His brother? Friar Lukas is brother to the bishop? He never said. However, there seems to be a lot she failed to ask about. Like where she would live.

Friar Lukas's mouth narrows. "I don't owe the bishop any . . ."

"Oh, spare me your family quarrel. You need his approval. We all know it. Or you'll bring nothing but trouble upon your order. And on us, if you drag us into this business. A girl who abandons a contracted marriage to join a band of men? Why would we invite such scandal under our roof? A real scandal? When half the town tars us with lies? And our wool contract!" She claps her hands to her wimple. "Why in heaven's name, Mistress Sophia, would we take this girl in?"

"Because, Sister Katrijn, Friar Lukas is our confessor, and he has asked it of us."

"We don't owe him obedience."

"No," she agrees, "not obedience. But we do owe him our trust. If Lukas brings us a girl who's dedicated her life to that of an apostle, we will shelter her. Imagine if he had brought us the Magdalene, Katrijn. Would we turn her away? Christ's favorite?"

Katrijn exhales sharply and looks toward the church. Mistress Sophia places her hand on Katrijn's elbow. Katrijn softens at her touch.

"Sister." Sophia's voice is gentle, but its authority unquestionable. "I have already decided."

"Mary Magdalene better earn her keep," grumbles Katrijn.

Sophia ignores this. "Very well," she says to Lukas. "We will put Sister Aleys in the dormitory."

"And she will work where?" demands Katrijn. "I don't suppose she can handle coin." She looks hard at Lukas. The thought is plain on her face: You Franciscans, too pure to handle money, but quick enough to let hardworking people fill your bowls.

Aleys decides she doesn't like Sister Katrijn.

"Enough, Katrijn," says the grand mistress. "There is ample work for her."

Sophia claps her hands. "Cecilia!" Across the courtyard, the girl with the blonde braid brightens and passes her carding paddles to the others, dusting her hands on her smock. As she nears, a frizz of wheat-colored curls escapes Cecilia's cap. She wears a dress of the sort a country girl might wear to church.

Cecilia beams at her. "Hello, miss." She bobs a curtsy. Aleys inclines her head.

"Sister," Sophia corrects Cecilia. "We are one family in the begijnhof." Aleys senses that the message is meant for her as well. "Sister Cecilia, please show Sister Aleys to the dormitory."

Cecilia's eyes dart to Katrijn, seeming to check her approval. Katrijn's lips tighten but she gives a small nod.

"Now," Sophia adds.

Cecilia takes Aleys's arm and guides her down the path, but not before Aleys hears Sophia's next words. "The girl can stay, Lukas. But Katrijn asks a good question. What exactly does the bishop know of this?"

11

The Bishop

It is the year of our Lord 1298, and the Church is uneasy, a fat beast circling itself, snapping at its tail. Jan Smet, Bishop of Tournai, is in his manor house, counting all his money. His accountant, a thin man with a scant moustache, leans over the books he's lugged into the dining room, squinting up for approval as his finger traces ruled columns. The man looks like he eats nothing but bone broth. Good. Accountants should be thin. It shows they haven't been skimming the coffers.

"Your Grace." The accountant's finger shakes as he reaches the figure at the base of the page. "This last venture, well, it was not as profitable as usual, though . . ." His finger steadies as it moves to another column. "As you see here, they did retrieve some relics we could sell." The accountant taps a list of plunder from the recent crusade: saints' bones and splinters from the cross. *The* cross, if you're gullible. His accountant is right. The relics could bring in some cash, as long as the buyers believe they're genuine. The bishop knows better. If you added up every holy bone that a knight has pulled from a dusty saddlebag, you'd deduce that Saint Peter had four legs and two heads. The cross must have been the size of three longships. The bishop retains the best relics for his cathedrals. Long bones of saints attract tithing tourists. The rest—well, the bishop views the sale of minor relics as a sort of holy lottery. Some buyers take home miracle-working bits and ends of martyrs. Others will be praying to the knuckles of sheep farmers. Their coin is the same.

"Your Grace," murmurs the accountant, "it is not enough."

It never is. Crusades have their charms, but they've been growing ever more expensive and less and less productive.

"Well?" he says. "You're my accountant. What do you suggest?"

"Sir, there are always indulgences." As if he's read the bishop's mind, he adds, "We could pardon the blasphemers and moneylenders."

"Perhaps." Taxing the blasphemers who complain about the Church is satisfying, but not especially profitable. Lofty morals, shallow pockets. Better to tap the moneylenders. "What's the going penalty for usury?" The Church runs a brisk trade in pardons to men who lend with interest. Notorious usurers, as the pope calls them, are forbidden communion or a Christian burial. Unless they obtain his, the bishop's, forgiveness. The solution is simple: The Church sells its indulgence, and the moneylenders hike interest rates and count the price of pardon as one more cost of business.

"Three guilders, Your Grace." The accountant hesitates. "But you may want to lower that, sir. The market is growing a bit . . . restless."

Jan already knows this. His men on the street have told him that the mood toward the clergy has shifted. They should have seen it coming, but the Church was looking the other way. The pope insisted that the threat was from Acre, from Constantinople, from Moors at the gate. While they were busy raising levies and armies, funding knights under Christian banners—*Deus vult!*—they failed to see the quiet threat festering at home. It came back from the Holy Land in bolts of silk, in jars of spices. The hubbub and babel of markets and ports, of couriers and tutors. The bishops looked up from the crusades and suddenly, merchants were everywhere. And merchants must read, and reading, they question.

The bishop sighs. "The merchants are demanding we repay their loans."

The accountant nods quickly. "Yes, Your Grace. They see that the knights are almost all come back. The patrons hope to recoup their investments."

"We are unable to pay them." The bishop states a fact he already knows.

The accountant stares hard at the ledger as if a miracle might change the bottom line. Then he adds, reluctantly, "Your Grace, this morning someone asked to return his relic. He complained it didn't cure his gout. He wants his money back." The accountant looks up at the bishop, eyes worried. "He doesn't believe it's real."

"Who doesn't believe?" The bishop puts up his hand as soon as he speaks. It doesn't matter. It could be any of them. Half the town is challenging the legitimacy of the Church, grousing about corruption. Meanwhile, the other half grows ever more pious, wailing about the coming apocalypse and looking for his clergy to grant miracles on demand, as if it were in their power to conjure favorable winds and healing waters. He's not sure which half is worse, the doubters or the believers. The bishop gives a puff of exasperation. "Never mind. Just exchange it."

"For?"

"Give him one of Ursula's kneecaps." There are half a dozen in the storeroom.

The bishop runs his hands through his thick curls. When did everything become so difficult? It used to be manageable, just the monasteries that run themselves and send lovely fruit brandies at Christmas and joints of lamb at Easter. A handful of quiet nunneries for spare daughters of the nobility. And, of course, the diocesan parishes he oversees, with their biddable priests whose names he can never recall. Jan Smet supervises all of it, a scarlet-clad king with a peaked cloth crown. Clerks scurry at his whims. Sovereigns weigh his opinions. He has spiritual dominion over a city of nearly forty thousand souls, or so his friend the mayor brags. Granted, they're not as cultured as Paris or as powerful as Venice, but men call Brugge the market of Europe for good reason. Wool. Most of Europe's wool is made or sold in his diocese. The city may be laced with canals, but it is built on wool. Fleece comes in on barges, wool goes out in carts. The cloth of Flanders is famous for a weave so dense and a nap so soft that it draws merchants from Germany, Genoa, France. In Brugge, they sell to princes. Shame he can't tax them.

The bishop squints into the dimly lit chamber. He should have had them light the candles. Even at noon, the manor is in permanent twilight. He looks toward the window. No, it's not so simple anymore. Everyone is questioning the Church. Everyone wants something from him. He taps his ring on the table before him, impatient.

Just the other day, his own brother was in here asking for money. Lukas, head of the Franciscans of Brugge, one of those new preaching orders that shuffle around in their robes and sandals, flaunting their *vita apostolica*, claiming to live as Christ's apostles. The friars' gaudy poverty makes even his most impoverished clergy look flush. They tell his people it's not enough to have nuns pray for their salvation, not enough to be baptized, to tithe regularly and confess rarely. No, they must actually live like Christ. Extremists.

If their father had lived, he'd have bought Lukas a bishopric, and that would have been the end of that. The banker had intended to seed two bishops, buying a promise of heaven and permission on earth in one fell swoop. No sooner had he secured Jan's seat than he dropped dead. From an excess of blood. Too sanguine. Cheerful as a chicken. Who dies of sanguinity? Jan knows his own humors are tempered by choler. He lifts a glass to himself; his ruby winks in the light. Choler makes the sun go round. Too bad Lukas lacks any spice to balance all that damp melancholia. No fun at a banquet. Not much of a preacher.

Mother always treated Lukas like she'd birthed a saint, fawning over his prayers. "How lovely," she'd sigh, and raise her chin to heaven, while Jan burned in a furious boyish hell beside her. Mother, with her soft eyes and hard glances, had made perfectly plain which son she preferred. No matter. He had his father's approval and his purse. It irks him how Lukas wants it both ways now, how he parades his poverty, then comes calling with his hand out. He loves his brother, but it's too much. Those ghastly open sandals. You can see the man's toes. Jan curls his feet within his slippers.

He's not alone. All the bishops of Europe are plagued with wandering preachers. Friars are suddenly everywhere, sprung from nowhere, like weevils in a sack of grain. There are not just one, but two sects infesting all of Europe: the Franciscans and the Dominicans. The pope finds them useful. They make good inquisitors, since the people see them as honest brokers. If the pope tolerates them, then his bishops must, too. But the friars stir up the people with their notions of apostolic poverty, with the idea that they, too, might get close to God. That the Church has grown too fat. And then Rome expects its bishops to tamp down the religious fervor and raise money at the same time. The pope wants it both ways. Friars to keep the Church honest, bishops to keep the Church profitable. Bless him.

The accountant looks at him with blinking eyes.

"Go on, then. Tax some moneylenders. Just not the wool merchants." The mayor won't like that. "And send Willems in."

The accountant lifts the books and nearly trips over his feet in his haste to leave. Jan rubs his temples. He could have gone to a monastery and lived a life of ease as a monk. He pictures a sleepy abbey, with vineyards and pigs, a library, busy bursars counting rents. Though the monasteries are poor in theory, he knows he would have been comfortable. A monk may not own the cup he drinks from, but he will never want for wine. They own plenty of property, communally, and live long lives far from town and plague. They can pull shut their doors when God's hand gets too near. It's not a bad life. Guaranteed a place in heaven, better fed than most on earth. The monks are God's field hands. It's not for Jan, the humble life.

And the wandering friars' humility puts the abbey monks to shame. It's its own kind of pride, he thinks, humility. Take the beguines, those self-righteous burrs beneath his saddle. They're as bad as spring mushrooms, popping up all over Europe, from Florence to Frankfurt. Groups of women—the bishop shudders—unsupervised women, who form their own communes and make their own living and won't answer to the Church. They refuse to operate under papal rule. What's worse, they're in bed with the friars, and his own brother ministers to the largest begijnhof in Brugge. They multiply like rabbits, those holier-than-thou women who won't answer to him. There are more beguine colonies in Flanders than anywhere else. Like lepers, he thinks. They ought to wear bells. He's surprised the pope hasn't banned them. He supposes Boniface already has his hands full of radicals who complain the Church is corrupt and heretics who claim it's wrong.

Jan stretches and walks to the window looking over the cathedral square. His blue and gold flags stand at stiff attention, announcing his dominion. Even the secular church that he leads, all the parishes across Tournai, well, that used to be easier, too. It's unfortunate how shorthanded they are. The people complain his priests are barely literate, which is true enough, but it never used to bother anyone. Few fathers read Latin, fewer still can recite the hours. Water on the forehead, dirt on the coffin. These are the services they provide, for a fee. He imagines the clink of coins in the offertory, how they slide and jostle as they gather from village to town, gathering tributaries flowing toward his cathedral. These are streams of copper, not rivers of silver. The parishioners complain that the required tithes are too high. But they aren't enough for the Church. Rome requires gold.

If only he were in Rome. All Jan needs is one more promotion, and he could join the ranks of the curia as a cardinal and spend his time choosing the next pope and sampling the wines. He hears the Roman vineyards are extraordinary. To be promoted, he needs the favor of the seated pope. Money would help, but he doesn't have it. He has other ideas, though.

A click of heels on the stone, a pause at the door, a cough. Without looking over his shoulder, Jan says, "Approach, Willems."

Jan spotted Willems in a company of traveling players in the square outside the cathedral some years ago. It was a chill November day and his assistant had forgotten the furs. Jan had seen the annual mystery plays so many times that he could recite the lines of God and Lucifer and every good and evil angel. He was required to give his annual blessing. That year's God was tiresome, overacting and heavy-handed. Jan had half a notion to sweep up onto the wagon stage and banish God before he could exile Lucifer to hell. But he was too late.

"In mischief and menace ever shalt thou abide, in bitter burning fire, in pain ever to be put." God's grimace was comical, reaching for the back of the crowd.

But Lucifer, a dark-haired actor dressed in black, skin so ghostly pale, delivered his reply with subtle defiance and despair: "Now I am a devil full dark, that was an angel bright."

I could use a man like that, thought Jan. As the troupe packed the wagons for Antwerp, Jan sent for Lucifer. "I need someone," he told Willems, "to be my eyes and ears in the market. Someone who doesn't call too much attention to himself, but who can deliver a chill to those who require"—he cleared his throat—"chilling."

Willems approaches through the shadowy hall with feline grace. Cloaked in black livery with the bishop's small golden crest on his shoulder, the man retains something of hell about him. It's most satisfying. Willems bows beautifully. "Your Grace?"

"Willems." He does not need to be delicate with Willems, not after all these years. Their motives are aligned; Willems will come with him. The bishop will enjoy the loose Roman women. He pictures them ripe and soft as olives for the plucking. His servant will enjoy the—well, Jan doesn't really know what Willems prefers. Some mysteries are best left untouched. Jan pinches the bridge of his nose. "I've been contemplating the pope's interests. The materials you apprehended."

"Yes, Your Grace." There is a glint in Willems's eye. He's been quietly purchasing contraband from back stalls in the market, the sort of goods slid behind curtains or exchanged under bridges. Yesterday, Willems produced several sheets of cheap parchment, set them on the table and stepped back quickly, fingers spread, as if even the devil found them godless. The bishop looked at his man, normally so cool, then down at the pages. Then he looked more closely. They were lettered in Dutch, the letters slanted, scrawled in haste, which was unremarkable enough—until he realized he was reading a psalm. In Dutch. Right there, on the page, in common language. The bishop sat up.

"Where did you get this?" Rome abhorred translations. *Not without reason*, the pope had written, *did it please Almighty God that Holy Scripture should be secret*. It took years of training to interpret the Bible. It was one thing to allow people their psalters and books of hours; those were carefully curated, and the people only half understood the Latin anyway. It would be another thing entirely to give them free access to the entire Bible in their mother tongue. People would start reading scripture on their own, without the supervision of a priest. The pope has clearly forbidden these *occultis conventiculis*, hidden gatherings in which people treat gospel like it was written for them. Rome wants to strangle this movement in its cradle. It didn't end well for the translators in southern France and eastern Germany.

"I thought you should know," Willems had said. "These are circulating in the Markt."

"There are more?"

"New ones every week, apparently. And they're being copied."

This is what comes from whipping up devotion. It's the fault of men like Lukas who plant radical ideas. He doesn't think the friars are actually doing the translations—they live literally hand to mouth, they have no means—but they provoke unnatural desires in his people, insinuating that they, themselves, can know God. Good luck with that.

Jan has enough experience of God to know he is absentee, hardly paying attention. His people have been kept safe from any real knowledge of God—until now, happy enough to cross themselves at Mass, never mind they don't understand the words. Lately devotion has been spreading like wildfire. He shudders. The grotesqueries that people come up with. Now they treat God as their mother or as a maiden in a castle. They're so full of longing. It horrifies him. It was better when they were full of fear. Not that the bishop fears him. God is, to the bishop, a benevolent uncle who has left a bequest and disappeared; the rituals must be observed, but he has withdrawn his gaze. The bishop imagines an elderly God, nodding asleep at the banquet, his beard in the soup.

But his people want a young God, a handsome God. They demand a courtship with God, they want God to be their lover. They want to read scripture as if psalms were love letters.

Tracts like these could get him in trouble, if Rome were to learn of Dutch scripture circulating in his diocese. He must quash this quickly. He pauses.

He's not the son of a banker for nothing; he can calculate his interests here. Is there a way to flip this to his advantage? He turns back to the window and twists his ring, letting his eyes travel beyond his fluttering flags to the Lakenhalle tower. He adds up all the illegal parchment being passed hand to hand. What a spectacular bonfire it would make. No people, mind you. They don't have to be fanatic about it. Just heresy in print. In Lombardy, they burned pages of Saint Peter in French; in Metz, they burned Saint Paul in German. He heard those bishops were promoted. What's to stop him from building a bonfire in Brugge large enough to be seen from Rome?

"Willems, gather the Dutch scripture. Quietly. And find out who the translator is."

12

Aleys

Cecilia pulls Aleys across the begijnhof courtyard, toward the lowest and longest of the buildings, where the other girls are carding wool, or at least pretending to. The *scritch scratch* of the wire brushes pause. Aleys feels the girls' eyes upon her back as Cecilia pulls her up a narrow wooden staircase that opens to a dormitory. Here, the light from the courtyard filters through leaves and reaches into the window, so that the whitewashed walls flicker green and gray as the laundry snaps below. Within, all is as one might expect: for each woman, a chair, a cot, a stiff prie-dieu with an unpadded kneeler. Upright furniture, straight edges, no embellishments. Simple in the extreme. Aleys thinks about Mama's psalter hidden beneath her robe in its scarlet silk pouch. How gaudy the little book would look on the sloped shelf of the bare prie-dieu, a gem of temptation. She glances around. Possessions are few, cloaks on pegs, a comb on a chair. Despite what she's heard about beguines' unholy acts, she doesn't think they steal. Besides, there's nowhere to hide even a pin.

Or pray. Aleys regards the prie-dieu with dismay, jammed between chair and bed, the plainest of crosses nailed to the wall above. She tries to imagine herself kneeling there, offering her soul amidst chatting, sighing, snoring girls. Cheek by jowl with breathing beguines, how is she expected to pray?

"Here, next to me," says Cecilia, patting the empty cot. The other five are taken. Cecilia is a large girl with dimpled hands and a voice deep as molasses. "I've been here just a few months, you mind, but Sister Katrijn has already said I can come live in her house, once I take the gray dress. This dormitory's for the girls as not yet committed. Some of them leave to get married, the beguines don't mind. It's not so bad, living here. The girls are friendly. And it's comfortable enough. I didn't know much more fancy from home. You aren't from the farm, that I can tell." She tilts her head, hesitates in the way of people who know better but can't stay their tongues. "Miss, if it's not prying too much, everyone's wondering. They say you were about to wed the head of the drapers' guild. You'd never have wanted for wool, that's for certain." She looks at the robe. "I suppose you do have that. But silk, you could have had silk dresses and furs on your bed. So, if it's not too forward, miss, why ever did you do it?"

I should have gone to the convent, thinks Aleys, at least they keep silence. Aleys knows there's no point in trying to explain herself. How can she say what she seeks? That she has left home to find God, that he cloaks himself in plain sight, that she wants to catch him like children hiding in the apple trees. It would be like asking someone to help her find the sky. They all call it blue, but she knows it's truly gold, if only you look at it the right way. It is gold and green and shot through with angels. She looks at Cecilia's open face and knows the girl could never comprehend. How can Aleys explain that she already knows she won't find her beloved in the begijnhof? She parries.

"First, tell me. What brought you here?"

Cecilia colors, looks at her feet. "My parents, they'd had enough of me."

"What? Why?" It's hard to believe that Cecilia wasn't beloved, with her round cheeks and toothy smile.

"Well, I wasn't so easy for them."

"They sent you here?"

"I didn't know where else to go." She twists her pretty mouth. "My father, he turned me out, miss."

Oh. Cecilia was probably caught behind the barn with the baker's son. Or the butcher's boy. Or a field hand. Why they didn't just marry her, Aleys wonders, but doesn't ask.

"Anyway." Cecilia brightens. "It's all right here. I like the city."

They stand there, looking at Aleys's cot. She owns nothing beyond the psalter that she can place on the bed or chair to mark it as hers. Cecilia screws her forehead into a knot. "And to think you could have had furs." Then she shakes her head and clears the frown. "I suppose there's nothing for it. I'll have Marte get you some bedding." In a nimble move, Cecilia hoists herself onto the chair between their cots, places her hands on the windowsill, and leans out. "Marte!" she bellows, then looks back at Aleys with a grin. "At least we have a servant. You can be sure there was none of that where I came from." She turns back to the window. "Marte! Hurry up!"

Aleys hears the door's hinges below, and an uneven tread ascends the stairs. "She's new," says Cecilia, as if that explains her slowness. It takes a long moment for the servant to reach the doorway, but then she is framed in the greenish light, a woman with a plain, weary face, already running to jowl. Her eyes are unremarkable, a watery hazel, but for the purple bruise across her left cheekbone. She meets Aleys's gaze and scowls before she looks away, whether from shame or defiance, Aleys can't tell.

"Marte!" commands Cecilia. "Get Sister Aleys some proper bedding."

Marte doesn't smile. Her face is unreadable. She probably wonders why Sister Cecilia didn't spare her the climb. The sheets, after all, are hanging in the courtyard. Marte only grunts. As she turns, her foot drags. She leans on the wall as she prepares to descend.

"And bring water!" Cecilia yells after her. She waves her hand at the space vacated by Marte. "From the farm," she says dismissively, as if she herself were not fresh from the fields. "That is all she knows."

"She is . . . ?" Aleys intends to ask about the limp. Cecilia answers another question.

"Married." She points her chin after Marte. "But you see how he treats her. She ran away. Sister Katrijn says we'll keep her so long as she earns her pottage."

When Marte returns, she bears a sheet, a blanket, and a small towel. Atop this, a wooden basin filled with water that threatens to spill as Marte lurches to the chair. She lowers her burden carefully, then lifts the bowl for Aleys to wash her hands. She twists her head away, almost painfully.

Aleys dries her hands with the towel. "Thank you," she says.

Marte sniffs and gives the smallest of nods, then leaves with the basin. Aleys hears the water slosh onto the stairs.

There is an awkward moment as Cecilia and Aleys regard each other, not sure what to say next. The voices of the girls carding wool drift into the window. Cecilia dips her head their way. "I best be getting back to my work, miss. When you hear the bell ring, that's for supper. I'll save you a spot next to me, don't you worry."

Aleys imagines her life beside Cecilia, sleeping, waking, eating, praying. Cecilia's abundant energy more than fills this close room: It rebounds from wall to wall. And there are four other girls, in this space alone. She was better off with just Griete. The thought of Griete is a stab in her side. She should never have left home. But that wasn't a choice.

And she will need to recruit some of these women.

After Cecilia clomps down the stairs, the rhythmic sound of wire brushes scraping each other stops for a moment as the others make room for her. Then one of their voices picks up, resuming a story.

Aleys pulls the sheet out from under the blanket. She'll prepare her bed. Then she'll pray. It may be her only moment alone all day.

"She loved him," floats up a voice.

"I don't understand," says another. "If she was in the convent . . ."

"There are ways."

"No," says the first, "that's not what I meant. She'd been in love with him since childhood. Since they were twelve. They pledged to each other the night before he left with the Templars."

She hears Cecilia's voice. "If I could have married a knight, you can be sure I wouldn't be carding wool."

Aleys spreads the sheet over the bed.

"Listen, in the Holy Lands, the knight fights with valor. It's afterward, on the way home, that he slips from his saddle. His man at arms rushes to his side, but the knight's wounds have opened, and he's bleeding all over the ground. There is nothing they can do. He tells his comrades to go forward, gives his man a rose to bring to Beatrice, and a message. 'Remember me, always.' When his man comes to the house of Beatrice's father, her heart breaks at the news. What's she going to do?"

"Take vows, of course."

"Unless they had a begijnhof in her town."

"No, they didn't have any. She went to one of the convents devoted to Saint Mary."

Aleys folds the blanket over the end of the cot. Then she kneels at the narrow prie-dieu, crosses herself, begins the Lord's Prayer.

"Anyway, listen," the voice drifts up, "in four or five years, she's the bell ringer for the abbey, and she's perfect, she never once misses the prayers. But then the knight returns . . ."

Aleys tries to concentrate. How is she supposed to hallow his name when she can barely hear herself think?

"I thought he died."

"That's what's so tragic. He survived. And he comes back and she's just taken her final vows. At evensong, he comes to see her. The mist is rising, and they whisper through the iron grill. 'Do I dream?' she asks. 'Is it you?'

"'My lady,' says the knight, 'day and night, I yearned for you.'"

Aleys rests her forehead on her clasped fists. This is impossible. Will they talk all day?

"'But, sir, I have made the solemn profession. I am sworn to chastity. For life.'"

Apparently, they will.

"'Damsel,' he says to her, 'you wound me! Better my heart had been quartered by infidels! Now it is condemned to beat as your prisoner, forever.' Then he reaches through the lattice. Their fingers touch."

The sounds of carding stop.

"'Kiss me, lady, for old friendship's sake.'"

"Ach, he's a scoundrel," says the third girl.

"No, he's not," says Cecilia. "Keep going."

The voice resumes. "Sister Beatrice prays to Our Lady. She does penance, she fasts for days. 'Release me from this temptation!' she cries. But it doesn't work. She loves him still. And then one evening, she's in the cloister alone, gathering roses to set before the Virgin's statue, and the knight breaks in. He seizes her and lays kisses upon her, and her veil falls off at the foot of the Virgin, and then he rips off her habit and covers her in silks and furs and jewels and puts her before him on his horse and rides off with her!"

"Pffft. This story's not true. You can't just tear off a habit."

"It is true, wait, there's a miracle in it. The knight and his lady go to a new town, and there they live happily as man and wife. Then, at the height of their happiness, the knight is struck down by fever. In the morning he kisses her. By noon, he's dead as a doornail. She's left alone in a strange place."

"She'll have to go to the brothel," says Cecilia.

"Get your mind out of the gutter."

"Well, what choice does she have? She can't return home and she can't go back to the convent. Even if he was a knight."

"She ends up in the brothel. But through it all, she prays to the Virgin daily, the seven hours of Our Lady."

"Even Matins? She wakes up for midnight prayers?" Clearly, Matins is the height of piety.

"All of it. Every day. And her carnal sins? No lust. She does it in the brothel without any lust."

"It's not mortal if you take no pleasure," says Cecilia.

"The devil ceases not. Who told you that?"

"The butcher." Ah, thinks Aleys, it wasn't the butcher's son, it was the butcher himself. No wonder he couldn't marry Cecilia: He already had a wife.

"Finally, after seven years, the lady can't even remember all the vile acts she's done or whom she's done them with. 'Mother of God,' she cries, 'take pity on me for my sins. Let me return home to my sisters.'"

"She expects the convent to take her back? They'd never."

"Wait. She drags herself back to the town. A widow living beside the convent takes her in out of charity, for the night.

"Beatrice asks the old woman, 'What news, mevrouw, of the convent?'

"'Ah,' says the old woman, 'the nuns there are pure and stainless, and their rosaries are a blessing for the town. None have given cause for criticism.'

"'Not even the nun who eloped, seven years ago? The bell ringer. Her name was Beatrice.'

"'What say you? Sister Beatrice, eloped? No, do not slander that good lady. Listen, there she is now, tolling Vespers. Sister Beatrice, the most devout of sisters.'"

One of the carders gasps. "How is that possible?"

"But it is. That night, Sister Beatrice has a dream. One of those ones that seems as real as waking?"

"Ja, I had one of those the other night, about a pudding."

"Shhhh. Let her finish."

"In the dream, Our Lady comes to the sister and says, Faithful Beatrice, I have heard your prayers and I have interceded for thee. Go to the cloister, the door is open. You shall find again your veil, where you dropped it at my feet. And cowl and shoes. And habit."

"And?"

"And she goes there and discovers that the statue of the Virgin has come alive and has worn her habit and rung the bells every hour of every day for seven years. And none of the other nuns, not one, noticed it wasn't Beatrice."

"That is a miracle," breathes Cecilia.

"I told you."

And then, in reality, the begijnhof bell rings, and the carding stops and so does the talking and they rise to go to chapel, where they will contemplate Saint Mary or Sister Beatrice, or, quite possibly, the finger touch of a knight at evensong.

Aleys whispers, "Dear God, what have I done? How will I find you here?"

13

FRIAR LUKAS

Friar Lukas hitches his robe as he takes the stairs of the manor two at a time. God will provide. But will the bishop? He finds his older brother in his dressing room, a servant helping him don the heavy vestments. Lukas wishes Jan would dismiss the attendant, but the man stands back against the wardrobe, stiff as a poker, extending his pointed green slipper and allowing his gaze to slide to Lukas's sandals, which poke out beneath his robe. The man tosses blond hair from his eyes and wrinkles his nose like he's detected dog shit. Even the bishop's servants feel they're above the Franciscans. *Dies irae*, thinks Lukas. Come Day of Wrath, those fine Venetian shoes of yours will dance you straight through the gates of hell.

"Ah," says the bishop, "it's my brother with the begging bowl. You must need something. Let me guess what it is this time: You have the girl, and now you want me to buy her an abbey. First the hen, then the henhouse? Has she laid any eggs for you yet, this girl from Damme?"

"Jan, stop. We just need a small house with an enclosed yard." He looks around the dressing room. He could sleep two brothers in each of these closets.

"I have enough convents. Put her in one of those."

"We need a Franciscan sisterhood. It's time. Brugge is thirsty for our message."

"Hmm. And where are they, all these sisters of yours?"

"You know she's our first."

"You think more women will want to play at apostle? You know you'll only attract the girls without dowries."

Lukas refuses to take the bait. "She'll inspire others."

"And exactly how will she do this?"

"You haven't met her." Why must Jan question everything he says?

"It sounds like I should. You've put her in the begijnhof? All those unsupervised women." Jan shudders. "Maybe she'll win over some widows for your friars."

"Brother, I tell you. She won't just draw women from the begijnhof. She'll bring in women from the town and the villages around."

Jan laughs. "You think you have a Saint Clare, then? Oh my. I do need to meet her. Is she going to start performing miracles? Look at you, you're blushing."

"It was in our father's lifetime that Clare came to Francis."

"Oh ho—I see now! You fancy yourself a Francis! Is my little brother a saint-in-waiting?"

"It's not like that, Jan."

"No, no. It's marvelous. We can use a saint in the family. Good for you, Brother. You'll outstrip me yet."

"Jan, I don't covet your crown."

Jan laughs. "That's plain enough. You follow a man who preached to birds."

"I seek only God."

"So you say. But does God seek you?"

The manservant smirks.

Lukas sighs. "Just come see her. Judge for yourself."

"I'm a busy man, Lukas." Jan signals to his attendant, then bows his head to accept a heavy gold cross around his neck. He pats it as a man patting a full stomach. "I'm expecting an envoy from the pope."

Lukas wonders if it would be easier if the bishop were not his brother. Jan enjoys needling him. *Just help us out. Sell a few of these candlesticks and give us a house. I'll train her, and she'll bring more women to God. They only need a place of their own, separate from the world.*

Jan studies his reflection in the glass. "Let's see if your Sister Aleys can win over even one beguine. Show me two women in the brown robe"—he casts a glance up and down his brother, and Lukas feels his disdain like a lazy whip—"and I'll consider it."

14

ALEYS

Aleys sits beside Cecilia at supper, simple broth and bread, silent but for the muted clink of wooden spoon on wooden bowl and Sister Katrijn's prayers in strident Latin from the front of the room. The words, about lilies of the field, appear to be wasted on this audience. Aleys wonders how many beguines understand them, if any. She's impressed that Katrijn reads Latin. Not many women do. "She hired a Latin tutor from her very own earnings," Cecilia whispers, "back when Katrijn's business with her husband started to turn a profit. Katrijn loves scripture." You wouldn't know it to listen to her read. Katrijn's rendering sounds like she's pounding the milk to punish the butter. She bludgeons the psalms.

Aleys glances to her right at a taciturn young woman, small as a swallow, with dark hair and black eyes and the sobriety of someone much older. Aleys thinks her name is Ida, but maybe-Ida's severe countenance forbids even a whispered question. It's not like Aleys can just lean over and whisper, "You look like you'd enjoy a life of prayer. Care to join the friars?"

Aleys finishes her soup quickly and looks up to find the beguines taking measured sips from their spoons. She's still hungry. She thinks of her family at home, the boys forking second helpings of lamb, Griete laughing, Papa leaning back in his chair and stretching his stomach with his hands to make more room. At least, during the good times. She pushes the thought of them away and watches the beguines consume their meal prayerfully, seemingly grateful for each spoonful. Even Cecilia sips quietly, one with the silent communion.

When Katrijn stops reading, the women set down their spoons and rise together. They file out behind Sophia. Cecilia glances back to beckon Aleys before she turns the corner. Aleys is alone. She grabs a half-empty bowl and downs it, the salt broth sliding down her throat. She reaches for another. Marte limps into the room with an empty tray. Aleys sets the bowl down quickly.

Marte grasps a heel of bread left on the table, hands it to Aleys.

"You're hungry," she says. It's a simple statement. Aleys feels a shock of shame to be offered food. It's one thing to ask for alms, but no one's ever held out a bread crust like she's a pauper. She backs away. "No," she says, "you keep it." Marte shrugs and puts the bread on the tray and starts gathering up spoons. Aleys hurries out after the beguines.

She finds them gathering around the hearth in a nearby room, shifting chairs here and there, though it's clear everyone has their own place. She hesitates at the door. Is she meant to join them? Atop each chair sits a workbasket full of skeins and spindles. The women nestle baskets at their feet as they settle. There's an air of intimacy in this close room, a shift in key from the starched meal. Some of the beguines stretch their legs straight out before them in a way that's mildly shocking. Aleys looks around, but no one seems to notice.

Katrijn is seated at Sophia's right hand, beside the hearth. All Aleys can think of is the chink of that coin purse. She knows they pledge simplicity, not poverty. Still.

Katrijn stiffens when she sees Aleys. "Magistra." She leans over to Sophia. "Is this wise?" Several women stop talking and look up.

"She's one of us, Katrijn."

"But she might—"

"Sister, we do not love in parts."

Katrijn looks as though she wants to protest but thins her lips and bends over her mending. Cecilia waves from the far side of the hearth, where there's a chair and a stool beneath an oil lamp on the mantel. As she weaves a path through their workbaskets, pulling close her brown robe, Aleys feels the women's eyes like dozens of pinpricks of curiosity. Lukas told her to impress them with her faith. How is she supposed to do that?

A sheaf of parchment lies squared upon the chair. Cecilia smiles shyly at Aleys as she picks it up. "It's my turn to read tonight." She has the air of a child about to recite her alphabet. Aleys is sure Cecilia wasn't taught to read on the farm. She assumed the beguines' schools were just for children. Maybe they teach their own.

Cecilia gestures Aleys onto the empty stool beside her. All around, women have resumed chatting amiably, pulling work into their laps. Aleys folds her hands, hoping to disguise their idleness. They're still watching her, though they hide it well. Sure enough, a middle-aged beguine reaches over. "Sister," she says, thrusting a needle through some mending and handing it to Aleys. At least it's work she's being offered, not bread. She examines the men's cap in her hand. A mouse has chewed a hole in it. How is she meant to close that? Sew around the edges and gather it in like a hay bale? Or stitch across the hole and leave a scar? Aleys looks at the quick hands of the other women and knows her work will be wanting.

As the magistra offers the evening prayer, the women pause to bow their heads and cross themselves. As a test, Aleys searches for dust motes above them, but the air is flat. She's not surprised. God wouldn't flirt with her in this place. Does he even know she's here? She sighs and knots the thread and slides the needle through the fabric. Around the edges it is.

Cecilia takes a deep breath and begins haltingly. "As she stood behind . . . behind him . . . weeping she began to wet his . . . his feet with her tears."

Aleys looks up, needle poised in midair. Cecilia is reading scripture. In Dutch. She looks over, and sure enough, the words are plain on the parchment, in text any schoolboy could read. Aleys raises her eyes to find Katrijn's gaze hard upon her, daring her to object. Aleys doesn't object. She's just bewildered. It never occurred to her that a psalm on a page could be as simple as this. The words are simultaneously so native and so foreign that it takes Aleys a moment to recognize the story of Mary Magdalene, the disciple who needed Christ most and loved him best. Aleys knows this gospel to heart, in Latin, has envied Mary the chance to touch his feet, has imagined the bowl of warm water, in Latin, the alabaster jar, *alabastrum*, her copious tears, *lacrimae*, the fragrant ointment filling the room with nectar and balsam. His fond gaze upon her. But never in Dutch. Aleys closes her eyes to listen to the story as Mama might have read it, if Mama had known how to read.

Except that Cecilia jolts from word to word like a cart between ruts.

"Then she wiped them with her hair . . . kissed . . . them and . . . and poured oil on them."

She is making a hash of the sacred passage. Aleys wants to grab the parchment from her, to read it as it deserves to be read. To savor the story in her own language, how it would roll off the tongue, so easy and free. It would burst with meaning into the air like the head of a dandelion. The wind could carry the seeds anywhere. It would be so beautiful. But Cecilia lumbers along, her finger jabbing the page.

"Jesus said to Simon the . . . the . . ." Cecilia scowls at the word.

"Pharisee," inserts Aleys. Immediately, the beguines look up from their work. A small disapproval ripples through the room. Aleys is right, of course it's the pharisee. Needles hover. Cecilia raises questioning eyes to the magistra.

"You were about to get it, Cecilia," says Sophia. "Please continue."

Cecilia glances around the room, takes a deep breath, and bows her head to the paper. "Jesus said to the . . . pharisee. See you this woman? I entered your house, you . . . gave me no water for my feet. But look, this woman has . . . bathed my feet with her tears."

Katrijn's cold stare cuts through the hazy room. Aleys feels she has transgressed, but she was just trying to help. And maybe to impress them.

Her gaze slides to the fire, where Marte is adjusting smoking logs with a poker. The spring night is too warm for the chimney to draw properly and smoke is wafting into the room, already hot with all the bodies crammed in. The beguines wear light wool. Her own robe is coarse and heavy. Sweat beads in the small of her back.

Aleys remembers the mending in her hand, tries to focus on that and not on Cecilia's butchery of the gospel.

"You gave me no . . . kiss but she has not stopped . . . kissing . . . my feet."

Aleys can hardly bear it. She accidentally stabs her thumb with the needle and a drop of blood stains the cap, which now has a bunched hillock instead of a hole. She looks around. Everyone is listening appreciatively, pausing to turn a piece of work or nip the end of a thread.

Even Marte is listening, paused with one hand on the mantel, leaning toward the chimney. Old sweat stains at Marte's collar point down her back. Those would be from the farm, she supposes. Marte is nodding along with Cecilia's words. When she bends to rest the poker against the wall, her hip hitches and the poker falls to the hearth with a clatter.

Cecilia starts, her finger slipping down the page.

Marte scowls and bends to retrieve the poker.

"Cecilia, go ahead and finish the passage," says Sophia. "I do love this part."

Cecilia reads on, now from the wrong place, gaining momentum. "Her sins, which are many, are forgiven, for she loved much."

She's skipped the part about the debtors. She's missed the point.

"And he said to her, 'Your sins are forgiven.'" Cecilia looks up from the text, cheeks pink, eyes round. "Just like that!" She has the word *vergheven* pinned beneath her finger like it was about to take flight. "Right here, it says so. He forgave her, in front of all those men."

"But you skipped half of it!" Aleys protests.

Katrijn makes a disgusted sound, throws her work into her basket, moves to stand. Sophia stays her with a glance.

"As we see, Cecilia has understood the words and their meaning," says Sophia. "Well done, Cecilia. You've read it for yourself." Cecilia beams at her praise, and Aleys sees that the girl has found forgiveness, twice over, once in the text and once in the eyes of Sophia.

Outside, a mist rises from the courtyard, so that each beguine appears in her own pillar of smoke as they separate to their homes, bobbing lanterns casting faint halos of rainbow. Aleys didn't think to bring a lantern to supper. She'll have to feel her way to the dormitory. No one waited for her. Even Cecilia, buoyed by fresh revelation, was carried off by her friends and forgot Aleys. She stands in the dark, feeling the mist slick her cheek. Doors close around the begijnhof and lanterns glow, one by one, in the windows.

Aleys thinks of Candlemas, of the village girls dressed in white, bearing candles to the church to be blessed. She remembers shielding the flame with her hand as she walked carefully, tending it, watching the flame falter on the black wick, pausing to let it revive like a little resurrection. Griete beside her, hair in ribbons. Griete loved red ribbons for the holidays. Claus used to steal them from her hair and tie them on Farrago. Mama would pin Griete's silky blonde braids up like a crown. Aleys imagines Mama behind her now, quick fingers plaiting her hair with firm tugs. Mama would smooth the stray ends into the braid, then give two brisk taps on her shoulders when she was done. It leaves a hollow feeling, the thought of home.

"Sister Aleys." It's Sophia, closing the door to the reading room behind her. "If I might have a word." She steps forward and the aura of her lantern envelops them both. Sophia's face emerges distinct from the dark veil and the black night.

"Of course, Magistra."

Sophia lets the silence settle around them. Above the trees, the dormitory windows show as lit rectangles, silhouettes of girls passing between them. None of them are Griete. None of them understand her. Neither did Griete, Aleys reminds herself.

Sophia's lantern burns a small break in the weather. Aleys wants to reach out to warm her hands above it, imagines leaning in so far that she would tip into Sophia's arms and be held for a moment. Just a moment. She wonders if Sophia could plait her hair, then remembers she's given that up, too. She slips her hands within her sleeves, grasps cold wrists with chilly fingers.

"Aleys, what you heard here tonight."

"The reading?"

"We don't speak of it outside these walls."

"But where did you get the translation?" She imagines monks in their scriptoria, penning Dutch and adding red capital letters and other flourishes. She imagines Finn leaning over a desk, translating the Song of Songs into Dutch. But the parchment Cecilia held was crude, the letters plain. Hardly abbey quality.

"Translators have had trouble, elsewhere, so we keep our source secret. For their safety."

She wonders what Friar Lukas would think of reading the gospel in Dutch. She could ask him whether Franciscans are allowed to read translations. The friars are almost as unconventional as the beguines. But she doesn't want to point a finger at Sophia. In this moment Aleys only wants the magistra to plait the hair she no longer has.

"It's beautiful, Magistra, in Dutch."

"Even from the mouth of a beginner?" Sophia arches an eyebrow. "You know Cecilia's just learning. It's not easy for her."

Aleys feels a wash of shame. She shouldn't have corrected Cecilia. It's obvious now.

"I won't do that again, Magistra."

The magistra closes her eyes briefly in a small nod.

"Aleys, would you consider a piece of advice from an old beguine?" There's a touch of irony in Sophia's voice. Aleys feels her hackles rise. She doesn't answer to Sophia Vermeulen. She is not one of them.

"I don't—" she begins.

But Sophia gently places two fingers across Aleys's lips in a gesture that feels like a benediction. Sophia's small smile is almost mournful. She waits. The muffled sounds of night canals—quiet oars in water, the bump of boats moored to landings—seep into the courtyard. A dog barks in the distance. Finally, Sophia speaks.

"Dear child," she says, "only this. Try to be simple."

Sophia peers into Aleys's face, to see if she's understood.

Aleys waits for more. There must be more.

"That's all," Sophia says. "God be with you." She pulls back, and with her the light. As Sophia retreats across the courtyard, the lantern illuminates the length of her figure in the mist. Aleys is left alone in darkness, but for points of light from windows that feel distant as beacons from unreachable shores.

Simple. It's like elders who tell you to be calm. So passionless. So uncommitted. As if you could find God at the bottom of your bowl. As if God would notice you if you were simple.

15

The Bishop

Jan Smet, Bishop of Tournai, waits for the pope's emissary at the city gates, the gathered clergy of Brugge arrayed behind him like geese in flight. At his shoulder stand his archdeacons in their sumptuous vestments (though less sumptuous than his own), behind them the parish priests in white (if they own white) or green (if they don't own that; he must see to it), the abbey monks still stinking of hogs and ale, and at the back, jostling for position as the most humble, the wandering friars, the Franciscans in their sandals and Dominicans in their black hoods. The friars form a nice backdrop to his own clergy. Only the nuns have been left at home. He just hopes the beguines won't show up.

They wait under a June sun, shifting their feet, eyes trained on the road from the south, watching for the first puff of dirt that will announce the arrival of the papal legate. As the sun crests, scarlet banners appear above the fields of maize where the road leaves the woods. There are a half dozen in the party. The legate rides a handsome steed with a coat like polished chestnuts, the white reins of his office resting across its flank. As the hooves clatter to a halt, Jan sees that the legate is perhaps less magnificent than his mount, despite the scarlet cape and gilded shoes. The legate looks down on them with a pinched mouth and a stray eye. It's most unsettling. How do you meet the gaze of a man like that?

Off his horse, the legate seems small for a prince of the Church. Jan kneels before the man, who blesses him with one eye. Jan is hoping to be doubly blessed by day's end. A *nuncio* had ridden ahead to deliver the message this visit from Rome was a *legati missi*, no routine social call or tax collection, but a visit with a mission. Jan wonders if he might be called to Rome. To be a cardinal, perhaps? He imagines himself in full scarlet regalia, barrel chested and thick haired, more impressive than this legate who delivers a nasal prayer outside the city gates. From the back, the friars lean forward to hear. It's difficult to imagine this as the voice of the pope for whom he speaks.

Jan hums to himself as the cortège enters the city, smiles beneficently at the people lining the way, who are bowing as if he himself has choreographed their movements. Which he has. He's ordered the streets cleared, flushed the drainage ditches so that Brugge sparkles. The water of the canals sparkles. Everything sparkles. The architecture, he must admit, is impressive, especially his stately churches with their soaring towers. The guild halls with their statuary. Even the common architecture touches him today, the arched bridges over the canals and the half-timbered homes leaning into the streets. And the markets! It makes him almost sad, leaving this most cosmopolitan city of Europe, where Muscovites barter furs for barbarian ivory that is sold by Arabs. He's seen amber rosaries traded for lustrous silks, pigments for paintings. He reminds himself that the Silk Road also leads to Rome. And in the burnished sunshine of the Roman hills there are raven-haired women trampling grapes. He'll get over it.

He'll dine with the legate at his manor after the cathedral service. Jan has ordered his household to prepare as if for a prince. He supposes it will be after the meal, flush with wine and goose, that the legate will announce his promotion. Jan feels like he's getting a free pass. He won't even have to make a show of burning illegal translations in the square. If the pope is promoting him to Rome, the heretics of Brugge are the problem of the next bishop of Tournai. No tithes to collect. He'll be done selling relics and indulgences. No more of these petty city politics, just the weighty concerns of popes and kings. He'll be well rid of Flanders.

The legate celebrates Mass in Our Lady, under soaring vaults, and Jan feels his spirits rise with the wafting incense, imagining the ceremonies he will witness in Rome. For a moment, he is so transported that tears spring to his eyes at the beauty of his own thoughts. To be at the side of the Holy Father, one of a handful of God's most chosen. From the son of a banker to the elector of popes. It is more than his father even dreamed. His one hand squeezes the other in congratulation.

Back at the manor, Jan brushes away the servants, except for Willems, who blends into the shadow like a black cat. This will be good news for Willems, too. Jan rises to pour the legate's wine himself.

"Not, perhaps, what you're used to," he says. "We had it brought up from the Rhineland. After dinner, I believe you'll find the liqueurs produced by the monks of Flanders equal to any."

The legate is a man of few words. He puts out his hand to stop Jan. "I take only the wine of communion."

Jan almost jokes that, in that case, they should switch posts, but stops himself. The man is unsmiling. Jan sits, suddenly wary. Perhaps this visit isn't what he thought. He glances nervously at Willems, who twists the corner of his mouth.

The legate hoists his leather pouch to the table and fishes inside. One eye seems fixed on the bag; the other rolls heavenward, as if God is guiding him through its innards. Finally, his eyes reconvene and he extracts a sheet of parchment. The legate slides it across the table with one finger, reluctant to touch it.

"This has come to our attention."

Jan squints at the parchment. He knows immediately what it is. For a moment, he hopes he's wrong, that perhaps it's a bill of sale; maybe some rent on church lands is due. Has he failed to declare all the diocesan property to Rome? He looks up at the legate, who waits with pressed lips.

"Bring me light," Jan bellows.

Willems opens the door and signals to the staff. A servant rushes in with a pair of candles, another lights a spill from the fire and touches it to the wicks. All the while the legate keeps his eye glued to Jan as if he might pull a conjuror's trick. Jan draws one of the candles close to examine the parchment.

His heart sinks. It's the gospel of Saint Matthew, in Dutch. *And he saith unto them, "Follow me, and I will make you fishers of men."*

Jan can feel Willems tense in the shadow against the wall. Damn it, they should have moved faster. They should have been the ones to whip out the parchment and to drag forward the translator for questioning. If he admits now that he's been aware of the translations but failed to act, he'll appear weak. Uncommitted. He doesn't want that to get back to the pope. Behind the legate, Willems gives a subtle shake of his head. Denial is their best strategy.

"I don't know—" Jan starts.

"How this can exist?" interrupts the envoy. "We have given no dispensation for a Dutch translation."

"It must be a mistake. It must be one of my parish priests." He racks his mind for the least of them, the one he could sacrifice. "There are those whose Latin is wanting." He falters. "Where did you get it?"

"It was purchased here, from a stall in the Markt."

"You have spies in Brugge?" Willems should have told him.

"We have men who concern themselves with the health of the Church."

"I'm sure it's an anomaly."

The legate looks at him long. One eye, then the other. "Anomalies seed heresy."

"I assure you there is no heresy in my diocese."

The legate gives a dry laugh. "That's what they said in Strasbourg. Our inquisitors found the place crawling with heretics. They were preaching without ordination." He squints both his eyes as if he cannot bear to face the thought. "They had women preaching."

Jan knows he speaks of the Waldensians. "But you've chastised them." They burned eighty of them. It's said that when the breeze shifts in Strasbourg you can still catch the whiff of singed flesh.

The envoy sighs. "Perhaps. We must be alert. There can be no more translations. Heresy breeds where butchers read the Bible."

"I don't think that—"

"Of course not. No one sees it coming. It starts with this." He presses his finger into the table, beside the parchment. "Then there are secret meetings. Laypeople begin interpreting scripture on their own. They are unqualified. They haven't spent their entire lives training to understand God's intentions for us." The legate taps his finger. "These translations. Before you know it, the people reject the word of their deacons, their priests, even their bishops. You've heard the Waldensians are threatening to excommunicate the pope? The pope!"

Well, the pope has already excommunicated the Waldensians, so perhaps that's little surprise. Now that they can read the Bible, the heretics claim they can't find the word *pope* anywhere in it. Not *ad literum*, thinks the bishop, they stand on a technicality, but he does understand the pope's impatience with translations. "That will not happen here, I assure you."

The pope's representative falls quiet, eyeing the document. He sighs, and an unguarded emotion flickers over his face. He raises his hand to rub his eyebrows. When the legate speaks again, there is a wistful note in his voice. "They claim to communicate directly with God." He pauses, looks up at Jan. "No one can do that. Right?"

Jan isn't sure how to respond. For a moment, the pope's man seems a child who's run all the way to the fair to be told the fire-eater has left for the next town. He stifles the urge to lay a consoling hand on the legate's shoulder.

"We are but the pope's shepherds," he says. "And he the messenger of God on high."

The legate gives his head a little shake. "Of course." He is silent a moment longer.

Jan hears the muffled sound of laughter from the kitchens. "You were speaking of heresies?"

"Yes. Yes, I was." The legate gathers himself, straightens his shoulders. "Someone in your city is distributing the Bible in vulgar language." The legate stands. "You must stop them."

"Your Excellency." He must show strength. They missed their first chance. Now it won't be enough to destroy the documents and merely frighten the translators. He has no desire to roil Brugge, to trouble this commercial city with trials and acts of faith. It won't win him any favor with the city leaders. It will make it harder to raise money. The whole thing is distasteful. His hand is forced. "We will see the authors tried."

"I assure you, the pope will take note." The legate gathers his bag. "We await news that the sanctity of this city has been restored. You must bring your translators to account." He focuses both eyes on Jan. "If a bishop can't root out heresy, well, then, what use is a bishop?"

16

Aleys

The sun peaks high. It's nearly Midsummer, thinks Aleys. A year ago she was learning Latin from Finn in the fields. Just before they moved to the orchard to read the Song of Songs in the trees. *Canticum Canticorum*. The world brimmed with promise and blood rushed through her veins like a spring-fed river. She knew where she fit. Or thought she did. And now? Finn's in some scriptorium, copying out Latin, dipping his reed in a pot of red ink and embellishing the *D* in *Deus*. He's adding flourishes to words that need no embellishment, that were perfect and sacred and their very own. *The beams of our house are cedars, and its rafters are firs.* Does he think of her as he copies? Will someone explain the meaning to him? Maybe to them he's nothing more than a hand with a quill. Either way, he's risked nothing, she thinks bitterly. She's better off forgetting him. Finn's safe within his monastery.

Whereas she's a novitiate nearly two months into her probation, already running out of time.

She's supposed to be recruiting other women. Friar Lukas seems to think it would be easy, like she could bang her spoon on her mug and announce that she's looking to form a women's order, would anyone care to join? She'll have to approach the candidates one by one. She figures she'll have better luck with the ones not yet pledged.

Aleys steps from the dormitory into the sunny courtyard, where she nearly trips over a pair of young beguines seated on a ground cloth spread across the path. They've pulled their skirts above their knees and stretched out their legs, stockinged feet nearly meeting to create a diamond of space. Between them is a pile of sheep fleece, straight from the sack, still tightly curled in locks, still full of seed and bramble. The girls clutch long willow switches, poised to beat the curl from the fleece so it can be carded. Aleys smiles. Wullebreken. She and Griete used to chant as they broke the wool, their yellow switches whipping the locks into a churning cloud of wispy fleece angels. And sure enough, the girls nod to each other and begin singing as they snap their switches into the fleece.

Wullebreken, Wullebreken
Send me a dowry
Wullebreken, Wullebreken
Send me a man
If he's not handsome, I'll go to the convent
Wullebreken, Wullebreken
Fast as I can

Wullebreken, Wullebreken
Nun in the convent
Wullebreken, Wullebreken
Send me a priest
If he's not holy, take me to the begijnhof
Wullebreken, Wullebreken
We'll have a feast

Wullebreken, Wullebreken
Priests want your money
Wullebreken, Wullebreken
So do the nuns
The beguines will make you work for your living
Wullebreken, Wullebreken
Till the fleece is done

Within moments, the air is full of angels. These girls look way too happy to join the Franciscans.

The problem is that they *all* seem happy. So Aleys has decided Marte should be her first target. She's stalked Marte through the laundry, spied as she sweeps the church, watched her kneading dough. Perhaps a life of prayer would be a relief from constant toil. She's noticed how Marte lingers at the evening readings.

Marte is on her knees, scrubbing a doorstep.

"Marte? Do you have a moment?"

Marte pauses to wipe sweat from her forehead but doesn't look up. "What's on your mind, miss?"

"I've been hoping to talk with you."

"You've not wanted for opportunity." She puts down the brush and sits back on her heels, wiping her hands against her apron. "You've been on me like a brown shadow all week." Marte hoists herself to stand. "What do you need? You can just ask."

"Well, I . . ." Already the question seems preposterous. Marte, limping down the lane with an alms bowl? Aleys has to start somewhere. She claps her palms together. "I thought you could join the brown friars." She waits. Marte frowns. Aleys rotates her palms against each other. "With me," she adds.

"The friars?" Marte squints. "Why ever would I do that, miss?"

"To get closer to God?"

"Hmph." Marte snorts. "If you'll pardon my saying so, God seems to prefer me at a distance."

"But . . ."

"You forget that I'm married."

"Oh." She had forgotten.

"I don't know that your brown friars are recruiting any wives. If God wants me closer, he'll need to make me a widow." She rubs the back of her neck. "I might thank him for that." She picks up the scrub brush. "Until then, miss, I'm grateful to be here with the beguines."

Aleys next considers Cecilia, who's carried herself with fresh confidence since the reading of Mary Magdalene. Perhaps she's looking to go deeper. At least she's friendly. But Cecilia's never alone. On a wet afternoon, Aleys finds her among the dormitory girls winding skeins onto niddy-noddies that look newly made. Katrijn must have recently ordered them. Aleys picks up a spare one, examines the slim rod of beech crossed by bars at the top and halfway down; it's well-made, neatly polished so the wood won't snag the yarn that's wound in figure eights over the crossbars. Ida nods curtly as Aleys takes some yarn from the pile and perches at the end of her cot, away from the rain splashing off the windowsill. Aleys loosely knots the yarn onto the top cross and begins wrapping. There's not a woman in Flanders who doesn't know how to wind yarn, how to keep the tension even and the twist constant so that the skeins won't tangle when they're slipped off. They can wind yarn while walking, while minding a toddler, while talking. As usual, it's Cecilia who's doing the latter.

"Well, he was just the worst man, stealing and cheating and beating his wife and children. To hide his sinfulness from the priests, the man forbade his son to go to church, but of course the boy does go, and he confesses, and when the father hears about it? Whoa! He's so angry he grabs the boy and throws him into the village furnace. Just like that, right in there with the bread as it's baking."

"His own son?" gasps a nearby girl.

"Yes, Sister. And you know what happened? When they pulled that boy out, he was unharmed. Completely fine. Not even a hot blister. He said the Holy Mother came to him in the fire and placed her blue mantle about him and that protected him from the flames."

Aleys pictures a swirl of sky, softer than silk, impenetrable as iron, around the child.

"She can do that?" another girl asks.

"She can do anything."

Several of them nod.

"What happened to the father?" asks Ida, suspicious.

"Course they threw him right inside, where the devil was waiting." Cecilia leans in and her large eyes grow larger. "They say that fire still burns and if you look in, you can see the man in agony. The town had to build another furnace, on account of the bread always coming out burnt."

They do love their miracles. Aleys believes in wonders, at least the ones in scripture. Those happened a long time ago. Cecilia's miracles, she thinks, might be tall tales.

The noon bell rings. Cecilia puts down her winding and looks out the window. The rain has picked up, the hush dampening the sound. The dormitory feels like a small drowsy ark swaying above a green sea. "I'll go fetch the beer," Cecilia announces.

"Again?" says one of her companions. "Didn't you go to the brewery just yesterday? Besides, it's pouring."

"It's a warm rain."

Hardly, thinks Aleys.

"Cecilia, you can't go alone," says Ida. "It causes too much gossip."

"I'll take Sister Aleys with me." Cecilia looks straight at her. "You'll come, won't you?"

Aleys has to run to keep up, skirting puddles.

"Cecilia, wait!" Aleys pants. "I have something to ask you."

"Right now? In the rain?"

"Yes, can you please just slow down a moment?"

Cecilia stops, but her head leans toward the brewery. She shields her eyes. "Maybe you can ask me later?"

Cecilia tugs down her dress and sets back her cap, allowing a few wheat-colored curls to escape. She pushes into the brewhouse, where they are met with a warm gust of yeast and rosemary. Sawdust covers the floor. Housewives and errand boys are bargaining over barrels. Cecilia cranes her neck, searching. At the back of the hall, a door to the side yard opens. A gangly young man strains to push a large barrel over the lip of the doorway, putting his thin shoulder to the staves.

"Rolf!" cries Cecilia. Rolf straightens at her voice, and the barrel rolls back against his foot. He winces as he smiles, reddening to his jug ears. Rolf doffs his cap, pressing it to his chest as the rain plasters ginger hair to his cheeks. "Miss Cecilia?" he calls out, his voice cracking.

"Rolf! More ale!" she commands, and Rolf abandons the barrel in the doorway. "The juniper flavor!" she bellows after him.

Cecilia looks at Aleys, reads her eyes. "He's the brewer's apprentice." Aleys frowns at her. "No, really, it's not like that. Rolf just knows me from fetching the small beer." Then she grins. "But he always gets me the best." Aleys doesn't doubt it.

Rolf returns with a cask in his arms. Water sluices from his orange eyebrows. "Shall I carry it for you?" It looks as though Cecilia could bear the load more easily than Rolf. Pit the pair of them in an arm wrestling contest, and Aleys would put her coin on Cecilia.

"Yes, Rolf. Follow me." Cecilia lifts her chin and sails out the door.

"You see?" she says to Aleys over her shoulder. "The city is good. Just," she says, "maybe don't mention it to Sister Katrijn."

Wouldn't matter if she did. Cecilia won't last any longer at the begijnhof than Aleys.

"Now what did you want to ask me?"

"Oh, that?" says Aleys. "Never bother."

Ida, she thinks, Ida might say yes. Every evening, Ida gathers the parchment of the reading with great care. She loves the psalms like Aleys loves her psalter. Someone that serious about scripture might be open to a life of prayer. But Ida is dedicated to her work at Sint-Janshospitaal. Aleys doesn't want to follow her there. Hospitals are magnets for demons; everyone knows that. Aleys imagines invisible leathery creatures with fast, rank breath that hover over the dying, waiting to snatch their souls. Aleys was afraid to face them in Mama's chamber when she was thirteen. She's not sure she can now.

But Sophia assigns her to work in the hospital, and so she must follow Ida there. People narrow their eyes as Ida passes. Aleys remembers how her brothers said that beguines speak with demons, that they negotiate with the devil's agents as they pray the dead through purgatory. She didn't know whether to believe them or not. Aleys looks sideways at Ida as they weave their way through the city. Does she talk to demons? Unlikely. Ida hardly talks to humans.

It's a short walk past the brewery and over Maria Bridge. Sint-Janshospitaal dominates its square, an imposing building of ruddy brick, its roof a series of steps that meet above the entrance like a double stairway to heaven. Ida jerks her head toward the large doors. "Sister, go ahead. I'll be right behind you."

But Aleys has no intention of entering alone. She watches as Ida crosses the square, dwarfed by the large basket she carries on her small arm. Halfway across, Ida turns back to shoo Aleys toward the hospital. Odd behavior from the woman who chided Cecilia not to venture out alone. What's Ida doing? Aleys sees her enter a shop. Aleys waits. When Ida emerges, she's rearranging the cloth on her basket. Aleys ducks inside the hospital doors.

Inside is a vast space with enormous leaded windows that soar to a vaulted ceiling. You could fit a lot of demons in here. The ground floor is split into two sections, lodgers to the left and patients to the right. The section for travelers is boisterous with the buzz of hearty men. Cecilia had warned her to steer clear of the merchants who use the Janshospitaal for lodging, wine purveyors from France and traders from Germany, mostly. "Quick with a feel, they are," she said. "And anyway, we're meant to serve in the infirmary." Now that she sees the clear barrier separating the sinners from the sufferers, Aleys wonders how it is that Cecilia discovered that the healthy men are so handsy.

Cots disappear into the shadow of the infirmary. On that side it's quiet, except for a man moaning softly. Beguines in gray move between bedsides, bearing trays and pitchers. The air is thick, a humid fug pierced with an unholy smell. Aleys breathes shallowly.

Ida joins her. "Are you all right?"

"It's a hospital."

"You're afraid of blood?"

"No," she whispers, looking up to the vault, "spirits."

"Oh, for heaven's sake," says Ida. "The devils don't want you. Only the patients."

Maybe Ida does speak with demons.

Aleys stops beside an old man with skin so pallid he could be a marble effigy, but for pearls of sweat that dot his brow. Aleys can't tell if he's breathing. An elderly woman sits by his side, shredding a kerchief in her hands. "Sister?" she says. "Can you help?"

Aleys looks up for Ida, but she's bent over the next bed, unwrapping a bandage.

"Please, Sister." The woman's voice cracks in desperation. Aleys has no idea what she should do. She should leave. She doesn't belong here. She doesn't belong with the beguines, she doesn't belong with Ida, she doesn't belong in the hospital. The look on the woman's face is naked supplication. Aleys feels tears of frustration prick her eyes. "I don't know, I . . ."

Ida grabs her wrist, wrenches her around, whispers fiercely, "Don't you dare cry. If you weep, what will they think?" She takes a cloth from the basin, wrings it out, hands it to Aleys. "It's God's will, whatever happens. Make yourself useful."

"But I don't know how—"

"Then pray. Isn't that your specialty?"

Aleys considers a retort, something sharp about being called to worship, not washcloths. She bites her tongue. Ida looks pointedly at the rosary on Aleys's belt, watches Aleys unloop it. Ida waits. Aleys crosses herself, searches her memory for a prayer for the sick. She can think of none. Her mind is entirely blank. She stands there, her rosary drooping from her hand.

The prayers she knows by heart are joyful, they speak of union, they are ecstatic and entirely wrong. She bows her head.

"Aloud," says Ida. "We need to hear you pray."

Then simple words jump into her chest, and with a rush of relief, they flow through her tight throat: "Lord, have mercy on us. Lord, have mercy on us . . ."

"That's better," says Ida. She touches the shoulder of the old woman. "Come, Mother, pray with us."

As Aleys watches Ida bring comfort to the hopeless, she knows she'll never recruit her. Ida has found purpose right here in the hospital.

By Midsummer, Aleys despairs of recruiting even a single beguine. They're too content. Happy in work and worship. They've not been schooled in a convent, but every evening they gather to consider what the psalms ask of them and what they give to them. There's Cecilia, who holds her head a little higher since her reading; Ida, asking questions; Sophia, pushing them deeper. *As iron sharpens iron, so one person sharpens another.* They pause in their stitches to contemplate the meaning. *A cord of three strands is not quickly broken.* The verse knits the women together. Their hopes, their labor, even their disagreements, are all strands in a single weave. Aleys sees that. It's just that she wants to be more than another thread in the cloth.

Aleys has learned to slow herself at meals, to mete out her soup and tear her bread into morsels. She prays with them, attends their readings. It's all so muted. Where's the ecstasy? Where are the trumpets? Aleys left home to fly. The roof is bolted solid over the begijnhof. It's not going anywhere. These women seek, but it seems like a trudging sort of seeking. *Dear Lord*, she prays. *You called me, but did you mean to call me here?*

Aleys sighs. Tonight is the solstice, but this evening will be like every other. The summer nights have infused her bones with restlessness. The voices of children playing in the courtyard vault the sill and land in the reading room. She's had the urge to run out and join them, to climb trees and race along the canals. At home on Midsummer, they'd had bonfires and merriment. What are Griete and Claus and Henryk doing this solstice night? She hasn't dared ask how her family has fared. She's afraid to.

But tonight, even the beguines are restless at supper. Cecilia whispers something to Ida, and Ida whispers back. Katrijn seems in a good mood, smiling benevolently at them all. After the meal, instead of the reading room, they move as a group to the church. Aleys considers slipping to the dormitory. She wants to pray on the problem of how to tell Friar Lukas that she's recruited exactly no one to their order. But Cecilia beckons, and Aleys is curious, so she follows.

Inside the church, the beguines are scraping the benches to the walls. They've placed a few stools before the altar, where a middle-aged woman is settling a lap harp on her knees. Beside her, another wets her lips and pipes a few notes on a recorder. Someone has a small drum. A fourth beguine enters with a clipped bang and shiver of tambourine. What is this?

Aleys stands aside as the youngest women, those not yet pledged, gather beside the musicians. The color is high on their cheeks. Aleys is unsure what is happening. A tambourine in a church—it seems like it shouldn't be allowed. Where is the magistra? Sophia is smiling at the musicians. There is a mounting undercurrent of excitement. The girls are stirring, removing their headscarves. She looks up to the crucifix. Does Friar Lukas know about this? Just how many secrets do they keep from him? Aleys feels she should leave. She shrinks against the back wall.

The side door opens, admitting an evening breeze. Katrijn enters, ushering a frail beguine that Aleys has never seen. That must be old Agnes, who lives in the infirmary. The woman is so birdlike, so tiny and clawed, it seems she could fly to the ceiling and perch on the cross. Aleys can't help but think of Christina Mirabilis. From Sint-Truiden, just south of here. At Miraculous Christina's own funeral, as the priest sang the *Agnus Dei*, she rose from her coffin, sprang to the church rafters, straddled a beam, threw back her head, and laughed. And that's not even the strangest part. Saint Christina returned from the dead with a death wish. She threw herself into the icy Meuse, staying under the water for hours, then days, at a time—some report she was carried downriver to the mill and spun about the waterwheel—until she stepped out, dry and complaining of thirst. Or she'd step into furnaces to pray. There's something about Christina's mad miracles that frightens Aleys, maybe because they happened so close to here. Aleys eyes the birdlike beguine warily as Katrijn guides her to a wooden chair. Old Agnes stays firmly seated.

At the front, the girls are chattering loudly. They wear their dresses from home, blue dresses and red, vests of green, ribbons of yellow, a festival of color. Such vivid hues belong in a psalter. Cecilia unpins her cap to let her yellow hair spill down her back. She nestles her head between Ida's shoulder blades as she loosens the ties of Ida's sleeves. Aleys stares. These might be the lewd rites people talk about. What is she about to witness?

Cecilia uncoils Ida's dark hair and smooths it down her back. Ida reaches back to take her hand and Cecilia whispers into her ear before they separate. Aleys is torn between horror and fascination. She should retire to the dormitory, resume her prayers. She edges to the exit. From here she can make a quick escape. She gathers her robe about her ankles, as if loose morals might seep up from the flagstones.

The drum and harp begin in measured pace. The girls separate into pairs. Two by two, they bow to each other. The beguine with the recorder lifts her instrument to her lips and issues a high and mournful melody. Aleys feels a longing kindle in her throat—for what, she's not sure, only that the loveliness pulls at a thread deep in her chest. The girls link arms and promenade. The pairs sweep before Aleys, sedate and slow, so close she can hear their dresses brush the stone. As they pass, each couple is silhouetted against the wall torches. The girls disappear, then reemerge into light, brighter than before. Cecilia is partnered with Ida, their hair gleaming flaxen and coal. The two regard each other in profile, Cecilia's round face and Ida's sharp, and Aleys feels the chill of the stone against her back. She's nothing but a flat shadow pinned to the wall.

The tambourine joins. The pulse quickens. Around the circle, the older beguines begin clapping a staccato rhythm that fills the space, reverberating from the walls as if the church itself keeps time. Aleys feels the beat in her feet, feels the urge to stand and join the women. She must resist, she must not be drawn in. The dancers begin to turn about each other, palm to palm, eyes locked. They weave a pattern, ribbons of pigment in a tapestry of sound, a quilt of music. The beguines laugh. The music quickens. The voices grow loud. The women call out. Old Agnes is waving her hands like she's conducting. Even the magistra seems to have forgotten herself, is shouting, "Faster, faster!" The tide of music carries them forward. Aleys leans in, wanting. Within her, something bursts like a cloud of tears.

Then the tune ends and the girls collapse to the benches, breathing hard, and Aleys is left to gather herself alone. She clutches her hands together, to keep herself from joining the beguines. Now she will leave. As she reaches the door, she catches Katrijn's triumphant look. Katrijn be damned, Aleys thinks, I will not be made witness to unholy rites. As her fingers touch the handle, she hears the harp's flourish, and she turns. Like Lot's wife, already tasting salt on her tongue, she turns back.

Ida has stood. With her cheeks flushed from dancing and her hair smooth down her back, Ida is beautiful. She opens her mouth and from her comes the purest sound Aleys has ever heard.

"Look!" Ida sings, and her summons fills the chapel, rises to the rafters. Ida the silent is become a herald, alighted in their midst. The women look above them, as if Ida's voice has lifted the roof and they see heavens above. Aleys pauses, her hand glued to the latch. She cannot bring herself to open the door. Somehow the precious sound must be contained in the church. She must not let it escape. When the note fades, a hush descends upon the women, like snow falling to field.

Ida sings again: "The winter is past. The rain is over and gone."

The notes shiver delicately from her lips, dancing through the air of the nave. You can practically see the song of Ida. The voice makes you want to hold the girl, you want to shelter her. The voices of the beguines swell in chorus.

"Come, O sisters of Jerusalem!" they sing in response.

Then Cecilia rises across from Ida, folds her hands over her breast, and sings.

"Blossoms appear in the land, the time of the songbird has arrived."

Their eyes meet across the space as their voices merge, the light meeting dark, diving and soaring. Aleys lifts her head to listen. It is so achingly beautiful. The words and the notes weave a nest, complex and particular, twig and grass and feather, a home in the heart of the music, and she is held fast by their song. *Oh, Mama*, she thinks, *this is the melody you sought.*

"The cooing of the dove is heard in our land."

"The green figs open."

"The grapevines bloom and yield their sweet fragrance."

The voices reach for each other, interlacing in harmony, yearning and truth entwined and humming through the space. Tears well in Aleys's eyes. It is as if the sun has risen in the music. She knows these words. They sing in the language of their mothers. She drops her hand and raises her head and sees she is not alone. The cheeks of the most elderly beguine are wet, too. Aleys see that old Agnes is not birdlike, not fearsome, but majestic.

And when the women respond, "Sing, O women of Jerusalem!" and rise to their feet, the thunder of their noise shakes Aleys.

"Come, O sisters!" sings the angel Ida. The women join hands. They are radiant and alive and dancing as Cecilia offers up the last line, and Aleys understands they all yearn as she does. She has been stingy, hoarding her prayer. It is not only between her and God. They are all beloved.

"Arise, my true love, and come with me."

It's the Song of Songs, the Canticle of Canticles, so joyful it makes you weep.

She has misunderstood. They all can fly.

17

Friar Lukas

On Sundays, Friar Lukas performs Mass for the beguines. Sophia Vermeulen meets him inside the begijnhof entrance. He's always liked Sophia, has been glad to see her rise with the begijnhof, now nearly fifty women strong. There are as many beguines in the begijnhof as nuns in most convents. She runs the place with a steady hand. She is the best of her sex, practically a man. It occurs to him that she has more beguines than he has friars. Well, women are more inclined to religion than men. Maybe his Aleys will recruit a hundred women to the Franciscan order. What a tribute to God that would be.

"Magistra." Lukas bows his head to Sophia and scans the courtyard for Aleys. He will spend some time after Mass to instruct her, perhaps try out a variant of his sermon about the coming end of times. It's a sunny morning, with buttercups poking through the lawn and children running around. Several beguines are trying to corral them for church. Aleys is not among them.

"How fares my new friar?" he asks Sophia. He means it as a joke.

"Good day, Father." She nods. "Walk with me?"

He falls in beside her. As Sophia speaks, he continues to look for Aleys. Perhaps she's already in the church, praying. Perhaps she's at her prie-dieu, with that little psalter of hers. Good. They will see her exemplary devotion.

". . . want to limit our trade in English wool, prohibit us from selling . . . Father, are you listening?"

"How is Sister Aleys?"

She sighs. An exasperated tone enters her voice. "Aleys is"—she pauses—"well educated. Now, we need your help with the guild."

"Yes, of course." Wool is their livelihood. "But has she won over any converts?"

"Converts?" Sophia stares at him. "You've sent her to convert us?"

He realizes it doesn't sound good. "No, of course not." He'd have thought no one would complain if a few beguines set down their spindles and took up the robe. Beguines leave the begijnhof all the time, they turn left for marriage or right for the convent. No one seems to mind. They are free women, after all. "I thought perhaps she would inspire others. If enough seek to join us, I'll secure them a home of their own."

"Father, you are welcome to evangelize among my beguines. If you find any who would prefer Aleys's company to ours, they are free to go. We wouldn't hinder any woman from joining the Franciscans, if that is her calling." She lowers her voice. "But I don't think Aleys is winning you any converts."

"Why not? She is brimming with faith, she is learned, she is . . ."

Sophia looks at him. The look contains a warning. "She has a calling, Lukas, I can see that. It doesn't mean she has charisma."

He winces. People have said the same of him.

After the service, Aleys cuts across the courtyard, trampling buttercups. *Be careful with such new life*, he thinks.

"*Pax et bonum*," he greets her. "Peace and goodness to you, Sister, and may you spread faith where it's needed." Which is everywhere. "How have you been?"

He remembers the moment he first saw her, the wild desire in her eyes. Now it seems subdued. This is good, he thinks, her passion is finding channels of obedience. At least he thinks it's good. He's never been spiritual advisor to someone like this. Usually, his work has been to whip up faith among people, not transmute it. This is like taming a wild horse to the plow. The girl was left on her own for too long, reading, interpreting, praying without guidance, hallucinating angels. A feral faith, really. He will pray on it.

"Father, I know it's Midsummer." She's already shaking her head. "I've not found many who want to become Franciscan."

It's as Sophia described. "Why not?"

"I'm not sure." She looks at her hands.

"This is about a calling to serve God. Are you not presenting it correctly?"

"They already serve God. In the hospital, at deathbeds. In the school."

"So you've convinced none of them? Not one?"

"It's just that they're happy here. Maybe I could recruit from town. If I could preach like my brothers . . ."

"Women don't preach."

"But that's what Franciscans do."

"Franciscan friars."

"You revere Mary Magdalene. She spread Christ's message. You said she was a model of womanhood."

"To be venerated, not imitated." Aleys has a quick way of turning his words. She'd make a good theologian if she were a man.

"But—"

"If you preached in public, you'd be teaching men. That's forbidden."

"Father, didn't you tell me women are more likely than men to reach heaven?" Her voice rises. "Maybe men should heed us."

"Like Adam did Eve? We'd still be in paradise if she'd kept her advice to herself."

Aleys gives a huff. A verging-on-disobedience huff. "You know the magistra instructs us. She's perfectly capable."

He puts his hand out. Stop. He's heard rumors about those meetings. He respects Sophia and doesn't want to know more. "That's teaching, not preaching. A woman has never given a public sermon in Brugge."

"That's because there's never been a Franciscan sister here. How am I supposed to find recruits? Could I at least go door-to-door like my brothers?"

"And who would accompany you? One of the men? Sister Aleys, where did you get such notions?"

"But Saint Clare?"

"Saint Clare was enclosed with her women."

"She wasn't by the side of Saint Francis? Like Mary Magdalene beside Christ?"

"Of course not. Francis established a convent for her."

"Oh."

"The brothers supported them at first, then the town, once they realized the power of their prayers." How could she not know this? He supposes he could have told her, but it seemed too obvious to say.

"But how will I recruit if I can't preach?"

She has a point, but he can't have her wandering about with his men. "You must try harder here. You can . . . impress them with your Latin. I'll ask Sophia if you can perform the evening oratory instead of Katrijn."

"No." She frowns as she twists to look for Katrijn. "Please don't. I'll think of something."

A burst of laughter rises from a knot of young women as a pair of toddlers chases a group of pigeons and the courtyard explodes with rising, flapping gray. Aleys's gaze catches on the women for a moment, and when she turns back, he glimpses longing in her face. It strikes him, for the first time, that he could lose her to the beguines. That she could find something here. He watches the flock disappear over the roofs. He can't let that happen. God sent her, he can't lose her. Aleys has something he needs, something he can't quite name. He can't let her go.

"Sister," he says urgently, "you have a calling as a Franciscan. Take the time you need. I will pray for him to show you the way."

18

ALEYS

The reading chair has migrated to the window to catch the evening light. Aleys has asked permission to read. She hopes to make up for the night that she corrected Cecilia. She hopes that they will like her if she reads. She feels the contradiction, that she wants to belong even as she tries to recruit them away. But there you have it.

Katrijn pushes aside the spindles in her basket to extract a sheet of parchment. It's riddled with holes where the parchminer scraped the goatskin too thin. The translator, whoever he is, uses cheap materials. The readings are always in the same cramped hand, hastily executed, words crammed onto the page in uneven lines.

Katrijn passes the reading to Aleys. For a moment, they're face-to-face, gripping the parchment. Aleys looks down. Katrijn's hands are blemished with liver spots. Even her cuticles are stained brown. Aleys starts. On her right hand. Just her right hand. When Aleys looks up, Katrijn's eyes are stern. She releases the reading.

Aleys's eyes follow as Katrijn resumes her seat and pulls cloth work from her basket. Every nail on Katrijn's right hand is stained brown; her third finger bears an angry red callus, as if she's been gripping a pen too long. It's a sudden realization: Katrijn is the translator.

Aleys's head reels. How is it possible? Katrijn must work through the night by lamplight, Latin to her left, blank parchment to her right, the words *gloria*, *pax*, *fides* flying across the gap, landing on the new page as glory, peace, faith. This page she holds is written in Katrijn's hand.

How had she missed it? She hadn't imagined that the woman with the coin purse could also cherish scripture. But it makes sense. Katrijn reads Latin. Now Aleys understands why Katrijn is so wary, why she watches Aleys as if she were an informer. Aleys could bring down the Church upon them if she reported the translations.

"Let us pray." Sophia gives the benediction, her voice as calm as a compress. Sophia—she's been harboring a translator in the begijnhof. For Sophia knows, of course she does. Katrijn and Sophia are always together. They're close, closer even than sisters. You can see how they lean on each other. They may disagree, but there's some understanding between them, a tenderness. They protect each other.

The women are waiting. Aleys holds in her hands the parable of the mustard grain, the tiny seed that grows into a towering tree to delight the creatures of the air. She imagines the Dutch syllables springing into forests of words. As Aleys begins reading, Katrijn tips back her head to listen, intent as a composer hearing the first notes of her own music.

Later, Aleys corners Ida.

"Katrijn translates scripture, doesn't she?"

Ida looks at her sharply.

"You don't have to say. But why?"

Ida frowns. "If you don't understand, I can't explain."

"No, I do. Just, why her? Why does she do something so dangerous we can't even talk about it?" Aleys thinks of the martyrs in her psalter. Is Katrijn that brave?

Ida lowers her voice. "If you must have a reason: Her old father is gone deaf, but he can still read. She makes three copies. One for us, one for the townspeople, and one for him." Ida looks Aleys straight in the eye. "She doesn't want him to die without joy."

"But it's so risky."

"You learned Latin to read the psalms"—she purses her lips—"to yourself."

"But that's not illegal."

"You think we can all study like you? That we all own psalters? It's hard enough to read in Dutch. We can't master Latin, too. Some of us have to work."

It's the most she's ever heard her say at once. "Ida, I could teach you."

But Ida is shaking her head. "You still don't see, do you? It's not just me. Look around. God rules our lives, our deaths. He judges whether we will spend eternity in heaven or hell, but Rome won't let us read his word?" Ida grips Aleys's arm and the look in her eye is fierce. "She does this for us."

Katrijn's translation is a gift. Sure as bread on the table, she's given them meaning. She's offered Cecilia forgiveness. She's given Marte the solace of stories of the afflicted. Katrijn brings her father poetry when he can no longer hear. Some want to understand so they can follow. Sophia, so she can lead. And Ida? Ida just thinks no priest should stand between the people and their God. And Aleys realizes that it's not just her, not just the beguines—there are people all over the Low Countries who would hold the word close if they could.

"Magistra? Might I seek counsel?" Aleys knocks on Sophia's door.

"Advice from an old beguine?" Sophia smiles. "Come in."

Sophia's home is modest, with nothing more than a prie-dieu, a painted wall cupboard, and a table, but there's a thick rush mat on the floor and the chairs before the fireplace have good wool blankets across their backs. On a table lies open an accounting book, ink still wet on the page; Sophia has just been making an entry. A narrow stair leads to a bedchamber above. It's not the largest house in the begijnhof, but the magistra doesn't take in boarders as some others do. It would be nice to have a room like this, thinks Aleys, all to yourself.

Sophia gestures her into one chair and takes the other. "What's on your mind?"

"I wanted to ask you"—Aleys hesitates—"about the translations. I know we don't discuss the source."

"But you've figured it out. I thought you might."

"Yes." Aleys releases her breath. She adds, hurriedly, "No one told me."

Sophia nods. "And you want to help."

Can Sophia read her mind? "Exactly! If I could get parchment and ink, then I could—"

Sophia leans forward and puts a hand on Aleys's knee. "I'm sorry, child. I can't permit that."

"Why not?"

"This is a matter between you and Friar Lukas."

"But the friars don't translate."

"Exactly, and for good reason. The Franciscans are so radical, their commitment to poverty and love so uncompromising, that it makes powerful men uncomfortable. You know there are those in Rome, right now, trying to persuade the pope that the friars must be forced to own property? As it is, the Franciscans dance on the edge of papal approval. They don't dare translate, even if they're sympathetic. If you did, you'd be putting your own order in danger."

"Then why do you risk it?"

"The Church isn't concerned with the activities of old women who mend stockings."

"We could keep it secret, if I helped."

Sophia gives her a long look. "That attitude is in neither the spirit nor the law of your vows."

"It's the only thing I know to do!"

"Child, there are many gifts of the spirit. Prayer, charity, devotion, healing, teaching, among others."

"But what's my gift?"

Sophia laughs. "Such impatience! You've been in religious life for what? Two months? Not even prophets foresee their own gifts. God will call your talent from you when it's needed. Until he does, child, serve with a full heart. It's all he asks."

It's what Friar Lukas said. Be patient. She doesn't want to be patient. Aleys harnesses herself to the prie-dieu, prays and prays harder to be shown her gift. A real gift. She has to prove herself. More than fasting, more than a hair shirt. If she can't attract followers and she can't preach and she can't translate, there must be something she can do. She prays for a calling to serve God that's as clear as a clarion. Something big.

19

ALEYS

"There's fleece on the quay, a shipment of English." Katrijn stands before Aleys in the refectory, her leather bag slung across her chest. They haven't even finished breakfast. "I suppose you can grade grease wool? You are a draper's daughter."

The reminder of Papa sends an icicle down her back. Aleys swallows the last of her bread. "I *was* a draper's daughter."

"Well, you still have two arms. We need help with the sacks."

"I—" Aleys wants to protest. She left home to pray, not pick wool.

"I assure you, Sister, God resides as much in the marketplace as he does in the church. Follow me."

There's little point in arguing with Katrijn.

Ida waits for them inside the archway, basket on her hip. She recently took the gray dress, which makes her look even smaller, her dark eyes even more intense. Aleys wonders why Ida's not at the hospital today. It makes no sense for Ida to haul bags of fleece when they could have Cecilia.

Katrijn and Ida walk with purpose, scattering pigeons. A fishwife squints at them and spits to the side. Another draws her apron over her child's head, and Aleys recalls the baker's wife back home claiming that death hung in the folds of the beguines' skirts. Outside the apothecary a group of men watches them pass. "Mertens's wife," someone sniggers. Even though she's tailored her robe into a brown habit more fit for a woman, people still recognize her. Sophia was right. They need better stories.

They cross the city toward the loading docks of the canal that runs north to the seaport and the channel to England, where the fleece is sourced. The poor English have such bad soil, she's heard, there are more sheep than men. It's here in the Low Countries, where people are plentiful and labor is cheap, that the drapers turn filthy fleece into a wool so fine it's coveted by kings and bishops.

The plaza is loud with horses pulling pallets across cobbles and hawkers shouting the price of eel and herring. The air is flecked with sheep dust. The familiar grassy scent of fleece spills from burlap sacks that line the plaza. That smell takes her home. For a month every year, the house smelled like a barnyard until Papa farmed out the last fleece to the professional wullebreken, who would beat out the sheep shit until it was clean enough to card. It occurs to her that Papa might be here to meet the English shipment. If she saw him, what would she say? Part of her shrinks at the thought, but another part yearns to run into his arms. Would Papa even greet her? He might turn his back. *Let her be God's child.* Her heart twists at the memory. Aleys takes a few steps into the plaza, scanning the fleece stalls on the other side. Katrijn and Ida are making their way across the crowd, but there's no sign of her father or brothers.

Aleys turns to check behind her and stops short at the sight of the wharf crane. She'd walked right by it. The huge wooden structure leans over the canal like a great heron scanning for minnows, but instead of legs it has enormous treadwheels on each side. A rope with a large hook snakes from the crane's beak like a strange tongue. Bobbing below is a barge stacked with barrels. Workers clamber over the stack, loosening ropes. A man grasps the swinging hook and fixes it to the topmost cask and yells "Klaar!"

There's motion within the treadwheels. Aleys squints into the nearest one. Inside the dark wheel is a pair of boys. At least, she thinks they're boys. They appear misshapen, with the thighs of men and the chests of children. The boys lean forward and begin to trudge up the inside of the wheel, which groans like a donkey. Slowly, the wheel turns, the rope tightens, and the top barrel rises from the stack. It's stamped *Gascogne*. Fine wine. These barrels journeyed under sail up the coast of France to the Low Countries before they were put on this barge to the center of Brugge.

"Quite the marvel, is it not?" A man beside her is watching the crane. He is pale, with deep-set eyes and dark curls under a black velvet cap. "I'll never forget the first time I saw it. The ingenuity!"

"The children," she says. "It seems cruel. Why don't they use horses?"

"Inside the wheels?"

"Or men?"

"Dwarves, maybe. They pay the boys."

A carter on the quay uses a hooked pole to fish the rope that holds the barrel, walking back until the strained line is bent in two and the barrel hovers above his wagon. "Laat los!" he shouts. The rope quivers with tension as the barrel twists in midair. The pair of boys stops, balances, and turns carefully. It looks for a moment like the momentum of the load will drive the wheel into a violent backward spin, and the boys with it, but they are precise as they walk in tandem, reversing the direction of the wheel. The barrel drops into place and the carter scrambles up to release the load. The children turn again and trot forward quickly as the hook swings up and back over the barge. One of the boys stumbles; the other catches his shoulder. Aleys shudders. If God is in the marketplace, he hides himself well.

"Spinning squirrels," says the man. "That's what people call them. By any name, the machine is magnificent. The *magna rota*."

"The great wheel," echoes Aleys.

He turns to her and raises a brow. "Latin?"

"Mmmm." She turns over her shoulder to look for Katrijn and Ida. Ida is clutching her basket as if she fears pickpurses in the jostling crowd. Aleys should rejoin them. They won't like her idling with a strange man.

"Ah! I know you! You're that woman in the begijnhof. I should have recognized your friar's cloth. So what does that make you, exactly? A nun or a beguine?"

"I'm not a nun," she says wearily. "I'm a Franciscan sister."

"But where are your brothers?"

"They are—" She falters. She knows only two of them. Lukas and Hervé. She couldn't even say where the friary is. It's awkward to claim she's joined the brotherhood. "They will be teaching me once they secure me my own place." It sounds absurd, she realizes, the idea of a woman living on her own.

"I see. And what will you do? Preach Latin to the ladies?" He smirks. "You might as well lecture the sparrows. Women can't possibly understand." He affects a dramatic shrug. "But then, I suppose Saint Francis preached to birds."

"You think I'm the only woman in Brugge who's lettered? There are two others in the begijnhof alone who read Latin."

He chuckles. "Their psalters, maybe. Nothing more."

"You find it impossible that a draper and a magistra could be so accomplished? Sophia Vermeulen and Katrijn Janssens are both fluent."

He raises a single eyebrow. "Ah, well, the world is changing." He sweeps his palm toward the wharf crane. "Wonders abound."

"Aleys!" Katrijn's voice cuts through the crowd.

"It seems you are summoned, Sister Aleys."

Aleys rises on tiptoe to find Katrijn and Ida huddled together at the far side of the plaza. They look exposed, two women in gray, surrounded by men. Aleys feels a prickle of guilt. Maybe she shouldn't have spoken of begijnhof matters to a stranger. She was only repeating what Cecilia told her. When she looks behind her, the man in the black cap has vanished.

Aleys slips sideways through the crowd. Near the stalls, the sour smell of fleece is strong. Katrijn gives her a scalding look. "You can't even manage to keep up." She gives a huff, then turns to the trader behind a wooden slab erected as a counter. Ida remains facing the square, watching the crowd, hand clamped over the basket.

"Sister Aleys." Katrijn snaps her fingers. "Pay attention."

The trader speaks a graveled jumble of English and Dutch syllables. He leans toward Katrijn, his eyes bright, full of mevrouw and milady as they argue over the cost of long staple. He nods to a group of sacks in front of the stall. Take your pick.

"Aleys, test the cores for britch."

Some of the Dover packers hide nasty nests of coarse hind clippings in the heart of their sacks. Aleys sinks her hands deep inside, knowing she'll come out smelling of pasture. She'll have to wash her sleeves out with lye. Sure enough, buried beneath the soft long staple is a hard ball of short, curly fibers that would be impossible to spin. She's withdrawing her hands from the sack to tell Katrijn to find another vendor when she sees Ida step away from the stall. Katrijn's hand shoots out to grip Ida's forearm.

"Ida, no," murmurs Katrijn. "Look. Over there."

Aleys's eyes follow. The man with the velvet cap is across the square talking with a carter, but he's only half listening, his gaze trailing a third man, a shopkeeper fast approaching the fleece stalls. Ida quickly turns her back to the square and hugs her basket close. As Aleys straightens, she sees the shopkeeper frown and veer off. The pale man tracks where he was heading. His eyes land on Ida. He starts over.

"Aleys, keep your head down," Katrijn hisses. To Ida, she says, "It's the man I told you about. Who's been buying up translations."

"The bishop's spy?" Ida goes rigid. She shoots her eyes at Aleys. "You were exchanging words with him. By the wheel."

Katrijn turns on Aleys. "You spoke with the bishop's man?"

"I didn't know who he was!" Aleys protests. "I didn't say anything."

"Ida, draw close." Katrijn slips her left hand into Ida's basket, extracts something that she slides up her right sleeve. She closes ink-stained fingers around her cuff. Katrijn glances coolly at the English merchant, who studiously looks the other way.

"Can't trust a friar to judge wool," Katrijn announces, pushing Aleys aside with her hip. "I'll just have to do it myself." She plunges her hands deep into the bag of fleece, then rises and dusts them off. "These will do," she says. "Here, take this." She lifts the sack and thrusts it at Aleys and grabs another. "Let's get out of here."

They walk briskly from the plaza, their gray cloaks sweeping the cobbles. Aleys follows, her cheek against the burlap, her beating heart only inches from a piece of parchment that she knows is sacred, Dutch, and illegal. When she looks back, the man in black has paused in front of the crane. Behind him, the children in the treadwheel change direction. His eyes never move, trained on the backs of the beguines.

20

The Bishop

From his barge, the bishop admires the mayor's glass windows set into his three-story timbered mansion on the main canal. The upper panes capture the image of the harbor crane, never at rest. Jan would like to outfit his own windows with glass, imagines them reflecting the shiny weathercock atop the steeple of Sint-Salvator. He'd need more funds for that. Besides, he hopes to be long gone before glaziers could finish the project. He's one heretic shy of Rome. With Willems's new information, he's getting closer. He need consider only the *optica* of the angles, how his choices bounce off city, guild, church.

Willems bangs the oars against the gunnels. He's no boatman, though he plays one well enough to mingle in the mayor's kitchen and sample the scullery gossip. The bishop regrets that his barge isn't more kingly, but it's long enough that he can recline under the canopy that bears his sapphire and gold crest. As they approach the landing, the mayor's men open the boathouse doors and Willems manages to slide the boat into the open bay. Willems makes a joke with the servants and saunters off to the kitchen. Jan mounts the curving stairway. At the top, the mayor greets him with open arms. His round chin and polished cheeks are topped by a peaked hat that makes him look like a jovial acorn. Bite that nut, though, and you'll break a tooth.

"Come in, come in! We'll walk in my garden. The cherries are ripe."

It's a tidy city garden, with herbs outside the kitchen and fruit trees lining the back wall. A child's swing hangs in the apples. The mayor has many children, six from his wife alone. Willems says there are three younger ones hidden around the city.

The mayor slaps the bishop's shoulder, then winces and cradles his elbow. "Ouf. Gout."

"The disease of kings," says Jan. "It's all that French wine you import. You should drink less and sell more, my friend."

"You sound like my apothecary. He says Bordeaux taxes the joints. I tell him it's what fills the city coffers with levies." He chuckles at his own joke. "No matter. He says brandewijn will cure it." The mayor nods down the central path, between ornamental shrubs. "Jan, how did we get to be so old? I'd swear that yesterday we were playing knucklebones."

Jan chuckles. "You always cheated."

"No more than you! Your brother was the only one who played it straight. I could never figure out how he won."

"Yes. Well. Lukas has strange luck, I suppose."

"Listen," says the mayor, "I have a small favor to ask." He rubs his fingers together briskly, then laces them in a gesture of prayer. On him, the gesture speaks more of retail than reverence.

The bishop bows. "As always, I am at your service."

"My daughter, Mechtelt, the one with the, ah, large eyes?"

Yes, he knows the girl. On the street, they call her the frog. Children are known to hop in her wake.

"Mechtelt would very much like to join the Benedictines." He puts out one hand. "Now I know the convent is full, but I wondered if there is any way to make room for one more nun. Might you speak to the abbess?"

Jan nods. "I am sure the abbey would welcome any daughter of the mayor." He gives a subtle emphasis to the *any*. Willems reports that there is at least one girl among his bastards.

"Very good. Very good."

Jan feels the scales tip. It can be profitable when the city owes the Church a favor. "I was hoping I might ask you about a troublesome matter."

"My advice is free."

Better be, if you expect me to pull strings for your bug-eyed daughter.

"You are aware that Dutch scripture has been circulating in the Markt?"

The mayor purses his lips. "Illegal scripture? In Brugge? I know nothing of it."

Old fox. He's lying. "Yes. Pope Boniface has charged me with finding the translators."

The mayor's head jerks. "You're not going to make a Strasbourg of us?"

"Most assuredly not. We merely seek to keep the city in the good graces of the Holy See."

"I don't want any executions in this town, Jan. It's bad for business."

"No more do I." Jan uses his most soothing note. "That's why we must nip this in the bud. The Church doesn't burn people for translations. Just bad translations. We need to stop them before they make any unfortunate mistakes. Heretical mistakes."

A squirrel chatters from the trees. They've reached the intersection of the groomed paths.

"There's reason to believe that the beguines are the source," says Jan.

The mayor stops. "I have a niece in the begijnhof. I am very fond of that niece."

"No, no, no. You misunderstand. We needn't disturb them all. I need identify only one."

"I know who you're going to name."

Does he? "Lord Mayor, you are always one step ahead of me."

"My niece won't say who, but you can read that girl like an illustrated alphabet." So he does know about the translations. "You're talking about the Janssens widow. Katrijn Janssens."

As Willems told him. "The draper."

"But you can't touch her, Jan. Have you considered how much of your income comes from the guild?"

"But aren't the beguines a thorn in their side? Mertens has been slapping new regulations all over them. I don't know why they didn't reclaim the stall when old Janssens died."

The mayor chuckles. "They tried. Katrijn told them she was a widow, not a half-wit."

"But she's a woman."

"A guildmember is still a guildmember." The mayor removes his hat and rubs his forehead with the back of his wrist. "You know what they say: Blood ties, but wool binds. Besides, her fabric is among the best, what keeps the Genovese in port. You know our generosity to the Church depends on the city revenues. No wool, no tariff, no tithes. You'll lose a quarter of your income from the city and all your income from the guild if you harm Katrijn Janssens."

The bishop is so tired of walking the tightrope between city and church, between mayor and pope. He struggles to keep the exasperation from his voice. "Boniface insists." He swallows and corrects himself. "If the translations continue unchecked, I will be forced to act."

"Jan, the pope is fighting a losing battle on the translations. You know that."

"Maybe. I hear your advice. I'll leave the widow Janssens to her wool." They stop at the back of the garden. "Perhaps someone else in the begijnhof is doing the translating."

"Do you care for cherries?" asks the mayor. "These sour ones are the best. Now, let's discuss Mechtelt's dowry."

21

Friar Lukas

Heat lightning illuminates the evening sky. Friar Lukas senses a tension in the begijnhof, a tremor among the steady congregation. He's administered the sacraments to this community for nearly a decade, since Sophia took over and invited him to be their pastor. He knows them so well. He knows how Ida mouths her prayers and Katrijn barks her *amen*. That Sophia, who once knelt so fluidly, now lowers first one knee, then the other. He's never seen them so on edge. Instead of laughter as they take their usual places, there are whispers. Even Cecilia, boisterous Cecilia, is muted. The air feels charged, like the lightning is inside the church walls. Lukas raises the wafer: "Take this, all of you, and eat of it, for this is my Body, which will be given up for you." He forces himself to concentrate on the miracle of communion. He sees Sophia clutch Katrijn's hand. A chill runs across Lukas's shoulders as he raises the cup. "Take this, all of you, and drink from it, for this is the chalice of my Blood."

Afterward, Sophia, Katrijn, and Ida approach him as he is wrapping the cup in the altar cloth. Katrijn scowls. Ida has her chin tilted high.

Sophia speaks. "Father, we think you should know. We're being watched."

"Watched? By whom?"

"Several times now, when we go out—the fleece stalls, the Markt, the Lakenhalle—the bishop's man has followed us."

"I very much doubt that."

They stare at him. These aren't fanciful women, he reminds himself. "But why?"

"Lukas, you take our confessions. I think you know. He follows Katrijn often. Sometimes he trails Ida to the hospital."

He does know. He's warned Katrijn to stop translating. Many times. She always returns with the same confession. He's given Ida *Ave*s in penance for smuggling contraband text. But he's been half-hearted in his admonishments. Part of him rejoices at the thought of the gospel flooding the Low Countries. He's parsed it finely for himself. Strictly speaking, Rome has forbidden only certain unauthorized translations. The pope hasn't yet forbidden a Dutch translation. Not *per se*. If it's an accurate translation—and he has told himself he trusts Katrijn not to distort the Dutch—then there's virtue in allowing the people to read it for themselves. How can he deny them the word? Lukas knows what these women do, and he thinks them brave.

Sophia interrupts his thoughts. "Lukas, are we in danger? How far does the bishop intend to go?"

When he leaves the church, the rain is just starting. The beguines hurry into their homes. Except one. He has a glimpse of Aleys in the middle of the courtyard, her head tipped back, tasting raindrops. He pauses to watch. He senses there is something there for him, some message, an insight. He doesn't know what it is. She looks like she would swallow summer lightning.

Lukas storms into his brother's dining chamber. "Why are you following the beguines?"

Jan dismisses the servants with the back of his hand. The table is laden with the remains of dinner, threads of mutton hanging from a half-eaten bone. A loaf of fine white bread lies untouched. His brother's leftovers would be enough to feed a small household. Jan pulls over a goblet, pours wine for Lukas, motions him to the seat at his right.

"To what do I owe this pleasant visit?"

"You've set your man to harassing them. I protest." Lukas pushes the wine away.

Jan rolls his eyes. "I thought you might be glad to see me." He stretches his fingers before him. "Perhaps not. I will say your timing is excellent, if your manners are lacking. You see, I find myself in a . . ." He searches for the right word as if choosing among fragrances. "A position. A position that inclines me to meet your needs."

"You've always been in a position to meet our needs."

"If," continues Jan, "it advances the work of the Church."

"How could housing faithful women do anything but advance the Church?" It tires him, always having to justify his decisions, his order, his faith. It's been three months since Aleys joined them. This has gone on long enough.

"I think it would, Brother, as long as your women truly answer to you. The Church has many needs. Other needs."

When they were boys, Jan didn't have this silky tone in his voice. When they wrestled in the yard, their elbows and words were sharp and unoiled. The bishop's crown has changed him into a politician.

"Be plain," says Lukas. "I'm a simple servant of God."

Jan looks to the ceiling, rolls his neck to crack it, then brings his eyes back to Lukas. "You know I've been visited by the papal envoy."

"Of course I know. I was there." He stood in the back with his friars.

"He delivered a disturbing message. It's come to the notice of the Holy See that there are cells of unorthodoxy in Flanders. A tract, written in Dutch, purporting to be gospel, has reached the pope's hands. He is asking how Brugge could harbor such activity."

"You know the answer. People want to understand the scripture."

"They have their priests for that."

"Your priests barely read Latin!"

"You criticize the Church."

"You should welcome the Dutch gospel." Lukas rubs his hands on his thighs. The coarse wool reminds him who he is. He must not let Jan get under his skin.

"God's word is subtle," says Jan. "Translations are easily corrupted."

"We could supervise them."

"No. Once the tracts get out, people will copy them, they will get into every household, in the hands of shoemakers and bakers. The sacramental mysteries aren't meant for scullery maids."

"But the people yearn for their God."

"Whose God? The people's God?" snaps Jan. "Or the pope's God?"

Lukas shuts his eyes, gathering himself. "Worshippers deserve the truth."

"They have no idea what that is."

"They do, brother, better than you think."

"Better than Rome?" Jan slams his fist on the table. The dishes rattle. "You contradict the pope? Sometimes, Brother, you sail perilously close to the wind." A servant looks in. The bishop, annoyed, brushes him away. He spreads his hands on the table as if calming unruly waters.

"Look. You need a house. I can give you that house."

"You want something in return."

"Don't look so offended. We're sons of the same banker. I require only one."

"One what?"

"One heretic. I propose a trade. A heretic for a house."

"What?" Lukas stands abruptly, pushing back the chair. Not here. Not in this town. "Jan, no. These are good people in Flanders."

"Good people reading the Bible? Where do you think the heresies of the south came from? The Waldensians? The Cathars?"

"It's not the same."

"It is exactly the same. My priests complain that people are asking why they can't speak directly with God. Parishioners have become scornful. The value of indulgences has fallen. People are starting to claim they understand the scriptures better than their own clergy. It's certainly not my priests giving them these ideas." He gives Lukas a pointed stare.

"You're saying we are."

"I'm saying that you and your brothers need to stop whipping people up."

"Is that a threat?"

"No." He drums his fingers on the table. "I won't touch any friars. Though I could."

"Then who are you talking about?"

"Listen, we won't be excessive. An arrest or two should suffice. A short trial. I'll let them recant any heresy, and then release them. It's their own fault for resisting supervision. You need to govern those women."

Lukas feels a pit in his stomach. "You want me to name a beguine."

"Why not? The people already distrust them. Plenty will come forward to witness. There are many who would be happy to see their wings clipped." Jan puts his palms up. "Though I can't touch their draper. The guild protects her."

"But the beguines are faithful! They're more devout than your merchants."

"Precisely. They're pious fools. They err in their excess. I know they're writing tracts."

Lukas stands. "Jan, I'm their shepherd."

"Then be a shepherd. Cull the diseased to save your flock. I promise it will be quick and easy. No one will come to harm. Bring me a translator, just not the Janssens widow."

"You want me to betray them."

Jan snorts through his nose. "Don't be deliberately naïve. It doesn't suit you."

"I won't betray my own."

"Either you will or I will. And I'll be less generous. I understand there are two lettered women in the begijnhof besides the draper. The magistra and your girl. I'm letting you select who will serve as an example. Or I could take them both. We require, the pope requires, that we teach the people a lesson. They need to stop seeking that which is too high for them."

22

ALEYS

The women start at small noises: the cat in the hall, the settling of logs. They build the fire high, though it's August, in case words must be burned quickly. Marte keeps watch outside. The readings grow short, but they don't stop. Katrijn looks strained.

"Our mission is service," the magistra reminds them. "Let us focus on our work."

Sophia had been wrong. The bishop is interested in the activities of women who knit. Aleys wishes she hadn't let his man goad her into speaking. She tells herself that she said nothing about translations. Still she's uneasy.

Aleys walks with Ida to the hospital. "What's going on?" Aleys asks. "That man on the quay—"

Ida looks around. "We're not sure."

Aleys gestures to her basket. "You're not . . . ?"

"I am. We're being more careful."

"And Katrijn's still translating?"

Ida nods. "We can't live by bread alone. Nor can the people of this town."

Aleys is assigned permanently to Sint-Janshospitaal, where she performs the lowliest tasks, changing bedpans, holding cloths to wet coughs. Disease is so damp. Piss and blood, pus and mucus. Sores creep like living things across limbs. She swabs a wound and it opens like a cut of raw meat. She is forever wiping her hands on her apron. Aleys no longer watches for demons. She's too busy. She observes the other beguines, and her admiration grows for their stamina. They are fast in their faith and they are frank; they do not shrink from the facts. We will all go to God when he calls, they say, but we can ease each other's way in the passing.

A girl is brought in who looks like Griete did as a child, with a blonde braid to her waist and eyelashes so pale they're barely visible. The girl's chest rattles and she spits blood, but her eyes follow Aleys around the ward. When she can, Aleys sits with her, tells the girl saint stories as she smooths her hair. The child asks over and over again for the tale of Ursula and the eleven thousand companions who chose to die rather than yield their chastity. The girl seems more impressed by their number than their virtue.

"How much is eleven thousand?"

"They would fill the whole of Markt square. There would be no room for anyone else."

"All of them friends?" Probably not, thinks Aleys, it would be more complicated than that. But she nods.

The girl is consumed by a fit of coughing, the sharp bark of it and the heavy wheeze. Aleys places her hand on the child's back, feels the fever against her palm, and squints above the bed. She hopes it's angels, not demons, waiting for this one.

The last day, the girl fades quickly, dissolving into air. Though she can no longer ask for Ursula's story, Aleys tells it to her anyway. In heaven, she tells the girl, there's a special maidens' garden, trees bent with pink and golden pears. And so many friends. She hopes it's true, what she's saying. The girl draws a long ratcheting breath. There are swings in the trees. The girl moves her hand to Aleys's wrist to quiet her. *Stop*, she seems to be saying, *I don't need this now*. She opens her eyes and Aleys reads something deep that says, *Still. Be still.*

Once, when she was a girl, Aleys happened upon roe deer in the meadow where the slope of larkspur and bishop's lace spilled from dark pines. The morning light fell on the red doe and her spotted fawns, just so. The doe raised her head, measuring Aleys. A moment, another moment, and the world stilled, the trees holding them, the sun holding the trees. It was as if the slender doe had stepped from the pages of the psalter to this spot at the edge of the wood, silver and red ink come alive. The fawns continued eating while the doe watched Aleys, until, at some mute signal, the three deer moved into the woods. At the margin, the red doe turned back, and there was something in her liquid eye; an understanding passed between them, between Aleys and the doe. An acknowledgment. A silent, sure gossamer thread between them suddenly visible. *We are made of spirit.* And then the doe left.

Aleys returned to the meadow later. She lingered on the path. She sat beneath the trees on a carpet of rusty needles. But she never saw the doe again. She had been given one glimpse, and she came to understand it was meant for a lifetime. A single note from which to build a song. Yet she yearns for more. She knows the doe is there, watching from the trees. Aleys does not speak of this to anyone.

The girl squeezes her hand, and in the child's eyes she witnesses a sudden opening depth, like mirrors upon mirrors receding into dark, a knowing. The soul of the child looks out, ancient and benign, and whispers, "I shall endure." Aleys slips into her open eyes as she would into a clear pool, enveloped by perfect silence beneath the surface. She does not know how she knows. Somehow, beyond phlegm and pulse and swallow, beyond touch and thirst, the essence of this child will live.

And then the child coughs and gasps for breath, and Aleys surfaces into the ward. The girl's eyes close and she withdraws into her body, which will struggle, one breath, the next, shuddering and grasping. Though the soul travels ahead, the body fights to stay. Aleys sees this and wonders. The air above the child shimmers. She looks about the ward; it is dense with waiting spirits. She cannot see them, but she can sense them. Perhaps she is becoming beguine, after all.

Ida pulls her away to help splint a leg. When Aleys returns to the girl, there is no more wheezing. Aleys feels a sudden vertiginous drop. She cannot stop her tears from welling. Though she knows the child is gone, though she has seen the certainty in her eyes, still she would pull her back from the woods. *Come back. Don't leave. Wait for me.* Aleys stands, searching the margins of the world for the child who is not there, but everywhere.

All that evening, through the dinner and the reading, Aleys holds a thought as if she's protecting a Candlemas taper, a glimmer of some understanding that could flicker and die if she doesn't tend it. She carries it to the begijnhof chapel to sit alone. As she passes Sophia's window, the magistra is just turning down her lantern. Her hair is loose, the wimple set aside, and Aleys sees with a shock that Sophia's hair is streaked with white, like it's painted with chalk. The lines in Sophia's face are cast into relief by the shadows, and Aleys sees what she had not seen before, the effort. Sophia's eyes flick up, sensing someone outside, but Aleys treads quietly the dark path past her window.

Empty, the church echoes. A faint moonlight sifts through high windows, rendering the nave in black and silver. Aleys's robe reads gray in this light, as if she is beguine. Aleys pauses and rubs her hands over her thighs. It wouldn't be so bad, she thinks, joining the beguines. They have purpose and they have faith, and even if they lack glory, they do have each other. Their mending and their mutual understanding. Their laughter. It might not be the quickest path to God, but she would have good company.

The night she left home in her blue dress, the moon following her between the trees. It feels ages ago. She had thought it would be different, this journey to find her beloved. More certain. She had thought it would be easier. What does she know of God? What does she really know?

Aleys stands before the bare altar, taking account. She feels she's been given glimpses, sparks that are proof of fire, quickly extinguished. It's so hard to keep his light before her, always. To never lose sight. "Beloved"—she falters—"why do you hide?" The darkness is so vast, the light so fleeting. "Why hide from me? From all of us?"

He is silent, up there on his cross.

Behind her, the door squeaks. For a moment, her heart leaps. Is he come? But it's Sophia, bearing a candle. The magistra stops to cross herself before the altar.

"I thought you might need this," she says, placing the candle on the step.

"You knew I was here?"

"It's the work of a magistra to see."

Sophia sits on the step, pats it. Aleys sits beside her. The candle casts an egg of light over the two of them. Christ hovers above them like a nighthawk.

"How goes it, the running toward God?"

Aleys checks to make sure Sophia is not making fun of her. She can't tell. "It sounds foolish."

"Not to me." Sophia looks up to Christ. There's a small smile on her lips.

"Were you . . . ?" Aleys has never thought about Sophia's experience.

The magistra doesn't move her eyes from the cross. "Was I once on fire with love of him? Yes, I thought the world would burn if I couldn't find him." She places her palms on the stair, straightens her elbows. It is a gesture more girlish than matronly. Her loose hair spills down her back, silver in this light. "Everything was urgent. I needed proofs and showings."

"And now?"

"Now"—she sighs and looks at Aleys—"I am become more his hausfrau than his lover."

Aleys feels sorry for her.

"No, no. Don't mistake me. I am content, most of the time. It almost makes me miss it, watching you. The desire. I once wanted him for myself. All for myself." She laughs. "I was sure I was his most ardent lover. I thought I was special."

But you are. "Did he come to you?"

She looks back up at the crucifix and doesn't answer for a moment. Her capable hands lie quiet in her lap. Finally, she speaks. "You know, I believe he did."

The magistra stands, smooths her dress. "Blow out the candle when you leave." Her eyes contain an equal measure of joy and sorrow. "And Aleys?

It's not enough to be in love with love. You must be willing to suffer with him, too."

The light seems to dim when Sophia leaves. Aleys suppresses a shiver and slides her hands deeper into her sleeves. How is she supposed to suffer with Christ? She thinks of the suffering lying in the hospital now, their moaning and thrashing, the awful final stillness that comes over them. She can witness their pain, she can give comfort and tell stories, but she doesn't want to inhabit their suffering. Not the way Sophia means. And if she can't manage even that, how is she supposed to understand the suffering of God?

Aleys regards Christ's hanging head, his seeping wounds, and feels—what? Reverence, yes. Always. But mostly fear. She hardly recognizes him. This is not the playful God, the divinity in dust motes and birdsong. She's wary of this Jesus, imagines him raising his head and fixing her with disappointed eyes. *Why can you not gaze upon my wounds?* She turns her head away from the gory thorned Christ. He frightens her, and she's ashamed of that. She knows he sees her cowardice. Just as a horse will buck a frightened rider, she is sure that Christ sees into her heart and feels her shrink from his agony. She presses her hands into her ribs. She cannot bear to look at him. It's too big, his sacrifice, incomprehensible. It's too much to witness.

A whisper seeps into her head, Sophia's voice: *If you cannot comprehend, imagine.*

But what should she imagine?

His last night.

So she shuts her eyes and pictures him at the end of the meal, his last with the apostles. Christ knows that he will be arrested in the morning. He has already given them bread and wine in remembrance, has initiated them into the rite of his bodily sacrifice, has named his betrayer. Judas has slunk from the house. What does Jesus feel? She doesn't know. She searches inside, finds nothing.

You are an apostle. Follow.

Aleys trails them through the streets of Jerusalem, back to Gethsemane, where they have their camp outside the grove. Some of them, the younger ones, are giddy after the good supper. They throw their arms about each other as they go up the hill. The older disciples are sober, they have understood his meaning, and they turn inward in contemplation, ignoring the shouts of the youth. The evening air bears the kiss of spring. Crickets call softly.

She waits outside the camp until she sees him emerge alone. From the darkening shadow of olives, Aleys follows Jesus, sees he is barefoot, has left his sandals behind, is stepping out with naked sole over flinted ground. She looks back, sees Peter, James, and Paul settling against gnarled trunks, where sleep will take them soon. She wants to slap them awake but knows she cannot. Jesus looks back at them, hesitates, then moves on. He is sad. She can feel this much. She will walk with him.

The stones are sharp as barbs, they lie hard upon the ground and pierce his feet. He does not flinch. And then she understands. He knows what is coming, and it's not only scourge, thorns, lance, nails. These are the least of his sorrows. It's the eyes of Judas. What are these bodily pains compared to the betrayal to come at dawn?

Aleys follows him deeper into the grove as the heavens glow indigo and ink. He stumbles, then grasps a tree, and he goes like that, from branch to branch, tree to tree, the olives his last companions, until he passes even them, at the edge of the grove, overlooking the valley. And there he calls out a single word: "Abba." It rings over the valley, his anguish drifts down upon sleeping creatures, the cry of the child whose father is fearsome and far. "My Father, if it is possible, let this cup pass from me."

His fear, she feels it now. It's the fear of any mortal creature, the love of self and life and body, the love of heartbeat and breath, the love of tongue against roof, of sweetness of sleep, of warmth of the fire, of cricket song. She presses her hands to her face and loves the soft grab of flesh to flesh and finds that tears have made her cheekbones slippery. How could God ask this of his son? God asks too much. More than she has.

Then from Christ's mouth, a soft cry: "Thy will be done."

How? she asks him. *Why?*

Draw near, he says. *I will show you.*

He looks at her then, her Christ, with his wounded eyes, and she sees what she had not seen before. He is in love. He is in love with her, he is in love with the sparrow and the river, he is in love with the root and trunk and flower of it all, the entire creation, and his fear and his love are inseparable. He has love even for the fear, and it is through the vulnerable door, the portal of fear, the spear in his side that will come tomorrow, that Aleys glimpses, for a fleeting moment, the unutterable vastness of her beloved.

She returns to the dormitory, shaken. She had no idea who she loved.

23
Friar Lukas

Friar Lukas walks to the shore and stares at the ocean with unseeing eyes. Seagulls squabble over shells on the rocks but he doesn't hear them. He has come to contemplate Jan's request. One heretic. He wants to reject it outright, but if he does, he will abandon both women to his brother. Sacrifice one, save the other, his brother said. Sophia or Aleys. It's not a real choice. Both are impossible. The waves creep up the shingle, recede. Each comes closer. If he stands here, just stands here and does nothing, he will drown.

Jan is a wolf. A wolf with a pope nipping at his heels. Only a king dares defy a pope.

The gray water mirrors a flat sky. Lukas tastes salt on his lips. The choice wraps like a vise around his chest, so that it is hard to draw breath, even in this open air. He is thinking of Judas and the thirty pieces of silver, how the purse would have weighed in his fist, the coins stamped with the head of a Phoenician god. Thirty shekels from the high priests to name Christ in the garden, to kiss Christ in the garden, so that he could be stopped. So that his radical truth would be silenced. After, when Judas saw what he had set in motion, that Christ was condemned, he returned to the high priests. "I have sinned," he said to them. "I have betrayed innocent blood." But they did not take back their coins. Blood money, they said. Your responsibility, they said. So Judas cast the coins to the temple floor, where they rolled and fell to stone while the priests and elders watched with cold eyes.

The bishop doesn't care who he names.

The betrayal of Judas had been foretold. God had whispered the plot to the prophets. Zechariah, buried before Judas was born, had already predicted the price: thirty pieces of silver. Christ knew it was coming. The betrayal was necessary. And so Lukas wonders, what choice did Judas really have?

24
Aleys

They brought him to the hospital in the night, a boy with a wound to his head, leaking pus. Fever like a hot iron. The senior beguine *tsk*s her disapproval. "If they'd come in sooner, we'd have bled him. It's too late now."

Aleys bends over the boy, sees his downy fuzz of new moustache, barely visible against his skin, which is an indeterminate gray, blending into the shadows. Though it is morning, the light barely reaches the back of the ward. The boy's wound has seeped into the bedsheet so that a yellow crescent blooms beneath him, edged with brown, like a halo. The smell is putrid, a mix of sick and stool, and Aleys knows from this that the boy will die today. She puts her ear to his mouth. His breath is barely audible. His open eyes fix on the ceiling, as if the gateway to purgatory opens above them. He is half in the next world.

"Not a thing we can do for this one but pray. Sister Aleys, stay with him. I'll get the priest."

Aleys hitches her dress to kneel beside the boy. She can feel the fever rise from him as she leans her elbows on the edge of his cot. His limbs are already stiffening, fingers rigid on the blanket like he's seeking his maker in a blind man's bluff. He doesn't know she's there. He's already far away, alone in his passage. She thinks of running after him, of grabbing his elbow and saying, turn around, you're too young to go, turn back, let's play. Come chase me back to life. But he is far down a corridor she can't enter. She presses her ear to his chest and recoils, because his body is light and dry as a husk. He still breathes, but barely. There's not much time. She doesn't know what to do. She thinks of Sophia. Of Ida. They'd appeal to the saints to illuminate his path. They'd call on Mary.

Aleys bows her head upon folded hands and begins the *Ave Maria.* The words are starched and stiff in her throat. She feels like a fraud. She has no gift. Who is she to summon a saint? "Holy Mary, Mother of God, pray for us sinners." She looks up. The boy shows no response to her voice. He is inert as the lead in the windows. Can he even hear her? She screws her eyes shut and finishes. "Now and at the hour of our death." It's not enough. She knows it's not enough. What else does she have? "*Ave Maria . . .*" Aleys utters the syllables over and over, again and again, until repetition renders them supple and the prayer grows tender and round. She sees the boy's eyelids flicker. Aleys abandons herself to the graceful coiling words, and ribbons of prayer curl into the air. Gradually, she feels the boy's breath, the infinitesimal rise of his chest fall in tandem with the verse. She slows to make it easier. *Lonely boy, child of God, peace be upon you.* The smell of his death is ripe and sweet in her nose, too much, so she sips the air, tiny sips of death and prayer. She does not stop when her vision grows murky, her hands begin to tingle. She sinks further into the prayer and the edges begin to blur and she bleeds into the boy and he bleeds into the prayer, and the prayer beats with his heart and she breathes the prayer. The spiraling words draw them together, deeper, into a space that is blue and gray, bound and unbound. "*Ave Maria . . .*" Aleys feels a swimming in her head and grips the edge of the cot to steady herself. She sways as she grinds her fingers into the coarse weave of the linen.

Abruptly, the cot disappears, the entire bed fallen away, and she opens her eyes and finds that all has changed.

The ward has receded like an echo into the blue-gray haze. Around Aleys, around her knees, around the boy, who stands before her, a honeyed light drapes and pools, bathing them in warmth and grace. A humming sound, of bees, fills her ears and her heart, as if they float in a midsummer meadow. The smell of death has vanished, and a verdant scent, of fern and moss and soil, fills the humming, and the boy smiles. She can see inside his chest, which holds neither organ nor bone but three sparrows, hovering, silver shining through trembling feathers. They soar from his chest and she watches in wonder as they circle to a blue dome above.

When her eyes descend, the vision is gone, and she sees again the injured boy on the cot, only he has turned his head and is looking at her with eyes like a clear stream. She can see pebbles, brown and green and blue, through the water.

Rise, she says, though she does not know why, and he does. He sits, and the bed linen comes with him, stuck to his wounds, so that he appears for a moment to be winged. When the sheet falls away, it bears only a faded shadow of his wound. Her fingers are ice cold, sparking like crystal flint. She is suspended in confusion. The boy looks as surprised as she does.

A man moans from the next bay. "Touch me, Sister." The voice startles her, breaks her reverie. What did they see? And then the voices rise and merge, from around the bed, from around the ward. "Heal me, Sister." A whispering murmur spreads like contagion. "Sister, Sister. Touch me, nurse me, bless me, Sister." Aleys stands, but in the time it takes to cross to the next bed, the marvel in her hands is gone, and she can only collapse and weep.

Has Christ answered her? Is this her gift?

Outside, the storm gathers and lepers inch their way to the begijnhof gate.

News of the miracle settles upon the town like a snowfall in August. Flurries of whispers float from the hospital entrance. "Did you hear?" Through alleys, the words eddy and swirl, and the people look up. Zephyrs of wonder dust steeples and sills. Priests gaze from their windows and raise their eyebrows at the swollen flakes and ask themselves, "Is it? Could it be?" Sailors in port feel the wind shift and cross themselves. The rumors reach the marketplace and become a blizzard. *There's a saint in the city.* Beggars rejoice and barren women fill with hope. News of the miracle drifts and piles. Chickens lay double yolks and gamblers triple stakes. Blind men dream of blue. In the taverns, tankards are raised to Sister Aleys. Bread and coins, salt and flowers, rabbits' feet and squirrels' tails pile up outside the begijnhof gate and the swan pond grows foul with offerings. Only the children are unimpressed, for they see miracles everywhere.

They must have carried her back to the begijnhof. When Aleys wakes, she's in the infirmary. Old Agnes is the only other one there, asleep, her clawed hands clutching the sheet. Aleys tries to rise but cannot. Her head splits with questions as she struggles to recall what happened, as one does from a vanishing dream, grasping at fragments. A meadow, and sparrows, and . . . a boy with limbs of light. A beam of remembered ecstasy breaks through the film of pain.

She must find the boy. Aleys runs into the hallway in her nightshift, her shorn head bare and prickling. A young beguine carrying a basin drops it with a clatter, and cold water spills over Aleys's bare feet. The girl bends to dry them with the hem of her dress, and Aleys pushes her away. She doesn't care about her feet. Sisters emerge from every door. Seeing Aleys, some cross themselves, some bob a curtsy, one falls to her knees. She sees herself in their faces. How she must look to them, disheveled, half naked. They see a wild-eyed John the Baptist, a Moses stumbling down the mountain waving tablets of stone. They think she is lit with revelation, that she has just risen from lying with God. The senior beguines clutch each other. They've been waiting for this since they were children.

"Get up," says Aleys to the girl on her knees. She isn't a prophet.

The girl doesn't rise.

"Where is he?" Aleys demands. "The patient, what happened?"

"Sister," says the matron, "he is healed; it is marvelous."

"No, I want to—I must talk to him."

"But Sister," says another, "he collected his bag and walked whole from the ward. It was a true miracle."

She doesn't know about that. "You didn't stop him?"

No. They shake their heads. It didn't occur to them. One adds hopefully, eyes wide, "We saved his linen?"

Aleys feels more alone than she has in her life. There's no one to corroborate, no one to help her remember the details. None of them saw what she saw. She knows only that it was . . . glorious. Like the moment the roof lifted from the beams and an angel whispered in her ear. A dream more real than reality.

But still, a dream?

Aleys retreats to the empty infirmary, sits on the edge of her bed, looks at her hands. She bites into the pad of her thumb, gnaws at the flesh. The boy lived, they say. She believes that much. He wouldn't be the first to rise from a deathbed. Her teeth find a hangnail and rip it off, and she is glad of the sting. A pink stripe, the color of coral, is laid bare beside her nail. It begins to well with dots of blood.

Aleys throws herself back across the cot, her head hanging over the edge, and covers her face with her elbow. It was magnificent, she should be grateful. But what was it? What is she left with? Her head pounds. Her hands begin to throb. Her entire heartbeat is in her fingertips. She has no idea what is happening. Maybe Friar Lukas will. She is sure of only one thing: People are hungry for miracles.

25

Friar Lukas

Friar Lukas hears the news from his brothers. They are back from collecting alms and have gathered to observe Sext. They enter in silence from the friary yard and assemble in the chapel, each one to his place. For years, twenty of them have gathered here to observe the hours, eight times a day. They know each other's subtle signs. A cough, a sigh, that when Brother Baldric rubs his nose it means his devotion has drifted, the trouble brewing when Brother Albert scratches his neck. Today, though, there is something in all of them. As they chant the *Kyrie*, Lukas senses a restlessness in their limbs, and not just the young ones. He sees eyes dart, one pair to the next, as they hold the notes. Even Hervé is shifting from side to side like the floor is hot. Something is up. They file out, their hands clasped before them as always, but once outside the doors, hands are flying everywhere. They're acting like they're from Florence, not Flanders.

Lukas goes to his most trusted source. "Hervé, what is it?"

"You haven't heard? Our Sister Aleys. She has healed someone!"

He pauses. "She works in a hospital."

"The youth was close to death. Some say he'd already passed. He rose from his deathbed. There are witnesses."

"Our Aleys? Hervé, you're sure?"

"I've seen the linens. Clean as newly washed." He shakes his head. "Lukas, when you inducted her, I had doubts. But this. This changes everything."

He looks around like he hardly dares to release his thought into the friary. "Don't you see? God smiles upon us."

Hervé, the most steady of friars, is looking at him with the wide eyes of a boy who has glimpsed the ocean for the first time. Lukas wants to reward him, wants to say, *Yes, it is she. Yes, we have been blessed.* He wants to gift the miracle to Hervé.

"I must go to her," he says.

Hervé nods, then closes his eyes and tips his head back to the sky.

As Lukas walks through town, he tunes his ear to the chatter, taking the pulse of Brugge. There's an excited tone he's not heard before, every voice is raised half a note. People turn and stare as he passes. They stop what they're doing, catch their neighbor's eye, point their chins toward him. He pauses on the corner of the Markt, and immediately a group assembles. He hasn't attracted a crowd like this since he brought the tambourine. And it's not just the widows. Before he opens his mouth, they are clamoring.

"Is it true, Father? Did she raise the dead?"

"Can she heal my son?" A woman grips the shoulders of a young boy, thrusting him forward. The child lurches, and Lukas sees his twisted foot. He thinks of Simon Peter healing the lame beggar, twisted limbs unbending true. And Paul. Cloth that brushed Paul's skin had healing powers. Lukas thinks of the clamoring crowds in the dusty marketplace, the half-crazed people waving dishcloths like flags as they pushed to rub them against the apostle's forearms, his ankles, the back of his neck.

He, Lukas, has preached such miracles. Here, on this very corner. So why doesn't he believe one could happen now?

"Where is she?" someone shouts from his right. The crowd is growing.

"Can we see her?"

Lukas raises open palms to tamp them down. "Wait. Slow down. It's all rumor."

There's a grumbling. The crowd shrinks back a step. He can't lose them. Not this fast.

"Father, are you saying it's not true?"

It would be better if he believed. "We just—we must verify." He's making this up. How do you verify a miracle? He has no idea. They would call the authorities, he supposes. From Rome.

"We'll test her!" shouts a man waving his cap. "Bring her out!"

If Aleys walked through the square right now, the crowd would turn from him. He pictures Aleys, not in the brown wool, but in her maroon cloak. She'd appear in the far corner of the plaza and lift her head and his people would flock to her. Though he's been preaching to this crowd for decades, they'd forsake him in a moment for a miracle. Why can't he be enough for them?

"Father, you believe." The mother with the lame child looks at him closely. "Don't you?"

Lukas takes a quick inbreath and feels something flare in his chest. Of course he believes. He believes in the Father, the Son, and the Holy Spirit. His faith doesn't require present-day miracles. There is wonder enough without them. But Brugge doesn't want the truth. He feels tendrils of smoke rise up the back of his throat. Brugge wants cheap miracles.

From the back: "The friars are hiding their saint!" People raise fists. "Show her!"

Lukas feels the heat burst from his chest. "I am not her procurer!"

Even as he says it, he recognizes the half-truth. He remembers the weight of her severed braid in his hand, his pride when he presented her like a sacrificial lamb to God in that church in Damme. He was her eager agent then. He brought her to Christ's door. That was different, he tells himself. That was for God.

But he never expected God to grace her with miracles.

When Lukas reaches the begijnhof, he shouts to the first beguine he sees: "Get her. Bring her to the church." The woman is alarmed. The friar has never raised his voice. She drops her linen into a basket and scurries off.

Inside the shadowy cool, he paces the flagstones. This time, he won't hide in the transept. This time, he'll face her, he'll see what God sees in her, he'll have certainty who she is. Who he is. God will show him, Friar Lukas, the miracle. After all, he brought her to the altar. God owes him that much.

The door opens and a band of yellow light precedes her, striking a path across the floor. He sees her blurry shadow before he sees the girl herself, and he wonders if he'll be able to tell saint from sinner. He reminds himself how she relished the drama of running from home, back in the spring, not even six months ago. This could all be the playacting of a child.

Aleys leaves the door open and crosses herself as she faces the altar. He shudders. She must not pretend at this. Her eyes are large in her pale face, the black of her pupils nearly eclipsing the blue. "Oh, Father," she says.

He braces himself. "You've heard what they're saying, in town?"

She is shaking her head. "Father, I need to talk to—"

"Deny it." Even as he speaks the words, a voice within him whispers, *Please don't.*

"I—"

"It's not true." *Let it be true.*

Aleys pulls her head back, suddenly wary, as though unsure she can trust him. That's not the question. Can he trust her? His jaw tightens. He draws in a breath and holds it like a discipline. His discernment, his judgment, his duty to protect his order from charlatans are all held in this breath. He's aware that he's trembling.

A sudden gust sweeps through the open door, as if invisible attendants have joined at her shoulders. He waits. She must speak. Everything hangs on her answer. Her cheeks color, and he doesn't know how to read the blush. Boldness? Shame? Humility?

Did she, or did she not perform a miracle? He can't let himself be duped by a child. But if it's true—if it's true—he hardly dares think of it. Lukas feels boyish wonder rise. It threatens to fill him, and he must resist. He wants to believe. His faith shivers, cautious and hungry, out on a limb. She's the apple at the tip of the branch. He wants to lunge for the fruit. *Please*. Everything, everything, depends on her answer. He is waiting for God to speak to him through a woman.

But he remembers Adam, seduced by a woman. "I order you to deny it." He lets the words hang like a challenge.

"Please, Father. Listen." She hugs her hands to her stomach. "I don't know what happened."

"How can you—?"

"I was just praying. And the boy woke up."

"No. It was more than that." He hears himself. "There were witnesses."

"It was a dream."

"It was more than a dream." What is he doing? He's leading her.

"I don't know." She won't meet his eyes. "I don't think so."

"God spoke through you."

"Father, I've prayed my whole life to meet God. But not for this. I don't know if it was real."

"God guided your hand." He stretches for the fruit.

Her face contracts in confusion. "You just ordered me to deny it."

"Tell me the truth!"

Frustration floods his hands, bursting open his fists. Before he can help himself, he grabs her arms. He knows he shouldn't touch her, he knows he's out of control. He starts shaking her. He can't stop. Roiling waters surge within him, press through his chest, spill over his shoulders, course the length of his arms. He jerks her as if he would shake loose devils. How dare she? "You think you're Saint Clare? That you can perform wonders?" He hears her teeth rattle. "You wicked child."

She turns her head, tries to pull away. Wool slides through his hands until he is gripping the bare flesh of her wrists, so small he could snap them. "Why won't you tell me the truth?"

He is breathing hard, and she is, too, gasping for breath.

He feels it then, a vibration. A buzzing coming from her clenched hands. He turns them over. Her knuckles are white, her small pink nails pressed hard into the heels of her palms.

"What are you hiding?"

"Nothing."

"Open them."

She shakes her head.

"Don't make me force you."

She flashes her hands open like a slap. Her palms are empty. And buzzing.

"What is this?"

"Since the hospital. Like I hold wasps."

He touches his thumbs into the center of her palms and she winces. The humming grows stronger as he clamps her hands, a kernel of vibration, just where . . . He is picturing iron spikes driven through tender flesh.

Lightning judders up his arms. He drops her hands.

She raises her eyes to his. He sees not defiance, not pretense, but fear, clear and icy.

God help him, it *is* true. The impossible . . . has happened? Lukas feels himself on a precipice. He presses his fingers to his temples, hard, to form an axle for his spinning head. A miracle, here? In this mercantile city so far from any remotely holy land. Here!

He drops his hands, feels doubt drain from his fingertips. He's a pauper woken up to a banquet. He has yearned for this, worked for it, prayed for it. But he never thought it could happen. Not in his lifetime. Such blessings were for other eras, more deserving times. Braver men. Through his amazement, Lukas feels the whisper of green belief. A miracle!

Aleys stands away from him, looking frightened. This must be awe, not fear. Overnight, she has been transformed from a girl to a vessel of grace. Wonder rushes through his mind, overturning carts, ripping thatch from rooftops. He knew she was special. He must protect her. Lukas runs his hands over his tonsured head. The Lord has come to redeem this city. They have been blessed.

He remembers how she was lit like a lamp the night he gave her the brown wool and cut her hair. How she made him feel like Francis. Lukas feels his chest inflate with raw, clean air. He spreads his arms to heaven.

"Hallelujah!" His voice is resonant. He is uplifted, standing on the headlands of the rock of the church. Above him, the rafters sing. He thinks the roof may rise from the church. The sun will come out and flowers will bloom across the land.

His eyes descend to her face. The girl is crying softly into her hands.

"Child, what is it? This is a time to rejoice!"

"It's gone." She opens her wet palms.

He reaches out to take her wrists. They're wooden as wheelbarrow handles.

"No, no, no," he says. "It will come again. The grace will return."

"How do you know?" She stares at him.

"Because you're chosen."

"Chosen?" Aleys shifts her blue-black eyes between his. "Do I have a choice?"

He could wring her with his exasperation. "Did Moses have a choice? Did Mary?"

"But I'm not sure it's true."

He takes a deep breath. Patience. The girl has just worked her first miracle, of course she's confused. That doesn't give her leave to doubt. Or spread doubt. This must be nipped in the bud, for the sake of the city, for the sake of his men. For her own sake. He thinks of his brother. The bishop can't arrest a miracle worker. He doesn't think.

Lukas feels his feet on the church floor. He roots himself in his own faith, back to the fundament. He remembers his knees in the cold soil of redemption. If ever there was a call to obedience, this is it.

"It's God's will," he says. "I order you to believe."

26

Aleys

Aleys returns to the hospital in procession as if she were a holy relic. Beguines encircle her like a protective guard. The citizens of Brugge drop their tasks, bow their heads. Crowds trail them, emptying whole plazas, and entrepreneurs gather the dust from her footprints. They want her now, in the wards, all the time.

Sint-Janshospitaal stills to a hush when she enters. People freeze mid-gesture, mouths agape. Aleys wants to yell into the strange silence, *Return to your tasks. Resume your conversations. I'm just a girl! Stop gawking.* From the lodgers' side of the hospital, merchants crane to see her, cross themselves when they do, remember to doff their caps.

There are so many sick people.

Her mouth is dry with doubt.

They guide her to the first bed, a man with yellow skin and lemon eyes. She feels the tingle start in her hands, and when she prays, the *Ave* spreads like a balm. The man blinks and pink blooms in his cheeks. She doesn't know what's happening.

They lead her from one bed to another. Sometimes she feels something. Sometimes she doesn't. Fever consumes a child, a woman miscarries, and Aleys's hands are useless. She has no understanding, no idea who will rise and who will fall back on the pallet. It seems random.

"God is mystery," says Lukas that evening, like she doesn't know. Her nights are more real than her days.

It is the same the next week and the one after. Friar Lukas is hovering, too attentive, overjoyed at the recoveries and suspicious of the losses, like Aleys could conquer death if she only tried harder. He makes excuses to touch her hands, testing for the buzz, and she has taken to drawing them back into her sleeves when he approaches. Lukas steers her toward patients who aren't that sick. He's afraid I'll fail, she thinks. He presents florid men with dyspepsia who sit up in their beds and undress Aleys with their eyes. Indigestion is a waste of a miracle. She wonders if she has the power to smite them.

People cram into the hospital, two to a bed. Patients have taken to bringing their own pallets, so there is hardly any space between cots and Aleys must inch her way to the heads of the sick without kicking the suffering on the ground. Fingers clutch at her hem, grab at her ankles. She wants to heal them. But there are so many, and she feels like an imposter, like she's donned holiness like a costume. Like she's playing at being a saint. Because she can't trust her own hands. The gift is quicksilver, running through her fingers, pooling in her palms one moment, evaporating the next.

Aleys cures a shepherd of dropsy, a carter of a sprained ankle. With each healing, she grows less and less substantial, as if she's thinning at the edges, becoming transparent as wavy glass. For when the feeling comes, there is nothing better, a rush of golden honey followed by a glorious shiver, particles of light shaking loose from her body. She could dissolve in the glory. She touches foreheads and drives out demons. Cords unfurl and infants gasp. Food repels her. She wants only this medicine in her veins. Aleys wants more and more and more. She prays for more. Her need only grows, shooting through her thinning vessels, the light replacing blood and marrow until she is laced with canals of light that flow toward the sea. She is a city of light, and afterward, when she goes dark, she is exhausted and craving.

For just as quickly, the gift lifts like a flock of sparrows, and Aleys is dropped from a great height, fallen boneless to the floor. She tries to summon the light to her hands, blows on them to kindle sparks, but she clutches only mud. And as the glow fades from her bones, doubt fills her marrow. It slinks through her limbs and sidles into her heart and curdles her gut. She crouches at a bedside and feels nothing. Her tongue swells from salted prayer. Ida clutches her hand, knowing. Ida, who has healed and failed to heal so many. Aleys tries, she tries so hard, but nothing comes. The eyes of the suffering beseech her and she knows herself a fraud. Has he abandoned her? Is she unworthy?

Or maybe she's imagined the whole thing.

"Father," she whispers to Lukas as a patient turns to the wall, coughing, "you best give him last rites." She is heavy with silt. Nothing is coming. Still they pull her toward the next bed. Aleys would cry with frustration, but she's too spent.

She believes. She doubts. If only God would clarify. Why can't he make himself plain? If she's chosen, as Friar Lukas insists, why can't he send an angel to explain? But there's no angel, no message. Everyone around her is so sure, so desperately certain, and she's so bewildered. So lonely. People think she has the power of judgment, that she is choosing to save only the righteous. She thinks, I prayed for a gift, but I didn't ask for this. I didn't ask to *be* God.

Later, in the hall, Lukas tries to comfort her. "Child, it is not ours to question his choices. Do not despair. You've already saved two souls this afternoon."

Has she? A palsy stilled, a breech delivered safely. She'd been a distant spectator, not a healer. Her hands had been dead. She'd have been more useful if she'd held a washcloth.

"I had nothing to do with those."

"What are you saying? Of course you did."

"No, I was numb."

"Let me feel your hands."

She shrinks within her robe. "No," she says. She doesn't want his touch.

He stiffens. "What do you want from me?"

"To teach me the difference between coincidence and miracle."

But he can't. He sees only God.

At night, Aleys washes in the basin and falls, near dead, onto her cot. Every morning, someone collects the water from her basin. Somehow, it ends up in the street, for sale, in little vials bound with red thread.

When she wakes, the magistra is at her side, keeping vigil.

"When you first came"—Sophia traces her finger gently across Aleys's cheekbone—"you didn't have these shadows." She puts the back of her hand to Aleys's brow, testing for fever. Aleys wants Sophia to keep her hand there, and reading her mind, Sophia does. "Child, he asks much of you."

"Lukas? Or God?"

"Both." A fast twitch in the corner of her mouth. "Neither knows much about limits."

The weight of Sophia's hand is like an anchor. "Magistra, I'm tired."

"I know." Sophia turns her palm over, smooths Aleys's brow. "Do you want to stop?"

Aleys just wants to lie here, to rest. Yes. No. "I don't know."

Sophia nods. "You're only human. Come, sit up and eat." She reaches for a mug of barley and milk, puts the cup in Aleys's hands. Aleys wraps her fingers around the cup, tilts it back, and tastes honey in the still-warm gruel. Sophia is looking out the window, across the courtyard. She appears lost in thought.

"Magistra?"

"Mmm?"

"What if it's all in my head? If it's not real?" Sophia tips her chin, studying Aleys. "I don't want to be false."

Sophia takes the empty cup. "Whatever gift God has or has not granted, I know you're in earnest." She holds the mug in her lap.

"Sometimes I feel things, in my hands. Then I don't. I can't tell whether I'm imagining it."

"You don't know if they're miracles."

"No."

Sophia considers this. Her gaze returns to the window.

"Maybe that's the wrong question," she says, nodding toward something across the courtyard. Aleys leans forward. Marte has stepped outside the kitchen and is crouching to feed an orange cat. She wipes her fingers on her apron and waits while the cat finishes the fish head. Then she reaches out rough knuckles to rub behind his ear. The cat leans into her hand.

"You see," says Sophia. "We're all miracles to someone."

They try to let her rest. The magistra orders Katrijn to give Aleys her spare room, the one Katrijn intended for Cecilia. Katrijn follows Aleys with narrowed eyes that say she's not buying any miracles. Aleys wants to tell her, I didn't will this upon myself. Not this. Katrijn only shakes her head and retreats when Aleys opens her mouth.

Below the two small bedchambers is a bare sitting room. They bring a second chair so Aleys can receive visitors. She turns them away. Except one. On a rainy afternoon, Cecilia bangs on the door to announce that Aleys's sister has arrived.

Griete stands in the open doorway. Behind her, a sheet of rain blurs the courtyard, the leaves of the trees pointing to the ground. Griete lowers her hood. Her hair is in a simple plait that she must have braided herself. She looks older. Aleys rises from the table. She can feel the invisible maze between them, full of false starts and dead ends, no sure path to each other.

"Sister," says Griete.

"You're here." To slap me, kiss me, break my heart? Aleys thinks of the clapping games they used to play. Of cat's cradle, their hands bound together so tight that they cried for Mama to cut them free.

"I had to come."

"Why? Is someone ill?"

"No, Aleys. It's just—" She looks at her hands. "I've missed you."

Something in Aleys breaks open and suddenly they are in each other's arms. Aleys silently thanks God. Her sister, her real sister. The heavens outside have washed the world clean. The smell of wet wool, of home, fills her nostrils. She mumbles into the cloth, "I thought you hated me."

Griete pulls back. "I did, at first. You abandoned us."

"You know I—" She stops herself. It doesn't matter if she had to.

"We lost the Lakenhalle because of you. It was bad."

"But you've forgiven me?"

Griete shrugs. Maybe.

"Why?"

"Papa. After he left you at the church with that friar, he went up to your prie-dieu and stood there, staring at it for hours. When he came down, he said it was the biggest mistake of his life, forcing his child into marriage. He said losing the Lakenhalle was his fault, not yours."

"Oh." It feels like a gift. Like more miracle than she deserves. "But why hasn't he come?"

Griete looks at her likes it's obvious. "You live in a community of women."

"I could still see him."

"I don't know, Aleys. I think he's ashamed. It's been a hard season. We sold the buttons from your wedding sleeves. Henryk traded his green cloak." Griete rubs her forehead. "But it wasn't enough. Claus started dicing. Remember those pardons he bought? *Miserere mei*? He used every one of them."

"But that's terrible."

"Less terrible than starving." Griete lifts a shoulder. "Turns out Claus has excellent luck. Especially now that you're so famous."

"What do you mean?"

"Claus sells your prayers."

"My what?"

"He took the cross from our altar and charges a guilder to touch it. Marie van der Blein got pregnant off it." Griete leans in. "So is it true, or not?"

"Is what true?"

"What they say about you."

"That depends what they're saying."

"That you're raising the dead." She gestures out the window. "Causing the rain."

"Griete . . ."

"They say you cure livestock of rinderpest." In Griete's voice is an accusation: *You never used to heal cattle.*

"Then they know more than I do."

"Aleys," Griete says, "are you some kind of saint?"

"No!" It comes out sharper than she intends.

"How do you know?"

"That I'm not a saint?" Aleys is momentarily stunned. How would she know? "I'm just not, that's all."

"But you can do miracles, anyway? When you want?"

"Griete, no. I mean, it's hard to explain." She flails for words. "It's just that sometimes something comes over me."

Griete squints. "That sounds like a yes."

"It's not my doing. I can't ask personal favors of God."

"Why not? Everyone prays for something."

"Yes, but . . . this is different. It's God's will, not mine."

Griete draws back, disappointment on her face. "I was hoping you could help."

"With what?" She can't be sick. Her sister is healthy as a horse.

Griete hesitates, and Aleys wonders if she blushes. "You see, I want . . . I want Pieter Mertens."

Aleys gasps. The man she jilted for God? "Griete, not him. He denied Papa the license."

"We broke the contract, Aleys. Besides, you humiliated him. What else was Pieter going to do?"

Pieter? There's more going on than she's saying.

"Plus," Griete continues, "now that you're, well, all saintlike, he's glad he didn't marry you."

Is he, now? "Griete, be careful."

"Aleys, don't you see? I want this. I can do what you couldn't. It's my turn to help the family. Plus"—she grins—"he's quite handsome."

"Griete, he's not pious."

"Aleys, we don't all want what you want." She twists her ring. "What you want scares me."

Griete's question lingers in the air. Could Aleys request a miracle, personally? There are moments in chapel, with everyone staring like they expect her to levitate, that Aleys wishes she could fly to the rafters like Christina Mirabilis. Just for the fun of it, to watch Katrijn's jaw drop. There *is* one healing she really would like to try, though she doesn't want witnesses. So on the way to morning prayer, Aleys feigns that she left her rosary beneath her pillow. Katrijn *tsk*s her impatience, as if to say, *Some saint*. Aleys turns back from chapel. The courtyard is empty but for rows of linens. Water seeps from the hems of the sheets, peppering the dewy grass. Finally, she finds Marte pinning up the last of the laundry.

Aleys pauses at the head of the alley, watching Marte limp between basket and line. A bee, one of the small hard ones, hovers beside Aleys like a silent chaperone. Another joins, so that Aleys has a bee at each shoulder. She doesn't brush them away.

Can she do it? Aleys looks around. Except for the bees, they're alone.

"Marte, come here."

"Miss." Marte bobs from a distance. She seems wary.

"It's all right, Marte. It's just me." Marte scratches her shoulder, deciding. "I won't hurt you."

Marte approaches reluctantly, one hand on the laundry line, her awkward gait making the line dip and rise. Aleys doesn't want to frighten Marte, so she begins the prayer internally. Aleys feels the bees settle to her shoulders like she's a winged creature. Marte's feet leave uneven green prints behind her in the silvered grass. She stops before Aleys, her face closed. When Aleys drops to her knees, Marte starts, but she doesn't pull away. Aleys places her hands on Marte's bad foot. Marte inhales sharply. Aleys can't tell if anything is happening. Then she feels the faintest coolness in her fingertips, followed by a rush of triumph. She knows it's God's will. But this time it also feels like it's hers.

When Aleys rises, Marte simply nods.

"You won't want to be late for prayers, miss."

"Thank you, Marte."

"Thank you, miss."

"We won't speak of this."

"No."

She watches as Marte returns to her work. The limp is gone. Or is it? She's not quite sure.

When she turns back to chapel, Katrijn stands outside, watching.

That night, Katrijn herself takes the reading chair, stained fingers drumming the parchment. Cecilia tries to coax some vigor from the desultory fire with the hand bellows. Marte stands guard in the courtyard. Aleys looks toward the window and yearns for the cool of the water's edge. Even Sophia seems distracted, fingering a slub in a strand of yarn that will have to be smoothed or sacrificed. She reaches for scissors, then changes her mind and sits back, clasping the back of her neck. Katrijn stands to rub Sophia's shoulders. The magistra gives Katrijn a grateful glance and a small, pained smile. Aleys thinks, Only Katrijn can do that. Katrijn won't allow anyone else to touch Sophia. The other day, Aleys rounded a corner and found them standing close beneath the eaves, sheltering from a sudden downpour. They were laughing at their sodden headdresses. Sophia raised Katrijn's wet hand to her lips. Their foreheads touched, and Katrijn whispered something that made Sophia close her eyes and nod. Then they parted.

Now Katrijn moves from Sophia's shoulders back to the reading chair. She clears her throat: "He went to Nazareth, where he had been brought up, and on the Sabbath day he went into the synagogue." Christ has come home. Aleys imagines the elders' eyes following young Jesus as he strides to the front, sandals worn thin with travel and the hem of his robe in need of washing. Jesus pulls the prayer scarf over his head and reads: "Today this scripture is fulfilled in your hearing."

Right here. This is the moment that Christ claims it. *The Lord has anointed me.*

To the old men of the synagogue, the elders, he claims to be the foretold Messiah. It is so bold. So incredibly bold. They've heard crazy rumors—loaves and fishes, healings, walking across a lake—but isn't this just Joseph's son? Joseph the carpenter?

"Show us," they say. "*Medice, cura te ipsum.*" Physician, heal thyself. Heal us. Raise our dead of Nazareth. Show us these miracles you claim. Prove it.

But that's not what happens. Jesus refuses to heal them. "'Truly I tell you, no prophet is accepted in his hometown.'" Will not or cannot heal them? How Aleys wishes she could ask. There's so much she wants to ask.

Katrijn raises her voice: "The people were furious. They drove him from the town and up the hill to throw him from the cliff."

Katrijn slaps her hand onto the parchment, and the women look up from their work, startled. Their eyes go first to Katrijn, then to Aleys. They all hear the barely veiled threat: We don't tolerate fraud.

"But that's not what happens, is it, Katrijn?" Sophia says quietly. "That's not what it means."

"Here's what I don't understand," says Cecilia, puzzling out loud, the bellows dangling from one hand. "If he wasn't ever going to help them, why did Jesus go home to tell them he wouldn't? It seems prideful."

"No," says Sophia. "I do not think it pride. Christ is telling us that we must be open to wonder if we hope to witness it." She looks around the room, her gaze skipping over Katrijn. The magistra brings her fingers to the arches of her eyes, presses hard. "I'm sorry. I have the headache tonight." Sophia draws her hands down her face. When she lifts them, Aleys sees something uneven about her mouth, something broken in her smile. She's in pain, thinks Aleys. I should heal her.

Then Sophia seems to recover. Even under duress, she is a teacher. "What, my friends, is the opposite of pride?"

At once, two answers. From Cecilia: "Humility?" From Katrijn: "Shame."

There is a silence as the women weigh these words. One as plain as bread, the other with the bite of mustard, but they are kin, somehow. Handiwork settles into laps as the women consider. A log collapses into the fire with a murmur of sparks.

Finally, it is Ida who speaks into the quiet: "Neither. The opposite of pride is love."

An hour later, Katrijn accosts her, storming up the stairs to the landing between their rooms. Aleys is in her chemise, about to turn in to her chamber, bearing a candle. She's too tired to deal with Katrijn. Tomorrow is another day in the hospital. She turns to face Katrijn. The landing is small.

Katrijn speaks without preamble: "What do you think you were doing?" The flame on Aleys's candle rears back from its wick. "To Marte?"

Aleys doesn't need this. "Sister, I'm going to bed."

"I saw you." Katrijn points her finger. "This morning. In the courtyard."

Aleys feels annoyance flare. "What? I can't help our own?"

Katrijn scoffs. "If you did."

If she did. Aleys is so tired. All she wants is sleep.

"It's bad enough, you exploiting the dying. But this is the begijnhof. We live here. When you're in our home, you need to keep your holy hands to yourself."

"If you're accusing me of something, say it."

"I see how you profit."

"From what?"

"Chicanery." Katrijn doesn't blink. "Fraud."

This is outrageous. She's pursued by believers and attacked by nonbelievers. She can't win. "Explain to me, exactly, what I gain from this."

"My free room. The magistra's attention. Sophia's hardly sleeping, she's so concerned about you. Did you know that?" Katrijn slices her palm through the air. "Her hands went numb yesterday, she told me. Her headache is back. She's worried sick about you."

"I never wanted this."

"Didn't you, though? You come here parading about as a friar, the talk of the town, when you could have just joined as a woman. A regular woman. Like the rest of us. But no. You were too good for the gray dress, weren't you?"

Aleys is stunned into silence.

"Just say it. You think you're better than we are."

"No. No, I don't." What comes from Aleys's mouth surprises her. "The beguine life is beautiful." The quiet pleasure of the company of women and the solace of the word of God. It *is* beautiful. It's just not what she's seeking. She wants the fast path to God, the shortcut that runs straight up the mountain. It doesn't make her better than them, just different. She appreciates their ways.

Katrijn scoffs. "Really? You've been a threat to us from the day you arrived. The wool contract canceled. The bishop following us around."

"You can't blame me for that."

"No? What were you doing with his man in the market? By the wheel?"

"Nothing."

"So it was coincidence that he approached us after speaking with you?"

"I had no idea who he—"

"Tell me this," says Katrijn, "how do we know you're not the bishop's spy?"

Aleys can't speak. There's nothing she can say to this woman. She turns on her heel, slams the chamber door behind her. The action extinguishes her candle, and she's left in the dark, the walls ticking. After a moment, Katrijn storms down the stairs, but not without delivering a parting shot: "If you want to prove yourself, get the bishop off our back."

27

The Bishop

Miracles are an issue for the bishop. He paces the nave of Sint-Salvator, avoiding the withering gaze of Christ over the altar. The peaked miter perched on his head begins to slide to the side, so Jan yanks it off and ruffles his hair. He can't think straight in that hat. He resumes walking, turning the hat in his hands.

First, there's the matter of his staff. Everyone is talking about the girl. Jan has heard the rumors; his priests, his cook, his footman all speak of the saint in the begijnhof. They can't stop talking. The kitchen help are concocting false ailments to get into Sint-Janshospitaal just to see her; the scullion went so far as to stab himself in the thigh with a carving knife. Jan thinks to remind them that no one is a saint until he says they are, until Rome agrees, and certainly not before they are dead, but he holds his tongue. A surge of faith is swelling over the Low Countries like a wave that will swamp them all. Even in Brugge, especially in Brugge; today's Mass was so crowded, they ran out of altar bread. It has been a week since anyone was murdered. He needs to stop this. They might wake God up with their fervor.

Jan reaches the end of his pacing before a small door set in the wall, the entrance to the old anchorhold where the recluse Gunther lived. Another fanatic. They're all over Europe now, these hermits, pretending they're the original desert fathers who abandoned their earthly possessions, shouting that they were off to commune with God. Madmen. Back in the first centuries of Christendom, before there were more comfortable ways of showing devotion. Like becoming a bishop. But today's hermits, the anchorites? God, they're even more unhinged. Instead of wandering free in the wild, they volunteer to be walled into cells hastily slapped on the sides of churches and abbeys—for a life of prayer. Especially women. There are over a hundred anchoresses in England, even now. It's too strange. He remembers, as a boy, how they'd throw pebbles at Gunther's window, daring each other to peer through the panes of shaved horn. Even though you couldn't quite see into the anchorhold, Jan always feared that Gunther's leering shadow would pop up in the window like a jack-in-the-box.

Jan turns the corner, setting his back to the empty hold. Gunther died years ago. He has more immediate issues with the living zealots. People thirst for wonders. The problem is, he can't arrest Lukas's girl now. He doesn't believe she's actually performing miracles, but as long as the people do, the girl is untouchable. He might not even be able to arrest the magistra who houses her. He still needs an arrest. This miracle business is complicating everything.

How ironic it would be if the miracles were real. Just as he was about to round up the heretics, God raises his head from his soup and makes one of them a saint? No. He can't think like that. It's unproductive. Why would God get involved in the affairs of his own church? He's turned a blind eye to the corruption for centuries.

No, the thing that needles Jan the most is the missed opportunity. There must be a way to monetize the miracles. He needs to meet her. Either she's as accomplished an actor as Willems, or she's a bona fide miracle worker. If she's the real thing, he'll present her to the pope. If she's a good actor, he'll present her to the pope. If she fails, if she's a bad actor, he needs her to fail flagrantly, publicly, so the people see her scam, and he can arrest her and close down the whole begijnhof for fraud. He can throw in translation to make it stick. Problem solved. No matter what, he's going to Rome. He just needs to think of a test.

28

The Bishop

The bishop's carriage comes to a clattering halt at the footbridge as the last wandering stars fade above the rooftops. The bishop descends, his red cloak billowing, followed by Willems like a black echo and Lukas like a muted shadow. Jan would storm over the bridge, break through the doors into their stronghold, but it's as impregnable as a fortress with a moat. He will have to knock. It's annoying that the cobbles are smeared with sodden loaves of bread. He refuses to soil his slippers with their offerings.

"Clear this!" he orders. Guards jump from his carriage and start shoving food into the canal with the blades of their spears. Below, the swans beat their wings in displeasure, but they have grown fat and fickle on white flour, and none rise to defend the beguines.

The begijnhof doors crack open to reveal the face of a small woman with dark hair and sharp features. Her eyes dart among the men and land on his pectoral cross. She admits them with a frown. The bishop is reminded how much he dislikes these beguines. They should be put into convents. Or wed. Once he gets to Rome, he'll have them outlawed. The girl's heels click on the flagstones as she leads them through the passage into the courtyard. *I'll marry you to a ratcatcher*, he thinks.

Jan had expected to surprise the women in their beds. Not so. Though the sun is just visible over the red-tile roofs, the yard is already stretched end to end with linens. The bishop is confronted by the industry of women, a labyrinth of taut cloth, forbidding and female. Above the dawn laundry looms their gray church. A handful of startled women emerge from the linen maze, then scatter like mice into doors that look identical. Good. Fear is first cousin to reverence.

A broad-shouldered woman marches toward them. She halts and dips her head in a gesture that manages to convey more disrespect than respect. Willems raises a subtle eyebrow and looks pointedly at her large hands, and he notices the ink stains on her fingertips. The widow Janssens, then. Draper and translator. A very busy woman. He'd like to arrest her for the look in her eyes.

"Where is your magistra?"

"At prayer. You can deal with me."

Oh, believe me, I would if I could. "Summon her. And bring out the girl."

The draper furrows her brow. "Which girl would that be?"

God, he wishes he could arrest her. "Sister Aleys."

"She also is at prayer."

"Get them!" he barks.

Katrijn holds her ground for a moment, glaring. Finally, she gestures to the small woman to go to one house and Katrijn crosses to another. Around the courtyard, women peer through lace curtains. How he would love to shut this whole operation down. It wouldn't please the mayor. It wouldn't please the guild. But it might make the pope happy.

Lukas stands to the side, his arms up his sleeves. On the way over, in the carriage, Jan thought Lukas looked frayed. His brother kept rubbing his hand along his rope belt. It's a rather disturbing tic. A strange film of nervous excitement is newly layered over his brother's melancholia. He needs to be careful, thought Jan. Melancholia can seed delusion. When Lukas raised his hand against the window frame, Jan saw that the webbing between thumb and forefinger was pink and weeping.

"You should have her fix that for you."

Lukas looked at his hand like he was surprised to find it on the end of his arm. He scowled. "She doesn't perform on command. She's not a jester."

"More's the pity. But even you must appreciate that we need to examine her."

"Why? Why can't you accept a miracle?"

His brother was so blind to politics, it was almost charming. He sighed. "Because, Lukas, we are the Church. This is our job. Besides, if she proves herself before the town dignitaries, I won't arrest her for translation. I might not need to arrest anyone for translation." Because that will be the next bishop's problem.

"God will protect her."

"What, you think she's real?" Jan peered at him. "You do, don't you?"

Lukas looked back out the window into the twilight. Rectangles of light were beginning to appear in windows.

"At least I believe in something," he said, raising hard eyes to Jan. Their mother's eyes. "Do you believe in anything?" he asked. "Anything at all?"

Poor man. What favor has belief ever granted him?

"You'll see," said Lukas. "Her faith will convert you."

Across the courtyard, a door opens to reveal a tall woman. Katrijn Janssens walks quickly to intercept her, blocking the path. They argue briefly, urgent whispered words he can't make out. The woman places a hand on the draper's shoulder with an unmistakable authority. This must be their grand mistress, Sophia Vermeulen. The magistra steps around Katrijn.

"Your Excellency." Sophia bows. "To what do we owe this visit?"

That's more like it, he thinks. He notes a tremor in one hand, sees her silence it with the other. Does everyone have a twitch today?

"Magistra. We have been made aware of certain activities at the begijnhof"—he circles his hand lazily and watches Katrijn and Sophia exchange alert glances—"and Sint-Janshospitaal."

He pauses. Clearly, they think he has come about the translations. He doesn't mind letting them stew. Behind doors, he imagines women hastily stuffing parchment under mattresses and spilling inkpots out back windows into the canals.

Lukas breaks the tension. "Magistra, it is marvelous. The bishop is here to announce a public demonstration of Sister Aleys's gift." Jan has the distinct impression that Lukas is signaling to them. *That is all—you are safe.*

Sophia nods. "Your Excellency, we will arrange for you to visit the hospital. There are many there who have been cured."

"That won't be necessary. We will hold a demonstration in the Markt before local authorities. I've invited the clergy, the monasteries, the abbeys, and the heads of the guilds." He might even let the nuns out for the day. "All the burghers and merchants of the town. Everyone should witness the wonder."

Sophia frowns and puts a hand to her temple. "We must ask Sister Aleys, I think." She turns to Lukas. "Father, as her spiritual advisor, should you not counsel her?"

"I have already discussed this with Friar Lukas," says Jan. "All is set for this evening. They assemble the platform as we speak."

Another door opens to reveal a young woman in brown. This must be her. Jan glances over and is startled at the eagerness on his brother's face at the sight of his girl. Lukas is such an innocent. He needs to be more careful.

As the girl approaches, Jan is struck by her strange eyes, the bright blue rims swallowed from within by black pupils. He once saw a boxer stagger to his knees after a hard blow—his eyes had the same dazed quality. And then he collapsed. This woman stands upright.

The second thing he notices is the translucent quality of her skin, as if the early morning light bends to pass through her.

The girl has a certain beauty, he supposes, if your taste runs to elves. Jan is unimpressed by beautiful women. Beautiful women serve him wine, warm his bed. And he's seen virgins with visions before. Marriage cures them of imagination. But there is something different about this one, unearthly, a vapor wraith from the woods.

"Sister Aleys," he says, "we have heard much about you."

She says nothing. He has a feeling she's judging him.

"You claim to work miracles."

"I make no such claim." There is a hint of defiance in her voice.

"Yet you lay hands upon the ill."

"As do your priests."

"My men are ordained to perform sacraments." She's quite slippery. "But you have healed patients in the hospital."

"I work there."

He didn't expect this. He didn't expect denial. It's good. A show of humility, a certain attractive reluctance could be part of the act. He glances at Willems. *What do you think? Good enough for the stage? For the pope?*

Willems jerks his head toward their guards. Jan looks around.

The guard behind him is making a surreptitious cross over his throat. The other is gazing at the girl with his mouth agape. God help him. He wonders if the pope could be this gullible. Infallible, but gullible.

"You are too modest. The esteemed Friar Lukas"—he nods at his brother—"has witnessed your healings. It seems you have been given a gift of the spirit. You can bring people back from death?"

He's giving her an opening. She doesn't take it. Instead, her eyes graze his finery, the costly fabric, his belt paved with precious stones. Her gaze, focused to a pinpoint, rests on his pectoral cross like she could melt it.

Well, he has plans for her and her insolence. "The Church, as you can imagine, is interested in all powerful manifestations of the Holy Spirit. Witnessing such gifts can"—his eyes flick to Lukas—"cause faith to flower in desert rock and streams of belief to turn into oceans." He is laying it on a bit thick. He wants to see what she's got.

"I am a simple servant."

Simple, my foot, he thinks. *There's nothing simple about you.*

"Good. I have arranged for you to perform a public healing. My carriage will collect you this evening at the tolling of the Lakenhalle."

She blanches. "Your Excellency, God does not require human tests and demonstrations."

"You instruct a bishop on God's requirements?"

"My gift is capricious."

I bet it is.

She looks to Friar Lukas. "If someone is healed, it is God's will, not mine."

"Well," sighs the bishop, "then we will rely on God's will to prove your virtue."

"And if I refuse? Or fail?"

"Then it would appear to be God's will to close this begijnhof. In addition to harboring a possible deceiver"—he gives Aleys a long look—"we have reason to suspect that one or more women here—women lettered in Latin—are making unsupervised translations of scripture." He nods at Aleys, Sophia, and Katrijn. "It's enough to make some arrests, perhaps close the whole enterprise." He opens his palms. "Such a shame. It's really quite lovely, what you have here."

He smiles at Willems. *Your work, come to fruition. I hope you are enjoying this theater of our making.*

Aleys twists around. Her eyes narrow. "The man from the *magna rota*."

"How the wheel turns," Willems responds, doffing his black cap and extending a leg. He replaces it on his head at the perfect angle.

Such style, that man, thinks the bishop. He will do well in Rome.

"This evening we look forward to your demonstration of God's will on earth."

29
Aleys

As the men leave, a breeze blows over the rooftops and the sheets lift from the lines. They float in the dawn light, impossibly lovely. As they settle, one by one, the beguines emerge from their homes, until Aleys is surrounded by women in gray. The only noise is the children, who have begun their games, unaware of their mothers' plight. I want to be a child again, thinks Aleys. Several of the beguines have bowed their heads before her, believers who think her capable of anything. To the side, Katrijn, who thinks her capable of nothing, stands with arms crossed. Only two beguines can begin to understand the impossible bind she's in.

Ida murmurs, "I'm so sorry, Aleys." Ida has been beside her at the hospital. She knows Aleys is helpless to control this thing.

Sophia steps forward to take Aleys in her arms. "Child, come here."

"I might not be able to heal them," she whispers.

"I know." Sophia looks around at the community she's built. A band of sunlight illuminates the first lines of laundry. "I know."

"I can't do it," says Aleys. "I can't, I can't do this."

"Shhh. It won't be your doing. It will be God's choice, whatever happens."

"But why? Why would he do this?" Isn't he supposed to protect them?

"I wish I knew."

"But if I fail—"

"It's not in your hands. You've told me so yourself. You can't will what happens."

But can't she? She thinks of Marte. Aleys wishes now that Marte still limped as badly as the day they met. It would have been better if she'd failed that day, if her hands had been inert, if there'd been no rush of sensation when she placed her hands on Marte's foot. Then she'd know she had no power to heal at will, that her own desire had nothing to do with it. What will happen to Marte if she fails? To all of them? Where will they go?

A thing so precious and beautiful as this place, these brave women. All of it in her hands.

She mumbles into Sophia's shoulder. "I didn't ask to be chosen."

But she did. She asked for a big gift.

Sophia shakes her head. "We're all chosen, child. Some are chosen to the cross and some to feed the chickens. There's no second-guessing God's intentions. You know that."

She does. Sometimes.

"Well, at least we should give you the day off from the hospital." Sophia gives a weak smile. "I think you should pray."

Aleys positions herself on her knees before the altar. She starts a prayer. She stops. She begins again, stops again. Here in the nave where the women sang and danced at Midsummer just months ago, where their voices wove music from verse, she can find no rhythm, no beauty. She wants to prepare. She wants to lose herself, as she has before, in the twilight of poem prayers that curl through her like smoke until her spine is made of whispers. She wants to disappear.

But that doesn't happen. The light ticks across the stones.

Father, if it is possible, let this cup pass from me.

She can't manage the words that follow: Thy will, not mine. She wants too much. She wants to save the begijnhof. She wants to save Sophia, Ida, even Katrijn. Herself. What if that's not his will? Can she pray for that?

Please, she beseeches, *just make this go away*.

She tries harder. She sends her prayers to heaven, but they fall to ground, their wings bare assemblages of bone without feather, useless.

At noon, she gives up. She's too angry to pray. "Why?" she asks. "Why are you doing this to me? To us?" If she could reach out and touch God's fabric, she would rip it.

She needs to calm herself. Aleys fumbles for her psalter. It's there, as always, under her dress, the pouch smooth against her skin. She slips out the book and opens it to Saint Ursula. There's the miniature Ursula in a blue dress, russet hair loose around her shoulders, a soldier's arrow pointed at her breast. Around her lie eleven thousand slain maidens. What is in Ursula's heart? Her expression is placid, but so is that of the archer and of the virgins bleeding to death at her feet. Did she rage against God for sending an assault on the women he'd commanded her to lead? Or did Ursula still call him beloved? It seems to Aleys, now, that the tale couldn't possibly be true. Or maybe that's what makes you a saint: the ability to face the worst and pray, *Thy will be done.*

I don't understand you, she thinks. *When I was a child, you hid messages in the clouds and love notes in the psalms. But I'm a woman now, and I see your cruelty and wonder what you are. You create, you destroy. You plague, you heal. You've made me your fickle instrument and I don't understand your mind. Show me, face-to-face. I want to know you.*

This is her prayer. *Show me where to find you.*

She collapses back on her heels and opens her palms. *Show me.*

She feels it come on this time. A blurring of her edges, a fuzziness in the light, the smell of charred rosemary. The light on the floor ticks backward. Aleys lurches like she's leaned into the wind only to feel it slacken. She opens eyes that were already open and sees before her a windswept vista of hard-packed sand. It is a solitary place. A single tree stands in the center of this plain; its shadow is precise in the glare. She walks toward the tree and halts. She has found him. She knows this. He is the sun and the shadow, the perfect solitude. The beautiful, perfect solitude. She knows she will find him if only she can stay here. She doesn't know whether she's calling him or he's calling her.

Let me stay with you, she says to this Christ. *I will dwell in the desert, if only you will let me find you. Forty days, forty nights, forty years.*

Then the Lakenhalle bell tolls and Aleys is pulled back into a world that makes no sense. *You have broken my heart*, she thinks.

30
Aleys

As the bell echoes, Aleys walks through the twilight courtyard. The laundry hasn't been taken in. No lamps shine in the windows, except for the reading room. By this, she understands her sisters have spent the day together, in prayer. They fear, too. But will they not walk with her? No one has come to see her to the carriage. Not Ida. Not Sophia. It's a long way through the courtyard, alone. She passes under the archway and steps onto the bridge. The bishop's carriage waits on the cobble, its black door open. The swans twist their necks to follow her. As she steps up into the carriage, Aleys hears raised voices from the courtyard behind her and turns to look. But the footman has shut the door. There's no escape.

Inside is Lukas with a friar she's never met and Brother Hervé, whom she hasn't seen since the day of her induction. How odd it feels to be surrounded by her order at this moment, how little they understand what's at stake. Hervé reaches out the window to slap the carriage roof. It begins to roll.

"Sister Aleys," Lukas says, smiling, "are you ready for this day?" He looks overexcited, slightly demented. "Our day of victory?"

"Father?" Surely, he understands the risk of this? He has witnessed the limbs that didn't heal, the wounds that festered, the babies who died. He knows her gift can fail.

"You're nervous," he explains. "It's only to be expected."

"I'm more than nervous! How can you be so sure of miracles?"

"Have you prayed today?"

"Of course!" And he sent me a vision I can't interpret.

"Good, good. All will be fine."

"Why do you think that?"

"It's God's will. He will not fail his chosen."

Hervé watches her closely. "Perhaps," he says, "we should ride in silence."

The buildings close in as they approach the plaza through narrow streets, until only the peak of the Lakenhalle belfry can be seen over the roofs. The way is lit with torches, as for a holy day. The streets are already crowded; the progress of the carriage to the Markt is slow and halting. Voices are pitched high. Aleys wishes she could crawl under the bench. She wishes she were anywhere but here. She reaches to the back of her neck, to yank at the spiky nubs of hair under her veil. To feel something, anything, other than fear.

The carriage turns into the plaza and the noise grows. Aleys clutches at her brown dress, rocking back and forth, trying to contain herself. People bang on the carriage, eager to reach her, straining to touch even the horses, and the animals grow nervous, starting and stopping, so it takes them an eternity to reach the middle of the plaza. Aleys's heart is beating so hard she can hardly hear. A high buzz has entered her ears. Please let that be God, she thinks, please let that be his presence.

The carriage door is yanked open, and the bishop stands there in full regalia, the golden shepherd's crook in his hand, the white miter on his head. He is holding an azure cape embroidered with the insignia of his office, the crenellated tower topped by three golden fleurs-de-lis.

"We are ready for you." He leans forward to wrap the cape around her.

"What are you doing?" says Lukas. "She's Franciscan! She doesn't wear a bishop's costume."

"Tonight she belongs to the Church," says the bishop.

Aleys is too dazed to care what men want her to wear. As the bishop fastens the cape about her neck, she cranes around him at the platform erected in the heart of the plaza, trying to see who she's been called to heal. She focuses on her hands, trying to feel the tingle, the sense of wasps in her palms. They are bundling her out of the carriage. Just as she is stepping down, there's a commotion. It's Cecilia, out of breath, broken through the crowd, shoving people aside.

"Aleys!" she cries, and Aleys can't make out what she says next, but she sees wild desperation on Cecilia's face.

"Stop!" Aleys says to the bishop, who's taken her arm and is leading her toward the platform. "Wait!" Cecilia is speaking to Lukas. He looks quickly up at Aleys, his face ashen. "What is it?" she shouts back. The bishop tightens his grip and pulls. "I said to stop!" He pulls again. Aleys steps on his foot, hard, wresting her arm away and turning back through the crowd toward Cecilia. The people want to touch her, she feels them tug on the accursed cape, but Hervé and the other friar hold them back until Aleys reaches Cecilia and Lukas.

"Aleys, we need you!" Cecilia's voice is desperate. "Sophia. She's taken ill. She rose from prayer to see you out, and she just collapsed. She can't move, Aleys!"

"Sophia?"

"Yes, we were all in the reading room praying on our knees. When the bell rang, the magistra stood and her hands went to her head like she was struck by lightning, but from inside like, and she crumpled and couldn't get up. Oh, Aleys. It was horrible. It's like only half of her is working, like the bolt struck her right side. I'm not even sure she can see!"

No. Not Sophia.

Cecilia yanks on her arm. "Katrijn said to bring you back."

"But Katrijn doesn't believe . . ."

"She does now." Cecilia gives Aleys a pointed look. "She'd believe anything to save Sophia."

Aleys faces Lukas. "We have to return to the begijnhof."

The bishop reaches them. He is glowering. "The people are impatient."

The crowd has begun to chant her name. It starts out as Aleys, a sound that ripples through the crowd with a hiss, until someone, somewhere, changes the word, and it comes back as a whiplash: "Sint!" They are calling for a saint. Aleys is not a saint. She is far from a saint, but the chant grows louder.

"Sint! Sint!" It fills the Markt like an arena. She thinks of Perpetua's death in the emperor's stadium. She thinks of Mama wrestling with demons the night she died.

"I have to go back. Turn the carriage around."

The torchlight catches the gems on the bishop's miter. His crook glows. The bishop shakes his head.

Lukas speaks up. "Jan, it's the magistra. She's been struck down. You see your people. They'll wait all night for Aleys. Let her go to the begijnhof. We'll bring her back."

Aleys feels panic in her throat, a hot acid. She has to get to the begijnhof. She thinks of Sophia on the floor, unable to stand, unable to see. She remembers the moan that snaked under Mama's door. She has to be there. Whether or not she can help, she has to be with Sophia. She can't lose Sophia.

But the bishop is angry. "Don't be ridiculous. It's one woman. Look at this crowd!" His eyes narrow as he focuses on Aleys. "On that platform are three gravely ill souls who have been waiting for you for hours. They could die while you dither."

Behind him the raised platform is illuminated with torches. In the center are three people. One is on a litter, covered with a blanket. Two are standing, bent, shivering. They're dressed in rags. Their eyes are large in their faces, turned to her. She realizes with horror that one of the standing figures holds an infant.

The chanting grows even louder, the crowd impatient. The bishop bends too close to Aleys's ear. She feels his spittle on her cheek as he enunciates, each syllable crisp and quiet. "If you leave, the test is aborted. Failed." He straightens. "Your choice. You can save the begijnhof and these three souls." He gestures to the platform. "Or we arrest you and your magistra. I don't care if she can't see. I don't care if she can't walk. She can still burn."

Aleys hates this man with a perfect fury. She doesn't know if he will keep his word, but she thinks he will keep his threat. For all her prayers to God, he's sent her a devil in a bishop's robe.

She wants desperately to flee to Sophia. The magistra could be dying. But if she can heal these three people quickly and get to Sophia in time, the begijnhof would be saved. If she fails, they're all condemned. If she leaves, they're condemned. She knows what Sophia would say. *Try. You have to try.*

"Lukas," she says. "Go to the magistra. Run. If she requires last rites . . ." It's hard to say. "Cecilia, go with him. Tell them I'm coming." Cecilia turns and starts throwing elbows to clear the way. "Hervé, get this carriage turned around."

Aleys turns toward the platform.

The crowd is baying now as one animal. Aleys walks past the bishop, not even glancing at him. She reaches the stairs, fumbles with the fastening at her throat, tears off the bishop's cloak, and throws it behind her. She runs the last steps. The scene on the platform is infernal. A dozen torches frame the stand, their caustic tar stinging her throat. She can hardly draw breath. She thinks she hears someone cry "Aleys!" in a familiar voice. Even in the midst of everything, she startles. Finn? But the sound is swallowed by the mass of people chanting "Sint!" The stage is lit so brightly that she can't see beyond the first row of people who are reaching up to touch her hem. She steps back from the edge and turns to face the patients. They are shivering, though it is hot as hell, cowering in the center of the stage, their eyes huge, like the souls in the devil's cauldron in her psalter.

On the litter is an ancient man struggling for breath, his chest shuddering with effort. His eyes are clear, though, and they follow her. There's a boy on a crutch, his leg twisted beneath a cloth wrapped around his waist. A battered cup hangs from the crutch. They must have found him on the streets. Beside him, the woman with the infant has sunk to her knees, cradling the child with one arm, reaching toward Aleys with the other. She is lovely and dressed in blue and looks so like paintings of the Virgin that she could have a halo. Aleys peers at the child. The woman quickly pulls the swaddling to cover the infant, but not before Aleys glimpses a babe with pink cheeks and bright eyes. Odd. It looks like teething is the worst he's ever suffered. She can't tell which of the pair is the patient.

The bishop sweeps up behind Aleys and bangs his shepherd's crook so hard the platform shakes. As he spreads his arms wide, the chanting dies down. Aleys can hear the horses snorting, a panicked rattling sound to their breath. She looks back at the carriage. They've turned it around. She faces the patients, wishing she felt something, anything, in her body. This is the moment. She concentrates herself around the kernel of flame in her core, willing it to spread through her spine, into her arms, to burst into sparks in her fingertips. She feels strangely fearless, now that the moment has come. Aleys steps toward the patients, but the bishop blocks her path with his crook.

"People of Tournai," he booms. "I stand before you in humility and awe for the act of God we are gathered to witness, his divine power made manifest in the person of a simple maid." He clears his throat. "The woman before you has been chosen as a channel of the Holy Spirit." He sweeps his free arm toward Aleys, and the crowd cheers.

What's he doing? It sounds like he's going to canonize her.

"It is with profound joy that we bring these patients to be healed by her miraculous touch."

Her signal. She pushes forward, but he blocks her again.

"It is with gratitude to the Almighty that we share this momentous event with the faithful of Flanders. What you are about to witness"—he steps toward them—"is no less marvelous than Peter healing the lame and Paul raising the dead. For Christ gave his twelve apostles authority over unclean spirits, to cast them out, and to heal every disease and every affliction." He bows his head. "This beneficence marks a new era of grace in the bishopric of Tournai. We are blessed. In the name of the Father, the Son, and the Holy Ghost, let us pray."

He is drawing this out. She wants to be let at the patients, to cure them or fail to cure them. But his eyes say to her, *Down on your knees, or I'll make this even longer*. She drops. The patients fold their hands in supplication. Beyond the lights, she hears the murmur of a thousand people who have bowed their heads.

She prays, *Lord, please watch over Sophia. Please let me get back to her.*

She's startled by sudden steps behind her. It's Willems approaching with the azure cloak. He drapes it over her shoulders and knots the tie hard around her throat. The bishop intones "Amen," and makes a grand sign of the cross over her, as if this is an investiture. The Church is claiming her as their own. She doesn't know why. She hasn't done anything yet. When she rises, there is a ripple through the crowd, a collective "Ah." The weight of the cape pulls at her throat.

Finally, the bishop steps back. Aleys turns inward once more, hoping for the rush in her fingertips, searching for the feeling. Nothing. This won't work. But she has no choice. She steps toward the patients. The man on the litter begins to thrash in death throes. There's no time to waste. She kneels beside him and begins the *Ave*. "Hail Mary, full of grace." She trusts this prayer, has seen it uncurl in ribbons of grace through the hospital, but before she even finishes one round, the patient sits up, then stands, from his cot. The crowd gasps. The old man, suddenly young, bends to grab the litter and raise it over his head. The people cheer.

But she felt nothing. Nothing at all.

The woman with the baby is sobbing, curled over her child. The lame boy limps toward Aleys. "Heal me, Sister!" he cries, and he reaches out to touch her robe. Instantly, his leg straightens. He drops his crutch. He bounds to the edge of the platform. "Look! I am cured!" he shouts, tears flowing from his eyes.

She suddenly understands. They are actors. This whole thing is a charade, a farce. Aleys pivots to look at the bishop, horrified. She could be with Sophia, but he has her here on this stage, making a mockery of God's will. The bishop is triumphant. *Go ahead*, he seems to say, *heal the last one*. He jerks his head toward the carriage. *Then I'll free you.*

She wants to run. She wants to go far from him, from this faithless man, from this world that he and his kind have created. She thinks of the desert. The tree. The quiet. In the midst of madness, is there no refuge? For a fleeting moment, as the people chant, she can feel the stillness. Just here. Just beyond. And then it is gone, and the stench of tar fills her nose and the roar of the crowd fills her ears and the terrible, cynical task is before her. *Oh Lord*, she thinks, *won't you take me to the desert?*

The woman has raised the infant to Aleys. The fraud is stunning, this act so craven, Aleys has no words. Is the child even hers? Aleys turns back to the bishop, shaking her head.

"Heal the babe!" he announces. "Drive the devils from this woman and heal the child!"

The woman begins convulsing and Aleys fears for the infant. The woman could dash the child to the boards in her wild contortions. Then Aleys feels a tingle in her hands. She looks at them with astonishment. What is this? She knows it can't be her will. Whatever she does, she must do fast. Aleys steps forward and lays hands on the woman's head and feels some strange flow of grace travel from her palms into the woman, who looks up, startled. Their eyes meet. The woman forgets her part. They are frozen, Aleys and the actor, in some strange meaning that neither understands. The child begins to bawl. Willems steps forward and grabs it, quickly unfurling the swaddling and raising the healthy infant high for the crowd. Aleys shakes her head at the woman, who is now crying in earnest. "Go in peace," whispers Aleys.

"Today we have witnessed miracles!" shouts the bishop.

Aleys turns and runs for the carriage. Hervé slaps the roof and they start back to the begijnhof, while she struggles to get out of the bishop's awful cloak. Hervé reaches forward to help her. She raises her chin so he can undo the knot. "You are very brave," he says.

"Burn that thing," she says.

31
Aleys

Inside the begijnhof, lamps are turned up in every window in vigil. Aleys senses the beguines at their prayer benches within. She can hear their murmurs flowing together, merging into a fast-pleading river. Cecilia's grip on her arm is so fierce Aleys can feel her nails bite through the wool. They run through the courtyard. The door to the magistra's home swings open on silent hinges. Inside, three women look up from preparing poultices, their cheeks flushed. The room smells of vinegar and rosemary. Marte stands before the fire, urging the flames with the bellows, though the heat is already stifling.

The sisters regard Aleys with relief, as if now all will be well. She feels their hope climb onto her back, and she could collapse under the weight of it. Their eyes all bear the same message: *Save her for us.* The oldest gestures her poultice toward the stairs. *Go.*

Aleys feels the heat rise with her as she mounts the narrow stairs, palms against the walls. It's a long climb. The hopes of the beguines trail her up, plastering her ribs like bandages. It's hard to breathe. God is not at her bidding. They have no idea how willful he is.

Sophia's bedchamber is lined with candles. They must have brought every beeswax taper from the church stores. Aleys sees, surprised, that the walls of Sophia's bedchamber are painted a golden mustard. The wavering half-light casts shifting pools of amber and ochre. So the magistra allowed herself this one luxury. No lace, no tapestry. Just this cocoon of warm light. Something in that thought makes Aleys glad. Her hand travels to the small rectangle of the psalter she wears beneath her dress.

Katrijn is bent over the bed, her strong back flexed taut as a bow. Just inside the door Lukas is murmuring prayers. Her heart sinks. He has delivered last rites. He raises his eyes. They are bloodshot and troubled. He shakes his head. *It's bad*, his eyes say.

Katrijn cradles Sophia's head with one hand, strokes her brow with the other. There's a great tenderness in the gesture. Sophia's form disappears beneath the blanket. Katrijn twists to look at Aleys. Her eyes are desperate.

"You have come," she says. "Finally."

"Yes."

Katrijn can't bear to relinquish Sophia. So Aleys waits, her hands folded, breathing vinegar, which stings a throat already raw from the torches on the bishop's stage.

Katrijn bends to press her brow against Sophia's, and Aleys can tell she is trying to pull the affliction from Sophia's body into her own, like drawing a splinter from the flesh. Finally, Katrijn pulls herself away and stands to face Aleys. "Please," she whispers, "please." Katrijn's anguish is plain on her face, a naked despair that is willing to bargain. *Heal her, and I will believe you. Heal her, and I will do anything.*

Aleys holds her breath as she approaches Sophia. The magistra is childlike against the pillow, pale and hollow, perfectly still, waxy but for the spot of color on her forehead where Katrijn has pressed her own. Her hair is spread out like a silver corona. Has she already passed? Then Aleys sees, with a bolt of horror, the magistra's eyes wheeling toward her with the terror of a frightened horse, overshooting Aleys's face.

"She still can't see," says Lukas, "nor move. She couldn't take communion."

Katrijn moans. She hugs her elbows to her waist and bows her head, a gesture that belongs to another woman.

Aleys leans toward Sophia. "Magistra, can you hear me?" Sophia's eyes train on her voice, latching to a rope thrown down a well. "Yes, Mother, I think you can." She concentrates on her hands, strains to feel the spirit within them. She thinks back to the evening the magistra brought her the lamp in the church. Nights when she woke racked with pained spirit, to find Sophia at her side. *He asks too much of you*. Aleys bends to her ear and whispers, just for her, "Magistra, I will pray for you as you taught me."

And so Aleys removes herself to Gethsemane, to the garden, and she prays his word so quietly that only Sophia can hear, over and over again. One word to animate her frozen body, one word to bring her home, one word to bring her back: "*Abba. Abba. Abba.*" She hears Christ's anguish over the valley and she feels his wonder and she tries, she tries, to let the magistra feel what she feels. Into that word Aleys pours all her desire so that it channels a route; she carves with that word like a pickaxe, "*Abba*," flint and pull and rock and mud, "*Abba*," and the beguines' prayers quietly fill the canal until it swells and spills over its banks. She can see the way, opening to the sea; it is ahead and it is light, and she takes Sophia's still hands and warms them and murmurs, "We are there, Magistra, it is just ahead." She can feel the miracle descend. They will save her, this cup of suffering will pass. And then . . . nothing.

The vision dissolves and Aleys is back in the room with the cloying scent of rosemary and the magistra's eyes now closed, and there is no safety, she knows, because the world is flat again. Her hands do not tingle, her spirit is damp. She is empty of miracles. The beguines' prayers have watered fallow ground.

Katrijn covers her face, stricken. She knows.

Aleys has failed.

Sophia issues a rattling sound and Aleys pulls back. She feels a weariness in her bones.

Sophia opens her eyes, searching. "Katrijn," she murmurs.

From the corner, Katrijn lifts her head. "Sophia?" She pushes Aleys aside, takes Sophia's hands.

"Katrijn?" It is a hoarse whisper, barely audible. The two women lock gaze, hazel eyes searching brown, as if in this moment, they both see each other. Then Sophia closes her eyes, exhales, and it is over.

Katrijn stiffens. She does not move for a long while. No one does. Silence expands to fill the room.

Then the beguines begin to sing. It is Ida first up the stairs, then Cecilia, then they are all there, around the bed. They sing *Ave Maria*. Their dresses are spotted with raindrops and they smell like wet wool, but their song opens the shutters and Aleys feels Sophia slip out the window. *Do not go.* But it is too late. Katrijn sobs quietly, her broad back heaving.

Aleys looks around the room at the tearstained faces. "I'm so sorry . . ." she begins, speaking to Katrijn's shoulder.

"Get out," says Katrijn, never moving her gaze from Sophia.

"I tried—"

"Get out," she repeats louder, turning. Her eyes blaze. "You fraud. Sophia believed in you, thought you were something rare, like some kind of"—she spits out the word—"angel. It was all about you. Since the day you arrived it's been all about you. And you didn't even save her." Katrijn nearly chokes. "You didn't deserve her."

None of us did. "Katrijn, I love her as you do."

Katrijn shakes her head. Her eyes are raw. *No one loves her as I do.* And Aleys sees it is true.

"Get out of here," Katrijn whispers. "You are no saint to us."

There is a shocked pause in the song as Aleys pushes her way from the room and stumbles down the stairs. Below, Marte raises her head from gathering the sodden poultices. Silent tears wet her ruddy cheeks. The sight of Marte crying pierces Aleys as nothing else can.

Aleys runs. She races across the dark courtyard, through the arch, pushing open the double doors and passing onto the bridge. A thin thread of cobble is visible through the offerings, mush and glistening cabbage heads. Flower petals float below in a browning pink and yellow quilt. A quiet rain is falling into the small square outside the begijnhof, empty in the dead of night. Somewhere, the bell of Matins rings. She is startled. Sophia is gone. Time should have stopped.

Aleys stands there, on the bridge, in the rain. Behind her, above her, the begijnhof bell begins to toll. The first stroke rises sudden, swells, fades into a watery echo. Then the second. It will be Ida ringing the bell, pulling with all her small solemn might on the thick rope. Over and over, clapper strikes metal. Peal after peal is born and dies. It is so senseless. Aleys begins to cry, there on the bridge, among the offerings to her worthless gift.

A man exits his home across the way, wiping sleep from his face, looking up at the steeple. The bell tolls on and on, and with each clang, another person enters the square. Their eyes graze Aleys, then rise above her. Aleys sees the wondering in their faces: Death has chosen a beguine. Which one?

The best. Death took the best.

A small girl in the hand of her mother is watching Aleys, brown eyes under a white cap. All the adults are gazing upward. But not the girl. Her eyes glint with recognition, with the triumph of young children who have found the right word. The girl mouths it. *No*, thinks Aleys, *don't. Please do not say it. Not that. Not now.*

But the child speaks her claim: "Sint."

The mother looks at Aleys. Her eyes spark with the quick flint of opportunity. She drags her child forward and presses the girl's shoulders until both are kneeling before Aleys, demanding her blessing. Can't they see she's not a saint? If she were, the bell would be silent. Sophia would be alive. Aleys looks down at the woman. *You throw sheep knuckles onto the ground for a scrap of luck. You require miracles to feed your faith. What in God's name do you believe in?*

Aleys opens her empty hands and looks up into the rain. *I have nothing for you.*

The mother grabs Aleys's wrist and twists it to place it flat on her daughter's head. Aleys pulls away, but it's too late. The crowd has noticed them. Murmurs of "Sint!" rise from around the square. Aleys feels the people closing in, like she's a magnet drawing sharp filings toward her. She pulls back, but the woman already has a handful of her robe, and then there are more, more voices, people slipping on the bridge as they push to be near. She glances back at the begijnhof door, but there is already a man behind her with a gray beard and tearful eyes. "Sint," he says, touching a finger to her shoulder. *Don't touch me*, she thinks. But the sibilant hiss of "Sint!" surrounds her, until it licks across her palms and kisses her ear. They claim her with the intimacy of ownership, like she's a lucky rabbit's foot. They have encircled her now, on their knees in the offerings, hands clasped, heads bowed. Their desire coats her limbs like ointment.

And then, from behind, hands grasp her hem. A tug, another tug. Her dress slips down her back until the front grips her throat. She claws at her neck to pull it away.

"Stop!" she gasps. But there are other hands now, scrabbling over her. They pull her robe away from her until it is extended like a bell. Cold rises from the cobbles up her thighs. Before her, a man on one knee grabs a knife from its sheath, and with two flicks, nicks off a bit of cloth. He folds it into his fist and brings it to his heart. "Sint," he murmurs. "Sint." His eyes are closed. The rip in the fabric is enough. Other hands begin to tear at it, yanking, pulling threads, grabbing handfuls from her garment. They seize her belt, and it tightens around her waist like a vise until it too falls away, severed, and a small crowd fights over the knots.

When they look at her, their eyes are blank. They are breathing hard now, chanting "Sint! Sint!" and she feels their wildness. She pushes, but there are hands on her arms, fingers around her ankle.

"Stop!" she yells, but no one hears. Her heart can't keep pace with her shallow breath, it's all too fast. She's engulfed by the crowd.

A knife nicks her shoulder and slices a ribbon from her sleeve. She feels someone else run a knife through the other so that both sleeves are rent into brown wings that hang limp down her back. Her arms are naked now, her legs exposed. The drizzle is chill against her skin, hands hot where they slide along her limbs. The people grab at the wings. She slips on their offerings and falls backward. Fingernails bite into her calves. A fishwife is wringing her ankle as if to unscrew it and she realizes: They will tear me apart for my blessing. A large man grunts as he pulls hard at her arm and she feels her shoulder skip its socket with a quiet *ping* and her back torques in pain. Panic sharpens her thoughts. She struggles, but there's nothing she can do. *I'm only seventeen. I don't want to be martyred.*

Then she's groping air as they lift her above them. Her sandals have vanished and her feet dangle far from her as they raise Aleys like a rag doll. They will carry her somewhere—perhaps the cathedral, perhaps a bonfire—she knows not. She is in the grip of something animal and frenzied, a wild sacrament.

Then someone slips and Aleys is falling, from their hands, from the bridge, and as she strikes the surface of the water, she knows no more.

32

FRIAR LUKAS

Lukas feels himself split. One piece is at Sophia's side. "Go forth, faithful Christian," he intones, commending her to the saints and angels. But another piece of him is already following Aleys, to stop her flight, to demand, how—how did you do that? For this is what he saw: He saw Sophia's features soften as Aleys prayed over her trapped spirit. He saw Sophia's spirit set free from its cage of flesh, in the moment when her eyes met Katrijn's, and he knew that she could see, though she'd been blind moments before. The women, all three of them—Katrijn, Sophia, and Aleys—were paused in tableau, captured in unconscious glory. Though it was not the miracle they sought, nonetheless a holiness had descended upon them. Or had risen from Sister Aleys, for she was lit with grace. His eyes are wet. As the bell tolls, Friar Lukas is shaken with grief and wonder. And as Sophia's sisters lay out her body and begin the prayers of purgatory, he takes his leave of them.

Outside, he shoulders his way through a crowd gathered on the bridge and all around the shore of the begijnhof pond and down the canal. The bell stops tolling. The crowd is strangely hushed, everyone facing the island. The moon hides behind racing clouds, so it takes him a moment to understand what he sees. In the center, there's a mound of brown wool. Then he realizes it's Aleys, collapsed. Swans surround her like guardians. Her robe is torn, her sandals and belt gone. Even her veil has disappeared. With her hair half grown in, brown and spiky, she looks like a street urchin. When he wades into the waters, mud sucks at his sandals and an animal smell wafts up; he is wet to his thighs. The swans part. He lifts Aleys easily, gathering her in and tucking her head against his chest. As he wades back, his robes trailing, he knows he holds a living saint in his arms. The crowd surges toward him, but he shouts, "Stand back!"

Some of them clutch scraps of brown wool in their fists; he wants to hit them. He reins in his wrath and storms across the bridge. The people give way. They look ashamed.

At the begijnhof entrance, Ida has one hand on each of the enormous doors. She shakes her head no. Her eyes say she's sorry.

"I'm to stop you," she says.

"She needs attention." Ida is birdlike, he could easily force his way in.

"Katrijn doesn't want her here."

"The magistra promised her shelter."

"Sister Katrijn is the magistra now." Ida backs through the doors and closes them. He hears her slide the bolt.

33

The Bishop

Jan swirls the burgundy in his goblet, admiring how it glints like dark gems. He'd been too exultant to sleep when he returned from the Markt, had called for his finest vintage to savor with his victory. Might as well drink it all. He'll be heading to Rome after this triumph. Willems has dispatched couriers to carry the news of the miracle to Rome posthaste. The actors were superb. That boy with the crutches, genius.

After the demonstration, notables—abbots and counts and the mayor—gathered around to congratulate him, as if it were his own merit that caused God to grant a miracle worker in his diocese. The only one who stinted on praise was a squint-eyed Dominican from the university in Paris. "The pope's men will want to test her," he said. "Independently."

Well, that's tomorrow's problem. Tonight, he celebrates. But his ruminations are interrupted by a pounding on the door. His staff are asleep, so he goes down and finds Lukas outside with the girl limp in his arms. Her hair is uncovered, indecent, with small patches torn out. Her robe is in shreds; she has gouges down her exposed legs. What happened? She belongs in the hospital. Why bring her here? He doesn't want her. But he can't have his brother holding a woman on his doorstep. He admits them.

"What's this? It looks like your girl's been brawling. Put her on the bench."

Lukas pushes past him, lowers the girl carefully. "The crowd attacked her outside the begijnhof. They've kicked her out."

That makes no sense. Not after he staged her healings. "Why?"

"Aleys tried to save Sophia Vermeulen."

"Ah, that's who died." He heard the bell. It only confirms his opinion that the girl's just an actor.

Lukas is shaking his arm. "Jan, we need shelter. The town will destroy her with their fervor."

"What?" There's something in his brother's voice. Jan peers closer. "Look at you. You're jealous!"

"I am not."

"No, it's there. You would love them to tear you asunder. Oh, poor Lukas."

"Just give me the funds, Jan." Lukas sounds weary. "We must have a house now. We'll be turning applicants away."

More Franciscans? That's the last thing he needs. He takes stock of the girl. Even unconscious, even with hair like a hedgehog, she is strangely alluring. Lukas has dropped to one knee, cradling her hand in his. Jan has the impression that he's watching a hapless knight who plights a hapless love. His lady is distant, pledged to another. He should get Lukas away from her.

The inspiration comes to him out of nowhere. He should have thought of it before. It's so obvious, he laughs.

"I have the solution." He claps his hands. It's elegant. Simple.

"What?"

Oh, he's brilliant. In one stroke, he will get her away from Lukas and under his own control. "We'll put her in the anchorhold."

"No." Lukas stands abruptly, dropping her arm. "You can't mean—"

"Just listen. The cell on Sint-Salvator's been empty for years, since we carried out old Gunther. It needs to be swept, and the chimney cleaned, but it's perfectly adequate. Hear me out. I'll fund her keep."

"For life?"

"Of course. You think I'd seal her in and leave her to starve?"

"She'd be entirely alone."

"Lukas, you know better than that. She'll be walled in with God. Exactly where she wants to be." Exactly where I want her to be. "The town could still access her counsel through the window."

Hold the horses, he wants to tell Willems. In the same letter declaring miracles, they'll announce that the holy woman has dedicated herself to the life of a recluse. In his own cathedral. Whatever miracles, prophecies, or showings she comes up with will be credited to him. He couldn't bring the girl to Rome—he'd have to excommunicate her if she left the anchorhold—but he doesn't want her in Rome, anyway. Too risky. Willems doesn't know the actors there.

All he has to do is make a hermit of his saint. There are anchoresses all over Britain, why not Flanders? It's simple: You build a cell onto your church, conduct a funeral rite, give everyone a last look, lock her in, and throw away the key. She lives a life of constant prayer, and you have a holy woman literally attached to your cathedral, like a sanctified barnacle on a whale. He likes the idea. Popes like anchorites, towns like anchorites. Why shouldn't he, Bishop of Tournai, have an anchorite? And a famous one, at that. It's perfect.

Lukas is shaking his head. "She's not yours," he says. His meaning, its obverse, hangs in the air like a philosopher's puzzle: *She's mine*. Ah, the truth will rise. He watches Lukas scramble to correct himself. "She's pledged to our order. Her place is with the Franciscans."

"You would hoard a saint to yourself, Friar Lukas? I shudder to think what his Holiness would think of that." This Franciscan order has papal approval, but barely. If the pope wants the Church to take credit for the saint, the Church will win. It always wins.

No, this is perfect. He'll get Willems to hire some minstrels and compose them a ballad. "The Song of a Hundred Miracles." He rubs his palms together. "Of the Anchoress of Brugge." They'll send rumors south on fast horses.

"You can still be her confessor." Jan throws his brother a bone, though he knows he doesn't need to. What else is Lukas going to do with his supposed saint?

34

ALEYS

Aleys wakes with a start, a crawling sensation all over her limbs as she surfaces from nightmare. Slowly, her eyes focus. She's in a dim chamber with slot windows that admit vertical bars of yellow light. It must be midday. She has no idea where she is or how she got here. She's been laid out like a corpse on a bed canopied with heavy hangings. She forces her breath to slow. She is, for now, alone. She grabs fistfuls of the blanket beneath her.

Her psalter. Where's her book? She fumbles and finds the twisted cord beneath her shredded robe, follows it around her waist, tugging to get at the pouch wedged beneath her. The ruby silk is water stained. Carefully, she extracts the psalter. Oh, thank God. The book is intact, its leather cover smooth and familiar. Her fingers trace the embossed vines. She presses one hand on her prayer book and the other into her stomach.

The loss hits her like a millstone falling straight through her core. "Sophia?" Her voice is swallowed by stone and fabric. No one answers. Aleys feels the cracks open within her, the edge of the great howling void, the abyss she knows too well. She squeezes her ribs to make it close, but she can feel it there just beneath her skin. It feels like losing Mama all over again.

Aleys rolls over, buries her head between pillows, and breathes in her own darkness. She bites the pillow for something solid between her teeth, a predictable, trustful thing. A sob forces its way through her chest.

Take my gift away, Lord. Please take it away. I failed.

Aleys cries hard into the pillow until she can cry no more.

She rolls over, wipes the snot from her face with the remains of her sleeve. She's tired of being a vessel. She feels brittle as a pot, as if her body were made of cheap clay, expendable. Maybe it is. Maybe she's not meant to last. This strange grace that has inhabited her for a month has made her fragile. Aleys knows this: She can't go out there again. The crowd will kill her.

She needs to be alone.

Beloved, what do you want from me? Where does this end?

Aleys presses her psalter to her forehead until she feels its clasp indent her skin. Though she's not sure she trusts, though she feels anger scrape against hope, she opens the book to find the answer.

The psalter falls open to the illustration of the spreading oak. Every branch bears a bird: scarlet cardinals and black crows, brown wrens and yellow finches. Mama's tree. From the bottom margin, an auburn fox peeks from a dark den. Aleys reads the text that Mama never could. *The foxes have holes and the birds of the air nests: But the Son of Man hath not a place to lay his head.* It's Christ warning his apostles. *It won't be easy for you if you follow me*, he warns them.

But what does that mean, now, for her? That she must go back out there, when what she needs is shelter?

35
FRIAR LUKAS

Friar Lukas watches as she descends the stairs in a dress, some fine green thing. Her hair is short and bristling. She is a changeling. The dress restores her as female, abruptly, violently, before his eyes. He can hardly look at her. He wonders how his brother owns such a gown, but he knows better than to ask. He cannot object, not when her robe is in tatters. She is not herself. She does not seem Franciscan. She gives his brother the coldest look he's ever seen anyone dare give a bishop.

When Jan suggests, in his oiliest tones, the anchorhold, Aleys looks up to the ceiling and laughs. She says, "You mean a fox den?" When she looks back at them, she is wiping tears from her eyes. "Or a bird's nest?" Lukas wonders if the violence of last night's mob has deranged her.

"Tell me," she says, "about it."

He needs to talk her out of this. He'll find some other solution. His brother is pressing his case, adorning the argument. Jan tells her she will live the *vita angelica*, the life of God's favored angel. Her prayers and meditation will rain blessings upon Brugge.

"Like last night," she spits at Jan.

"You will be a recluse," says Lukas. "For life."

"Yes, I understand." She nods, too eager. "I am willing."

Lukas cannot believe she understands. "You'll never leave the anchorhold. Not for illness, not even for madness." She may already be mad. "You'll be interred."

"Symbolically interred," corrects Jan.

Lukas presses. "You will be permanently enclosed in the cell. You'll never come out. You'll never touch another person. Your family, your friends . . ."

"They can visit through the window," says Jan.

Aleys regards the bishop with a look of disdain. "I gave up that life already."

"If you set foot outside the anchorhold," Lukas warns, "you'll be excommunicated." He wants to command her to remain in the brotherhood, though he knows it's not a viable alternative. Jan has backed him into this corner. Still, he wants to order her to stay. If he could change her into a falcon and tether her to his wrist, he would. His urge to demand her obedience is strong and irrational. He has no counteroffer, yet he presses.

"Excommunicated, Sister! You would be denied the sacraments if you left."

"If I leave the hold, I will be banished from the Church," she says calmly, "and society. I understand perfectly. I would be a pariah. But what need will I have to leave?" Lukas feels her tense, ready to fly.

"Friar Lukas will be your confessor," says Jan, "and your hold has a squint onto the cathedral, so you can watch him celebrate Mass." Lukas knows it's a concession to let a Franciscan preach in his church. "You will receive communion from his hand."

Lukas has seen the squint from inside Sint-Salvator, the narrow window carved into the wall that separates the church from the anchorhold. It's cut in the shape of a cross, barely wide enough for a hand to pass through to administer communion to the hermit within.

"You need to see the hold before you commit." But Lukas can tell. She's already left him for God.

36
ALEYS

The enclosure ceremony is a few days hence, but Aleys wants it to begin now, if only to get her out of the bishop's manor. She's resisted Lukas's entreaties to visit the cell and has kept to the bedchamber with the draperies drawn shut. A piece of her is afraid that if she sees the hold, she will lose nerve. Or worse, that if she sees the sky, her spirit will rush up to meet it and refuse to be drawn into the enclosure. She will miss the sky. Perhaps more than anything, she will miss the sky.

Of course, that's what Lukas is testing. His entreaties become a demand. It's her first trial. She cannot truly consent to enclosure until she sees the hold.

Aleys follows Lukas to Sint-Salvator. She keeps her eyes fixed on her feet until the last moment, when she can't resist a glimpse of the belfry, of the golden weathercock on its peak. The rooster atop the cathedral is still, pointing north. *Surge aquilo*, she thinks—rise up, north wind! She wonders if she'll be able to sense the weather from her cell. Then she thinks back to the vision of the solitary tree on the desert plain. She will have no need for the weather.

The cathedral is empty but for an orderly lighting the standing iron candelabra. Aleys pushes back her hood and feels the volume of the cool, vast space. She lets her eyes trace the soaring arches that taper to infinity. The altar itself is grand, solid. The Christ in this temple hangs from the cross gracefully, the weight of his body pulling his outstretched arms into a gentle arc. His head bends toward the wound in his right side. His eyes are closed;

it is the moment past death and though he bleeds, his face is at peace. He will be looking away from her, she notes. For in the wall to the right of the sanctuary is the heavy oak door. Her door.

She considers the sliding bolt with an iron padlock. She hadn't thought about the lock, and confronted with it now, she frowns. Who will hold the key? She doesn't need to be told that the other side of the door has neither bolt nor latch. From the inside of the anchorhold, the door will be nothing but a wooden relief in the wall, an interruption of stone. A door that is no door.

This is what she seeks, she reminds herself. A sanctuary.

Beside the door is a small window into the anchorhold shaped like a cross, beautifully carved, with generous rounds decorating the foot, the head, and arms. Her squint. She twists back to the chancel and sees that the squint is cut at the perfect angle so that from the hold you could see altar, priest, and Christ on the cross. It's just wide enough to admit a hand with a wafer, but cut at a slant, and narrow enough that all anyone can see inside her cell is a sliver of gray stone wall opposite. It buoys her, this precisely carved squint. It is lovely.

They stand before the door. Lukas shows her a heavy iron key. "This has been opened only twice in forty years. To admit the anchorite Gunther, and to remove his earthly remains."

"So, inside, there are no . . ." She doesn't want to say it.

"Graves?"

She nods. He inspects her face. "That would frighten you?" Like she's not strong enough. She resents his doubt, so she stares hard at him to prove it doesn't frighten her, the possibility that the anchorhold contains graves, might even have a pit already dug to her precise length and breadth. Some anchorites live with their own open graves inside their cells, a *memento mori* to prevent them forgetting, for a moment, what they owe to God. *You must pray like your hair is on fire*, Lukas has said to her. He doesn't understand that she prays from desire, not fear.

"No," he says. "No graves."

Aleys is relieved. She knows she will die in the anchorhold. That part doesn't bother her. Somehow, though, she would like to be buried beneath the sky.

And there's a second reason she's glad that Gunther and the anchorites before him aren't buried under the floor. She doesn't want to share her cell with anyone. Aleys doesn't fear the dead; she's jealous of them. The hold is meant for her and her beloved. She doesn't want God's former lovers beneath her feet, like so many dead wives beneath the bed.

Lukas inserts the key. It turns easily. He slides open the bolt and pulls the door into the church. It swings wide. A cool, mossy smell emerges. He watches her. "You'll have wood for fire. It won't be so damp." He stands aside to let her enter.

Her first impression is that it's bigger than she thought. From the outside, the anchorhold is barely noticeable, two rooms pasted on the side of the church. One room is the public parlor, with a door to the street for her caretaker and for visitors. The parlor communicates with the anchorite's cell via a small square window obscured by black curtains, one on each side. Lukas has arranged for the beguines to bring food twice a day. "So you will see someone familiar." Apparently, Katrijn is glad enough to get her out of the way that she'll spare a sister to serve as maid. Aleys doubts the bishop knows she'll be attended by a beguine; he seems happy to pay for her upkeep and leave the details to his brother of exactly who will pass what through the parlor window into the cell of the anchoress.

Aleys pauses on the threshold. This room, this cell, will be hers, and hers alone. She feels like a bride meeting her spouse at the altar. They are committing for life, Aleys and this place.

Aleys crosses the doorstep and looks back over her shoulder. Friar Lukas won't follow her. Good. She wants to take in her new home, feel its dimensions, what it wants from her.

Aleys steps wholly inside, into a space defined by four walls of uneven gray stone, weathered and round. She runs her hand over them. They must have been pried from a riverbed, smooth as if oiled. The weight of stone is reassuring, speaks of the witness of earth and ground and true foundation. It feels loyal.

Behind her, beside the door that will be no door, is the squint. Faint light from the altar casts a cross, slightly askew, on the center of the packed dirt floor. Aleys inventories the room. First, she faces the wall shared with the church, which contains the door, the squint, and a narrow cot. Every night, for the rest of her life. She turns to her right, where the stone is interrupted by a square window with a black curtain. The parlor wall. Every meal, every chamber pot, every human word will cross that sill. She turns again. The wall shared with the street bears a small window with fixed translucent panes that admit a filtered light but not prying eyes. Beneath is a tidy table and stool. A stub of a candle, a quill, a dry inkpot. Aleys turns to the final wall, which hosts a fireplace with a simple stone mantel. An iron poker and a tripod for a pot lean against the stones like they expect Gunther to return any moment. She bends to pick up a knife which must have fallen to the floor. She replaces it on the mantel. Beside the fireplace, beneath a plain wooden cross, is a simple prie-dieu. Its kneeler is worn. She thinks of the anchorites before her. She hopes they found God here.

It's four paces from the squint to the street window. Six paces from the fireplace to the parlor window. Aleys lifts the black curtain to reveal a wooden shutter with a bolt. She can lock the world out when she wants. Aleys breathes into the room. It wants nothing from her that she can't give.

Aleys returns to the door and pulls it closed behind her. The cell darkens, but not completely. Noon light filters through the street window. Its panes are cow's horn shaved to a fine translucence, dark where they overlap, but glowing amber between. She thinks of Finn and his hornbook. It seems so long ago, back when God's word was a puzzle they could decipher together. She knows better now. Here, in this protected room, this simple, protected room, she will devote her life to understanding God. Her eyes adjust, and she finds herself happy.

At last. I am alone. No, she corrects. Not alone. Never alone. He is with me, always. What is it, then? I am sheltered.

She stretches her arms so that her fingertips nearly touch the walls. She turns slowly, sensing the contours of the space. Though there is a ceiling above and walls around her, she feels herself a hawk. Aleys spins, and feels herself expand, float, dissolve through the thick stone. What need has she of sun and clouds, when she finds a sky within her?

She hears silence.

She tastes nothing.

She shuts her eyes and feels herself open. She is everywhere.

Beloved, I am home.

37

Aleys

There's a knock on her door. Aleys has been keeping to the bedchamber in the bishop's manor. In part because she can't bear to lay eyes on the bishop, but mostly because she feels herself leaning toward solitude like a birch leaning toward sun. She would still herself, quiet herself, in preparation. They've announced her decision to the town. Tomorrow she will enter the anchorhold.

She rises to open the door. It's Lukas, and beside him, Papa. His hat is in his hand, silver in his hair. Her heart swells. She throws open the door so fast it bangs against the wall.

"Aleys?" he says. "Oh, daughter."

Papa takes one step forward and wraps her tight against his chest. Aleys feels tears spring to her eyes. There's nothing but his strong arms, his familiar smell, the scratch of his beard against her cheek.

"Papa," she mumbles into his collar. "I thought I'd never see you again."

"You won't, if they lock you up." Papa pulls back to glare at Lukas but keeps hold of her arm like he can't bear to let go. "How can you imprison this child?"

"No, Papa," she interrupts, taking his chin and turning his face back to her. "I've chosen this."

"These men are making a puppet of you."

"It's my desire."

"To become an anchoress?" His face falls. "You can't want that."

"Remember you said how Mama prayed to know God?"

"But—"

"I'll be free to go where she dreamed."

"To a cell? No. She wouldn't want that."

"What I seek requires solitude."

"They say you work miracles. Isn't that enough?"

She thinks, No. No, it's not. He courses through me, but he doesn't stay. "I've found awe, but not understanding." She grasps Papa's arms, makes sure he meets her gaze. "There's more, Papa, I know there is. I can feel it."

"You can't find it at home?"

"No."

He searches her eyes.

"Truly," she adds.

Finally, he sees. He sees her. He nods. "I didn't listen before. I won't doubt you now." He clasps her to him again. When Papa pulls back, his cheeks are wet. "I know God calls you." His words come out thick and rough. "Like Mama." He kisses her. "But you will always be my daughter."

38
Friar Lukas

Lukas stands at the altar of Sint-Salvator. Torchlight splinters the fog of incense. The church is full, the front pews filled with aristocracy, merchants in the middle, and peasants standing at the back. All eyes are on his brother in his finest regalia. Crimson and snow, the golden vestments, the peaked cloth crown, the crosier so ornate and curled in on itself that it is hardly recognizable as a shepherd's crook. Jan looks like God. Beside him, Friar Lukas is a brown mouse.

The balsam of frankincense pricks at his nose. Jan has brought out the best for the ceremony to mark the death of the girl who will be reborn as anchoress. Lukas glances toward the oak door in the wall, the entrance to her tomb. The anchorhold key lies on the altar, gray against white cloth. It makes him think of a relic, a saint's finger bone amidst gleaming gold and white. Lukas remembers the taper he lit for Aleys in the parish church. It feels long ago. That simple church. He looks up at the soaring stone vault, the stained glass, the crucifix above the altar. Who would have thought it would come to this? The funeral of Sister Aleys.

There is a stirring at the back of the church, a wave of rustling as the people turn. Framed by an arch, Aleys appears. At her elbow is her sister, as if Aleys must be borne up the aisle. It is tradition, scripted. Not that Aleys needs support; Lukas knows her resolve. He is awed by her resolve. In confession, at dawn in the bishop's garden, surrounded by daisies with browning petals, Aleys's voice was full of gratitude, not fear. He'd asked, again, for the hundredth time, "You're sure?" She'd turned to him with bright, impatient eyes. "Father, do you keep me from God?"

The sisters start up the aisle. The crowd bows heads as they pass. They move in unison; you cannot mistake the resemblance in their forms, the upright bearing, the long necks. Griete's fine sleeves sweep the cathedral floor as if she were a countess. Beside her, Aleys is a child bride in a black dress, carrying a burning candle in each hand. Her face glows bright above the flames. Her eyes, this time, are fixed on Christ over the altar. This time, she doesn't run up the aisle. This Aleys is not a breathless bride. She is the wife now, and Lukas cannot help but feel that she carries Christ within her, that the miracles have filled her with knowledge of him. The air between Aleys and Christ seems richly alive, as if invisible rays pull her toward him. Lukas must stop himself from running into the channel that crackles between them to—to what?—to keep them from fusing?

He has the key to her cell; she is the key to his God. He will lose them both today.

At the altar, Aleys hands the candles to Griete. He wonders at the dry-eyed sister. He wants to shake her. Don't you know how precious Aleys is, that you will never see her again? That this is her funeral? This is the end.

Aleys lifts the hem of her dress to lower herself, and her eyes brush past his, unreadable. Then she is prostrate on the ground, forehead to stone, arms spread wide so that she is become a black crucifix upon gray flagstone.

"Lord our God," Jan thunders in his best stage voice, "you summon this woman to the mountaintop of contemplation. You have raised her from the toils of Martha to the sweet tears of penitent Mary, and she shall at last come to rest in that best part, which will not be taken from her."

Lukas barely hears the Mass. His eyes are on Aleys, who doesn't move. She will be taken from him. Stop it, he chides himself. You are meant to rejoice.

His brother reaches for the holy water, which he will sprinkle over her. Aleys rises to her knees and looks at Jan. "No," she says quietly. "Not you."

Jan freezes.

She whispers so that only the three of them hear. "I don't seek your blessing." She turns to Lukas. "It must be you."

Jan frowns. But he is agile and alert to appearances. He swivels quickly and presses the holy instrument into Lukas's hand. Lukas looks at the filigreed handle with the pierced orb. She's asking him to perform her last rites. He doesn't want to, but he can't deny her the sacraments.

He steps forward. He sprinkles holy water on Aleys, and she spreads her palms open. The bishop hands him an alabaster bowl brimming with sacred oil. Aleys lifts her face. Lukas feels disturbed. To utter the benediction of death over this glowing girl is hideously wrong. And yet gloriously right. Lukas forms the shapes of the words with his lips, of *misericordiam*, of *Dominus.* "May the Lord pardon the sins you have committed by sight." He touches the oil to her eyelids with his thumb. The words feel both familiar and strange; Lukas has uttered them most weeks and just days ago over Sophia. But never has he applied them like salve to a creature so radiant with life. He smears the oil on Aleys's ears, her nostrils, her lips, pardoning crimes of the senses. He strokes the oil into her palms and forgives her the sins of touch, and thinks he is unworthy to touch her. Then he circles Aleys, bends to stroke oil down the soles of her feet: "May the Lord forgive you your faults in every step." It is a gesture so intimate that it sends a shock up his spine. Then it is done. Sister Aleys is faultless and prepared for death.

Somehow, he feels he's contaminated an angel. He resists the urge to raise her to her feet. He feels she would continue to rise and would hover over them, half in life and half in death. But Jan is already moving on, making the sign of the cross over Aleys. He sings out, "*Kyrie eleison. Christe eleison. Kyrie eleison. Pater noster.*"

Her cheeks glow with sunbursts of orange. Lukas smells flowers. In the midst of the frankincense, an aura of marigold surrounds the shriven Aleys. She looks up to the cross and he would swear Christ meets her eyes.

Look my way, he thinks. *Look at me.*

The bishop leads her, head bowed, to the door in the wall. Lukas bears the key. They form a small procession. The crowd follows them with their eyes. That's when he hears a cry. He looks back to see Griete sobbing into her hands. At the door, Aleys seems to stumble, to hesitate, but Lukas knows this too is part of the ritual. She would run to the cell if she could.

The bishop intones in full theater, relishing the drama, "If she wants to enter, then let her enter."

There's a pause. There is no sound but for Griete's sobs. *Turn back. Stay with us.* The crowd leans forward, and he feels their fascination at her sacrifice. Their breath is fetid with desire; they are eager to see a virgin entombed. Lukas wonders if it was thus, when Christ bore his cross through Jerusalem and the people lined the streets. The lust for death and spectacle, as if dogs have been set on the chained bear and blood is to be expected. It makes him angry. No one knows his private anguish. It's not too late. She can still change her mind.

But then Aleys nods her assent. It is her will. Lukas inserts the key in the lock, slides the bolt. He opens the door to her tomb. He stands back.

There is one last gesture. The bishop reaches into a velvet pouch hanging from his belt and exhumes a handful of dry soil. He throws it over Aleys. She raises her face to meet it. Dust to dust. She is dead to them now.

As Jan turns back to the congregants, triumphant, Lukas cannot take his eyes from Aleys. His last look. He tastes the dirt in his mouth. She steps into the cell, and he wants to grab her wrist, to stop her. Inside, she turns to face him. Framed by the door that will never again open, her eyes are calm. *Close the door*, they say, *leave me with my lover.* The dust has mingled with the oil on her lips, and somehow the sight is both ghastly and holy. *Bury me, Father.* And so Lukas closes the door, slides the bolt, and fastens the lock.

39

Aleys

Gone crowds. Gone words. Gone men. Gone children. Gone stars and moon and sky. Gone, gone, gone beyond, gone far beyond, gone to the distant shore. Aleys is free at last on the open sea.

Liber Tertius

40

ALEYS

Aleys wakes to the sound of someone rapping sharply on the window between her room and the parlor. She pulls back the curtain and unbolts the shutter. The other curtain is drawn open, but the parlor appears empty. It reminds her of peering into the decorated egg of Mary in the manger, the parlor plain but for an embroidered cloth on the side table and straw on the floor. It occurs to her that she's the one in the egg. If you looked through this window into her cell, you'd see fireplace, prie-dieu, cot. Anchoress.

The parlor door is half open and she can make out a wedge of cobbled street and, opposite, a wall. They appear oddly flat, like pieces in a puzzle. She dips her knees, craning to glimpse a slice of sky.

Marte appears suddenly in the window, startling and three dimensional. Aleys jumps.

"I'm to be your maid, miss." Marte does not look cheerful for it. But Marte never looks cheerful.

"I thought it was to be Cecilia. She's not ill, is she?"

Marte snorts. "Off to be married."

"To whom?" She recalls the scene at the brewery. "Rolf?"

Marte shakes her head. "No, miss, a Frenchman. She met him at the hospital, on the traveler's side." She scowls. "She'll be off to Paris."

"It was sudden, then?"

"As a pestilence."

Aleys laughs. "You think so well of marriage?"

Marte gives a dour grimace. "Head lice were better, miss. Your pottage." She shoves it through the window. "I'll just wait here while you eat it."

"Let us pray together."

Marte backs up a step. "I'm not taught in church prayer, miss. You pray. I'll just listen and be the better for it."

"You attend the evening readings."

"I like the stories, miss. Doesn't mean I know to pray like you."

"You could learn."

"The beguines' school is meant for those who will take the gray dress. Or children. One like me"—she shrugs a round shoulder, looks at the bowl on the sill—"I earn my keep."

"Well, then, I could—"

"That's kind of you, miss. I thank the Lord for my food and ask him to see me through the night. That's enough for the likes of me. The Lord needn't pay me extra attention. That's for you saints."

Aleys sighs. "I'm not a saint."

"Well, you're something out of the ordinary, miss. Healing them lepers and all."

"I didn't heal any lepers." Not that she knows of, anyway.

"That's not what the lepers say. Some of them have thrown away their rattles. You can't hear them coming anymore. Like as to bump into one of them round any corner." Marte clamps her mouth shut, like she's used more than her allotted words.

"Miss, you won't be letting your porridge go cold. I hurried over with it warm."

At first, the anchoress is a novelty. Crowds gather outside the hold, shove their way into the parlor, whisper plaints through the curtained window. Aleys might as well be the local apothecary taking orders for simples. She never sees the people; they speak to her through the dark square, and she must imagine them old or young or hale or infirm from the pitch and rasp of their voices. The windowsill forms the border between her hold and the disembodied, clamoring need in the parlor. Those who breach that no-man's-land, who try to brush the curtains aside, find that the saint in the box won't hesitate to crush their fingers with a snap of her wooden shutter.

From the street, people peer through the horn window, their silhouettes hovering indistinct against the panes. Aleys schools herself not to shrink back; she knows they can't actually see inside. But sometimes they knock to get her attention. It's unsettling. She tells herself that the town's fascination will wear off. It's like a first snow. People come out to gape at December's flakes, but soon her presence will be February slush, taken for granted.

They come for blessings, they come for kitchen table advice.

"He stole my goose."

"Her ill temper curdles the milk."

"There is this small matter of debt to the guild, nothing untoward, but I wondered if he might consider . . . ?"

"I have this carbuncle, see?"

She cannot see, thank heaven. She is protected by the black curtains. Without sight, without touch, the healing tingle comes less and less to her fingers. The people don't know that. They still believe. She yearns for nighttime, to be left alone with her prayers.

Lukas visits bearing exhortatory tracts regarding the hazards of loneliness. He warns her, through the curtain, that she must not succumb to the sin of despair. But her spiritual progress is more endangered by gossips than isolation, and she tells him that. So Marte is installed as gatekeeper. She is stern and forbidding, fierce, even. In the street outside the parlor, Marte plants her broom like a Templar plants a pike. None shall disturb the prayers of the recluse, be they saint's kin or devil's. Marte listens attentively for Aleys's *amen* before she admits anyone to the parlor. She shows them, one at a time, to a chair beneath the window, warns them to get to the point and keep their hands to themselves, then retires to the stool in the street outside the door, wrapping a shawl against the autumn chill.

Marte's is the only face Aleys sees. Twice a day, Aleys and Marte draw back the curtains. Marte passes the meal in; Aleys lifts the chamber pot over the sill. They are practical. Matters are concrete. Aleys learns every crease of Marte's brow, the subtle shades of her frown. The pursed frown, the resigned frown, the scowl that turns up in the corner when she tries not to laugh. It becomes a small sport, trying to make Marte laugh. Marte's plain face becomes the grounded touchstone to Aleys's reality. For with each passing week, the voices beyond the curtain become less corporal and the visions she receives more vivid.

Her hours are marked by prayer.

At Matins, in the black of night, Aleys rises to sing of his magnificence, of the sea, which he made, and of the dry land also. She pictures the swells and the vastness and the shelter of coves and relief of shore. Stars sing midnight hymns at Matins. His creation is revealed by candlelight, alive in her psalter. Cascades spill from the margins and pomegranates hang from the letters. The tiny book of hymn and lapis, psalm and leaf, contains his marvels. She does not need to have seen waterfalls to believe they exist.

At dawn, the hour of aurora and resurrection: *Lord, open my lips so that my mouth may proclaim your praise.* As the sun rises, the horn panes on her window glow, one by one, a ladder of praise. In her book, her fingers trace the images of spring, the robin's egg, the May lily. She is lost in the hour of Lauds, so that when she finally stands from the prie-dieu, her mouth is dry.

The first hour, Prime, holds pleas for strength, for truth, for mercy for the day to come. An enlargement of heart. *Hide not thy commandments. Teach me, Lord.* She remembers to eat.

At the third hour, as the sun bends toward its zenith, Aleys prays for charity to be poured into her breast, to burn with fire. To worship with mouth, tongue, mind, sense, action. She prays for the town, she prays for Sophia, for Lukas, for Marte. And when people come to her window, as they will at this hour, when they ask for her blessing, she pours unto them the warm milk of morning grace that is Terce.

Sext is the hour of crucifixion, the glory and the horror. Daylight turned dark as they nailed him to the noontime cross; this hour carries midnight in its soul. Noon is a trickster in splendid garb: The serpent beguiled Eve in this time without shadow. But noon is also the death that is victory, the fall that is redeemed. It is the hour where prayer bears paradox, where logic falters and faith must lead. At noon, Aleys prays for understanding that does not come.

It is in the ninth hour, Nones, the hour of his death, that the demons descend. The sun drops toward the sea and the spirit sinks with it. She prays the *Rerum*: *Grant to this day an unclouded end, an eve untouched by shadows of decay*. Some days her prayers are answered. But sometimes the horned beasts creep from the pages and her heart is unshielded. The demon, despair, and its servant, fatigue, hover at Nones.

Vespers is sunset. She sings the song of the gratitude that magnifies the Lord. Aleys sings with all her heart the words of her childhood: *Gloria Patri, et Filio, et Spiritui Sancto*. And always, always, as it was in the beginning, is now and ever shall be, world without end. There is a sweet softness to Vespers. From her cell, she conjures hills turning lavender, the last golden light on the oak. Her fingers trace the psalter waves as the sun slips beneath them, to where she cannot follow. Vespers is the hour of simple faith that the light will rise again.

She breathes trust into the last prayer, Compline. *Into thy hands, O Lord. You shall not be afraid of any terror by night, nor of the arrow that flies by day.*

She lingers over the image of the archer in her psalter who perpetually releases his arrow toward the silver-red doe curled at the foot of a monk in blue. The monk and doe are surrounded by a golden sky and framed in climbing ivy. The doe's face is lifted to the monk, who reads scripture from an open book. The doe is vulnerable and yearning; she leans in to hear his words. Aleys traces the path of the archer's arrow and cannot tell if it will pierce the deer. She doesn't know if the doe will live. She closes the psalter and sleeps a dreamless sleep in mystery.

At Matins, she rises for the midnight prayer. At Lauds she celebrates his dawn. Eight times a day she praises him. She feels him drawing near.

Her third night, in the unnamed hours, she hears spirits. Aleys lies rigid, her cheek against her sleeve, her ears as eyes into the pure darkness. Then, out of nothing, a whisper. She opens her eyes wide, as if she could see through ink. Then, again, she hears it, a rustling, quiet as the wings of bees on petals. Nothing. Then, once more, the sound. She laughs, for she realizes the commotion is her eyelashes brushing her sleeve. She blinks several times, and it is a flock of mallards taking flight. She rolls onto her back and laughs, imagining the ducks winging away. The air in her cell is dense as pudding. She feels, enfolded within stone, the stillness of the catacomb. She imagines the stone walls thick as miles, stretching on and on, so that there is nothing under heaven save the rock and this pocket of stillness, which is hers to violate with laughter and prayer and the flight of winged eyelashes.

But other nights, she is most definitely not alone, her cell porous to the world. Some nights, the echo of incense drifts through the squint like the sighs of angels. Sometimes, midnight creatures visit, loud as elk crashing through brush. These do not frighten her; she knows it's just mice crept in through the squint or dropped from the parlor sill. They patter the length of the cell, scouting for crumbs, their squeaks like shouts in the marketplace. She tucks her blanket around her feet. She doesn't really mind the mice. They're company in the dark.

That is, until the morning her eyes fall on her prie-dieu and she recoils, hands to her mouth. For the upper corner of her psalter—its sumptuous calfskin cover, silky to the touch, embossed with vines—is eaten away. From the once smooth and perfect edge, shredded threads of leather dangle. Aleys brings herself to touch the defiled leather gently, like she would the mangled ear of a favorite dog. Tears spring to her eyes; she kisses it. Oh, Mama, she thinks. How could I have failed to protect our psalter? I've been careless. I should have slept with the prayer book in my hands. Aleys clutches Mama's treasure to her breast, looks around for the villain.

When Marte comes, she receives the psalter from Aleys with both hands. "Miss, your book." She frowns. "'Tis the rats. They used to chew through our harnesses, at the farm. Once, Dagmar's boot . . ." She stops. Marte has seen too much of Dagmar's boot.

It's not rats, Aleys wants to protest, *it's just mice*, but she realizes she doesn't know that. The thought of rats in her cell, their long bald tails, horrifies her.

"Miss, shall I be taking your book to the saddler, then? I don't know if he can repair it to what it was, seeing as it's so fine, but he can round down the corner for you." She opens it. "At least your pages are whole, which is a miracle, since rats are like to eat anything." She turns a page and pauses. "Oh my. I didn't know as there'd be pictures." She looks up. She's actually blushing, stoic Marte. "Do all the prayer books have these?"

Aleys nods. "The better ones." She sees desire flare in Marte's eyes.

"They go with the stories?"

"Of course. See, there's the harrowing of hell." She points at a drawing of Christ, his robes flowing behind him, reaching down into a pit for the hands of Adam and Eve, first to emerge. They look stunned. The sinners in the cauldrons look optimistic.

Marte turns the pages. A hushed reverence falls over her. "And this?" She stops at an image of a woman pouring from a pitcher, while another woman sits at the feet of Christ. "This would be Martha?"

"Your namesake."

She nods, solemnly. "Martha, as was scolded by Christ for doing her work. I'll see that the saddler takes right care of your book, miss. But you cannot have such a book as this, alone in your cell, what with rats and all."

She tucks the psalter into her apron pocket and bangs out the door, and Aleys wants to leap after the book, through the parlor window, but it's too small. She's left rubbing the empty silk pouch between her fingers.

When Marte returns, Aleys hears a scuffle in the parlor. "Miss, open your window, quick-like!"

Aleys unbolts the parlor shutter, sweeps aside the curtain. Marte shoves something through, a stiff parcel of caramel fury. It jumps to the ground of the cell and immediately begins to hiss. The orange demon resolves into a cat the color of burnt sugar.

"There, miss. That should be the end of your rats."

Aleys skeptically eyes the animal, who eyes her back just as warily. He backs into the far corner, his back arched. Mama never let cats into the house. She said they were bad luck. But surely rats are worse luck. The cat's ears are pressed flat against his skull. His eyes are green unblinking globes.

"Here, give him this." Marte hands through a cloth with a fish head on it. "A cat'll never leave you once you give him a cod noddle." Sure enough, the cat lifts his nose, sniffs the air. "Ah, he's a hungry one," says Marte encouragingly.

Aleys places the napkin on the floor near the hearth. The cat hesitates, then walks over, grabs the fish head, and retreats behind Aleys's prie-dieu. She hears him rip apart the flesh. Perfect. She will pray over fish bones.

"He'll get in and out your window, miss, if you keep the shutter open. I'll leave the parlor door ajar. Just give him a fish head for a few nights, and he'll stay, I'm sure of it."

"Marte, thank you. It's a kindness."

"If he's a yowler, miss, then you might not thank me for it."

"As long as he doesn't chew my psalter."

"Oh, here, miss." She pulls the psalter from her pocket. The edge is smoothed. It will never be the same, but nor is it dangling flesh. "I looked at it. Your book. It's all in Latin language?"

"Yes."

"The stories, they're the same as those the beguines read after dinner?"

"The very same."

"The beguines' stories don't have pictures."

"No."

"But I could read them? The Dutch ones."

"If you were taught, you could."

Marte picks up the broom, begins sweeping the clean parlor with furious strokes. Her frown tightens. Then she stops, gripping the broom in both hands, and turns to Aleys.

"I could read the stories?"

And so the hours between Prime and Terce belong to Marte. She shuts and bars the parlor door and they ignore the pounding of petitioners. It is just the two of them and the cat. They begin as all reading lessons ever have, with letters that form sounds, words, a name, another name. Marte brings a charcoal. They write words on the sill between them and wipe them off, their palms and sleeves dark with dust. *Feet*, *hands*, *tears*, *cross*, *mercy*. *Child*. *Sky*. Marte writes *peas*; Aleys writes *porridge*. *The Lord eats peas porridge*. Marte smiles, a lopsided thing, quickly gone, but truly earned. The words lace them together.

Marte is the only real person in the world to her now.

There is also the cat—whom they call by its three-letter word, Kat—who jumps up to the sill that is both border and slate, so they have to shoo him off to write *dog*. Kat eats cod. Kat comes. Kat goes. Kat mostly sleeps. He claims two sleeping spots. By day, he sleeps on the ledge of the horn window, his orange back to the orange panes, as if all things orange in the world belong against the outside wall. At night, when he isn't prowling, he sleeps between Aleys's shins, his bulk a warm loaf from the oven. Kat weaves around her as she prays. He has one white paw. Sometimes he lifts it to her forearm. *I'm here*, he says. *With you*.

She cannot believe it sinful to love him, but sometimes she wonders.

Marte brings pages of Katrijn's Dutch gospel, hidden in her basket. They read together and Marte copies the text for herself. Her hand grows more and more steady, the letters take shape. She even adds some crude flourishes, pictures in the margins, illuminated letters. "I should ink these words in gold," she says. When she stands guard outside the parlor door, Marte recites the alphabet like a prayer, under her breath, over and over. She has great faith in the written word, does Marte.

Snow blankets the city. The canals freeze, unfreeze, freeze again. Aleys presses her hand to the amber panes. They are cool beneath her fingers, but Aleys is warm within.

She feels the change inside her, deep within, her body the hold within the hold. She is an ocean. From a distance, she appears calm and unperturbed, reflecting the shadows of birds. This is how the town imagines her. But it's far from true. Aleys feels herself in constant motion, full of swells and tides, insights that crash in sound and froth, then pull back across scoured sands, out of reach, lost. She empties herself of her own weather, waits. Still, still. *Come, my Lord, and stay awhile.*

He does come to her, in mysteries. The wave pulls back and back, drawing itself up, grinding across ocean floor, pulling pebble and sand, barnacled rock and bending coral. The fishes are drawn up into the mountain and all is laid bare beneath, a plain of rubble small and particular, and she but a grain of sand singing to the magnificence. The peaked wave contains the violence and the compassion, the trinity, and it flickers between him and her and spirit, poised, breath held, and it says you are grain and you are wave, you are mine, I am yours, and it crashes down in a terrible roar and she is crushed and uplifted and swirled into its waters, dissolved and free.

She lifts her head and tastes the brine in her mouth and knows herself grateful for the sheer, terrible beauty. Her prayers hold the fury and depth of oceans.

“Marte, I have received the most wondrous understanding!” She thinks, I must share this vision. It changes everything.

“Have you, miss?” Marte is busying herself with laying a fire in the parlor hearth.

“I have, this very morning. Christ came down and he was a wave, I cannot say, he was a mountain and ocean in one . . .”

“Yes, miss, I’m sure he was.”

“Marte, listen! It was so marvelous.”

“Pass me your pisspot, miss.”

“But Marte.”

“You best get back to your prayers, miss. I don’t know from visions, those things aren’t for my kind. The stories in the book’s enough for me, miss. You tell Friar Lukas, that would be best.”

But she doesn’t want to tell Lukas.

His visits are a scrape of chair and a voice behind the curtain. “You are well, Sister?” He comes to offer advice and take confession.

“Yes, Father, I am well.”

“Your prayers, are they . . .”

“I keep the hours.”

“Yes, but are your prayers answered? Does he visit you?”

No, not him. Not exactly. It’s even more wonderful. There are no words to explain the tides within her, the waves that crush and cleanse, that she speaks with God but can’t say how or why. She can’t bring herself to tell Lukas. Something in her resists the tone in his voice. He’s too eager, prying, like the people who try to peer through the panes of her window. She remembers too well how he would grasp her wrists to feel them buzz. Aleys composes her hands in her lap. She knows she shouldn’t fend off her spiritual director.

“I . . . I have been praying,” she says, “to receive him.”

"You must not despair."

I am quite far from that. "I will not despair."

"You—have you been healing people?"

"No, Father, I think that gift is gone from me." She doesn't tell him what a relief that is.

"It has." He is silent. "Well, we must not expect his favors always." Aleys waits. "Well, then." He sounds resigned. "You are eating?"

"Yes, Father."

"I will hear your confession. You must not give up hope."

She keeps the visions to herself. Though Lukas visits from field and flower, market and sky, she feels he sits in the empty cell. How can she confess that to him? It's too cruel.

She's not keeping secrets. Not really.

41

Marte

I can read.
I can write.

I can begin a new tale.

Marte fingers the scrap of parchment in her apron pocket. Throughout the day, in moments snatched from to and fro, between simmer and boil, punch and knead, this is her touchstone. Some keep saints' medals, some rabbits' feet. This paper, these words, are Marte's. She wrote them without even the help of Miss Aleys, and none, not Ida, not Katrijn, and most surely not her cur of a husband, have seen them. She didn't even copy this. She wrote it herself. At night Marte tucks the scrap between her forehead and upper arm and hugs it there, safe, until dawn, when she slips it back into her apron. She feels a new story, her own, gathering in her pocket. What it will be, she doesn't know. Sometimes she drops in an acorn, sometimes a coin, a sprig of thyme, to brush up against her first words, to see how they mix.

She has told Miss Ida that she is learning to read, in Dutch, and Ida replied, "That is very good, can you write, too?" Marte nodded. Ida is her favorite of the beguines. Ida doesn't throw words about like chaff on the wind. Ida asks where others bark. And while Ida doesn't smile overmuch, neither does she scowl at empty air like Katrijn. Marte is loyal to Miss Aleys, sure, and grateful, but Aleys can be powerful odd, and who can trust a saint? Marte flexes her foot. No, Ida is her favorite. Ida comes from the bottom, like her. Ida remembers the bottom.

Marte shifts her basket from her left hip to her right and blows on her hands to warm them as she steps onto Maria Bridge. There's just enough time to sweep the beguines' chapel and trim the wicks in the reading room before setting out supper. She leans over the rail for the fishmonger. He's on his stool in his flat-bottomed boat, whittling a dolphin from a piece of wood, surrounded by drying husks of saltwater fish.

"How much a mackerel?" she shouts down. The women prefer cod, but Katrijn has put them on a tight budget. Everything about the begijnhof has become tight.

"For the beguines? Or the saint?"

"Their stomachs growl the same."

"Then tenpence for mackerel and I'll throw in a cod and ask the saint to bless the catch."

Marte nods. He tosses up a rope and she lowers down her basket for the fish.

Miss Ida will be coming out of the hospital any moment now and they'll walk back to the begijnhof together. Ida says the hospital is less frenzied since Aleys left for the hold. Marte sees Ida's brow crease; she misses Aleys. There's some sort of fellowship among healers, Marte supposes. "You could come visit her," says Marte. Ida shakes her head. Katrijn has forbidden it.

Katrijn has forbidden many things. Second servings of ale, singing in the courtyard. They're in mourning. When they gather in the evenings, Marte feels a sadness descend upon the reading room; Sophia's absence is most present in this hour. Katrijn still translates, but it's only the begats, not the parables, as if to interpret any lesson without Sophia would be to betray her.

At least I can read the old stories on my own now, Marte thinks, those that have been translated. There's a stack of them hidden in the back of the reading room cupboard.

Ida emerges from the hospital, tucking a strand of raven hair into her wimple. "Marte," she says, brightening. "You waited. Can we stop by the Lakenhalle? Katrijn's set aside linen for the women's ward."

"Oh, miss, you don't want to go in there. It's full of men."

Ida smiles like Mistress Sophia did when she was amused. "They're no worse than the scoundrels in the hospital. You'll come with me."

Marte has never been inside the cloth hall. The enormous building reminds her of the night she limped into the city, her eye swollen tight and her heart bruised. Torchlight flickered over the wet cobblestones, which were strange underfoot and made her unsteady. When the great Lakenhalle bell tolled, Marte clapped her hands over her ears and felt her innards tremble. She kept to the edges of the square that evening, unsure where to go, fingering the two coins in her pocket. Finally, as the torches burned down and the plaza emptied, Marte crept under the arched entryway of the butchers' guild house and made herself small beneath the crossed stone cleavers. She stuffed her cold fingers under her arms and gripped her sides and felt waves of loss move through her. When the Lakenhalle rang in the morning, Marte stood and vowed to carry her grief silently.

No one in the city knows about her child. No one here saw the small shrouded body of Mathild strewn with straw and clover. As the first shovel of wet soil hit her daughter, Marte felt the last tether to Dagmar snap. She quit the village the next day. She left behind everyone who had known her as a mother. When the beguines took Marte in, she said nothing of the child who would spin round and round until she staggered against the hayrick, dizzy with laughter. Nothing about the endless night Marte ran a wet cloth over Mathild's fevered body, how she couldn't stop, even after her daughter's limbs cooled and stiffened. For how could Marte describe her daughter—how can a mother describe her child who is gone? Any attempt would be a falling away. Every word would make Mathild less real.

Now Marte reaches into her pocket to touch her parchment, to remind herself. I can read. I can write. I have the beguines. Everything is different now. Marte draws a deep breath.

I am not afraid of this city.

Ida takes Marte's arm as they cross the Markt, skirting beggars and money changers. The ring of hammer on wood is sharp in the cold air. Carpenters are knocking together a stage in front of the guild houses. "For the Nativity," says Ida. "The goldsmiths are sponsoring this year. Just wait and see. Everyone loves the Christmas plays." That's because they can't read, thinks Marte. If only they could see how their measly plays pale in comparison. When you read, you can turn the words over and over like a puzzle that is both new and familiar every time.

Half a dozen men in patterned hose and bicolor tunics burst from the entrance of the Lakenhalle, and Ida and Marte turn sideways to thread their way among them. Inside, the great hall is loud with the voices of drapers shouting in Dutch to their boys and in foreign tongues—German, maybe, or Italian—to well-heeled buyers with fat purses hanging from their leather belts. A dusty light filters from high windows. The hall is lined with the stalls of guildmembers, alcoves stacked to the ceilings with wool and worsted in indigo and green, but also in colors that simple folk aren't allowed, scarlets and yellows, even royal purple. Like a jumbled rainbow. In one stall, Marte glimpses rare silk.

"From Byzantium," whispers Ida over the hubbub, following her gaze. The stalls have doors that can be pulled shut and locked, and buckets of water stand in the corners. For good reason, thinks Marte. A loose spark in here would destroy the wealth of a small kingdom.

"The magistra has a shop here?" There are a few women drifting from stall to stall, followed by servants. It's hard to imagine Katrijn, even Katrijn, running her own business among these men in velvet tunics and feathered caps. Then, in the far corner, Marte spots a large woman with a leather purse strapped across her simple gray, in an alcove stacked with shades of brown wool that the beguines have beaten and carded and spun. The guild has slapped regulations on the begijnhof—no dyes—but even from a distance you can see that their cloth has a finer weave than most. On a stool beside Katrijn is the pile of linen for the hospital. Marte starts over.

"Wait." Ida grabs her arm, eyes wide. "I know that man. The bishop's spy."

Marte squints through the crowd. A slender man with a trimmed beard has slid alongside the magistra's stall. Katrijn looks at him, eyes narrowed. She reddens. She shakes her head. Marte makes out the words on her lips. *No, it's . . .* The view is blocked by people crossing the hall; when it clears, the man is gesturing. His back is to them. Then he's removing his cap and pressing it to his chest. He bows. *No, stop*, Katrijn seems to say, digging into her purse and thrusting a handful of coins at him. The man is backing off, smiling, before he turns and melts into the crowd.

Ida is already crossing the hall. "Katrijn!"

Their new magistra looks up, startled. Her hands are tight on her purse. She looks shaken, like she's just received very bad news. Or a threat.

"What did he want?" demands Ida.

"Oh." Katrijn looks away, up at the wool folded on the shelves. "Altar," she says. "Altar cloth."

Ida's eyes flick to Marte. "We don't make altar cloth."

"That's what I told him," says Katrijn, her face pinching. "Women are forbidden the sacred colors."

Marte shakes her head at Ida. *Don't ask more. Not now.*

That evening, Katrijn announces she can't translate anymore, not even the begats. The demands of draper and magistra leave her no time. They'll have to make do with rereading what scripture they have.

42
ALEYS

Aleys kneels at her squint as Lukas elevates the host, arms outstretched. Watching Mass through a small window concentrates the experience, she thinks. There's no distraction from fidgeters, no looking for dust motes over bowed heads. Nothing but the sacred ritual. She notices that the candlelight strikes the wafer from below so that it shines like a distant moon above Lukas. He takes in the body of the Savior, then drinks Christ's blood from the chalice, and she wonders whether he is filled with spirit or whether it is merely flour and grape in his mouth. Maybe she doesn't want to know. He places aside the paten with her wafer and blesses the congregants.

The church clears out, the people emptied of their sins, eager to fill themselves with dinner. Aleys watches Lukas utter some instructions to the altar boy, hears the child skip toward the door. The doors shut and silence falls. She remains on her knees.

Lukas approaches the squint, coming in and out of view as he walks toward her with the plate, so that it is startling when he appears large before her. "Sister," he says, "behold the Lamb of God. Behold him who taketh away the sins of the world."

Aleys leans into the squint, wedges her open mouth into the cross. She feels like a baby bird, stretched wide, yellow throat exposed. She doesn't like the feeling. She has to remind herself: You're receiving Christ, not Friar Lukas.

Aleys repeats to herself a verse from the Canticle. *My beloved put his hand through the window, and my inner self was moved by his touch.* She must be open to receive. And to give. She should tell him about the visions.

Next time.

Friar Lukas dips the wafer in the wine and places it on her tongue. "*Corpus Christi*," he says.

"Amen," she replies, pulling back into her enclosure with her beloved.

When God returns, he is Christ is mother is child is Aleys. She is the infant in the manger, she has entered the egg. She vibrates with life, without edges, seeping into the sheep, the kings, the sky. This nativity is made of layers and layers of moment, as dense and pointed as the six-tipped star above Bethlehem, exquisite beyond description. Her birth, his birth, all births in one.

And then the vision shifts. Mary the mother becomes Christ the son who reaches a hand to Aleys. *Come, beloved, we are waiting for you.* He kisses her hands, and she knows herself blessed.

When she opens her eyes, Mary is before the hearth. The blue of lapis surrounds her, a vivid aura emanating from her naked flesh; she is unrobed. This is not the doe-eyed Mary, not the humble Mary. This Mary is ferocious, hair radiating coiled and bristled from her head, teeth bared. She is swollen to the size of a mountain with Christ. Her hands present her naked belly. Mary's eyes are uncompromising. She smells of charred wood. *The priests are blind*, she says. *The pillars crumble. If you would join us, you must bear the truth.*

But what does that mean? What does all of it mean?

Marte comes bearing porridge in the morning. "Miss," she says as she passes over the bowl, "you look like you've seen a ghost."

"A ghost?" Aleys laughs. "Quite the opposite. Mary came to me in the night." Aleys knows Marte is wary of the visions, but didn't Mary just bid her to bear the truth?

Marte steps back from the window. "Christ's mother?" Aleys spoons the porridge into her mouth and nods. "You mean in a dream, like?"

"She was real."

Marte looks at her sharply. "You're sure?"

Aleys swallows. "As real as you."

Marte considers this, turning to straighten the cloth on the parlor table. She steps back and folds her arms. "Miss, can I ask you something?"

"Of course."

"Why do they visit you, who can read the Latin for yourself?" She nods toward the bound Bible on Aleys's desk, the Latin scripture Lukas brings her to copy for personal study.

"Why do they speak in showings? I suppose they have more to say."

"More than is in the book?" Marte sounds skeptical. It's a long book.

"Yes." Aleys hesitates. "It's not always easy to understand what they mean."

"Hmphph," says Marte. Then she adds, inexplicably, "I can see why Saint Mary has words to add. She lost her child. Seems like the scripture abandoned her like yesterday's bread after that."

The curtain is black, a gulf between. Aleys will confess everything to Lukas.

"*Confiteor Deo* . . . I confess to God and the Blessed Virgin Mary and to you, Father, because I have sinned exceedingly in life." Her voice is strong as it recites the formula. And then: "Oh, why do we waste time speaking of sin when the sun rises so splendid? I have much to tell you. Last night, I was shown marvels, I have seen . . . I have seen Saint Mary. And"—she hesitates—"God. He is love. We have misunderstood. Everything he does is love, everything is—"

"You have seen him?"

"Yes. He is magnificent beyond imagination."

"He showed himself to you? How?"

"He . . . she . . . they . . . I was Mother and Father, groom and bride, not even those poles, it was all encompassing, it was just . . ."

"Just what?"

"Oh, words are but watered wine. I could say *light*, I could say *glory*, I could say *Holy, Holy, Holy*. I should sing. Only music could approach his beauty."

"Show me your face."

"What?"

"If he has visited you, if he has entered your cell . . ." She detects a note of jealousy. "I need to see your countenance."

"Why?"

"I have to report this. If you have indeed received our Savior's touch, it will show itself on your body."

"I cannot."

"Aleys." He is impatient. "You vowed chastity, not invisibility. Don't make a disobedience out of virtue. Show yourself."

She swallows, pushes aside the curtain, and they are face-to-face. He recoils, blinking, like a man who has stepped from a cave into sunlight. As he inhales, the anger drains from his face, replaced with longing, as if he is seeing the sacred, as if she is the silvered angel in the January woods.

"Aleys," he moans.

"Father."

"You are alight with spirit." He closes his eyes. When he finally opens them, they are wet.

She can feel it is true.

"He has been with you," he says. "The King has brought you into his chambers."

She bows her head, feeling a blush on her cheek, unable to meet his gaze. "Father, what I have understood, I hardly dare say, for how can I explain it?"

"Tell me. You must."

"They showed me." She speaks in awe. "All is God. All. The good, the bad, we have misunderstood. There is nothing else. Nothing exists but is God." She pauses. "Father," she whispers, "my *me* is God."

43

Friar Lukas

It's more than he can bear.

He lets the black curtain fall back into place.

She prays, Christ answers. He begs, she receives. She asks, she receives. He preaches, people turn away. He blesses with cold hands. She strokes a brow, it heals. He asks, he begs, nothing.

Nothing.

Why? He's been obedient. Poor. Chaste. He's founded an order. Why would God raise the student above the teacher?

Aleys speaks of a love he's read about, yearned for, but has never felt. Christ kisses her. Lukas knows he shouldn't watch, that madness follows such jealousy. Yet he can't tear his eyes from the courtship of his protégée and his God.

Lukas knows his duty. He should be a joyful servant, not a covetous spouse.

And how is he supposed to respond to her ecstasy? He doesn't dare open his mouth for fear of what he might say, for fear that he might spew venom over the sill between them. He knows this is wrong. Envy is an error. A sin. He places his hands on the stone frame of the window, bends his head into the fabric of the curtain. She's just on the other side. For a moment, he thinks he should confess to her. But the shepherd does not confide in the sheep. He turns away.

When Lukas leaves the parlor, demons jump from the ledge to follow, keeping to the fringed shadows of the street. He glances at them and wonders that others can't see the darkness trailing him.

Hervé watches him with furrowed brow. Hervé puts extra rations in his bowl, observes that they go untouched. Hervé interrupts an argument between two young friars. Take that outside, he says, glancing at Lukas, who merely stares into the fire.

"You're not sleeping," he says gently.

There are demons in the night, Lukas wants to explain, but can't, because he leads these men. He can't speak of the fiends that crouch in the corners of the friary; how they whisper to each other in susurrus and go quiet when he looks at them. In the darkness, they slide between the cots, always toward him, toward him. He wakes with a start and knows he's not dreaming. The ash stirs in the grate and orange eyes wink from the cinder.

Hervé offers him wine and dishes of lamb. Lukas has no idea where he got such fare, what compromises he made to obtain it. Food has turned bitter on his tongue, and he knows its cause. He shakes his head at Hervé. There is no cure for his envy.

Lukas prays for days on end. Instead of joy, a beastly greed creeps into his penance. He fasts until his stomach screams. Nothing. He applies the strap to his back, opening wounds, so that something, anything, will hurt more than this. Nothing. He feels his obedience like a plug lodged in his chest, starving him of blood, of the pulse of matter, the flesh of passion. His tongue sticks to the roof of his mouth as if to a starched cathedral. He tastes the wafer, always the wafer. He thirsts for wine.

Lukas returns to the glade of his vows. He lifts his robe and sinks his bare knees into the dirt until the cold mud cups his bones. He flattens the tops of his feet against the ground. He will not move until he gets an answer.

My Father, who art in Heaven, you are the word, the rule, the beginning without end.

I am but your servant.

Help me understand.

Show me a sign.

He thinks, The girl's very desire, her lush desire, draws God like a magnet. Lukas reaches inside for his own passion, but it crumbles like dry leaves. He tries to recall what it felt like to be young, to be fresh as a sapling, to turn toward the sun. He wants to say, *You could have at least told me that my way was wrong. You could have told me there's another way.*

Let me feel, Lord. Make me feel alive, he prays.

He waits. There's no answer, save a breeze that rattles the bare limbs. He regards his hands. His palms are dry, his wrists dry, his fingers dry. If he were to cut himself, would he even bleed? He imagines drawing a knife over his wrist, the long slow slice parting his skin, pressing deep to find nothing but desiccated meat to the bone.

Finally, he speaks. "You made me, Lord. You made me a creature of reason." He is so frustrated. "Why do you require passion?"

He waits. A quiet rain begins. A drop here, a drop there, upon the ground, whispering as they strike the leaves. He doesn't look up. He bows his head. He waits for a sign. The patter intensifies; the rain is all around him now. The droplets are sprinkling his shaved head, running down his neck. Perhaps the skies will part, the rain will cease, he will be given a sign. But the water just keeps coming, until it's a steady hushed wash, until his hands glisten with it, until his robe is soaked. He doesn't see that every drop holds answers.

Then he thinks of her, in the begijnhof courtyard, face tipped back to meet the rain.

It occurs to him then. She is the sign.

There is an antidote to the daytime poison he drinks. The source of sickness is the source of cure. Only Aleys can heal him.

44

MARTE

Marte passes tied birch bundles through the window, then live coals in a bucket, so Aleys can rebuild her fire.

"You're lucky, miss, with the bishop providing so well for you. He doesn't stint on your keeping. You're warmer than the beguines, that I can tell you."

"You don't keep the fires burning in the begijnhof?"

"Well, miss, money is tight." What with the new regulations on the begijnhof wool, they barely make ends meet. "There's firewood for the cooking. And we keep the reading room warm. Though—" Marte breaks off.

"Though what?"

"It's just that it's never the same since Mistress Sophia passed. And Mistress Katrijn has stopped, well, you know. We have no new stories. We reread the old ones, over and over again. They're good, sure, but it's not like new ones."

"You want more."

"That's what I'm saying, miss." Marte can see Kat on the ledge of the horn window, eyeing the parchment on the desk like it might escape. "Maybe you could read me that?" She points at the scripture.

"In Latin?"

Sometimes Miss Aleys's head is too much in her prayers. "No, miss, I can go to church for that. I mean, maybe you could tell them to me in Dutch?"

Aleys smiles. "When I was small, my mother read me the saints' lives. Well, she wasn't lettered, but she knew their stories. I could read to you. Is there one you want?"

"What about the woman turned to salt?" Marte knows there was a wicked woman that God turned into a pillar of salt, but she doesn't know what for. It must have been something terrible.

"Lot's wife, you mean?"

"That one."

Aleys moves to her table and shuffles through the parchment.

"Here. Genesis." She plucks out a page and returns to her stool inside the window. Marte takes the parlor seat. She slides her hand into her pocket and rubs her nail along a small goose quill she picked up that morning.

"Go ahead, miss. I'm listening."

Aleys explains that Lot was a righteous man living in Sodom, a city known for its wickedness. A pair of angels arrived at his home. "He prepared a meal for them, baking bread without yeast, brood zonder gist, and they ate."

Marte tries to imagine angels at the door. "What were their wings like?" In Aleys's psalter, there are angels of many varieties. Most of them have white wings they keep pinned back like their feathers might get in the way of chores. Others bear luminous wings of green and red and gold raised high above their halos.

Aleys hesitates. "I'm not sure they had wings. I think these two came disguised as men."

Well, that's a problem, thinks Marte. How are you supposed to recognize angels if they hide their wings?

Aleys continues, "The men of this evil town clamored at Lot's door and demanded he hand over the strangers so they could have their way with them."

"Have sex with them? The angels?"

"I don't think the crowd knew they were angels."

That's what comes of leaving your wings behind, thinks Marte. But it would be rude, angel or no, to yield your guests to a mob.

"Lot spoke to the crowd." Aleys angles the page to catch more light from the horn window; it's too early to light candles. "'Look,' he said, 'I have two daughters who have never slept with a man. Let me bring them out to you, and you can do what you like with them.'"

"He said what?"

"Lot offered up his daughters in place of the angels."

To be raped? Marte doesn't understand. "Miss, I thought you said Lot was righteous."

"I know. It's . . . difficult. I think he managed to keep them safe inside."

Marte gives a snort. "This is the man God chose to save?"

"Well, the angels warned him to leave town with his family. He took his wife and youngest daughters. Just not their two married ones."

How they love their virgins in this book. "What was wrong with the married daughters?"

"Their husbands thought Lot was joking when he said God was about to destroy Sodom. They laughed and refused to leave."

"Lot's wife must have had words for her sons-in-law." Not to mention Lot, offering up her girls to the crowd. Marte would have left him, right there. That man was worse than Dagmar.

"Yes, well. The angels shepherded Lot and his wife and unmarried daughters into the hills. The angels ordered them not to look back, even as the Lord rained burning sulfur onto Sodom, and terrible cries rose from the city. But Lot's wife looked back."

Of course she did. Two of her children were in that town. How could a mother not respond to the cries of her daughters? Marte knows. She would have looked back, too.

"And so God turned Lot's wife into a pillar of salt?" Marte is incredulous. This is the crime that God smites her for?

"She was disobedient."

Marte gives a huff. "It's a strange story, miss. What does God want from us—obedience or love?"

Aleys frowns, unable to explain the Bible raining brimstone on mothers. But the answer seems obvious.

Marte points to the Latin scripture. "Men wrote this down, didn't they?"

"Yes."

"I don't think they wrote the whole story."

Marte fingers the quill in her pocket. People need the whole story.

45

ALEYS

Aleys tosses and turns into the night, pondering Mary's message. *You must bear the truth.* But what truth? The truth of the visions shown only to her, or the truth of the book kept by priests? They don't always agree. Both are hard to decipher. She dozes off, finally, open questions stirring her dreams.

In the small hours, between Matins and Lauds, Aleys wakes to the sound of weeping. It takes her a confused moment to realize the voice isn't coming from the parlor. Someone, a man, is outside her squint. People know the church is open, and some seek a companion in midnight sorrow. Their feathered cries flutter around her cell like trapped birds. Aleys swings her feet to the cold ground and draws her blanket about her shoulders, sending Kat to the floor.

An ashen moonlight graces the cross of her squint, so that it appears outlined in silver. Aleys edges quietly over. She will witness. She sets her head back against the wall and listens to the gasp, the poised silence, the spill and surge of breath as it cascades into sob. Aleys pulls her awareness inside. She inhales his anguish in long sweeps. The man's pain fills her lungs, hot and deep beneath her ribs, but she doesn't falter. She prays for the unseen man. And slowly, mercifully, in the far branch and flower of her lungs, in an alchemy of prayer, his heated breath cools, and she releases her calm as gift. She weeps and breathes with him for some time. The moonlight from the chancel has cast a blue cross on the floor at her feet. It is peace.

When the man speaks, his voice is thick. "Aleys," says Friar Lukas.

She recoils, stumbles back against her bed. The warmth drains from her. How can it be Lukas? Her confessor shouldn't come crying to her. Her skin crawls beneath her nightshift. It's an inversion of order, like father supplicating son, mother pleading to child. She has inhaled his pain into the depths of her lungs, where its tentacles have entered her blood.

"Aleys," he repeats. His voice is too close.

She could feign sleep, but he must know she's listening. She thinks of his tear-dappled face and feels not charity, but revulsion.

"I . . ." His voice catches. "I must ask you."

No. No more crying. You must not weep at me. You are supposed to be stronger. You are my spiritual director. You should have the answers, not the questions.

"*Ego sum homo malus uir* . . . I am a wicked man and hostile to my own self. I must confess to you."

"Father, no. Not to me."

"Ask our God to deliver me from evil, for I suffer the torment of devils."

What is he saying? This is so wrong. "You must confess to the bishop."

"The bishop cannot heal me."

"I cannot—"

"Sister, you must help me. Warm me with your prayers."

She hears him draw even closer to the squint. Then, through the cross, over the lip, his fingers curve, a long, pale spider on her sill. She looks away, but sees only the black shadow of his fingers inside the blue cross on her floor. He has breached her safehold. It is a trespass most foul.

"My hand," he pleads. "Take my hand." She doesn't want to touch him. "Have you no charity?"

"Father, don't ask this of me."

"Sister Aleys," says Friar Lukas, and it is the voice of authority. She feels the obedience rise within her like a raised stick, and she swallows her revulsion and takes his hand. It sends a cold wave up her arm. He is her confessor. She has vowed submission.

"Aleys, why? Why does God favor you so?"

46

The Bishop

Jan finds Lukas outside the Lakenhalle, sermonizing on the evils of capital to an assembly of beggars. He might as well preach to pigs about the dangers of flight. Jan will say this of his little brother, though. He never gives up.

Jan shoos away his men and waits for Lukas to finish. It's a warm day for February, the skies cloudless. He stretches his shoulders back. Lukas, he notices, looks worse. The skin on his face seems to droop. His robe pulls concave where his belt cinches it. How his brother eats from people's scraps every day, he cannot fathom. It's a recipe for flux. Perhaps he should call a surgeon for Lukas to let off a little blood.

He knows the sermon will end with the noon bell. It's contrived and predictable. The people know it, too. At the tenth stroke, they turn to scatter. When they see the bishop standing behind them, they make small bows and give him wide berth. He strides over the cobbles.

"I think you won over some widows today. Soon every crone will be wearing brown."

Lukas doesn't rise to the bait. Jan peers at him. The lining of his eyes is moist and scarlet. "Are you ill?"

A group of merchants look their way, and Jan raises his hand in benediction. They see him talking with Lukas and someone laughs. Jan bristles. He doesn't like it when they laugh at Lukas. It reminds Jan of how he had to stick up for his brother when larger boys would push him around. How he'd had to defend Lukas against their father's mockery. Jan doesn't like anyone to call his younger brother weak.

"Are you not well, Lukas?" he repeats.

Lukas bows his head. "Jan, it's worse than that. I'm bedeviled."

Oh Lord, it's another one of his moods.

"You just need a good meal." Jan slaps him on the shoulder. He'll bring him to the alehouse, order him some mutton stew. It's a shame Lukas doesn't indulge in women. A barmaid would be the antidote to his saint in a cell. She's wearing him thin. The idea was to get Lukas away from her, but he's worse now than when they entombed her five months ago.

"I need to confess. Will you hear me?"

"Nonsense. You're overworked." It's the services he's holding in the cathedral, in addition to this preaching on corners and shepherding his friars. And those beguines. Lukas still ministers to them on Sundays. His brother would have been better suited for the university in Paris. Jan knows the dean of theology—perhaps he could arrange for Lukas to study with the Dominicans, to debate Aristotelian logic until the sun falls from the sky. Once Jan's made a cardinal, he'll see about sending Lukas off. He'll assign one of his diocesan priests as the girl's new confessor. Someone less impressionable.

"Come, Brother. Walk with me. I have news to share." He takes Lukas by the elbow and steers him toward the canal, away from the square. A rower ferries timbers to the opposite shore. "The reputation of your girl has spread." With his help, of course. "Rome is sending an entire panel to interrogate Sister Aleys."

"Interrogate her?"

"Of course. Rome needs to document her miracles." It worked according to plan. Rome wants to try her for themselves, but they will do so here, on his territory.

"Jan, she says they've stopped."

"Have they? Really? That's a shame." Jan steeples his fingers before his lips, then rotates them to point downward like a dowser searching for water.

"No matter. We'll find people to attest to her healings." Willems will rally some former lepers. Willems knows the best players.

"She's been visited by God."

"Has she?" The girl must have realized that miracles will be found out, eventually. Showings, on the other hand, no one can prove. A smart change of tactic. "And what does God say to her?"

"Extraordinary things. Her words burn into my flesh."

Extraordinary is good. "You're recording them? She'll talk to the pope's men?"

His brother is staring straight ahead, like he's spotted something in the shadows beneath the bridge.

"Lukas?" Jan stops short. "Her visions are orthodox, aren't they?" He remembers now how the strange girl undressed him with her eyes and glared at his pectoral cross. "Nothing problematic?"

"She describes an unspeakable love."

Better she speak of sin and brimstone, but he can work with love. "What else?"

"Christ is a mother."

"What?"

Lukas turns to him with a look of desperation. "She's witnessed the union between mother and child, father and son, groom and bride. They are all one, she says."

"That's unusual," says Jan cautiously. Something is definitely off with Lukas. "Though not strictly unorthodox. Not necessarily."

"She says his voice is music." The yearning in his brother's voice is palpable.

Lukas could get himself into real trouble with the papal visitors. Jan knows the reputation of these inquisitorial boards; they have a tendency to hang the messengers. Or burn them. He can just see Lukas, red-eyed, hand on his heart, repeating heresies he's heard from the odd girl in the cell.

"Look, Lukas, maybe someone else should minister to her."

"No." He raises his head, alarmed. "I'm her confessor."

"I think it could be for the best."

"Jan, I must hear the showings. I must. I beg you." Good God, he might throw himself to his knees in the middle of the Markt. "Please. You're my brother."

"All right, all right." He feels like warning Lukas, but about what exactly, he doesn't know. "For now. Just be careful."

Lukas smiles through tears. "Jan, she says it's unspeakably magnificent, that heaven is on earth, before us, if only we can see it." His voice cracks. He sounds like he might sob in earnest. "Jan, it's hard to bear sometimes, I try . . ." His hands tremble as he grips Jan's sleeve.

The bishop puts an arm around his brother. "Steady, Lukas. You need to pull yourself together. The inquisitors are coming. We have work to do."

Far to the south, through the pines of Rome, the pope's legate leads the delegation through the city gates. The men are seated on fine horses with white papal reins. They feel the sun shines for them.

47

ALEYS

Aleys wakes with cramps and nausea. Marte brings her tea of fennel, removes her bloodied cloths. Marte never comments, just returns the fabric clean and folded. Aleys revives the fire and hangs a pot so she can wash. While it warms, she curves her body around Kat, whose fur glints cinnamon in the firelight. She scratches behind his ear, and he pushes into her hand. There's such pleasure in making another creature happy. Kat flips to expose the white diamond on his belly. Aleys strokes his silky fur and Kat traps her hand, scrubbing it with his gritty tongue as if cleaning her palm is of utmost urgency. His paw pads are pink like the insides of shells.

After Terce, Aleys rises from the prie-dieu and smooths her black dress, careful not to dislodge the linen strips she's drawn tight to catch her flow. Her eye snags on the cross on the wall. She sighs. She should pray for Lukas, too. For relief from whatever it is that's torturing him. There's something on the fringe of her awareness, a flick of a black tail in the dark, a shiver. She dismisses it. Friar Lukas is her advisor. She returns to her knees and asks God to give the man peace. *Just*, she adds, *keep his hands out of my cell.*

Marte raps lightly on the shutter to let Aleys know the first townsfolk have arrived. There might be a girl seeking advice about joining a nunnery or a laborer praying for his wife to be delivered safe from childbed. Her favorite return visitor is an old man who simply sits with Aleys in silence, his wheeze measuring out each moment. She's come to enjoy these visits. The showings have left her heart so full that it's a relief to pray with others. Like a new mother swollen with milk, she needs to share the blessings.

Friar Lukas's midnight visit, though, has left her uneasy. It's too much for him, she thinks. I should have held back. But what choice do I have?

"There's a monk outside," announces Marte. "A young one." Aleys can tell Marte doesn't approve. It's one thing for the wandering friars to give sermons on street corners, she says, but monks should stay where they're put, same as nuns in their convents.

"Let him in." Aleys laughs. "He probably wants me to bless the abbey pigs."

Marte huffs, snapping shut the curtain. "I'll be headed to the Markt. Don't let him linger overlong, miss. You promised to read me the flood and ark today."

"Then you shall have Noah and every creature, two by two, when you return."

"Least he saved the females that time," Marte mumbles. For a believer, thinks Aleys, Marte is shockingly irreverent.

Aleys takes her seat and listens to Marte's retreating footsteps. A scrape of the parlor door, exchanged words—Aleys sits up. She knows that voice. Her heartbeat quickens as new footsteps come closer.

"Finn?"

"Aleys." His voice is deeper, but still familiar. She pictures his lean frame, the flop of sandy hair. Of course that's gone; he's tonsured now. She restrains the impulse to rip the curtain from its rod to see.

She runs her hands into her own hair, dark and thick and uncovered. "What are you doing here?"

"I had to see you." He corrects himself. "To speak with you."

It comes flooding back to her, the hornbook, the meadow, the grasses with their miniscule globe raindrops. She's vowed never to let herself think of him—and she hasn't, not often, not here in the hold with her true beloved—but abruptly she's back in the apple tree. Finn's long fingers tracing the written lines as he reads. His gray eyes flecked with honey, looking up, astonished. Aleys leans into the window and inhales, despite herself, a faint scent of leather and earth. His breath stirs the curtain. She leans in farther and grips the sill like a fence on a cliff edge. "Speak to me about what?"

"I was at the bishop's demonstration."

The platform, the blinding torches, the stink of tar. It *was* his voice.

"I saw a performance," he says, "of players."

She stiffens. "You accuse me of acting?"

"No."

"Because I wouldn't do that." He's touched a sore spot. She feels her temper flare.

"I know—I know you, Aleys. I've seen the look on your face when you believe. The way you tilt your head when you doubt. I saw the exact moment you realized it was a charade."

"You know me." Her throat tightens. She looks up to the ceiling and can't hold back the beautiful, familiar words. "The beams of our house are cedars, and its rafters are firs."

"Our couch is green." There's a smile in his voice.

Her whole body starts to tingle, and she doesn't think it miracle. How? When she has God speaking into her ear, how can a mere boy still make her heart jump like this? "You remember."

"Everything," he says. "I wish I didn't." Her practiced ear, tuned to the laments and regrets that cross this sill, hears all that Finn doesn't say. I miss you. I think of you day and night. I made a mistake.

Well, it's a little late now. "You're a monk. In a monastery."

"And you're a miracle worker." She doesn't respond. Finn continues awkwardly, "I mean, I know you're not a saint—"

She feels a heat in her chest and can't tell if it's longing or fury. "What do you mean, 'you know'? What if I am? What if God called me?" *And not you*, she thinks, *after all.*

"Look." She hears the stool clatter to the floor as Finn stands. "I shouldn't have come."

"No. Stay." If he goes now, she might never hear from him again. They're silent. There's nothing to say; Aleys is seventeen years old and enclosed for life. After a moment, she asks, "Why are you here now? The demonstration was six months ago."

"To warn you. The bishop is using you."

She gives a bitter laugh. "Not anymore." She touches a round gray stone, feels the wall solid and sure. This is her home. Her choice. "I'm the safest woman in Brugge."

"Until the inquisitors arrive."

"The what?"

"I wasn't sure they told you. The abbot says that Rome is sending men to test your miracles. He's to sit on the panel."

A shiver runs through her. "Why?"

"That's what they do. They test for fraud."

How ironic. "The bishop called them?" He can't take her from her cell. That's not allowed.

"He's saying you've had showings." His voice drops. "Aleys, is it true?"

Aleys remembers the earnest boy in the dye yard, his urgent question. *There's supposed to be a kingdom of heaven on earth. Where is it?* Finn was searching, like her. He's still searching.

"I've been shown," says Aleys, "things."

"You have? What things?"

She sighs. Mary bade her bear the truth, but words are inadequate. Still, she tries. "They showed me this: We carry a heaven within."

"You make it sound simple."

"It is. That doesn't make it easy."

"You're saying a man could find God within himself?"

"Or a woman." The kingdom within. "I'm telling you what I've been shown."

"You know they've hanged people for less." Crucified them, in fact. "Aleys, be careful what you say to the inquisitors."

Be careful? About God? She doesn't know how.

It comes over her suddenly. She's not sure if it's love or obedience, right or wrong, but her hands are certain when they move. Aleys slides back the curtain so Finn can see the truth in her eyes. So he can see that there's no caution in simplicity.

And there he is, larger than she remembered, strange with shaved head and sandy fringe, but with true gold in his gray eyes. "What they've shown me, Finn—the good, the bad—all is love. All of it."

He leans in. Their foreheads meet, framed in the window, their bodies braced against the wall. Their lips are so close they could touch. Through the stone church, from the top of the spire, she feels the brass steeple cock turn in the breeze. Anything might happen. They might kiss, they might pray. They could fumble their hands together; he might run his tongue along her neck, she might grab his forearms. She shivers.

"All is love," he breathes.

"Yes," she replies.

There's a knock at the door. Another visitor. Startled, they pull apart. The moment passes; Finn turns away, and Aleys draws the black cloth.

That night, Mary returns. Aleys is at her prie-dieu when her prayers twist the air.

"Mother," she says.

Mary is before her, flat bellied and full breasted, larger than a man. *Come, daughter.*

Mary reaches to Aleys, gathers her into her arms. Aleys feels herself entirely enfolded. They will keep her safe. There's nothing to fear. She rests her head in the crook of Mary's elbow, her weight cradled in Mary's broad hand. The Holy Mother strokes her brow and Aleys sinks into a weightless joy.

She feels something warm splash onto her lips. She reaches for Mary's breast in the presumptuous glory of infants and opens herself to receive the communion of honeyed milk.

Mary slaps her hand away and spills her to the ground. Aleys falls hard, still reaching, mouth stretched open like a fledgling shoved from the nest.

Mary stands. Her dark eyes burn. She is enormous, filling the cell. Her hands are slick with ointment, which she spreads over her breasts and smears roughly across Aleys's lips. It is bitter aloe, sharp as lye on the tongue. Aleys's eyes water; she cannot swallow.

You have been suckled long enough, says the Mother. *It's time to walk the unmarked path.*

When Mary vanishes, she takes it all with her. Father, Son, Mother, gone.

Aleys knows it immediately, as if a presence has left the house. The way you sense, from signs and sounds, that someone is in the next room—you have only to rise and call out their name. The thrum of their presence and the sudden silence of their absence, the quick dropping away, the knowledge that you are completely alone.

The dust motes settle to the ground. Aleys reaches over to stir them up, to make them dance. They sift to the floor as the light in the amber panes dims, too fast.

Is this because of Finn? She doesn't think so. Why would they abandon her now, when she needs them, when the Church is coming to try her?

I always need them, she thinks.

She waits, hoping, hardly breathing. He must be here. His presence is subtle and pervasive as air. The hand cannot grasp it, as one cannot clasp the wind. She has merely to feel it, to empty herself like an open field beneath an opaque sky. He will show himself in the smallest blue gap.

Except he doesn't. The gloom descends like a blanket upon her, around her, and there is no shape in the gray.

He will return, she thinks. But she doesn't believe it. This time, she can feel, is different. This time, she knows, they test her faith.

48
MARTE

Friars. Monks. A bishop. What next? Marte shifts the basket on her hip as she crosses the begijnhof bridge. Even the pope is sending a delegation to poke their noses in Miss Aleys's business. Why they don't let her be, Marte can't understand. Men. Always pissing outside their chamber pots.

This morning, Marte brought dried red currants that she'd been saving since she gathered them from the edge of a willow grove last summer. Miss Aleys has hardly eaten since the showings stopped. It's as though, having feasted on visions, she'd rather starve than eat material food.

Aleys pushed away the fruit. "Gravel," she said. "Everything tastes like gravel."

"What is it, miss?" Marte was at her wit's end. "What can I do?"

"Nothing. There's nothing you can do."

Marte doesn't know what it means for a panel to judge a holy woman. She supposes Miss Aleys doesn't either.

In the courtyard, Marte pauses to test the sheets that she hung at dawn. They were damp; now they're damp and cold. Friar Lukas should be protecting Aleys from the Church's meddling. He'll be in the reading room, hearing Lent confessions, else she'd have draped the sheets in there, where they still keep a fire. The beguines like Lukas. But there's something about the man that Marte doesn't quite trust, the way nothing is ever enough for him. She once said that to Ida.

"But Marte," Ida said, laughing, "do you trust anyone?"

“Hmphph.” Marte isn’t used to people thinking about her. It’s best when they don’t.

Ida emerges from the reading room into the courtyard, her cheeks bright. Marte wonders if Ida’s ever confessed that she distributed Dutch scripture around town. Though that’s stopped, now that Katrijn’s no longer translating. There are no new stories to spread since they last took confession, what, four months ago? Ida can’t have much else to tell the friar. She’s not like Miss Cecilia, who must have entertained him for hours before she up and married.

Marte went to confession once. She was unimpressed. The village priest gave her the same penance he gave Dagmar, and Lord knows, her husband was a committed sinner. People say confession can heal body and soul, but it didn’t cure her black eye. And it didn’t save her daughter.

That afternoon, Marte asks permission.

“To read?” Katrijn doesn’t hide her surprise.

“Miss Aleys taught me.” Katrijn’s brow furrows. Marte adds hastily, “It never kept me from my work.”

“Very well,” says the magistra, “you may choose from the translations what you like.”

So Marte takes the chair by the lamp. The reading room is an oasis from the heavy spring rain. The beguines scooch their stools closer to the fire. Even old Agnes has been carried from the infirmary for the warmth. She sits, nearly folded over in the chair, her chin resting on her breast.

Marte begins. She reads in a slow farmer’s voice that recalls the smells of hay and clover, of manure, of the remembered scent of simple things. She reads of Abraham, whose wife was barren, aged beyond hope of a child. God beckoned Abraham from the tent and told him to look up to the heavens.

The women tilt their heads and imagine star-strewn skies.

“‘Count them, if you can,’” reads Marte. “‘So plentiful shall your offspring be.’”

Marte's heavy voice tethers the lofty words, so that the women think of their own constellations of children, of nieces and nephews, of grandsons and daughters, of the young ones laughing in the courtyard.

Katrijn is scowling at the page in Marte's hand. "Marte? Where did you—"

"Magistra, please," interrupts Ida, "let her finish." The women are nodding. They're eager for story. Katrijn purses her lips.

Marte reads on through Genesis, to Sodom and Gomorrah.

The women freeze when Lot offers his daughters to the men banging on his door. They look at each other, frowning. It makes no sense. Each one of them understands the fate that awaits those children. The hands of the crowd, pinning the girls to the walls of Lot's home, to the dirt in the plaza. No father, no good father, would serve his children to a mob.

"The priests read this?" one asks.

"Wait." Marte continues: "Lot's family follows the angels into the dawn hills as the Lord rains down a sunset of fire behind them." Then Marte pauses and looks up. "I will read the truth now."

And Marte begins a new tale.

Marte reads: "Lot's wife had a name. Her name was Irit. As they ran from the town, Irit felt pity for her neighbors and turned to look back. When she saw the roofs on fire and the people screaming, she fell to her knees and wept. Her daughters turned and cried out—all four of them—for Irit had marched to their homes, had pushed past those raving men in the public square, had pounded on her daughters' doors and shaken sense and warning into those girls until they followed. Irit is angry, so angry, at Lot. She'd have left him in town, tethered like an ass under flaming skies, if those wingless angels hadn't muscled into her business."

The beguines have set down their darning.

Marte continues, "As his wife and daughters wept for the bakers sliding morning bread from the ovens, for their neighbors at the well, for the children just waking to a sky raining fire, Lot looked to the angels for praise, for he was sure of his righteousness." Marte raises her gaze from the page. All eyes are on her. "The Lord turned Lot into a pillar of salt."

"What?" cries Katrijn, standing and spilling her work to the floor. "That's wrong. It's Lot's wife who is turned to salt. For disobedience."

From the corner, old Agnes lifts her head and rasps, "I like this version better."

"But it's not true!" exclaims Katrijn.

"Maybe," says a beguine, "one is true but the other is truer?"

Katrijn, outraged, snatches the parchment. "Where did you get this? It's not mine."

Before Marte can speak, Ida interjects, "I bought it. In the Markt."

"In the Markt? When?"

Marte stares. Ida knows the words are Marte's. Ida gives a quick shake of her head. Say nothing. "Yesterday," says Ida.

"But I'm not translating. Who is?"

"No one knows." Ida's been suspicious of Katrijn, ever since the Lakenhalle, when she was evasive about the bishop's man. Marte can't tell if Ida's trying to ferret something from Katrijn or just provoke her.

Katrijn brandishes the page. "This is corrupted."

"Is it? I'm sorry. How are we to know if we can't read Latin?" Ida stands. She puts a hand on her hip. "At least it's new."

The women stiffen.

"You're criticizing me for not translating?"

"We need the word. Katrijn, you know we need the word."

Ida, don't, thinks Marte. *You need to back down.* Ida doesn't see that Katrijn's a fox with a foot in a trap, snarling, half mad with pain. Grief can make a person vicious. Marte knows, anyone who's lived on a farm knows, never to confront a wounded animal. You have to sneak up on it to set it free.

"You think I can keep you safe," snaps Katrijn. "You're wrong. I can't protect you if you bring this into our home."

One of the women looks up. "Maybe we don't want to be safe."

Katrijn is shaking her head. "We can't outsmart the Church."

"Sophia did." Ida's eyes flash. "We were free to think when she was magistra."

The sound of the rain seems to intensify. No one breathes.

"I'm not Sophia." Katrijn takes a quick step toward the hearth. "I will never be Sophia." She flicks her wrist and the parchment flies into the fire. "But I know that Sophia would never have let us read this."

Not so, thinks Marte. Not so. She lunges for the page, too late. The parchment hovers over the flame, suspended in air, before it drifts toward the coals, where it lands gently. Tendrils of smoke rise from the center, through her letters, her very words. The edges of the parchment scroll inward and the sheet bursts into flame. My story is burning, she thinks. My true story. Marte lunges for the poker and drags the remnants to the hearth. An odor of charred parchment, of burning flesh, infuses the room.

Katrijn turns to Ida. "When you are magistra, Sister, you will make the decisions for all of us." She plunges her handiwork back into her basket. "Until then"—she looks around—"there will be no more reading in the begijnhof."

In the night, Ida comes to her, bearing sheets of parchment.

"Write it again, Marte," she whispers as she sets the candle between them. "I'll make the copies."

49

The Bishop

The bishop sits beneath the soaring gray ribs of the cathedral of Sint-Salvator, where he's come to think alone. Well, almost alone. His eyes stray to the cross-shaped window near the altar. The strange girl is just on the other side, praying, he supposes. He remembers her funeral, seven or maybe eight months back. *If she wants to enter, then let her enter.* She'd been defiant, refusing to let him administer the rites. He wonders how she likes it now, isolated in there.

Jan rubs his temples. Sometimes he envies the true believers. It would be so relaxing to believe in an all-powerful God. He wouldn't have to stage-manage everything. He'd just trust in divine providence, like falling back on a pillow at the end of the day. All the positioning, all the politics wear him down. This morning, heralds cantered into the city to announce the progress of the papal delegation, sooner than he expected; the legate and his men will arrive in just a few months, at Midsummer. They'll be expecting miracles, and Lukas tells him that the girl's run dry. Jan presses his fingers into his eyebrows. There's something wrong with his brother. Ever since he found the girl, or she found him, Lukas's mood has taken on an excited brittle glitter, like someone fevered. Jan's worried about him.

The bishop looks up at the cross. Maybe he should pray. *Dear God*, he begins, folding his hands before him. *If you're there*. Is he there? *If you're listening. Look, I've done what I can. I put a stop to the translations.*

He had Willems threaten Katrijn Janssens in the Lakenhalle, had him insinuate that the bishop would be forced to blame all translations on Sophia, would drag her name through the mud, would excommunicate her if they didn't stop immediately. "But she's dead," Katrijn protested. "Doesn't matter," Willems said, "we'll do it retroactively, she'll burn in hell for all eternity." At that, Willems recounted later, Katrijn paled. She tried to buy him off. "Blame me," she said. Willems shrugged and gestured around the guild hall. "If only we could."

Lord, perhaps my methods lack charity. I did what was necessary. And don't forget that I've shown people miracles! Granted, they were staged, but perhaps he'd spared God the effort. *There are more believers now than ever.*

Please, just make the legate's visit go smoothly. If you send me to Rome, then I won't have to stoop to—well, the levels I've stooped to.

He looks up at the cross.

And please help my brother. Grant him his desires or bring him peace, whichever you can do first.

Now would be a good time for God to make himself seen.

Jan waits. A bit longer. He sighs.

Show me the light, and I will follow.

There, he's prayed on it. And if God doesn't make his will known with trumpets and bells, then what is a bishop to do? Surely, not stand by idly. Jan glances toward the girl's cell. He needs her to perform miracles for the delegates. Or at least not to say she can't. He doesn't actually require her presence. Sister Aleys wouldn't be the first saint to cure at a distance. Technically, a saint's not a saint until they heal someone from heaven, so it shouldn't be a problem to convince them that the girl can work miracles from the next room. They'll set up a stage right here, outside her squint. Willems is rehearsing the players. He's found a fetching young woman who bursts into tears when her stammer is lifted and a mute boy who sings a lovely *Te Deum* on demand. Jan imagines the music filling the cathedral, the legate crossing himself in wonder. That's when he'll bring out the showings. He thinks of the legate's wistful voice: *No one can communicate directly with God. Right?* The man's a sitting duck for miracles and showings.

Lukas says he's recorded the girl's visions faithfully. Jan has yet to read her words, but if they require editing, Jan has a quill at hand. Nothing too on the nose, but it wouldn't hurt if her showings flattered Rome. He might even enjoy editing inspired verse.

Jan would love it if God would take over. But if he won't, God is said to favor the prepared. Jan is ready. It won't be long now.

50

Aleys

Aleys lays her arms on her knees and takes her head in her hands. It's been weeks with no showings, not even whispers, from God. She sighs and forces herself to sit back up and retrieve the psalter she dropped beside her on the cot. She traces the embossed vines on the cover with numb fingers. There's no solace in the calfskin. When she opens the cover she finds the illustrations mere paint and mineral, flat and lifeless.

Perhaps she imagined it. Perhaps she imagined all of it. The miracles, the visions. God. She looks around the cell. What if she is truly alone?

Aleys raises the book to her mouth, traces her tongue along a tree. Nothing. She turns the page and tips her tongue with pomegranate. No taste. The blue is not blue, the rose is gone gray. The deer and the monk are just pictures for children. The archer's arrow clatters to the ground, and with it the mystery. She stares at the deer without curiosity. She doesn't wonder if it will live. She doesn't care.

She looks at the door in the wall with no latch. She wishes she could go outside, just for a bit, to sit by the canal as the clouds roll in. If only she could see the sky, perhaps it would speak to her. Or perhaps even the sky is gone.

She thinks of the sheets flapping in the beguines' courtyard. She'd be glad to be there, to share a wooden bowl and crust of bread. The comfort of other women, their sure hands and round shoulders soft and strong against hers.

Until even that desire darkens and fades into dusk. She feels herself turning slowly to stone, one with her cell.

Her prayers fall from her lips like fragile moths. They litter the floor around her knees with their shivering, helpless flutter. Aleys forces them through her throat, but they're already half dead on her tongue. If no one is listening, her prayers have no life.

Why? she asks Mary. *Why did you leave?*

She hears only the echo of Mary's words. *You must walk the unmarked path.*

Kat stretches out his paw to touch her shoulder, then rubs his head against her spine as if to comfort her. It does, a little.

She prays. She prays harder. "Tell me," she pleads, "how to win you back. I will do anything."

Aleys pulls the candle close and squints at the text. *In the beginning, God created the heavens and the earth.* Genesis 1. *The earth was formless and empty, with darkness over the surface of the deep.* Like me, she thinks.

Aleys traces the line and wills the ink to seep up through her fingers into her blood and infuse her with spirit. God only feels farther and farther distant, receding back into the desert, where prophets call for a Christ who is not yet born, who will not be born for hundreds of years. In the old book, God is the Lord of vengeance, of tests and tokens. He is implacable and hard to please. Everything is not enough.

She perseveres. God calls for Abraham. *Yes, here I am!* So quick, Abraham. Then God's bewildering command: *Take Isaac, your only son, to the mountain, ibi offeres eum holocaustum. There you shall offer him as a burnt sacrifice.* Aleys rubs the space between her eyes. Abraham makes her weary. She's never understood Abraham. And Aleys doesn't want to read God's call to his favorite, not now. She wants Job, she wants the fellowship of the abandoned. Right now, she can hardly bear Abraham, too willing to bundle up his boy and lash together the kindling.

The candle gutters as if someone has opened a door. Aleys draws her blanket tight around her shoulders. Perhaps Kat has left through the parlor. She looks over her shoulder. Kat's asleep on the cot behind her, chin tucked, ginger stripes expanding and contracting with his breath.

Aleys has been gripping the page so hard her knuckles have gone stiff. She's given him all she has. Her vows, her freedom, her hours, her prayers, her youth. She has no son to sacrifice. She slaps her palms onto the desk. There's nothing more to give, no more to yield. The frustration of it makes her throat clench. An uneasiness, like ants, invades her limbs. She stands and begins to pace the cell.

What more could he want? He can have her pallet. She'll sleep on the ground. She grabs her blanket, shoves it out the parlor window. Fine. Take that. What else? The candles? Her lantern? He can have those too. She will live in darkness for him, if only he'll return.

It's not enough, she knows. He wants only what is precious to her. That's what Genesis says. She casts around the cell. Her psalter is nothing compared to his love. She hesitates only a moment before throwing it through the window, hears it land on the blanket. She paces her space, one wall to the other, slapping at the stones. If she could pry them out, she'd pile them into an offering. But there is nothing more.

Her eyes fall on the cot. Kat's ears flick. She steps toward him. He stretches his white paw, raises green eyes to hers, gives a small throaty sound of greeting. Aleys's gaze freezes. She's transfixed with sudden horror. No. God doesn't want this. He is not bloodthirsty. He is mercy. He is light and joy. Aleys twists the cloth of her dress. He is psalm. Hymn. Yet there is a voice in the back of her head: How well do you know him, really?

She shakes her head. He's not asking for sacrifice. Still, Genesis has entered her blood, is tracing its way from her fingertips to her heart. Ancient thoughts. She looks at the knife weighing open the pages of the Bible. If he uttered, *Be thou my Abraham*, could she slip the blade through Kat's fur, through the white diamond of his belly, slit him open? She imagines his guts slithering out, warm. Her raising them to the God of the old book. See? I will do anything for you. Whatever you ask. Aleys turns away, unable to look at Kat. Surely he is not asking.

Or is he? What is the sound of God's voice?

She thinks of Abraham. In the hollow night, Sarah asleep beside him. Did God whisper in his ear? *Wake, oh Abraham, I have a task for thee*. Did Abraham, arthritic and bent, a hundred years old, throw off his blanket and stumble barefoot into the yard and gaze up at the promised heavens? For God had pledged him milky galaxies: *I will multiply your descendants beyond number, like the stars in the sky*. And there was proof, too, Isaac behind him, curled like a fetus upon his cot, his childish loins the future of nations. His one child. The son whose name meant laughter.

How did God speak to Abraham? Did he appear in a storm of lightning? Or perhaps he was subtle, a sudden hush of sand falling to dune. Perhaps the moon swelled three times, burnished copper on a holy horizon. Abraham does not say what happened that night. Maybe he merely dreamed the voice that said, *Take now your son, your only son, whom you love, and make of him a burnt offering*. When he woke he said nothing to Sarah. He didn't ask his neighbors, *Have you ever heard God speak in your dreams?* No. He gathered the kindling and strapped it to Isaac's back and led his child toward the mountain. Abraham didn't question the voice in the night.

Aleys presses her troubled hands into the mantel above the fireplace to pin them to the wood. How did Abraham know it was God—and not the devil—who commanded him to kill the boy named laughter? She doesn't dare look at Kat. Is it God in her head? Or Satan? It makes her angry. He granted Abraham certainty, the gift of patriarchs and prophets. Noah, Elijah, Isaiah. They knew.

Why, my beloved, when I give you everything, do you give me doubt?

Perhaps it's not so simple. She has a resentful thought. *Your descendants will form a great nation*. Maybe Abraham already knew the ending. The test wasn't real. Maybe it was all a wink and a nudge—*Abraham, take your boy and bind him for sacrifice*—and a whisper behind a palm—*you know I'll send an angel to spare him. Haven't I already promised that you'll father tribes?* She pictures Abraham, swinging his knife high above Isaac, pausing at the peak, watching for the angel from the corner of his eye. And sure enough, here comes the winged creature, calling out: *Abraham! Do not lay your hand on the boy. Do not do anything to him.*

Was it fixed, this story?

She is exhausted to her marrow. *My Lord*, she begs, *do not play games with me. You don't need to make me promises or bribe me. Just ask*. She forces herself to look at Kat, who half opens his eyes, sleepy. When she picks up her knife from the Bible, the pages of Abraham fan out, releasing their words into her cell. Aleys lays the blade flat across her open palms, raises her hands. *If you show yourself to me, I will do it. Only this: Do not command me by subtle gesture and fleeting vision. Leave me without doubt, if you ask this of me. Use with me the voice that does not echo. Be plain with me, beloved. Do not let me confuse Satan's voice for yours.*

She listens. *I'll do it*, she tells him. *Come stay my hand*. She reaches for Kat, pins him to the cot, feels his narrow spine beneath silky fur. He squirms and then panics, claws into her forearm; beads of crimson rise on her skin. She raises the knife. Kat hisses. She looks up, waits for the angel. But there is none. No voice. Only her own rapid heartbeat, and Kat's fear beneath her hand. She looks down at Kat and sees the doe in the psalter.

The knife clatters to the floor, and she kicks it away. Aleys falls to her knees and drops her head on the cot and bites hard into the flesh of her own hand.

In the morning, Marte returns the blanket and the psalter. She says nothing, but her frown deepens. She takes the chamber pot to dump in the canal, and when she returns, passing it through, she asks, "Did you have another one of your visions, then? You don't look well, miss."

"No." She can't tell Marte that the whispers of the devil might be the commands of God and she's no longer sure she knows the difference.

"Well, something kept you up. You look like you haven't slept for days."

"I was contemplating Abraham and Isaac." I had the knife in my fist.

"The one where God tells Abraham to murder his own son?"

"That one." Aleys feels tired just thinking of it. "God was testing him."

"And he failed."

"Abraham? Failed?" Surely Marte has misspoken.

"If that was God's test, of course he failed. That man should have chosen his own child."

It stops Aleys short. Is that possible?

Aleys is pacing the hold when Lukas knocks on the shutter. He's come to explain the trial. He's saying it would be helpful if God would speak to her while the delegation is here. She's only half listening.

The last thing she needs now is to be interrogated about her faith. Not when it's at its ebb, when the miracles are gone and her own visions feel like someone else's stories. When the tests have no answers.

"Father, God no longer speaks to me. I feel like he's disappeared."

"That's impossible."

If only it were. "I tell you. I search for him, but I find nothing." There's only the emptiness of a sky with no birds, no clouds, neither sun nor moon nor star.

"Why? What have you done?"

Nothing, she considers telling him. *I didn't kill the cat. Should I have?*

"It's melancholia. I have warned you of this. You must pray."

"What do you think I do in here? I'm a living prayer!" A working, crawling, living prayer. She glares at the black square. It's so inadequate, his advice, it's cruel. He has no idea how cruel it is. None of his prayers have ever been answered.

"Prayer requires patience."

I can't breathe, she wants to say. *I'm drowning, my lungs are filling with dark water and I can't see the surface and don't know which way is up and you tell me to be patient?*

"Our God is everlasting," Lukas presses. He sounds resentful, like she's reneging on a promise. "He is ever present."

She's so tired of him relying on her. "Then why has he deserted me? Tell me that much!"

"You think you're the only one who has to wait? Be grateful for what you've received. You're a spoiled child crying for sweetcakes while the rest of us toil for crumbs."

"You wouldn't say that, Father, if you knew the infinite sweetness of his kiss."

His puff of exasperation stirs the curtain. "You say it is infinite. Let it be infinite. Where does it leave us, if the blessed despair?"

She has no answer. She's afraid of the answer.

"Aleys." She feels him lean in. His voice shifts lower, like someone in the parlor might be listening. "You must be vigilant. You must be wary."

"Of what?" He will say despair, he will say melancholy.

"Of demons."

"Father, no—" She doesn't need his fear on top of her desolation. Her shoulders tense. She pictures leathery imps dropping from the sill like rats, infesting her hold, surrounding her bed. She glances at Kat, who looks back at her unblinking. Can he sense demons?

"I've seen them," whispers Lukas. "In the corners."

"Stop!" She shoves back her stool. He can't do this to her. "I've told you. All is love." She grasps for the knowledge that was once as sure as her heartbeat. "Nothing exists except God." Yet she hears the desperation in her voice, her words clipped, struggling to fly. In this gray light, the truth is vulnerable. The truth is empty and gaping.

"Yes," he says, "so you were shown. Nothing but God. 'My *me* is God,' you said."

She could laugh. He speaks to her like she's something sacred. She's not even sure she's sane. "Father, I can't cure you." She remembers his hand in her cell.

"But you are the vessel."

Aleys feels more alone than she ever has in her life. More alone than when Finn abandoned her in the orchard. More alone than when Mertens ran his finger along her collarbone. More alone than she felt in the crowd that tried to tear her to bits. She wishes it was Finn on the other side of the curtain now, wishes she could confess her struggle to him. He would understand. She banishes the thought. Lukas is her spiritual advisor. He's all she has, her only lifeline. No one else is coming. She must not fight him, even if he scares her, even if he sounds half mad. She swallows her fear.

"Father," she says, "forgive me. I will be patient." He says nothing. "You'll come again tomorrow?"

"The day after. Aleys, you need to prepare for the pope's men. They'll want to know what you've seen."

She gives a brusque laugh. "You want me to tell the pope that God is fickle?" There. She's said it.

"Aleys," Lukas says softly. "I know you can't see him. But he is still here."

Aleys feels tears sting her eyes. She appeals to the curtain like the deer looking up at the monk. Her voice is small. She's tried everything. "Oh, Father. Help me see."

51

FRIAR LUKAS

Lukas hears her close the shutter. He sits on the chair a while.

Help me, she said. How?

God will return to her. He must. Lukas rubs his hand over his belt, catches himself doing it, stops. He looks at the black curtain. He's spent so much time at this window. If only he were the one in the anchorhold. Not outside, forever in God's parlor. A thought scurries through his mind. He doesn't just want to be near her. He wants to *be* her.

Lukas senses movement around him, as if the parlor is breathing, the furniture watching. His eyes land on a basket Marte left in the corner. He rises. It's a plain basket, covered, unremarkable. It seems to whisper to him. *Come*. Lukas looks around, edges toward the basket. He crouches and lifts the cloth. Beneath is nested more cloth, coarse linen strips coiled like snakes. A rich smell, something of yeast and mutton, wafts up. He sees, with mild shock, streaks of blood on the linen. Carefully, he unravels a piece, holds it up before him. It's striped with wet pomegranate, browning at the edges as it dries. He looks toward the curtain. She bleeds, even now? He thinks of the precious blood of the vessel of God. Mary would have bled, too. Lukas falls to his knees before the basket and stirs his hand in it and inhales the scent. He extracts a second strip, marked with clots. Lukas strokes his thumb along the cloth and it comes away dark, and when he rubs thumb and fingers, the ruby clot bursts, lustrous and slick. It comes from within her. It is a marvel. He takes his thumb and smears her blood into the center of his palm. His thoughts are spinning into a dark spiral of certainty. He decorates his other palm with blood. Then he yanks his sleeve to his shoulder and wraps a strip around his upper arm. Then the other. Lukas opens both hands to his God. *Come now*, he prays.

When he hears a voice in the street, he closes his fists and leaves quickly, with the sacred wrapped tight about his limbs.

52

Aleys

She prays. She prays more.

Aleys is at her prie-dieu when she hears the massive cathedral doors creak. Someone has entered the church from the plaza. Light footsteps, an altar boy sent to change the candles. But suddenly it's her sister at the squint.

"Aleys?" Griete whispers. "I have news! Are you there?"

Like she could be anywhere else. Aleys rises. She can make out pieces of Griete hovering on the other side of the window, the smooth skin, the blue eye, the golden hair. It's like looking at a cross-shaped puzzle of her sister. Griete's breath comes through the opening. She's had onions for dinner. The smell is at odds with the picture.

All is at odds, now.

"Aleys?"

"I'm here, I'm here. What is it?"

"I'm to be married! To Pieter!"

"You are?"

"Don't sound so surprised. It's your doing. You prayed for me."

Indeed she has, half-heartedly. Of all her prayers, this is the one God answers?

"That's marvelous, Griete," she manages. "You must be happy. And Papa? He's approved?"

"Oh, yes, he arranged it."

And yet you give me the credit. "Well, when will it happen?"

"Soon," Griete whispers. "Just before Midsummer. Aleys, the wedding will be here, in the cathedral! It will be so grand. You'll be able to watch through your window."

Aleys is stunned. Here? They'll wed before her eyes?

"Are you all right?"

"Yes, of course." She feels somehow hollowed out. Griete will get what she turned down. "Really, you must be very happy," she repeats.

"I am. Only."

"Only what?"

Griete leans into the window. "Aleys, I'm a little . . . afraid. About, well, you know." She takes a deep breath. "Consummation."

"Oh!" Aleys is surprised. Her sister, the flirt, is anxious about the marriage bed? Aleys supposes that, with Mama gone, there's no one to explain. Aleys is rather touched that Griete seeks sisterly advice even though that sister's a virgin anchoress. What does she possibly know about the topic? Their brother Henryk called it bedsport, which makes the act seem like jousting or archery. Of all the advice Aleys has dispensed from the hold, this might be the most awkward.

"I suppose," she starts. "I suppose it's like wrestling."

"It is?"

"Well, sort of. And also like ball-in-a-cup." She pictures the frustrating toy with the wooden ball on a string.

"It's not painful?"

Aleys thinks back to Mama's laugh when Papa would pull her onto his lap in the kitchen. They wouldn't have had so many children or been so happy if it hurt much.

"I don't think so."

"Hmm." Griete's not sure. "You could maybe pray for me."

She will. She'll pray for their happiness. She's glad that God seems inclined to grant Griete's wishes, even if it feels like he's abandoned Aleys.

"It must be hard, your life," Griete says. "I don't know how you do it, by yourself in there, all alone."

For a moment, Aleys isn't sure herself. She doesn't want what Griete wants. But she does, in this moment, think of the sky. "Are there clouds today?" She knows she shouldn't ask. It is temptation. "Rain clouds? I think I smell them."

Griete tells her about the flat gray slabs edging in from the north. She falls quiet. For a moment, there's only the two of them. "I miss you," Griete says, finally.

"I miss you, too."

Griete is wed two weeks later. The hired minstrels lead the parade to the cathedral, fife and drum, a motley fool throwing painted pins—Aleys parts the curtain and sees through the parlor, where Marte has pinned open the door to the patch of road. "See, miss, your sister marrying! That should give you cheer."

"You don't believe that."

Marte shrugs, turns to the door. "At least there's jesters."

The day is festival bright, the wedding party large and shivering with the sound of bells. Aleys's father and brothers ride by on their mounts, bearing shields with the family crest. She can see only their patterned stockings through the door. Claus leans down as he passes, doffs his cap and waves its red feather at her with a grin. Griete follows on foot and Aleys catches a glimpse of embroidered sleeves, the flash of fancy buttons.

Aleys smooths her hair, which has grown to her shoulders. Yesterday, she found a silver strand on her gray blanket and wondered for a moment whose it was. Her body has changed, too—it's more angular, her knees larger, the meat of her thighs less. Aleys washed this morning in a cold basin. If she'd been at home, they'd have drawn her a full bath and dressed her hair and attired her in furs for this day. If she were at home, she'd be married with an infant in arms.

The bells and drums fall quiet as the procession stops before the cathedral doors. The jester will be tucking the pins beneath his arm. Passersby will pause to admire Griete's sleeves and the colors of the party. The congregants are waiting in the street for the vows to be said before the Mass in the cathedral. She pictures the bishop waiting outside the doors to greet the wedding party, gathering in a half circle around him, Griete and Pieter stepping forward.

The bishop will perform the formalities, ask their consent, whether the banns have been properly cried through town three times. Aleys wishes it were someone else marrying them, someone less cynical. Griete will be looking up at Pieter as he says the vows. Whether she has a blush on her cheek or is bold, Aleys doesn't know. Pieter will place the ring on Griete's finger. And then she'll be married. Her little sister, a wife. Aleys sighs. She moves to the squint and observes the empty church. Christ looks away from her. "Beloved," she whispers. "Return to me." *This day would be joyful if only you were beside me.*

Then the cathedral doors open, the light on the altar shifts, and the bishop strides into view. People find their spots for Mass. It is loud; though she can see no more than a slice of the altar, she can hear the cathedral filling and the happy hum of people expecting a feast to follow. Mertens hired boys and put them in his household livery to raise a canopy of red velvet over the altar; the boys look toward the doors and Aleys knows that Griete and Pieter, husband and wife, are proceeding up the aisle. Which she, Aleys, last traversed for her own wedding. Funeral, she corrects herself. I am dead to them. Though not to Griete.

If she sits back and lets her vision blur, the squint becomes a mosaic of bright and shifting fragments. Griete comes into view, on her husband's arm, erect and pale. She glances toward the squint, her eyes troubled. Aleys wishes she could reach out and take her hand for a moment. She would hold Griete, comfort her, whisper to her that all will be well. Her life will be full. There will be feasting, and children, and dancing. Everything Griete ever wanted. For a moment, Aleys envies her desire for attainable things.

She imagines the bridal banquet, noisy with laughter. Claus will rise from the bench, his words slurred, raising a teary toast to their sister. She will miss it. As she'll miss Griete's first infant, wrapped in softest wool and smelling of lavender and milk. She will never hold that child, feel its fierce grip. From the anchorhold she misses the simple things, the everyday things. Farrago would meet her at the gate. She could sit in the garden and watch the birds in the hawthorn. Not just shadows of birds on her windowsill. The wondrous color of birds.

Aleys moves to the door that is no door. Only this panel separates her from that world. What keeps her here? What really keeps her here if God has left? Aleys curls her hands into fists, concentrates all her will not to throw herself forward. Not to hammer against the door. Slowly, she rubs her clenched fists against the wood, making circles, leaning into it.

She imagines the door swinging wide. The crowd gaping at her, curiosity and horror on their faces. They would back away from her, the fallen saint. She'd be excommunicated. She'd be a pariah. She'd destroy her family. Again. The bishop was clear. The conditions were plain. If she leaves the cell, she abandons God. There will be no blessings, no communion, no consolation. No heaven. And no showings.

But, she asks herself, does she have any of that now? Confession is hollow when he doesn't listen, communion turns to paste on her tongue. She might as well be excommunicated.

Aleys spreads her hands flat and presses her forehead into the door's surface until she feels the grain mark her brow. She feels a profound fatigue, a heaviness. She wants to scream.

And yet. She breathes into the door. And yet. She still wants him. In the depth of her bowels, the ember burns. Even if he is turned away, she wants him. Even if she is now widow, she yearns for him. She wants to know the world entire, heaven and earth, from inside her cell. It's an unfinished story. The only story she cares about.

The bishop's voice comes through the squint. "For our Lord God Almighty reigns."

She won't break her covenant with God. She removes her hands from the door.

"Alleluia."

53

FRIAR LUKAS

Lukas weaves on his feet. The day is hot, the bodies are close, they hold him up. Hervé is at his side. Jan is at the altar. The curtain above the couple is magenta, the petals at their feet are rose. The virgin wears blue, her golden hair swaying against her velvet shoulders.

The heat in the cathedral is making his head swim. He glances at the squint. Does Aleys pray within, as he instructed her?

Yesterday he visited the grove. He needed, once more, to return to the origin, to his covenant with God, to find it there in the damp soil. He cinched the sacred bloody strips against his arms until his hands tingled. *Come to me, Lord.*

Hervé grasps his elbow. The bride before them sinks to her knees to be blessed. The bishop places his palm on her head and she becomes Aleys. No. He is confused. Aleys was not wed here. She was buried here. He remembers the dirt upon her oiled lips.

His head swims back to the grove. Shafts of light cut through leaves and patches of moss glowed emerald in pools of sunlight. There was no sound, save the tap of droplets on the forest floor. Lukas bent to remove his sandals. He took off his belt, then lifted the robe over his head and cast it aside. *Even this*, he thought, *even this you may have*. A breeze sifted the glade and he shivered, his skin turning gooseflesh. Lukas was naked before God, but for the stained cloth biting his arms. He felt himself rooted in place, as if something pulled him into the ground, his knees, thighs, cock, chest, sinking into the loam. *Make us one*, he prayed. He unwound the strips from his arms and knotted them together and passed the length back over his shoulder and up between his legs, spreading the fabric over his crotch and winding it slowly, a holy dance, twisting it over his heart and around his chest until he was bound, like a Templar, with a maroon cross dark against his white skin. He spread his arms and looked up. Passion sang through him like lightning. This, this, was what was demanded of him. "Lord," he cried, "take me now." The trees shook water onto his shoulders, his back, his arms. He felt their cool kisses and knew himself blessed. Prepared. He donned his robe and touched his lips to his belt.

As he walked back to the cathedral, the light picked out objects and presented them for his attention, clear and beautiful and singular.

The bishop raises the wafer. The cathedral air shivers with symbols. The scarlet and blue, red teardrops on linen, the wine and wafer merging—union, God, Christ, Mother, Son. It is all one, she says.

He sways. Hervé's grip on his elbow tightens.

Lukas hears God whisper to him. He raises his head to listen.

"Alleluia."

His brother is blessing the union.

"Alleluia."

It all makes sense.

Christ's blood glistens above the altar. Jesus raises his head and looks straight at Lukas, and the friar understands. He has brought the bride to the bedchamber, but his work is unfinished. It's a test.

54

ALEYS

The church empties. Lukas comes to the parlor window.

"Where have you been?" Aleys demands. It's been days. Everyone but Marte has abandoned her.

"Fasting. In preparation."

"What for? The wedding?"

"No." There's an undercurrent of excitement in his voice. "I told you the swiftest route to God."

"You said it was obedience." She's annoyed. "I've been obedient."

"That's the broad path."

"The long path." And it feels like a dead end.

"I know you're weary, daughter. But . . ." She can sense him looking over each shoulder to ensure no one overhears, though the parlor is empty. He says, his voice growing animated, "There's another path."

"Sacrifice?" She thinks of Kat. She wants it in writing.

"Sacrifice? No." His voice is barely audible. "Aleys, I have been sent signs. He has spoken to me."

"To you?"

"You doubt."

Yes, she doubts. She resists the urge to tear open the curtain to read his face.

He says, "There's a hidden path."

"That you've kept from me?"

"It's shown only to the chosen."

But I *am* chosen, she thinks. Or I was. "What path?"

"What is the antidote to snakebite?"

"Just tell me."

"You must say the remedy."

"Viper's venom." She has no patience for games. Is he serious?

"Yes." He pauses, like it's obvious.

"I don't understand."

"The poison is the cure. You see, don't you?"

"No."

"To honor our vows, we must break them."

"That makes no sense."

"You have spoken of it yourself," he says. "You have the answer."

He waits as though he expects the answer to come to her. She has no idea what he means. But the skin at the base of her neck has started to crawl.

The curtain stirs with his breath. "Union," he whispers.

Deep inside her, a warning bell starts a wild clanging, her heart bashing against her ribs.

"Father, I don't understand you." Though she does. She wants him away, out of her parlor. Suddenly, she wants that more than anything in the world. She wants to be alone.

"I must pray," she says. She shuts the window and slides the bolt, hard.

55

The Bishop

The papal delegation arrives beneath bright banners under a blazing sun. Jan Smet bows low, ushers them into the deep shadow of his manor. "Rest well," he tells them. "Tomorrow you will witness wonders."

In the late afternoon, he's surprised when a servant announces a visitor at the door. "She refuses to leave, sir." Jan looks out the window. It's the Janssens widow, the begijnhof magistra. He hurries down himself. He doesn't want her anywhere near the legate, doesn't want the delegation to think he tolerates such women. *Out, out,* he gestures. "Go away. Whatever it is can wait."

"I need to tell you," she says. "It's not me. The new Dutch scripture in the Markt. They're not mine." She is pale, clenching her hands before her. "I swear to you I stopped. I kept my end of the bargain. I beg you, Your Grace." She drops her gaze. "Whatever you do, don't blame Sophia. Don't excommunicate my sister for my sins."

He's never seen her humbled. It's a bit disturbing. And what is this about new translations? He glances up. The legate could look out the window at any moment. "Away with you."

"But . . ."

"Such matters are decided by men of God, not women of the begijnhof. You are trying my patience. Don't try my mercy." He shoos her away with his hands. "Begone. Don't return." Jan watches her back recede across the plaza. "Willems!" he shouts.

56

ALEYS

Midsummer Eve. Torches illuminate the amber window as revelers make their way through the town, casting strange flickering shadows on her walls. A crew of men sing-shout in slurred voices, "Some be brown and some be white, and some of them be cherry ripe." The words fade as they turn the corner, but Aleys's mind finishes the verse: "Yet all they be not so." The carousing fades away. A part of Aleys follows them to the landing, where they'll light a bonfire to ward off demons that roam free on this night when the sun turns south.

She thinks of the beguines singing the Canticle tonight, if they still dance to tambourine and flute. Was that just a year ago? She remembers Sophia bending toward the harpist, whispering in her ear. It will be Katrijn now. Who will sing Cecilia's part? Even Marte will be dancing with them tonight. It seems her allegiance to Ida and the other beguines outweighs her skepticism of Katrijn. Just this afternoon she told Aleys she was thinking of taking the gray dress.

Longing constricts Aleys's throat. Though Sophia is gone, though Ida may sing solo, Aleys wishes she was in the company of women tonight. Midsummer is no night to be alone.

She thinks of Finn. The monks will be fasting to atone for the town's festive excesses and to fend off evil spirits, but at least they have each other. She wonders if Finn thinks of her; he hasn't returned to her parlor since his surprise visit in spring.

The bells of Matins fade. She clasps her hands before her, presses her forehead into them. *Venite, exultamus Domino*, she begins. These small hours were once her favorite, a solitary communion while the town slumbered and she sang glory unto the darkness. It was at Matins that she most felt the comfort of his presence. *In his hand are all the corners of the earth, and the strength of hills is his also.* She sang romance to the night skies. *As it was in the beginning, is now and ever shall be.* Now he no longer answers her, and though she reaches, tonight she feels no joy. She can't even rid the revelers' smutty song from her mind. She sighs and thinks of Job's words: *I am a brother to dragons and a companion to owls.* She keeps company with foul creatures, doubt and despair.

The outer door groans.

Not again. Someone's entered her parlor. Aleys sighs her *amen*. It will be a carouser booted out by his wife. She should have known this night would know no peace. Aleys shoots her thoughts into the other room. *Go home.* She hears a clatter as the man stumbles into the table. *Get out.* Aleys rises to check the bolt on the parlor window. Her heart stops. The shutter is outlined by light, the way sun rims the clouds. The fool has carried a torch into her parlor. A tendril of burning tar reaches her nostrils. Her eyes begin to water. She imagines the cushion on the chair smoldering, the tablecloth igniting, the curtain catching, smoke curving around her shutters, filling her cell. She looks at Kat, who sits alert, ears pressed back. He could escape through the squint, but she . . . If she shouts, would anyone hear? *Get the idiot out of here—please, God, get him out.* Aleys presses her hands against the shutter, willing him away. Her movement seems only to draw the man closer, his breathing fast and urgent just the other side of the shutter. "Go away!" she says. "Leave a holy woman in peace." The man fumbles with the parlor curtain, tearing it aside, and pounds his fist into the wood. The shutter slams against its bolt. Kat jumps from the cot, back arched. The visitor bangs again, and bright light bursts around the edges of the shutter.

Aleys tries to command the man. "Leave!" she repeats, but her voice is a hoarse whisper. She can hear his breath, louder, faster. He bangs again.

Then the man exits, slamming the parlor door behind him. The shutter fades black into the wall. He's gone. She blesses the bolt. She swallows, licks her lips, finds them dry. Her terror ebbs, her breath resumes. Kat's eyes glow in the dark, following outside, around the corner, into the road. Kat senses something Aleys cannot.

Torchlight flickers across the horn window. A silhouette is framed, ghoulish, swelling as the man peers into her cell, receding as he pulls back to look up the street. Kat gives a low throaty growl. The light licks the panes and the shadow pulses in and out of focus. Aleys backs against the opposite wall, pressing herself into the narrow strip between the door and the squint. The man can't see her, she knows, but she senses his eyes raking over her body. *Go to the devil*, she thinks, and the thought stops her. What if the devil has come to her? It is Midsummer's night—anything could happen. Uncertainty grips her gut. She edges toward her altar, touches the crucifix. *Protect me*. She lifts the cross from its nail and hugs it to her chest and it jerks with her heartbeat. She presses herself back against the wall, eyes glued to the window.

Then the creature steps away. The flames on the horn panes fade. All falls dark again. Aleys listens to the receding steps, then peels herself from the wall. Light, she needs light. She gropes for a piece of straw, her hand shaking as she lifts a shuddering flame from the banked hearth to her candle. She is not ready to let go of the cross, so she fumbles with one hand, must try twice before the wick catches.

"There. Better. Right, Kat?" Her familiar room jumps from the darkness, the comfort of her four walls like old friends. "Nothing to fear. No demons. Just us."

But Kat is in a crouch, ears pricked. Aleys listens, alert. Then she hears it, a small noise, the creak of the cathedral doors. No. A demon cannot enter a church. She moves toward her squint but knows she won't be able to see down the aisle. The thought of the devil's face, his leering red eyes appearing suddenly in the squint scares her, and she steps back, pressing the cross to her lips.

Footsteps approach. She cannot remember what the aisle looks like; she can only picture the diamond tiles of her home church, and she wishes she were there in her blue dress and brown braid, on the portal of the village church, full of love, safe. She *is* safe, she tells herself. These walls are my fortress, God is my keeper. But fear lights up her veins. The steps draw closer. She prays, *Exi ergo, transgressor. Give way, thou most horrible, give way, thou most wicked, give way.*

The steps stop outside her door that is no door. Her heartbeat runs shallow and fast and she tries to swallow her own breath so she can hear. The creature is fiddling with the latch. She can only clutch the cross tighter. Sulfur seeps through the squint; its open arms blink with fire. She looks down to see an orange cross pulsing on her shift. She tries to wipe it away, desperate, but she feels pinned in place. She is trapped within her sanctuary.

Then she hears the impossible, the click of a lock turning. It is quiet, subtle, but the sound inserts a key in her chest, slides between her ribs, as if someone spins a poker into her flesh.

"Go away!" she shouts, and this time, her voice is loud. "Leave me, Satan!"

A scraping of iron on iron, as the bolt slides away. The door swings outward, slowly. The hinges moan. No, she thinks. No.

The light of the torch casts an orange path into her cell. There is no one outside the door. Beyond looms an enormous space, an emptiness that rushes away and away into the blue-black cathedral. Leagues of air stream in, forcing her lungs open. She claps her hand over her mouth to keep from drowning. The altar recedes like a boat blown back in a gale. She feels lifted to her feet toward the gaping space beyond, abyss and tower, unfathomable. It is as if a devil's current would pull her from the hold, dragging her from God. Excommunication lies beyond the open door, and the devil knows that. He is tempting her to step out.

Aleys braces herself against the frame, digging her nails into the wooden jamb to keep from being sucked into the incomprehensible maw of the church. One step. One step and she would be out. The space unfolds like a map. The vaulted ribs of the cathedral are impossibly far. The crucifix above the altar shrinks. Christ is so small in the vast church.

She concentrates on her vow of enclosure, her small safe anchor. She shoves off to the back of the hold.

A hooded silhouette enters the doorway. Aleys's heart seizes. She raises the cross. "Get from me, Satan!"

The figure shakes its head. "I come in the name of God."

She knows the voice. It's Lukas. Her voice is a low growl. "You have no business here."

"I come in celebration."

"Go to the bonfire, then. I have nothing for you. Go to the bishop."

"We don't need the bishop." He steps inside. She can see his face now. There's something strange in his eyes.

"I beg you. Leave me in peace."

"Aleys," Lukas says soothingly. "Aleys, Aleys. Do not be afraid. We must celebrate. It is Midsummer and the groom is in the antechamber."

What? She is still dazed by the enormity of the space behind him. What is he saying? His eyes are frantic, at odds with his smile. As he lowers his hood, she can smell spirits on his breath. He tosses the torch into her hearth, where it smolders. He opens his arms to her. She steps back until she feels the stone wall brace her spine.

"For the glory of God, in his name, let us join in communion." He raises his hand in benediction.

"No." She is shaking her head.

He keeps talking. "Aleys, we will form a trinity." His eyes glisten with tears. "Sister, in his name, we will make a God between us."

"You're mad."

His head jerks back in shock. "Aleys, are we not wed to Christ? This is the path he has shown me."

"Leave, now." She has to talk sense into him. "Your vows," she says. "Lukas, you would never break your pledge to God." As she says it, she wonders if this *is* Lukas. He's like a man possessed.

"Don't you see? We've mastered our vows." He steps toward her, takes her forearms. She flinches. His touch is hot, scaled. "It's time we discard the servant."

"Lukas, no." She attempts a voice of authority.

His grip tightens to claws in her flesh. "You disobey?"

"I don't want . . ."

He laughs. "No, no, you misunderstand. This has nothing to do with desire. This is sacrament." He pulls on her arms.

"No." Aleys yanks herself away.

He looks, for a moment, like a hurt boy. Then anger stiffens his features, and he grabs her shoulders. She feels herself small, a rag doll in the hand of a mad child. He pushes her in front of the door. "Go then," he commands. "Leave this cell. Ignore his signs, everything you've been shown. Just throw it away. The door is open. Try to find him out there."

She imagines stepping into the church, fleeing down the aisle, pushing open the double doors into the square outside. There would be moon, and revelers. She could run to the bonfire.

He reads her thoughts. "Go to the devil, if you won't have God."

One step, just one step, and she could run free.

"Make your choice," he says.

She feels her heart stop; she can't breathe. Time shrinks, becomes layered, thick as the six-pointed star—every choice she has ever made, ever will make, collapsed into this moment. The space outside looms like a dark abyss. There's no salvation for those who leave the hold, who step knowingly from grace. She promised God she would never leave. What would happen if she did? She imagines herself plummeting, falling forever through a cold hell, an angel stripped of wings.

Aleys grips the doorframe and gulps air, her head swimming. The smell of incense engulfs her. Stained windows fleck the cathedral with flashes of ruby and sapphire, citrine and emerald. Into the bejeweled space, she feels her vows, sharp-beaked things, take flight. Enclosure. Chastity. Obedience. They circle her head, pinning her to the precipice. The vows shriek with fury and attack each other with beak and claw, until she cannot tell one from the other, her beautiful intentions at war. Blue and red feathers rain to the floor. She cannot save them if they fight.

"When the Godhead enters us," he whispers, "we shall be the church, the heaven, the soil, the river. We shall wash ourselves with snow water." He twists the words of Job, sacred words. From his mouth, they seem crazed, a vein of silver lost in rock.

She glances back at the table. Genesis lies open, her knife pressing flat the pages.

"Aleys, look at me." He moves to block the door, the church looming behind him. "Have your prayers been answered?" He knows they have not. "Has he not hidden himself, so that we may seek?"

She cannot answer.

"Do you understand all? It is written: His will is as high as heaven and deeper than hell."

She doesn't know his will. Not anymore.

"Aleys, I am your advisor, your confessor, your Father. It is no sin." She feels the weight of the church behind him, pressing. "Deck thyself now with majesty and array thyself with glory!"

The door is still open.

"You consent, then?" He rotates her, places his hands on her shoulders, presses down, as if willing her to root. She flinches. "Obedience," he says, "is faith. It is trust."

Trust even in madness? Aleys sees the wild conviction in his eyes, burning and cold.

"He showed me the way. As he once showed you. Did I call you mad when you spoke of waves and stars?"

"No."

"No, I did not. I called you holy. Do you not want him back?"

Desperately. She remembers her own words, spoken into this cell. *I will do anything.*

"Kneel," he says, "while I bless you."

She shudders as he anoints a cross of oil on her forehead, perhaps blessing, perhaps curse. There's no doubt in his gesture; his righteous hand does not shake. What if he's had a real showing? She's so confused. Down is up and up is down and the devil quotes scripture while God looks on.

Are you watching? Are you even there?

She is angry. At all of them. She is angry when he removes his belt. She is angry when he raises her and guides her to her cot, as if he is being gentle, as if this is a wedding night. As if he is giving her a gift.

"Stop," she says. "This is wrong."

"No. This is sacred."

Aleys twists away and loses her balance, hitting her hip, hard, against the corner of her table. The knife clatters to the floor, and she stumbles to one knee. Then Lukas is upon her, pinning her down, his acid breath in her face, and she understands that she is the offering to his God. Cold fear sweeps her. She is Isaac, the choiceless, bound to the slab in a game that is suddenly no game, watching his father unsheathe the blade he uses to gut sheep.

There must be an angel who will come to stop this. For a moment, she imagines a being of light, descended through the roof, muscled wings back-beating to slow itself. The voice: "Do not lay your hand on her." The voice should ring, it should say, "Do not do the least thing to her."

Her eyes find her knife on the floor. Her blade that shaves parchment, that sharpens quills. That fits so easily in her hand.

The understanding breaks over her like a wave. She's not Isaac; she's not Abraham. She's the angel.

Lukas sees her glance toward the blade. He hesitates. And in his hesitation, she feels his fear. Not just of the knife, but of her, of her body, of the flesh cave and passage between her thighs. The dark mystery of pillow and bone, of maiden and crone, midwife, blood. Anger. Hunger. Anything could emerge from her womb, anything. Snake or bat, milk or blood, wolves. A holy child. With her cheek pressed to the floor, Aleys feels herself become a new thing, a night thing, a creature of teeth and talon. She is bird-foot and pinion, feather and muscle.

A breath of air comes down the chimney and ash flies upward like snow.

The prophet Isaiah speaks of wilderness. In his voice is fear, of chaos, of the woman Lilith and other monsters. *She shall become an abode for jackals.* Beasts stir in her belly, raise their heads and sniff the wind. *Wildcats will meet with desert beasts, satyrs shall call one to the other.* The tambourine shivers and the hag and the maiden join hands and know themselves one. *There shall she repose and find for herself a place to rest.* Aleys is the owl within the tree, hidden in the hold. *With his hands he marks off their shares of her. They shall possess her forever.* But what Isaiah did not name is the share she keeps—the untouchable, unpossessable share.

God is not coming. Not for this.

She grabs the knife and plunges it into Lukas's side. He rolls off.

When she rises, she bears the wings of a nighthawk.

She flies to the door.

One step. Another step.

Nothing.

The cathedral does not crash upon her. The soaring arches hold their points, the glass panes cling to their holdings. No ribs crack, no windows shatter. She doesn't fall.

Aleys moves into the aisle. Everything is strangely slowed. She looks back. The hold is full of dancing bits of amber. The squint is limned with the colors of the cross, gray, blue, silver, black.

Then Lukas appears at the threshold, gripping his side, shouting words that are, somehow, inaudible. She sees them form on his lips: *You've broken our covenant.*

No. She remembers Mary. *The priests are blind, the pillars crumble.* Her covenant is with God, not men.

She runs.

Liber Quartus

57

ALEYS

Aleys sprints up the aisle, careening like a toddler, reversing her funeral. She shoves open the cathedral doors and the sky explodes above her. She stops in awe. The heavens are enormous, astonishing, as if God has lifted the roof off the city. A sickle moon hangs in the east, and the stars, the stars are white pepper scattered by a careless hand. So many. So bright. She looks at her feet. The cobblestones gleam like opals.

She must keep moving.

Aleys takes the deserted street beside the church, away from her hold. At the end, orange light flickers. She hesitates, reminds herself that it's people, not demons, in the next square, doing what people do on Midsummer Eve. She pushes on, turns the corner to a bonfire as bright as the sun. Aleys's hands fly to cover her face. The insides of her lids glow crimson. Only slowly can she open her eyes, peering through her fingers, spreading them bit by bit until she holds them to her temple as blinkers. The air before her seems smeared with paint. Colors jump from every object, the doors, the flags, the people. Was the world always thus? She lifts her face to feel the heat.

A man looks over his shoulder, then yanks the arm of his friend. Aleys realizes she's wearing only a thin shift. Her hair is loose about her shoulders. It's a feast day, and these men are drunk. She's not safe here. And, she realizes, the authorities will come after her. She's a fugitive.

Aleys slips back into the shadows. She hugs her arms over her breasts and walks quickly, keeping to the edges, dodging into alleys, heading for the canal. She can't leave the city; the gates are locked. She can think of only one place to go. She follows the canal until it swells into a pond cinched by a bridge patrolled by swans with inked eyes. The begijnhof, she knows, is shut for the night. She remembers a delivery landing on the side canal. The gate is too high for her to climb into the courtyard, but the dock is hidden from sight. She gains the small platform. The water is still. Behind the wall, the begijnhof church rises like a lighthouse, lit and glowing.

Though men may find her tomorrow, she's safe in this moment.

A breeze stirs, sifting the hairs on her bare arms; she'd forgotten breeze. Her every sense is raw, every fiber tingling like she's newborn. Aleys stands on her tiptoes and spreads her arms. The night air tastes of juniper.

A beat of drum and tambourine, fresh and sharp, comes over the wall. Her pulse quickens. Marte will be inside the church with Ida and Katrijn and the young pledges and old Agnes. Though it's late, they're still dancing. A plaintive flute, full of yearning, fills the night. Her throat catches. Somehow, the hollow reed knows how it feels to be forced from your home. Aleys closes her eyes and holds herself still in the flute and the juniper night and feels like she's hearing music for the first time. She's suspended in the sound when the voices ring out: "Sing, O women of Jerusalem!"

Oh, she thinks. Oh. I eavesdrop on angels.

Then she corrects herself. Not angels. This is the song of women.

Aleys presses the heels of her palms to her eyes to quell her tears. She wants more than anything to be with them. Not on the outside, looking in. Neither above nor below, but within. A strand in the weave. She thinks of Marte in the midst of the beguines. Plain, trustworthy Marte. A woman who will take the gray as her own. Who's been at her side every morning, every evening.

Aleys sees it now. She should have told Marte about Lukas. Marte would have helped her, would have raised an alarm that Aleys's spiritual advisor had become erratic. Dangerous. Aleys didn't ask for her help. Why? Was it some stubborn pride, some smug sense that God would raise her up through channels dug by men? That's crazy. It's like a sailor trying to discover new lands by canal when the ocean is beyond. Hadn't she been shown otherwise?

She had missed it. God was there, all along. In the hand of Marte.

As women sing into the darkness, Aleys slides her back down the locked gate and hugs her knees to her chest and grieves. She weeps for the hold. For Mama's psalter, left behind. For Kat. She weeps for the lost, unsung hours. She weeps that she couldn't keep her every vow. That she thought herself invulnerable within stone walls. Aleys cries until she empties herself and there is nowhere to go but sleep.

Through the night she dreams a dense forest, oak and evergreen, damp with leaf rot. Owls call through the dusk. She must find the doe. Aleys squints into the woods, looking for the rust amidst green and brown. Swans glide among the trees. She walks quickly, alert to the shift in the matrix of leaf and trunk that will reveal the deer. The forest grows only closer and more impenetrable. She begins to run through the gathering dark. She turns a corner to find her way blocked by a fallen tree, a gnarled and twisted trunk across the path, its majestic crown tumbled into the woods. A voice comes to her. *Build me a cathedral of broken limbs.* And so she gathers up the branches and leans them, one by one, against the fallen trunk. She drags thick boughs across the forest floor and fits slim branches between them. She weaves the wood together with green saplings. *The beams of our house are cedars, and its rafters are firs.* The sap of wounded limbs coats her palms. Fragments of leaf adorn her fingertips. And when the limbs are knit tight in shelter against the great trunk, she arches evergreen over the entrance and scatters golden needles to make a floor. It is a cathedral of balsam. *None shall see it but those who seek.* She crawls inside and falls asleep on a bed of thick fragrant needles within the hidden church. His voice, from the dream within the dream: *Thou shalt raise a tent of your failures, so that pilgrims may rest.*

58
The Bishop

The bishop is horrified. "I can't believe you entered her cell."

Lukas doesn't answer. He cradles his head in his palms.

"How could you? Do you realize what this does to the Church? To your order? If word gets to Rome, your friars will be disbanded." Lukas closes his eyes. *That's right*, thinks Jan. *Close your eyes. Close them to reality the way you always have. The way you have since we were children.* "How could you be so stupid?"

Not only did his brother break into the hold and set the girl loose, but he ran without covering his tracks. Like any sane man would. Like any man of the Church. One of his Franciscans helped to bandage his ribs, but that's not the worst of the damage. To himself, to his brotherhood of friars. And to all Jan's carefully laid program. He has no contingency for a missing saint. The sun is rising, and the bishop has no plan.

Willems reports that gossip is already flooding the town, coursing through the market, over the wharf, through the Lakenhalle. Jan pictures the dawn scene, as it's been reported to him: misty light, the streets filling with people, the smoldering remains of bonfires. The maid entering the parlor of the anchorhold to find the window bolted. She knocks. She knocks again. No answer. The woman drops the porridge and runs from the parlor, around to the cathedral entrance. Even from the nave, down the long aisle, anyone can see that the door to the cell is gaping wide. A small crowd gathers. The hold is vacant but for a thrice-knotted belt curled on the floor. The maid holds the rope away from her with loathing, like Eve throttling the serpent, as she marches from the church and yells for a hammer. With the fury of an avenging angel, she pounds nails into his brother's belt, anchoring it to the cathedral door.

I pay that woman's wages, he thinks.

The cat is out of the bag, he thinks.

"How could you be so careless?" Jan brandishes the belt that Willems pulled off his cathedral. Even Willems had been unable to mask his disgust when he tossed it on the manor table. "There are a thousand other women I could get you, and you pick the anchoress. Why, why would you do this?"

Lukas mumbles something into his hands.

"What? Speak up, man."

Lukas raises his head. "I thought she would save me."

Jan stops in his tracks. "Save you? You're her confessor! How could she save you?"

"She is with God."

Jan scoffs. "She is excommunicated." Or she will be. He has to work quickly. The legate will be rising soon, expecting the trial of miracles to begin. Jan's anchoress has vanished from her cell and his brother's belt has been seen dangling like a noose on the cathedral door. It's bad.

Lukas moans. "I thought she would bring me to him."

The woman has ruined his brother. "She bewitched you."

Lukas looks up. "No."

Jan is nodding, pacing the length of the room. "It's not unknown."

"Aleys is no demon," says Lukas.

"One of you is. And, Brother, I pray it isn't you."

59

OMNES

ALL

It is Marte who discovers Aleys crouched and shivering on the delivery dock, clad only in her shift. "Help!" Beguines come running from every corner through the dew-slick yard. Marte had roused them to search for Aleys, sure that the girl would return to the begijnhof. Where else could she go? It took them only minutes to find her.

Katrijn follows the commotion, her stride cutting a path straight to the dock.

"What happened?" the women ask. Aleys can't speak, but Marte knows. She nailed the belt to the door. She never trusted that man.

Katrijn stands back as they crowd around Aleys. When she speaks, her voice is grave; for once, her hands do not slice the air. "The Church will want to excommunicate her," Katrijn says quietly. For a moment, Marte wonders if Katrijn will shove Aleys from the dock. The enmity between them is no secret. Then the magistra bends to gather the girl in her arms and carries her through the courtyard, up the stairs to the bed in Sophia's room.

A hush descends on the begijnhof, a crouched waiting. There is debate. Should they hide her here? Should they spirit her away to the countryside? As long as she's alive, the Church will hunt her. They will cut her off. Afterward, she'll be a pariah, worse than any leper. No one will take her in. No one will feed her, not even pig scraps.

Someone speaks up. “Why did she leave her hold?”

Marte stares. “Friar Lukas broke in. I found his belt on her floor. What do you think happened?”

Their own friar. It seems impossible that the man to whom they confess would . . .

“We need to ask her,” says another.

“No,” says Katrijn. “Sister Aleys will have trials soon enough.”

Willems confirms the girl is in the begijnhof. The bishop orders him to marshal a group of armed men. They’ll surround the place, put the women under house arrest, rotate guards at the door. Then they’ll begin the trial. Jan can pluck the beguines away, one by one, for questioning. He wonders if he’ll be able to tell them apart, all those women in gray. It doesn’t matter. He has plenty to work with.

When Willems reports back, he says he can find no men for hire.

“What? Have they beaten all their swords into ploughshares?” That’s what comes of friars preaching peace and forgiveness on every street corner.

“That’s not it, sir.” Willems raises a subtle eyebrow. “It’s the wives. They’re angry.”

At what? the bishop is about to ask. Then he remembers the belt. So word has spread. He thinks of the tongue-lashing the brown friars will receive when they hold out their begging bowls to the women of Flanders. Those men should fast for a few days.

He also thinks, Now I will have to defend Lukas.

Jan sends Willems back out to find men without wives, the sort no one wants, the type too eager to invade women’s homes. In any town, there are always men willing to threaten women.

Lukas sits on the bed hung round by curtains. He hasn’t slept since Jan turned the key in the lock. “For your own good,” his brother said. Lukas hardly notices the wound in his side. He's focused on his fingertips, raw with splinters of hemp. He's spent the hours, Lauds and Prime, humming and picking apart the knots of his vows. The rope frays out from obedience, in a thousand directions, spread like a sun on the bed.

Aleys wakes in the chamber with mustard-colored walls. She thinks of Sophia's spirit rising through the window to the heavens. She gets up and pushes open the shutters, blinking. Too bright. Below, women cross the courtyard. She shrinks back. So many people. She closes the window, retreats to bed.

Midmorning, Marte brings a bowl of barley and milk. Sophia once put such a mug in her hands and from the window they'd watched Marte feed a cat from kindness.

When Marte sets the bowl on the table, Aleys catches her hand and brings it to her lips. Marte starts, pulls back.

"You were there for me. Always."

"Of course." Marte frowns.

"Every day, and I never—"

Marte interrupts, "Miss Aleys, are you . . . ? I know he entered your cell."

Aleys turns toward the window. The Midsummer sun rims the shutter like the devil's torch outlined her parlor window. Is she all right? She shakes her head, though whether she means yes or no, she's not sure. He didn't . . . but she feels his key in the lock, his hands on her skin, his hot breath in her face. The man forced her to abandon her home. She was violated the moment he entered the anchorhold.

"I want to wash," she says.

Marte brings water and a towel. The water is warmed. Marte cracks the shutter, allowing a beam of light to strike the basin.

Alone, Aleys strokes her cheekbones, presses her fingers into her jaw. It's easiest to touch the hard parts first, those backed by bones, the dependable ones. Her wrists. Her elbows. She wraps her hands about her upper arms and holds herself, still. Then she squats before the basin and reaches into it to fill her palms. The pooled water sparkles. She raises her hands to her temple and breaks the water over her head in baptism. The water trickles down her face, her throat, leaving rivulets of cool in its wake. She chants the cleansing words of Job to herself. *Though your sins are like scarlet, they shall be as white as snow; though they are red as crimson, they shall be like wool.*

God tested her. She doesn't know if she succeeded; the choice was no choice. She has a moment of pity for Abraham. His impossible, terrible test. How do you know whether you've passed God's trial? But maybe that's the wrong question.

Raise a tent of your failures. They came to her in the night. She knows it. That was no mere dream. It was a message.

What matters is now. It's what she chooses next.

She opens the shutters fully. When her hair dries, Aleys braids the strands and finds them softer than wool. When she rests, she sleeps on the balsam of hidden cathedral.

They have not abandoned me, she thinks. In my failure, they came. In my night.

Before the sun will set, this very day, the authorities will sever her from the Church. They will try to shame her.

She laughs. She remembers Sophia's voice. *What is the opposite of shame?*

And Ida's response. *The opposite of shame is love.*

She no longer seeks absolution from the hand of man. She has all the love she needs.

The first surprise is Katrijn. The new magistra, for Aleys can hardly bear to think of anyone but Sophia as magistra, appears in the doorway later that morning. The year has aged her. She looks, Aleys realizes, careworn. There's a slump to her shoulders and shadows under her hazel eyes, as though the burdens of leading the begijnhof have been literal weights pulling on her. And of course, Sophia's death. Katrijn's has been an angry mourning, not a gentle one, Aleys senses. When they were last together, it was in this room, over Sophia's body. *Get out*, Katrijn hissed. *You are no saint to us*. Perhaps Katrijn has come to remind her.

"I never thought to see you again." Katrijn is direct.

"Nor I." Aleys sits up in bed.

"Marte has brought you food." The statement is plain. It's hard to know what to make of the changes in the woman before her. Aleys might as well be frank.

"You've given me refuge. Why? I know you don't like me."

"No." Katrijn folds her arms. "But you're pursued by the Church."

"So you offer me shelter."

"It's what Sophia would have done. She protected me, and I'll protect you. You know the bishop threatens to excommunicate her, too."

"Sophia?"

Katrijn laughs bitterly. "Don't you understand? They'll hunt us all. The Church wants to silence difficult women. They'll use any means at their disposal. The bishop says he'll charge her with translation." She looks away. "He'll have Sophia burn in hell."

"But the translations are yours."

"Some of them. There are new ones circulating, too, that aren't mine." Katrijn flicks sudden tears from her eyes. "There's nothing I can do. I can't stop a bishop." She sags to the edge of the bed, and a small, frightened sound escapes her. "Sophia will suffer for my faults."

"Katrijn, no matter what the Church does, God won't punish her."

"How do you know that?"

What can she tell Katrijn? A year on her knees in a cell? Her conversations with God? "Trust me. Sophia is safe."

Katrijn takes a deep breath. "You've seen this?"

"Yes." Sophia has always dwelt in grace.

"I want to believe you."

"It's not your fault, Katrijn. None of it is."

The sounds of industry, the scritch of carding, the clunk of a laundry paddle, come through the window. "They don't like me," says Katrijn abruptly. "The women."

Aleys laughs in surprise. "Well, they never liked me either. We have that in common."

"Unlovable women."

"Who loved Sophia."

There's a moment as the older woman takes in her meaning, then adds, "Who will always love Sophia."

Aleys reaches her hand into the dense weave between them, which holds their past and present troubles and, somehow, Sophia's grace. The women's palms find each other. It's too much to meet each other's gaze, but it's enough.

"Sister," says Aleys.

Katrijn nods. They rest there in truce, in memory of Sophia. Then, as if overwhelmed, Katrijn releases Aleys's hand. "To business," she says. "I have a nephew on a farm outside Groenendael, over the border in Brabant, beyond the bishop's reach. If we move quickly, we can get you there."

Aleys shakes her head. "No. I want to see their eyes when they excommunicate me."

Another surprise, late morning. Griete breaks into the room, breathless. "Aleys!" Griete grabs her into a hug so hungry, so motherly, that Aleys can't help but think of Mama. "Are you all right?"

"I am." Aleys lifts her head from Griete's green velvet shoulder. "Really, I am."

Griete frowns like she's not sure Aleys is altogether sane, but twists to wrestle something from the pouch on her belt. "Look what I rescued for you!" She extracts the psalter and presses it into Aleys's hands.

"Oh, Griete." Aleys traces the vines and finds that feeling has returned to her fingers. Her sister has restored a piece of her heart. Aleys touches the rounded, chewed corner. "You entered the anchorhold?" Most people wouldn't dare.

Griete shrugs. "I had to. It was Mama's book." She looks wistfully at the psalter. "I loved the pictures so much."

Aleys cracks open the book. "Shall I read you Ursula?"

They curl into each other in the bed and Aleys reads the story of Saint Ursula and her eleven thousand maidens who defied the Huns. And then she reads Perpetua yielding her child to her brother and facing down an emperor. When she's done, Aleys murmurs, "Never could I leave you."

"Not even for God," finishes Griete.

Aleys closes the psalter. "You know they'll excommunicate me for leaving the hold."

"You'll stay with us. I don't care what people say."

"It would ruin you." Harboring an excommunicate would destroy her reputation, their business, her new family. "I can't do that to you. Or Pieter," she adds. Aleys hasn't even asked. "Griete, your marriage. How is it?" What she means is: *Did it hurt?*

Griete answers a different question. She closes her eyes and smiles, and when she opens them again, they shine with a light unlike any Aleys has seen from her sister. "I love him," she says. "I do. I love him like Mama loved Papa."

There's a third and final surprise. At noon, just before the bishop's men surround the begijnhof, a courier delivers a scroll tied with twine. Marte brings it upstairs to Aleys, who unrolls the parchment and knows immediately. The hand is trained, the verse familiar. *Rise up, my love, advance. For winter has now passed. The flowers have appeared in our land.* At the bottom, in the margin, hastily scrawled: *Come away with me.*

Aleys opens the psalter to the doe at the foot of the monk, the archer strained, the arrow in mid-flight. And all around them, the gold.

60

ALEYS

When they come for her, there's little time. The beguines procure what is at hand: a brown dress, a gray tunic. No one can find shoes. Aleys wraps a shawl over her head and throws the end over her shoulder. She clamps together trembling hands. The hour is Sext, the sun high and starting its descent into shadow. The guards lead Aleys across the bridge, through the streets, over worn cobblestones that had gleamed like cool opals in the night. Now they're warm, almost hot, beneath her bare feet. Her thoughts flick back to Christ crossing dark flinted ground, the kiss of Judas to come.

The priests are blind, the pillars crumble.

The Church will excommunicate her today for—for what?—for running to God.

The guards prod her through the streets, reluctant to touch her. People stop and stare. A murmur follows in her wake: "The anchoress is out of the hold." Those who have not already heard the rumors wonder why. Shopkeepers come to their doors. A fishwife drops the herring and swears, then crosses herself. These people nearly tore her apart when she was a saint. What will they do when the Church expels her from human society? Turn their backs? Spit on her? She wonders which is worse—to be idolized or despised.

The guards steer Aleys toward the court, a slim building behind the cloth hall, wedged between wool warehouses, as if criminals were less concern to the city than moths.

Aleys remembers how Papa teased that God stopped work when the Lakenhalle tolled, how Mama swatted his arm playfully. Aleys swallows, finds her throat dry. She won't go to her family. She nearly destroyed them once; she won't do it again. The court will release her into the Markt to beg or throw her in a cart and dump her outside city walls.

Or maybe she will run with Finn to the mountain of myrrh and the hill of frankincense, to the dens of lions and mountains of leopards. Into the Canticle.

Stop. Don't think about the future.

They enter the building and wait in a hall outside heavy courtroom doors. The guards stand rigid. She remembers Henryk playing soldier, Claus cast as saint. Griete looking over her shoulder. Children merry on the stake, bodies arched toward the sword. Cheerful martyrs.

Don't think about the past.

Aleys considers the doors, so burnished that the wood grain cascades in dark honey waterfalls. Aleys reaches inside, breathes deep, lets her fingers trace the falling streams. She must be her own alchemy of prayer. She must trust fully. She breathes faith into her lungs, slowly, and feels them fill with a humming, as of golden bees.

She chooses to trust.

From inside, a summons: "Admit the accused."

The guards open the doors to reveal the room in which she will be judged by men.

At the far end of a long aisle, behind a table, sit three figures in robes of brown and black and scarlet. They are sleek as starlings, sharp-beaked and hungry.

The pope's legate is at the center, small within the red cloak of authority. He leans toward her, and she feels him strain to detect whether she is come down from heaven or up from hell. He truly wants to know, and in that she feels the kinship of those who must sort the unruly angels, the fallen from the sent. As she approaches, she sees his stray eye. It gives her heart—a man who sees many ways. He regards her with his left eye, then turns his head to regard her with his right, then fixes her for a moment with both, like a three-headed guardian, a puzzled Cerberus with one eye fixed on law, the other on spirit. She can feel the weight of the scarlet duty on his shoulders. He speaks for the pope. She doesn't envy him the job. Before the day is out, he will have to excommunicate a woman who once worked miracles.

At his right is a Dominican in black, a friar. The man is young, dark eyed and dark haired, too eager, sharp. He wears the pointed shoes of the University of Paris.

To the left of the legate is an old Benedictine monk she recognizes, the abbot of Ter Doest. Aged and soft, his eyes seem clouded with mist.

Before the panel sits a clerk at a desk with a quill, a dun sparrow among glossy birds.

The bishop rises to clear his throat. Jan Smet is wearing the gold cross over a breastbone brittle with cynicism. A man who's given unto Caesar all that is Caesar's, but also all that is God's. He long ago forfeited his own treasure.

Behind him, collapsed on a bench against the wall, is a demon crouched in shadow, a gargoyle in a robe the color of beasts. When it raises its head, its red-rimmed eyes are those of Friar Lukas.

Aleys starts. For a moment, she's back in her cell, earth grating her back, fingernails scraping dirt. The horror of the open door. No. Stop. She shakes herself. Lukas is merely man, not demon. His power over her is null. She breathes. That was then. This is now.

The bishop signals to the guards to place her in the dock, a wooden platform surrounded by a rail to protect the court from madmen and criminals. She nods and mounts the stand, erect, and sets her hands on the rail.

None of this feels real.

The bishop presses the gold cross to his chest as he bows to the legate. He announces, loudly, as if to a full room, "In this the year of our Lord 1299, we convene in the name of our most holy father and lord by divine providence Pope Boniface VIII. We are gathered in the presence of God and the legatine counsel of the Holy See to try the accused, Aleys of Damme, arrested by the Bishop of Tournai"—he pauses to ensure the clerk records his participation—"for the stain of heretical depravity."

Heresy? He accuses her of denying God's truth?

It makes no sense. They're supposed to try her for breaking her vow of enclosure. Not for heresy. How? Why? The penalty for unrepentant heresy is death.

Aleys feels her composure shatter into bright flinting pieces. There is a retort, as of ice cracking. She falters. Fissures appear in the floor beneath her, chill water seeping through the cracks, wetting her feet. Cold fear mounts her legs and flushes her thighs. She grips the rail like she might drown. The bishop means to kill her. The raw water stings as it rises to her lungs, her breath becomes hoarfrost. Suddenly, the courtroom vanishes and she sees the stake, is tied to the stake, flame licking the hem of her dress. Her feet, her bare feet, shift as they begin to blister. No, she tells herself. This is no vision. She tries to resist the terror, but the burning tide wants to drag her into the open sea.

Remember, she wills. You are not alone. Even here. Even in this. Aleys reaches for the Mother that is Father that is Son that is She. *Help*.

And they come. From the dark mist, she feels women grasp her wrists, firm and sure. Their palms steady her bones. In their hands is the strength of Mary and Marte, Ida, Sophia. Of Mama. Her own strength flows to meet them. The mist thins. She breathes. She remembers herself and she remembers the God of these women.

I'm no heretic, she thinks. God knows I am no heretic.

But she might be made a martyr.

Aleys turns to face the judge.

61

The Bishop

The bishop registers, with satisfaction, the shock on the girl's face. He notes again that strange luminescence. The year in a cell has rendered her even more transparent. Aleys straightens and lifts her head. There's nothing repentant about her. She practically glows with shamelessness. Good. He'll trap her right in the middle of that self-righteous halo.

Jan waits impatiently. The clerk is scribbling the accusation as fast as he can. Jan wants to grab the quill from the boy, flip the page, scrawl *guilty* along the bottom, and put it under the legate's nose to sign. But they must follow the protocol; there must be a trial.

It's her own fault. If she hadn't resisted his brother, if she hadn't run, they'd be testing a saint instead of trying a heretic. She's forced his hand. As he said to Willems this morning, rolling a piece of parchment, "A trial of miracles would have made better entertainment." Jan passed the scroll to Willems. "One more for the bonfire." A blaze that will clear his brother's name. They'll forget his transgressions once they learn she's a heretic. There can be only one truth, and it must be the bishop's.

Willems placed the scroll with the other documents. "This evidence shall be kindling and branch." He patted the bag. "Most flammable." Willems will be good company on the road south.

The bishop surveys the courtroom with satisfaction. His contingencies are all in place. The only wild card is his brother. Lukas is on the bench behind him, fiddling with his frayed belt. *Stop it*, Jan wants to say. *Hold yourself like a man*. It was the Benedictine abbot who insisted that the accused's confessor be present at her trial. Jan regrets it. You can't help but contrast the composure of Aleys with the haunted appearance of Lukas. But the papal legate has hardly noticed his brother. His attention is wholly focused on the accused. Jan has the troubling sense that the legate is deciding now, that her guilt or innocence is writ on the air between them, plain to read. Maybe the legate is the wild card.

The clerk waits with suspended wrist. For a moment the court is poised, the judge and the accused locked in gaze, the others glancing nervously between them. This girl could seduce the court with her presence. He seizes the moment.

"The woman before you is charged with the following crimes against the Church."

He puts out his hand to Willems, who fills it with the first roll of parchment.

"First, that she has in her anchorhold entertained Satan."

The air in the courtroom grows sharp. He has their attention now.

"Second, that she allowed him to whisper abominations into her ears."

Jan raises the parchment.

"Third, that she disguised the words of the devil as showings from God."

He unfurls it.

"Here are her words."

He glances at Aleys. The girl has closed her eyes. But she doesn't flinch.

Jan turns back to the panel. "The evidence is before you."

The legate nods at the clerk and quickly recites, addressing Aleys: "I, legate of the apostolic see and inquisitor of heretical depravity, order and warn you once, twice, and three times"—he ticks the warnings off with a jerk of his hand—"canonically and peremptorily, that you swear upon God's holy gospels that you will tell the whole and plain truth about these charges.

"Though," he adds, his stray eye fixing on Jan, "this council finds it odd that a woman renowned for miracles would collude with the devil."

Damn it, thinks Jan, he should never have commissioned that song of the miraculous anchoress of Brugge.

The legate clears his throat and asks the girl, "Do you swear to tell the truth?" Jan thinks, What good is the oath of a heretic? Still, it's required. If she won't swear, they will imprison her until she does.

Aleys stands silent.

"Woman, speak!" commands the Dominican scholar.

She does not. Jan cannot help but admire her equanimity, her regal bearing. He sees the same admiration in the legate's face. "You refuse the oath?"

The scholar drums his fingers. "I have seen this before," he says. "Heretic's pride." The Dominican has already decided her guilt.

But the legate hasn't.

The moment draws out. Finally, Aleys speaks. "I swear to tell God's truth." Her quiet emphasis on the word *God* fills the room. As if the girl is privy to some lesson that the Church has yet to learn. As if God holds a truth greater than the Church's truth.

The legate frowns. The scribe pauses, uncertain what to record. The legate's right eye, trained on Aleys, narrows. It's so quiet Jan can hear him breathe, the long draw, the lingering pause, the short outbreath. Finally, the legate nods to the scribe, who letters *God's truth* on the parchment. "Bishop, you may proceed."

Good. Let the holy fool take her damned oath all the way to the stake.

"Your Excellency," Jan begins, "we have collected this woman's purported showings. I submit them now to the court." Willems slides the documents before the legate. The abbot leans in. The Dominican pushes back his chair and stands to read over the legate's shoulder. They form a tableau of judgment.

"I believe you will find them in grave error," says Jan.

Midmorning, he and Willems had scrambled to curate Lukas's record of Aleys's showings, redacting all that was irrelevant, keeping that which made its own case. It was easy. Out of context, and with a few tweaks for clarity, her accounts were blatant contradictions of doctrine.

The legate turns to Lukas. "Friar, do you attest that the accused reported these as showings from God?"

His brother nods, miserable.

"You must say it aloud," prods Jan.

"I swear it." The clerk makes the notation.

62

Friar Lukas

Lukas moans inwardly, crossing his arms over his belly. He suffers wounds of the spirit worse than pain of the body. Though Hervé came quickly in the night to poultice and bind Lukas's ribs, no one can heal his soul. Lukas confessed to Hervé that he entered her cell. "Brother," said Hervé, "that is grave indeed." Lukas felt his faults curdle in his gut like a mud so dense it had to be cradled, like a thing he might birth.

"You must pray," said Hervé. "Here, I will pray with you. We are all sinners, there is redemption for all of us."

It will not be enough, thinks Lukas. He still wants what she has. He can't understand where he went wrong. He did it for God. He thought her fire would course his limbs, consume him. That he would become clean as silver ash.

They try her for heresy, but Lukas knows she will be exonerated. As soon as they hear the beauty of the showings, they will revere her as the sacred vessel she is.

Lukas considers the man in scarlet who is the voice of the pope. It should be the real pope, thinks Lukas, not this stray-eyed envoy. She deserves to be heard in Rome. She has been with Christ. She is more precious than rubies. He loves her that much; he hates her that much. She's the fulcrum of his passion. His stomach spasms.

A bee flies in through the closed courtroom window. Only Lukas sees it. It hums of miracle; it hums of madness. He has lost the ability to tell the difference, if ever he had it. If there even is a difference. The bee circles her once and lands on the rail beside her hand.

Her words are holy. The panel is reading them now. They will find no heresy. They will find music.

The Dominican stabs at the document, then raises his head to stare at Aleys. "It says here that you claim that male and female are one. That spirit and flesh are one."

Her voice is steady. "So I was shown."

"That is in error," the Dominican states, as if presiding over a university debate. "And this: You say God is naught but love. Nothing else exists."

"No devil?" the abbot interjects, incredulous. "No hell?"

The Dominican leans forward to trap her. "All is God? Are sinners also God?"

"This is heresy sure," mutters the abbot.

The legate has been watching intently. When he speaks, there is interest in his voice. "It says here you claim"—he turns the document toward Aleys and points at the words—"that you *are* God."

Lukas is puzzled. She didn't say that. Not exactly. *My me is God*, is what she said. He will never forget when she swept aside the curtain. The illumination included not just her, not just him, but the windowsill, the chair, the sound of carts outside. The world stopped for an instant. He looked at her, and then at his hands, which sang with energy, almost dissolving in the soup of light. As if he were swimming in God. And for a glimmer, he, too, was God. Then, as fast as it came, the vision fled. His hands resolved into flesh and nail, the sound on cobbles only that. But he had felt it. He had felt the grace.

"Did you not?" The legate waits. "Say you are God?"

Lukas should speak up to defend her. Yet how can he explain? He reeks of sin. He's no longer an instrument of good.

He sees her hands tighten into fists, her knuckles pale. Is she angry that her words are turned to weapon, that men have beaten her showings into swords? Then her hands relax. She balances them lightly on the rail of the dock. He has the impression that she has just let go of solid earth. As if she prepares for flight. When she answers the legate, she speaks from far away, already gone.

"I was shown. To understand God is to be God with God."

"To be God," repeats the legate. "You don't deny it?"

She looks at him intently, like she would draw something from him. The legate leans forward. He wants to know. *Careful*, Lukas warns the legate silently, *be careful or you will touch the barbed faith. You will go too far.*

"Do you not see?" She lifts her eyes to the cross on the wall behind the legate. "The bridegroom calls you out."

Lukas follows her gaze. He cannot help himself. Even now, he strains to see what she sees.

"*Ecce tu pulchra es.*" She says the words softly. "Behold, you are beautiful." She is offering them the words of the Canticle.

"Only if you would meet him"—her eyes return to the legate—"you must die first. You must die to your desires." She pauses to see if the pope's envoy follows. She does not look at the others. The Dominican has pressed his steepled hands to his lips to stifle his objections. The abbot bears a knitted frown of bewilderment. But the legate has closed his eyes, listening. "In the dying, you will fill with honey. You are the hive and the honeycomb."

The echo of Lukas's best sermon returns to mock him. Pity these men. While they pursue riches, the comb lies broken open at their feet.

"He is as close as your heart breath."

Lukas sees Jan shift his weight. "Your Excellency," Jan interrupts. "Reverend Abbot, Master Theologian. May I speak my impression?" The legate nods but does not remove his eyes from Aleys. "The words this woman chooses are sweet."

The Dominican jumps in. "Indeed, I think they are much like the words Eve said to Adam."

The abbot agrees. "Or the serpent itself. 'When you eat this fruit, your eyes will be opened and you will be like God, knowing good and evil.'"

The Dominican opens his palms like a book. "Exactly! You will be like God!" He turns his hands over and presses down on the table, shoving heresy away. "Are these not her very words?"

The legate addresses Aleys: "What have you to say to this?"

"Insofar," she says. "Only insofar as we love God can we become godly." Her eyes flick to Lukas. "We cannot command God."

Her words are delicate as a paring knife. Lukas feels the edge of the pointed tip beneath his skin, and he is flayed, expertly, precisely, his skin sliced neatly away. His white ribs are bare, his windpipe is exposed, pink and striated. He grips his swollen gut so the worms will not spill onto the courtroom floor.

We cannot command God. With sudden clarity he sees his error. He wants, more than anything, to make God acknowledge him. For God to reach down and point a long finger—*You, Lukas, you are my most beloved.* To be named, to be chosen, to be honored. It's spiritual avarice. He sees the slender serpent, gray and strangely beautiful, weaving restless and hungry between his fingers. He turns it in his hand and feels a momentary pity. The worm seeks blindly. It will never still.

He understands. His ambition to be chosen by God is stronger than his love of God.

Her eyes settle front again. Those were her last words to him, he knows. Now she faces her accusers.

The Dominican is outraged. "This is sophistry! *Insofar* as we love God? Is she a lawyer, that she would parse the grammar of God to us? On what authority does she speak? She is neither monk, nor cleric, nor scholar. She is a devil with a clever tongue."

The legate puts out a quiet hand. "Did not the great Dominican teacher say much the same? Did not Thomas Aquinas write that the end of spiritual life is that man unite himself to God by love?"

"Yes, but a woman . . ." sputters the abbot. "The vessel is so, so . . . unorthodox."

"But her words, Reverend? Can we really say her words lack precedent?"

The legate does not want to kill her.

Lukas sees his brother go rigid. When they were boys and would wrestle, there was a moment when elbows became sharp, when claws came out and laughter turned to hiss. In that moment, Jan would pull back. He would go entirely still, and Lukas could feel the fury coiling within his brother. Now, as Jan gathers himself, Lukas knows he is about to strike.

"Admit the next prisoner," calls out his brother.

63

ALEYS

The courtroom doors swing open, and there stands Marte. Aleys sees her pale face, her hazel eyes fastened on the robed judges. She's still wearing her apron. The guards push her forward. Marte stumbles, then rights herself to walk the aisle alone. Her limp is back. She halts beside the dock, uncertain where to stand.

This can't be. Aleys swivels to the bishop. "What do you mean by this?" she demands. "My maid had nothing to do with the showings."

"Silence," Jan says coolly. "You have no standing here."

The legate frowns at the bishop. "We have traveled to try the anchoress, not her attendant."

Jan bows to the legate. "Your Excellency, you will recall that you alerted us to Dutch translations of sacred scripture circulating in our city. We have apprehended documents that are not merely illegal but anathema. Some are so perverse they can hardly be recognized as translations. Both the anchoress and her maid are implicated in spreading heresy."

Aleys is confused. Marte? It makes no sense. She can't translate. She has no Latin.

From the corner of her eye, Aleys sees the bishop's mouth crack a small smile as he tilts his head slightly toward Lukas. It's enough to reveal his motivation. This trial is retribution for the woman who stabbed his brother and the one who nailed the belt to the cathedral door. The bishop doesn't care whether the charges are true; it matters only that they advance his ends. He'll pin them on anyone.

"We found this in the begijnhof, among the maid's belongings." The bishop turns to his man. "Read it to them."

Willems carefully extracts a sheet of parchment from his bag. Marte gives a muted gasp. For a moment, Aleys thinks she's about to lunge for the page, but Willems whips it away. "You see she recognizes her work," he comments, then turns to read.

"Wait." The bishop raises his hand. "No man should suffer such words on his own tongue. Let the woman recite her own abominations."

Marte's eyes widen.

"No. Give it to me," says Aleys. "I'll do it."

The bishop nods, and Willems hands over the parchment. Aleys recognizes Marte's hand, the same cursive that once spelled out *The Lord eats peas porridge*. She looks up, but Marte has closed her eyes.

"Read it," orders the bishop.

Aleys begins. "So God created mankind in his own image. In the image of God he created them; male and female he created them." She remembers reading Genesis aloud to Marte in Dutch as the light climbed the amber panes of her window. Marte must have committed the words to memory and rushed back to the begijnhof to write them down.

The old abbot nods at the familiar text like it's a lullaby. Marte is clutching her elbows.

"Continue," says Jan. His eyebrows are raised as if he expects pleasure from the text.

Aleys reads Marte's next words. "God whispered to Eve: 'Taste the apple.'"

What? Surely Marte didn't confuse Satan and God—and surely she, Aleys, didn't tell Marte it was God who tempted Eve.

The abbot is bolt upright now. "Repeat that."

Aleys stops. "I don't wish to read further."

"You don't *wish*?" injects the Dominican. "What you wish doesn't matter. Any unwillingness will be interpreted as complicity."

Aleys is cornered. Her refusal will help no one.

"Continue," repeats the bishop. His eyes are gleeful.

Aleys reluctantly raises the parchment. "God said to Eve, 'Eat the apple and share it with Adam and you will set in motion all meaning.'" What has Marte written? "'For the apple will split and from its seeds will spring lover and beloved. When you eat the apple you will create desire.'"

The page vibrates in her hand. Marte is claiming that Eve created hunger because God wanted her to see him. It was an act of obedience. An act that split the world in two, setting in motion sin and redemption. Prayer. Forgiveness. It is all God's will, right down to Eve's sharp new teeth piercing the red skin and tasting, for the first time, the knowledge of God. The yearning to be one. One with a lover, one with a child, one in oneself, one with God.

Aleys read Genesis to Marte in the anchorhold, and Marte wrote her own story and committed it to the page. Like a revelation. Like a showing.

Aleys pronounces the last words. "God made Eve, the mother of all who seek."

Marte looks at her now. Their eyes meet in understanding. *Oh, dear Marte*, Aleys thinks. *I so underestimated you.*

The panel is stunned.

"This is an error so plain . . ." begins the abbot.

". . . that it cannot be countenanced," finishes the Dominican.

The legate turns to the bishop. "You found this in the begijnhof?"

The Dominican interjects. "We should burn the place down." He palms the table again. "And the author with it."

Marte turns to Aleys. *Miss*, she mouths silently, fear in her eyes.

Aleys sees the begijnhof on fire, the reading room filling with smoke. Flames shooting from the courtyard up the gray stone steeple. Women running over the bridge to be corralled in the square. The scene pulses before her, almost as if she has conjured it, and she feels a wave of nausea.

Aleys can't let this happen. She can't. Suddenly, she sees what she must do. Her heart stops. Her lungs, too, arrest between breaths. For she understands the test before her. She may have failed to save Sophia, but she can save

Marte. Ida. Katrijn. Her vision recedes to a pinpoint. This is not about miracle. This is not about visions or canals of light. It's about the strength of her heart. The choice is simple, hardly a decision. Aleys slaps her hands against the railing so sharply she feels the sting within her palms. The sound reverberates through the courtroom. All eyes snap to her.

"The heresy," she says, "is mine." She straightens, concentrating her will inside her. "I claim it." Eve did what was necessary. She took the fall.

You must bear the truth, said Mary.

All is one. It doesn't matter where the truth comes from.

"I wrote this," says Aleys. "I ordered my maid to hide it in the begijnhof until she could take it to the Markt for me."

"Then she is guilty of distributing heresy," says the Dominican.

"How is that possible? You can't blame her for harboring a heresy she can't read. The woman isn't lettered."

It's a betrayal. Marte looks at her, stricken. All their hours together, every letter that birthed a sound that spelled a word that formed an insight. Every new understanding, committed in ink. All of it, betrayed. But the lie will save both Marte and the begijnhof, and Marte knows it.

The legate looks searchingly at Aleys. She knows he seeks to understand, that he wants to understand. He must, however, represent the Church. He sees no choice. Rewriting Eve, rewriting the very nature of sin, goes too far.

"You swear that this work is entirely yours."

"I do."

"You understand that you must deny these words or be guilty of heresy."

She bows her head.

"And you do not recant?"

"No."

He looks to his left and right. Both men nod. "Then we are in agreement." He addresses the clerk. "Record this: By this present writing, this court excommunicates you and imposes on you the sentence of excommunication."

Aleys lowers her head and nests one hand inside the other. In the end, after all, she has no need to meet their eyes. Theirs is not the mystery.

"In grace and kindness, I grant you a delay from the present time until the ninth hour; a second delay from Nones until Vespers; or in our last and peremptory patience, until Compline at the day's end. I pray that in that time you humbly admit your error, and in our presence abjure it and all heresy, so that you may deserve to be reconciled and reunited with the Church." One hand of the legate wipes the other. "After sundown, if you have not recanted, we will decide your punishment."

64

Aleys

The jail cell is no bigger than an anchorhold. High up, a square window opens above the main canal; outside, men hawk herring and eel at twilight bargains. Moss grows over the sill, mold creeps down the wall. The corner smells of piss. Someone has tacked a crude wooden cross on the wall.

Aleys thinks back to the first moments in her hold, the dense silence, how she spread her arms and spun around, how she knew she was not alone.

Beloved, are you here? She approaches the plain cross. She will speak plain truth.

"I'm so afraid."

The first visitor, at Nones, was the bishop. He made it clear that, were she to recant, he'd be forced to charge Marte with heresy—"Someone has to die for this," he said—and to shut down the begijnhof, to put the women on the streets.

At Vespers, the clerk came. He nodded soberly. "They said you wouldn't." He turned as he left. "I am truly sorry."

Her last chance will come at Compline, after darkness has fallen, when her resolve will be at its weakest. Even now, her thoughts travel ahead, to a stake in a plaza and a torch that wavers slick and invisible under midday sun. The hour of crucifixion, the hour with death in its soul. Tomorrow. The tunnel in her mind is dark and cold and its exit so bright and impossible. Her pulse is in her throat.

"Beloved, I need you."

She opens her hands and looks at them. Perhaps, she thinks, perhaps tomorrow I will understand. She hopes she'll understand it all, on the other side. Maybe Mama will be there.

Or maybe she'll recant at Compline. She can feel the weakness in her, the desire to escape pain. I might die tonight, she thinks, here in this cell. Maybe the fear will grow in my lungs like chokeweed and squeeze the breath from me and I will escape the flames. Yet she knows that won't happen. She will need a courage she doesn't have, a martyr's heart.

"Help me."

Now and at the hour of our death. Aleys feels the prayer unfurl within her. Her throat is too tight to speak, so she hums the words until the verse fills her chest. *Ave Maria, gratia plena.* She drops to her knees beneath the cross, bracing her hands on the wall, finding her voice. *The Lord is with thee.* She sings the words over and over until they wreathe the cell like incense. The wisps form a curving labyrinth that draws inward, ever inward, circling. The prayer calls her on, beckoning. A glimpse of blue, the scent of juniper just beyond reach. She knows, in the center, is the courage she seeks.

As the last light ticks across the floor, Aleys enters the maze. Wind tosses the crowns of the trees above. She presses on, excitement pulling her heart. The way is stony, the way is plain. They are there, just around the corner. She is about to find them, again, to be fully reunited with her beloved. Then, before her, a wall. Impenetrable ivy, the psalter's ivy, the ivy that curls around the monk and doe of Compline. She looks up to a gold sky. She knows this place. She sinks her hands into the vine, feels its thick pulse, tries to rip it down. It will not yield. She turns to face the archer she knows will be behind her. He has stepped from the page, the man of malachite and cinnabar, ink arrows in his quiver.

The mystery crashes around her. Has she known, all along, this would be the cost? And yet—and yet. Her soul calls out. *Spare me, Lord.*

His voice, from above, from beyond, from within: *Have I not given you the gifts of apostles?*

Yes. It is but the first heaven.

And the treasure of prophets?

You know of what I speak. You gave them the second heaven. You are beyond.

You will be honored with the martyrs.

I do not seek honor.

What do you seek?

The third heaven. Beyond the joy of seraphs.

The archer raises his bow. *Nothing exists beyond their joy.*

Union.

You know not of what you speak. He fletches the arrow.

Then tell me.

You do not understand the price. The archer draws taut the string.

Name the price.

Your self.

Then where would I be?

Her soul answers: *The droplet in the ocean, the blue in the flame.*

He says: *Thou art by nature, mine, and I am thine.*

The archer awaits her order. Christ says to her: *Be thou my wounded doe.*

She offers all she has. *Take me.* Aleys looks down to her flank and sees crimson bloom.

Later, when Aleys wakes, her fingers grope for the wound. It is sealed, and within her, courage.

The last to come, at Compline, is Finn. His gray eyes are anxious. He seizes the bars of her cell as if he could bend them apart. She sees the chapped bunion on his third finger, where he's gripped the quill for long hours.

"It's all set," he says. "I have a horse. We'll go to the Black Forest. And then on to Freiberg, or maybe south over the Alps. To Assisi." He's speaking too fast. "Assisi would be good. They won't know us there."

"I thought you'd come." She rises to meet him. Assisi. The land of Clare and Francis, where basilicas dot the hillsides. They could find shelter there. She almost laughs. Like Beatrice, she thinks. Finn could sweep her away for a life of happiness. All she has to do is recant. She reaches through the bars and he takes her hands and turns them to kiss her palms. She feels his warm lips where she once felt the buzz of miracle. If she leaves with him, she could be a woman, just a woman, nobody's saint.

He folds her hands in his. "The abbot sent me to offer you the last chance before they . . . well, it doesn't matter. You'll recant. That's it, you'll be free. We leave, in an hour, together."

She hopes Finn can feel the weight of the decision in her hands. Between her palms is the fate of Marte and all the women of the begijnhof. The women learning to read, carding wool, gossiping about saints. If Aleys escapes the bishop, he will turn his fury on the begijnhof. He will destroy them all. She has seen it. And the town who have come to trust her touch, her counsel, her blessing? She would betray them, too. If she denies what God has revealed, if she refuses to bear Mary's truth, Aleys will sever herself from all she's ever prayed for. It would be worse than excommunication by the Church. She might as well excommunicate herself.

"You've risked so much to come, my friend." Aleys withdraws her hands from his, into her sleeves.

"No, don't say that. No." He slaps the bars. "You have to come with me."

"And let others suffer in my place?"

"They'll burn you! They'll kill you for words!"

"Finn, it's not just words. I can't deny God's showings."

Finn drops his hands. "You love him that much."

She does. And her family, and the beguines. She loves this glorious life, but she's found inside her a certainty. "Finn, I was always intended for God."

Finally, he lowers his head and nods. "So all you've said is true."

"Yes."

They regard each other.

"What shall I do?" he asks. "I don't know what to do."

"Only this," she says. "Try to be simple."

The abbot has given Finn the last task of record. When he returns to his room, Finn can hardly write for weeping: *We now on our apostolic authority bind the accused in the fetters of excommunication as intractable in her heresy because the accused avoids, refuses, and scorns obedience.* The legate will add his signature in the morning. And then they will burn her.

65

Aleys

The wind comes in earnest that night. It gathers in the streets, like rushing water, spilling and pooling, wish and wrath. Aleys lies awake and feels herself in the mouth of the whale, in the midst of a hurricane, enclosed and suspended, reviled by men, beloved of her beloved. She stops struggling, for what sense is the struggle against all that is? It simply *is*.

The wind roars through the town, rattling shutters and blowing sparks. A roof catches fire, then another, and the sound of running and shouting fills the alley outside the jail. Somewhere in the distance, a bell is loosed from its tether and begins tolling madly. Throughout the valleys of Flanders, church doors blow open and the name of God rushes down aisles to the naves. His breath purls through her jail, reaching even between the bars, and she knows he is with her. *I will keep you*, he says. She does not know yet what this means, whether he means to swallow her or spit her out. She is a minnow. *Crush me, for I am one with you. Crush me and use my bones for yours. Crush me and free my marrow to fill the heavens.* She is the wound of Christ, the bloody hole, and her terror and love are wide and gaping. She touches her ribs, feels her heart beat within, the faithful clock that will be stilled tomorrow.

The wind does not sleep that night. Trees bend and snap. In the harbor, anchors jump their housings and beat holes into the hulls of ships. People look to the skies where clouds slip over the moon like veils. They fight their way to barns to bolt the doors. Leaves blow sideways and the word is carried. Accused. Sentenced. Burning. Soldiers cross themselves. Mothers look in twice on their infants. Dogs howl the night through. The wind funnels through town and frills the water in the canals.

The sun rises, and with it, the knowledge that it's the last dawn she will see. Aleys waits. Faith and horror, courage and terror have been shifting within her like tides through the night. But not doubt. Her bowels are liquid, her spine is seaweed. She had hoped not to be afraid, but Aleys knows now that fear and faith are not incompatible, and that both will accompany her to the end. She is impatient for the end.

Finally, two burly men arrive. They are broad shouldered and strong. Do they think they will need to subdue her? She looks at the open door, thinks of running, but knows her place in the design. She offers her hands, wrist to wrist before her. She goes to God.

"Behind your back."

They bind her limbs together, careful not to touch her flesh. Aleys bows her neck and her hair falls across her face. She breathes into the dark curtain of herself. She will walk blind to her death.

There is a bustle farther down the hall, gruff voices. A woman has forced her way into the jail with the fury of a trapped wasp. Through the spill of hair over her eyes, Aleys can barely make out Marte.

"Miss!" In three strides Marte is beside her and Aleys is encircled in her arms. Aleys releases a breath she has been holding for days. She leans into Marte.

Marte spits at the guards, "Have you no shame? You didn't even cover her hair. And she can't see." Marte tears the leather cord from her own braid and grips it between her teeth as she reaches up to gather Aleys's hair. She moves behind Aleys and strokes her hair back, smoothing it once, twice, away from her forehead. Marte is murmuring something under her breath. It takes a moment to recognize that the incantation is the alphabet, and Aleys thinks that this is Marte's prayer. Marte begins again at *A* and plaits Aleys's hair slowly, carefully, chanting each letter with reverence. She reaches *Z* and Aleys hears "amen."

"Saint or no," Marte whispers, "you've been my blessing." She wraps the cord around the dark nub at Aleys's neck. Marte rests her forehead against Aleys's back, and for a moment Aleys thinks of Ida and Cecilia on the night of the Canticle. Marte's kindness drops into Aleys's hollow and fills it. She becomes solid again, steady.

"Our psalter," says Aleys. "It's in Sophia's room. Take it. Love it well."

Marte nods into her back. "Always."

The guards lead her to the door. It opens to cobble and canal and the path to the Markt, where they've driven a stake into the heart of the plaza. The Lakenhalle belfry looms above. Overhead, dense flat clouds press down upon them. It feels like a storm is coming, and the temperature is dropping. She will end there, before the wool hall. She remembers the day she sneaked from its doors, the light snow that fell as she searched the marketplace for Friar Lukas to ask him to explain: *I rose up in order to open to my beloved.* If she could, would she warn that girl? That child, that naïve and ambitious child, is no more. And perhaps that was always her path, the intended and only path, the necessary path, to her beloved.

The way to the Markt is short. A great mass of people line the street. The baker, the butcher, the seamstress, the cobbler, the children, fill the road in a murmuring sea of witness. Aleys cannot look at them, not yet. She turns her head to the left, toward her anchorhold and its beautiful hours, the warmth of Kat between her shins. And beyond that, the green court of the begijnhof, where the breeze stirs the laundry into sails. She looks to her right, at the canal that flows to the sea, back through her childhood. Perhaps she will see Mama before the day is out.

The great cathedral bell tolls deep and round and swimming. Aleys must face forward. Smaller bells join from all over the city, urgent and sharp, hammers on anvils. They come from every direction to this moment, and

Aleys feels herself the center of a swell of sound so beautiful it quickens her breath. Though the church may crumble, the bells will echo forever. It is time. She walks.

Her family breaks through the crowd. Griete grasps Aleys close. Henryk bows his head and Claus bends to kiss her hand. Papa's eyes are desperate. "I should never have let you go."

Aleys bends her head to meet his. "Papa, I gave you no choice."

Papa pulls from his bag her maroon cloak, wraps her in wool. "Sister," says Griete, fastening the claps. Then she can say no more.

The people part to let Aleys pass. She smells the first whiff of burning parchment, and flurries of ash fill the air. So they are burning her words, too.

People crowd the street, forming tributaries that stretch back through the alleys. As Aleys approaches, they fall to their knees. They reach out to touch her.

They say holy.

They say sister.

They say sint.

Their need rushes over her like a raw wave, and though she doesn't know whether she is the saint they crave, she sends them blessings in return. They carry within them flint and spark, the same as she, and Aleys loves them, these people, with their hurt and their hope. It is the secret honey on her tongue.

That is when she sees. She stops. The face of the laundress who kneels before her is lit bright, illuminated with the spirit of Saint Clare. How did she not see it before? There, but feet away, is a woman with two children and the stiff spine, the charisma, of Ursula. From the corner, a bent crone looks up and Aleys spies Christina Mirabilis, odd, defiant, cackling from the rafters. Aleys turns to look back at what she has missed, at saints all around her. A red-haired girl lifts her chin and looks Aleys straight in the eye. It is Perpetua in the arena, fearless, the gladiator's sword in her grasp. And she understands it is the people who are blessing her. There are others, too, the visionaries yet to come, in the crowd. Stubborn Marguerite, who will write and write again the books they will fail to destroy. Catherine of Siena, who will upbraid a pope; Spanish Teresa, who will build castles of spirit; the anchoress Julian, who whispers from the future: *All shall be well, and all shall be well, and all manner of thing shall be well.* Aleys is woven into the braid of those who sought the truth and spoke of the journey. She walks with them and knows she will join them, lionesses all, at Mary's side.

66
The Bishop

The bishop sees her from afar. The people bow before her, and she appears as a lit taper at the end of a tunnel. He squints past her, looking for Lukas. Jan doesn't know that his brother has closed himself inside the anchorhold, is just now bent in prayer. Later, Jan will bury his brother, will turn the key in the lock, will consecrate him to the hold, where he will spend his days praying to the saint he wronged.

The noon bells toll.

Jan is annoyed that the hastily erected dais was not properly squared; it swayed when he mounted it, and it feels insubstantial beneath him now. It's barely large enough to accommodate the six of them. The four churchmen are forced to huddle in the center like children hiding in a closet. The abbot and Dominican stand just behind him in their brown and black. The legate's red cap brushes against his shoulder. The bishop regrets the full gold and white regalia he donned this morning. It warmed him the day of her funeral; it is heavy on this, the day of her death. His hand slips on the shepherd's crosier. He just wants to get this over with and retreat to the shadow of his manor. The mayor stands to one side, frowning, as if to distance himself from these proceedings, though he will give the signal to touch torch to wood. The church mustn't be stained with actual blood. The mayor doesn't want this, either. "They won't like it, Jan," he said. "The people think she is theirs." Then he added, "So do I."

As the last bell fades, the crowd begins chanting "Sint!" The sound is faint at first, from the direction of the jail. "Sint!" A fury pushes the words along the street—"Sint! Sint!"—into the Markt. The voices are loud, the men angry, the women violent. The chanting reaches and runs around the fragile platform so that Jan feels adrift on a small raft in an ocean of frenzy. The abbot shifts his weight and Jan feels the creak of the wood rise through his feet. Only the legate is calm.

The bishop stamps his crosier hard into the dais for silence, three times, but the platform only trembles as the chant swells. The people are all craning to see Aleys. All but one. The bishop looks down and meets the green eyes of a small boy in a red jacket, holding the hand of his mother. He blinks up at the bishop. Then, though he cannot possibly know the meaning, the boy stretches wide his perfect ruby lips and he, too, mouths *Sint!* while looking straight at the bishop and the sight chills Jan to his bones.

"I will have them arrested," he says.

"No," says the legate. His voice is quiet. "The people need something holy." The small man presses his palms together and brings them to his heart. It looks as though he's praying. For a moment, Jan thinks the legate will step down into the crowd and join them in shouting "Sint!" Instead he says, "We have created a martyr."

"It's not too late," says Jan. "We could reverse the verdict."

The legate shakes his head. "The decisions of the pope are the decisions of God. We weave his design." Jan will never understand this man.

67

Aleys

The crowd parts and Aleys sees the stake. At its base is not just wood, but piles of parchment that form hillocks. Some are in stacks pinned down with stones. Some is tucked into the branches piled around the stake. She knows the parchment contains precious Dutch words inked by believers and copied by others. Marte's revelations. The showings of God that she whispered to Lukas. She has given the word to the people and knows that others will follow. In a century, in two, as the hidden copies surface, the world will read these letters of love. She mounts the platform. A breeze catches up a loose piece of parchment and the gospel drifts over the people as she's bound to the stake.

Closest in, encircling her, are the women in gray. The beguines are sober; they do not chant; they do not care if she is saint or not. The plaza is an ocean of people on their knees, but the beguines stand witness. All of them—Ida, Katrijn, Marte, even old birdlike Agnes—are there, and each is holding parchment, blank parchment, waiting for the word. Some, defiant, raise the sheets high. Others hold it to their chests. There is nothing between these women and their God. They simply love and are loved in return. As the pyre is lit, it is Katrijn who begins the *Ave Maria*, Katrijn who holds her eyes.

Aleys tips her head back to meet her God.

68

The Bishop

The flames lick her feet as ash lands softly on her cloak. Great snowflakes of ash, particulate and singular, show briefly against the crimson wool. Then the hem of her dress catches, at first playfully, then in earnest, and she is suddenly ablaze. The bishop has witnessed burnings, knows how skin will blush and blister and that flesh will hiss like a boiling kettle. The terrible smell. The screams.

But she is silent, eyes to the sky.

In the future, from Rome, he will wonder at what happened next. Robed men will ask him. He won't be sure, and the doubt will puncture his days and tatter his nights. For what he saw is not what others saw, and the paths that diverge from that moment are antipodal, inconceivable, cannot be held together. He saw what he saw. Others saw more.

In that moment, this moment, several things at once possible and impossible happen. Throughout the city, weathercocks twist on their steeples, gold and iron birds turning north, twisting south, wrenching to the east, pivoting west. A strange static excites the atmosphere. The faithful feel a tingle mount their spines. The chanting stops. Gray slabs of cloud and pearl begin to scrape against each other like layers of ocean current, moving out from the square, forming branching roads in five directions. The air flickers. Some will say it was a sudden haze, others remember a halcyon clarity. People look to the sky; people look to the ground. Jan feels his lungs fill with the smell of scorched flesh. His eyes burn with the reflection of Aleys's distorted face, the grimace of a woman consumed by fire.

But the legate sees what the bishop does not, that the flames are consumed by the woman, she is burning the fire, the glory is blazing and she is become a whirlwind of light and faith. A holy perfume, the smell of flowers, infuses the air. Sparks of spirit dance throughout the square in a contagion of wonder. The legate witnesses the people witnessing, the tears that course their faces. He wipes his eyes and is grateful.

The beguines keep their vigil. That day and that night, they are a gray wall, immovable. They will not permit the guards to approach. There are rumors later. She vanished. There were no remains, no relics. Some believe she was burned, entire, whole, by fire. Others saw, between the flames, the flicker of a cloak of the purest sky blue. They believe she survives.

69

The Beguines

They keep the blind beguine with their bodies and breath. When the damp creeps through the courtyard and slicks the whitewashed walls, and her hand slips along the surface as she gropes her way to the door, there is always someone who waits to take her elbow, to see her to the meal, the chapel, the reading. The women wrap warm stones in soft wool for her bed; the orange cat curls against her. But never a fire in her hearth, never the snap and sting of flame and smoke. They're careful of her, in that way.

The women in gray are quick with a poultice, they will teach you the alphabet, they will guide you through the gates of death. They know well the foggy shore between this world and the next, the sound of owls, the dancing light that beckons. Demons do not frighten them. Angels do not impress. They are practical and know the cost of herring and better than to question miracles.

Not everyone believes it is her. She lives for those that choose; she is dead for those that choose. The new bishop of Tournai would rather not know. He keeps his distance. In thirty years he will strive with the pope to bring down the beguines. They will cite disobedience as the cause. But the beguines will live on in flesh and in word. Movements will grow from their ideas. Their writings will be smuggled and hidden in convents, to be revived by poets and seekers.

For now, in this city of canals and wool, of markets and miracles, there is a secret courtyard of green and white and breeze. At Terce and at Vespers children laugh from the laundry.

At the blind beguine's side, always, is Sister Marte, who smiles, from time to time, at nothing much. She speaks little. Marte attends the small hours, the quiet hours, quill in hand. When God comes, they welcome him. And when he goes, they welcome that, too. They have a knowing together, these women in gray. They accept the shift in wind, the changing light, the play of perpetual apocalypse.

In every stroke of the bell, the world entire is born and dies and is born fresh again.

Acknowledgments

This is a work of imagination inspired by works of faith. I owe acknowledgment and thanks to so many.

Canticle relies on the lives and often the very words of medieval mystics. Readers may recognize the story of Saint Clare of Assisi running to meet Saint Francis on the eve of a marriage she didn't want. The witty autobiography of Saint Teresa of Ávila recounts a childhood full of mischief and longing (of the lives of the saints, she writes, "When I read of the martyrdoms which they suffered for the love of God, I used to think that they had bought their entry into God's presence very cheaply," *The Life of Saint Teresa of Ávila by Herself*, ca. 1565). Because I found no way to paraphrase them, I borrowed wholesale the necessary words of Saint Catherine of Genoa ("My me is God!" *The Life and Doctrine of Saint Catherine of Genoa*, ca. 1500) and Flemish monk Jan van Ruusbroec ("To comprehend and understand God as he is in himself, above and beyond all likenesses, is to be God with God," *The Spiritual Espousals*, ca. 1340, translated by James Wiseman). Such words could get a person in trouble. At his trial for heresy in 1328, Meister Eckhart defended his subtle insights with the word "insofar," which I borrowed for Aleys's claim "Only insofar as we love God can we become godly." (See Kurt Flasch's 2015 book, *Meister Eckhart: Philosopher of Christianity*.) I have, of course, interpreted the words of the mystics according to my own understanding; infinite interpretations are possible. I encourage anyone who seeks conversation with the mystics to read their original words.

A 2019 lecture at Radcliffe by historian Katie Bugyis, about the literary lives of religious women in the Middle Ages, lit the fuse for this novel; her sparkling scholarship spurred me to return to the mystics, whose writing I had first encountered decades previous. In researching the history of medieval devotion, I was delighted and surprised to come upon the beguines. The last beguine, who played the banjo to comfort the sick, died in 2013. Several begijnhoven (in French, *beguinages*) are still preserved in Europe, especially in the Low Countries. I chose Flanders as the site for this story in part because I'd spent several years living in Belgium and welcomed the excuse to return, but also because the Low Countries were a particular center of beguine activity. In Brugge (Bruges), you can visit the begijnhof "Ten Wijngaerde," which was founded in 1244 and is now run by Benedictine nuns. It is spectacular in its simplicity. I am particularly indebted to Professor Walter Simons, who not only wrote the marvelous *Cities of Ladies: Beguine Communities in the Medieval Low Countries, 1200–1565* but was kind enough to correspond with me about historical details (such as what quality of wool the beguines were likely to have been producing). I took some liberties with beguine life for the sake of the story (for example, most beguines ate in their private homes, not in a refectory); any departures from historical fact are my own. I also borrowed language from later centuries, following Hilary Mantel's advice to use plain, modern English in historical fiction.

Marte's interpretations of the Bible were inspired by the essays of Barbara Grizzuti Harrison and Rebecca Goldstein in *Out of the Garden: Women Writers on the Bible*, edited by Celina Spiegel and Christina Büchmann.

Rosalie Gilbert, historian and author of the website Rosalie's Medieval Woman, as well as several books about life in the Middle Ages, gave me generous and invaluable advice about clothing in 1300. (No, there were no laced bodices. Metal buttons, not pearls, would be on Aleys's wedding sleeves.)

The anchorites are another fascinating part of history. When I tell friends that there were people so devout that they would voluntarily commit themselves for life to a room tacked on the side of a church, they invariably screw up their faces in distaste and say, "Really?" I was incredulous, too, when I first learned about them. It seems insane to us, today, that someone would choose such strict enclosure. But choose it they did. In the high medieval period, there were hundreds of anchorites—mostly women—throughout Europe. In fact, it was such a popular vocation that a manual was written, the *Ancrene Wisse*, which warns the anchoress against being overly chatty with visitors and to avoid admiring her own uncalloused hands too fondly. The anchorhold was a chance for women who wanted to devote themselves to God to lead a life of contemplation. Still incredulous? There's a surprising amount of information about the anchoritic life on the internet; you'll find many historians and lay people fascinated by them.

My thanks go, most of all, to the colleagues, friends, and family who helped at every stage of creating this book. The community of writers at GrubStreet in Boston have inspired and instructed me from the beginning. Special thanks to Michelle Hoover, book whisperer and leader of the Novel Incubator, and to the generous souls in my writing group (Andrea Meyer, Bob Fernandes, Bonnie Waltch, Desmond Hall, Helen Bronk, Jennifer Johnson, Julia Rold, Julie Peterson, Louise Berliner, Michele Ferrari, Rachel Barenbaum, and, last but certainly not least, Tracey Palmer). Lisa Cron, Susan Bernhard, Lise Brody, and Eliot Harper gave me critical readings at critical junctures. Shout-out to Pam Loring for the Salty Quill Writers' Retreat. Jonah Straus, my agent and champion, is a man who knows his history and just about everyone in publishing. I am grateful to Cindy Spiegel and Julie Grau at Spiegel & Grau for taking the risk on this story and to Nicole Dewey, Jess Bonet, Nora Tomas, and Amy Metsch for their enthusiasm and for holding the hand of an overeager debut author with endless questions. My editor, Joey McGarvey, won me over when she said she loved that the novel takes faith seriously. I was at first skeptical of what I thought were her radical editorial suggestions, but she was right every time, and the novel is much the better for her imagination and intuition.

I would never have started writing without the support of my family. My daughters, my mother, and my brother and sister cheered me on when I was flagging. Kea Edwards and Laura Rich read and reread endless drafts and chapters and pages, helping bring Aleys to life. Finally, to Mark, the love of my life, thank you for believing in me and in us.

About the Author

Janet Rich Edwards is a professor of epidemiology at Harvard University and works in the Division of Women's Health at Brigham and Women's Hospital. A graduate of GrubStreet's Novel Incubator program, she lives in Brookline, Massachusetts.